RACHEL
&
LEAH

RACHEL & LEAH

WOMEN OF GENESIS

ORSON SCOTT CARD

SHADOW
MOUNTAIN

Visit us at shadowmountain.com

Library of Congress Cataloging-in-Publication Data

Card, Orson Scott.
  Women of Genesis : Rachel and Leah / Orson Scott Card.
    p. cm.
  ISBN 1-57008-996-5 (hardbound : alk. paper)
  1. Bible. O.T. Genesis—History of Biblical events—Fiction. 2. Rachel (Biblical matriarch)—Fiction. 3. Leah (Biblical matriarch)—Fiction. 4. Women in the Bible—Fiction. I. Title.
PS3553.A655W66 2004
813'.54—dc22

                                    2004008688

Printed in the United States of America   72076
Publishers Printing, Salt Lake City, UT

10   9   8   7   6   5   4   3   2   1

To Robert and D'Ann

By traveling together,

you're always already home

CONTENTS

PART I

LEAH'S EYES

CHAPTER 1

Bilhah was not born a slave. Her father was a free man, the son of a free man. He had skill, too. His fingers could fly over the pots of tile and find just the right color and he'd know just what size and shape it needed to be and he could tap just *so* on the tile and the right piece would chip off and he'd set it in the mortar.

It all looked like dots of color to Bilhah, watching him as a little girl. But when the day's work was done and he picked her up and carried her away, she'd look back over his shoulder and all the little bits of colored tile would suddenly *be* something. A horse, a lion, two men fighting, a beautiful woman, all made out of little bits of tile that had looked like nothing at all up close.

It was a miracle, to Bilhah. Her father worked miracles every day, for hours and hours, working too close to see the picture he was making, and yet it was always there, he never made a mistake. He was the best at such work in all of Byblos, Bilhah heard a man say that once, and she believed it.

Best in Byblos. And if that was so, then he must be best in all the world, because didn't the ships come over the sea from Egypt and all the islands? Why would they come to Byblos except that Byblos had the best of everything?

Mama wasn't born a free woman like Papa. She was a slave in a rich man's house. And a young one, when Papa met her—she told Bilhah the story many times. "I so young that nobody laying a hand on me yet, but your papa, he come to the house of my master and my master say, You make a picture here, you make a picture there, how much you want me to pay? And your papa he say, I just want one thing. I want that little Hittite girl you got there. And my master he say, She too young. And papa say, You give me her, I set her free, and she get old enough, I marry with her. And then he do his most beautiful work, and I think I see my own face in it three time, and when he finish, my old master come to him and say, Well you take her, because you give her to me three time in these pictures, so I give you *one*, I make a profit. And your papa take me away and put me in his mama house and he say, This girl be my wife some day, you teach her, Mama. And his mama teach me like she my own mama, and now I talk fine like this and I a free woman, and you grow up free all your life."

That was the promise of Bilhah's childhood. Then Mama died giving birth to a baby boy who died the next day, and that's when Bilhah started going to her father's work with him. Every day, learning more and more how to help him, and then at home, they cooked together and ate together, and she talked about everything and he answered her questions, and he often told her, "Someday, my beautiful girl, all the boys in

4

Byblos will come to me saying, I don't want a picture, I want that little girl of yours, and I'll say, You can't have her, she's my little girl forever."

"I'll be big then, Papa."

"Always my little girl, no matter how big you get," he said.

And then one day the king's men rode hard through the market and a man pulled his heavily loaded donkey out of the way, not seeing that Bilhah and her father were beside the animal. Bilhah tried to dodge out of the way, but she bumped into the wall of a house and the donkey bumped her from the other side and she couldn't find a way past the donkey's legs because it was stamping and snorting. And then she felt her father pulling her away, yelling at the donkey man. Then the donkey lurched again and Papa stopped yelling and after a couple of minutes his fingers let go of her and when the donkey moved away from the wall, Papa fell down.

The donkey man never saw what he did. Papa lay there dead in the street and people stepped over him while Bilhah cried, until finally along came a man who knew them. He was a man that Papa had once taught to work the tile, but he had no talent for it and now he made harnesses for animals. But he still knew Papa and he said to Bilhah, "Can you hold to my robe while I carry your papa back to the house?"

Of course she could. She was eleven years old, she wasn't a baby anymore! Couldn't he see that? She wasn't crying like a little lost baby, she was crying because her papa was dead saving her from the stupid donkey, crushed and broken against a wall by the donkey's load. Wasn't that a good cause to cry?

The friend picked up Papa's body and carried him back to their little house, Bilhah clinging to his robe the whole way.

She watched as the man laid Papa on the bed and covered him so gently. "What will happen now?" she asked him.

She meant, What will happen to Papa. But he answered her as if she meant, What will happen to me. "I know your father has a cousin who works for a man in Haran."

"But Haran is far from the sea, and Uncle No isn't a free man. He ran into debt and when he couldn't pay, he sold himself and now he's a servant."

"I know," said the man.

"If I go live with him, then I won't be the daughter of a free man, I'll be in the house of a servant and I'll have to be a servant, too."

"That's if you're lucky," said the man. "What if the master says, No, we've got no room for a little girl like this"?

Only then did Bilhah realize that with no father, with no mother, she would belong to a stranger, and become what that stranger was. A cousin she had never met, but only heard Papa and Mama talk about years ago, clucking their tongues and tugging at their clothing to show their grief for the poor man, who sold himself into slavery to pay his debts. And now she would have to share *his* lot.

"No," she said.

"Yes," said the friend. "You don't know, Bilhah, but in this city a girl like you, with no family, your life would be terrible and short."

"You be my family," she said.

"I can't," he said. "I'm only a harness maker, and no kin of yours."

"Marry me," said Bilhah. "Like my father married my mother, and then waited for her to grow up. Papa says I look like Mama, I'll grow up to be beautiful like her."

"I can't," said the man.

"Look," she said, and ran to the corner of the workroom and pulled and pulled at the big basket of tile chips until the man finally helped her move it, and then dug in the floor under the spot where it had been until she found all of Papa's money, the precious coins that he always told her would be her dowry.

"Here," she said. "My dowry. You take it and marry me and let me stay in Byblos. Don't make me go be a slave among herdsmen!"

"No," said the man. "No, that money isn't for your husband—a beautiful girl like you, men will someday pay a bride price for you, and not a small one. That money is your own, to take into your marriage so your husband will never have power over you."

"No one will pay a bride price for a servant girl."

"They will for you," the man said. "But let me take these four coins, to pay for the burying of your father. Two for the land where he will lie, one for the man who digs the grave, and one for the priest of Ba'al who will send him on his way to God."

"Then take only three," said Bilhah. "Papa did not serve Ba'al."

The man shook his head. "But the people who tend the graves *do*," he said, "and if the grave is not watched over by Ba'al, then soon his body will be taken out and the space sold again to someone else."

Bilhah had not known there was anyone in the world evil enough to do such a thing. But she saw in his face that he wasn't lying. "Four, then," she said. "Or five. For two priests."

"One is enough," he said. "And don't show this to anyone else. This hiding place, this dowry."

That night, neighbor women and the wives of some of Papa's friends took turns keeping vigil and keening over Papa's body, and at dawn the other tile workers, some who had been young men when Papa was young, and some who had learned from him after he became a master, carried him to the grave and laid him in it and Papa's friend gave a coin to the digger and then he and Bilhah stayed to watch him fill the grave with dry dirt.

Bilhah piled stones at her father's head, like putting a seal on a letter as the scribes did in the market. She memorized how the stones were, so she would know if they had been moved, if the body had been taken. And she looked long and hard at the digger, who nodded as if to say, I see that you will remember your father's gravestones, and I will make sure no one disturbs this place.

By noon the friend had her sitting on the back of a donkey. "The man who owns this beast, he gave me the use of her for three days, and I'll give him the harness work for free, so it costs me nothing."

"It costs you the time making the harness," said Bilhah, who understood perfectly well the sacrifice he was making. "That and the cost of the leather and brass, too."

"All that I know of hard work and honorableness, I learned from your father," he said. "Taking care that you are cared for, that is how I discharge my debt to that good man."

And at those words, Bilhah wept quietly on the donkey's back as the man led them out of the east gate of Byblos and took her on the dry, winding road up into the hills. She looked back again and again, watching as Byblos first grew very large, and then grew smaller and smaller, until there came a time when she could not see the city for the dazzle of sunlight from the sea beyond it.

Then even the sea was gone. She was surrounded by scrub oak and the occasional cypress tree, and the dust of the road clogged her nose and made mud of the tears on her cheeks.

Twice, chariots of the king's men came clattering along the road, once going up, once going down, raising a fearsome dust and forcing everyone off the road as they passed.

But when she complained, her protector only laughed at her. "It is because of those soldiers that we can travel like this, just you and me and a donkey. If no soldiers came by, then there would be brigands after us—they used to live in these hills thicker than lions—and soon I'd be dead and the donkey and you would both belong to them until they saw fit to sell you."

Bilhah shuddered at the thought.

Not long afterward, though, she realized that, going to live in a servant's care, she was entering slavery as surely as if brigands had taken her. The only benefit was that there would probably be less suffering along the way. And, of course, she had her dowry, tied up in a cloth and carried over her friend's shoulder because, as he explained, what if the donkey runs away or is stolen or falls off a cliff? Should he take your dowry with him when he goes?

They slept at a little inn where once again, apparently, the man had done harness work and there was no mention of paying. They had a good meal of lentils and carrots and old goat in a stew, and her friend slept at her feet with his knife in his hand, lest some rough traveler think that she was unprotected.

It was only two hours farther to Padan-aram, where her cousin's master camped. They did not pass the town of Haran—it lay on the other side of Padan-aram, said her friend. "But you will have plenty of chances to see it, I'm sure," he said.

The camp was not as bad as she had feared. Only a few of the dwellings were tents. The rest were houses of stone, along with pens for animals and stone-and-stick sheds for storing this and that. A much more permanent place than she had thought a "camp" would be, though it was nothing at all like the crowded, busy streets of Byblos.

They were seen coming in. A man walked out to greet them—only one man, which her friend said was a good sign. "They're peaceful people here," he said. "That bodes well for you."

Her friend explained why they had come, as Bilhah modestly kept her eyes averted from the stranger.

And within a few minutes, she had met her cousin Noam (who, she quickly learned, did not like being called "Uncle No"), and then met the great man, Noam's master, called Laban.

"Have you any skills?" asked Laban.

"I can mix the mortar as well as ever my father could," she said.

Laban smiled. "Nothing here is made with mortar, child. Can you spin? Can you weave?"

"I can learn anything that needs hands to do it," she said.

"A girl who can't spin," said Cousin Noam, shaking his head.

It made her heart sink with despair. They won't want me, she thought.

"The girl's a good one," said her friend. "She learned everything very quickly. She can cook. She can learn."

Bilhah kept wondering when the man would bring out her dowry. But after a while she realized why he had not yet done so. He wanted them to take her first for her own sake, or at least out of cousinly duty.

It soon became clear that while the master, Laban, was not averse to taking her, Cousin Noam himself was reluctant.

Until at last the cloth was unrolled and the coins exposed on the rug between them.

Cousin Noam shook his head. "This is her dowry. I'm not going to marry her! What good does this money do me?"

Bilhah saw how Laban's gaze grew dark, his eyes more heavy-lidded. "Why is it," he asked, "that you measure your cousin by how much of her money is yours, and I measure her by her usefulness to the camp?"

It was her friend the harness maker who answered first. "It's because both of you are blind, not to see the beauty and goodness of this child."

Cousin Noam whirled on him with a rebuke on his lips, but he was stopped by Lord Laban's burst of laughter. "You are a brave man!" he said, still gasping from the laugh. "And a true friend to your friend's child." Laban reached down and took five coins from the pile on the cloth and offered them to the harness maker. "Her father would want you to take this, for the days of work you have lost, and for your loyalty to her."

The harness maker took the coins, but then laid them all back down on the cloth. "I will gladly take a meal from your hospitality, my lord," he said. "But from her dowry I will not take even the flakes of gold that cling to the cloth."

Laban nodded again, and smiled. "We have good harness men here," he said, "or I'd offer you work."

"And I'd do the work gladly," said her friend, "because your animals are so well cared-for, and for taking in the daughter of my friend."

"Oh, I'm not taking her in," said Laban. "She's a free girl, though she's under the care of my servant Noam. *He* will take her in, and *he* will guard her dowry."

Cousin Noam nodded gravely. "She is now my daughter, and I am now her father."

Though he was nothing like her father, Bilhah understood that his words were the covenant, and she answered alike. "Like my own father I will obey and serve you, sir," she said. "I am your dutiful daughter now, and I put my dowry into your safekeeping."

The cloth was rolled up again, and instead of going into the harness maker's bag, it was tucked into the belt that cinched the loose robe around Cousin Noam's waist.

They ate in midafternoon, and after much thanking and honoring and blessing and promising all kinds of future kindnesses, her father's friend led the donkey away, heading back to the inn to spend a second night.

Cousin Noam introduced her to several people, warning her sternly that each adult had much to teach her as long as she was not ungrateful and served well. To each of them Bilhah bowed the way her father had always bowed to the men he worked for, and because they laughed a little she knew she was not supposed to do that; but the laughter was kind, she knew that it was not seen as a fault in her, and so she persisted. Someday someone would teach her what a free girl was supposed to do, if not to bow like a picture-tile man.

And that night she went to sleep inside a house made snug by tight walls and warmed by the bodies of four other girls, most of them younger than her.

In the morning, when she woke, Cousin Noam was gone. The dowry was too much temptation for him. It meant freedom, because with that money he could go far enough to escape the vengeance of Lord Laban.

But it meant the opposite to Bilhah, for now she, having been recognized as Noam's "daughter," was responsible for his debt to Laban.

She prostrated herself before him and wept the most sincere and bitter tears of her life, for now at last she truly was alone, and at the mercy of strangers.

"I know that I owe the value of my cousin's servitude," she said. "But I'm small and weak and have no money, either, and I don't know how to do any of the work of this camp."

"Your cousin Noam is a thief," said Laban mildly. "And I don't hold a child responsible for the debts of the man who robbed her. You are a free girl; I won't take you as a slave to pay for a slave's debt."

"Then where will I go?" she said, weeping and hiccuping because truly her life was without hope now.

"You will go nowhere," said Laban. "I will be your cousin now."

Oh, it was a fine moment, as her heart leapt within her to hear such a gracious saying.

But within a few months, it was as if the words had never been said. She did not think that Laban ever decided not to honor his word. She supposed that he meant them at the time, but they had come too easily to his lips to last for long in his memory. Soon she was just one of the servant girls in

Padan-aram, and if she got special treatment now and then, she knew it was more because she was pretty like her mother had been than because Laban remembered that she alone of the girls in her little stone house was free.

The end of my father's life was the end of my freedom after all, she thought, then and many times afterward.

And as years went by, when the pain of Noam's betrayal and Laban's forgetfulness had worn away, the thing that stung her most was her own ungrateful heart. For she remembered Cousin Noam's name, though he had robbed her and left her to take his place in servitude. But the name of Papa's friend, the harness maker who had refused to take even the flakes of dust that clung to the cloth, *his* name was lost in the darkness of memory, and though twice she had dreams in which she thought she remembered it, the name always slipped away upon waking.

CHAPTER 2

At first Bilhah was trained like any of the other girls. Learning to water the animals, to card wool, to gather dung for drying and burning, to hoe the garden and tell weeds from food, to sew, to cook, to wash whatever needed washing, and above all, to keep the distaff ever spinning in her hand.

It was weary work, and none of it drew upon her mind the way her father's work had, with the need to learn the fine gradations of color, what was a match and what was not, and how to imagine a shape to continue a line. Nor was she called upon to remember clients' names and all the things they asked for, or where they lived, or which shops provided the goods that were needed, and which shopkeepers were prone to try to cheat her when she came alone. Her mind was still full of all this information, which made her work here in Laban's household seem tedious and empty.

But the other girls thought that the things she knew from Byblos were useless. They asked about the city at first, hoping for tales of marvels and wonders from the sea. At first Bilhah was shy to talk about it, because the city brought back memories that made her cry. After a few weeks, though, she ventured a few comments about how things were in Byblos—only now the other girls weren't interested, and it wasn't long before one of the older ones said, "You're not in Byblos any more, so shut up about it."

The truth was that the things Bilhah knew from Byblos were useless here, and it wasn't many months before she found that she could remember the streets of the city only in her dreams, and then they never led where they were supposed to, and in her dreams she could never find anything, or if she did, the wrong people were there, or they didn't have what she needed in the dream, and more than once she woke up in tears, thinking, It's not my city, this isn't where I live. In the dream she was thinking it *was* Byblos, only changed; but when she woke, the words she found herself murmuring meant something else: that this sprawling camp in the grassy hills of Padan-aram was not her city, was not a place where she belonged at all.

And it was true. She did not belong. Oh, the tasks that took mere manual dexterity she mastered well enough. Spinning thread might drive her half mad, doing it hour after hour, but her work was as good as anyone's after a very short time. And she could clean and sew and cook as well as the other girls her age.

But the animals were impossible. She didn't have the feel for it, even with the small ones. She saw the other girls cuddle with lambs and frolic with kids, and watched the little boys

roll and play with the dogs of the camp. But when she came
near even the most docile animal, the stink offended her and
made her want to shy away, and when the animal moved she
leapt back instinctively.

She heard one of the old women say to another, "It's
because her father was crushed by a donkey," and maybe
there was something to that. She hadn't been afraid of the
donkey she had ridden all the way here, but that was because
she was on top of it; when she was down among the animals'
feet, then it was true, their stamping and shuffling in the dirt
made her uneasy. And maybe to her the smell of animals was
the smell of death, because it had been so strongly in her nos-
trils as she breathed along with her father's last labored
breaths.

What difference did it make, though, *why* she didn't like
being with the animals? This was a herdkeeper's household,
and everyone had to help with animals all the time.

Everyone, that is, except Laban's oldest daughter, Leah.
But that wasn't because she was shy of them. She'd hug a
lamb like any of the servant girls, and there were a couple of
dogs that everyone regarded as hers, because they ate from
her hand and when she went out in the camp, they trotted
along with her, sometimes running ahead, but always returning, as if she were queen and they were her guards and
servants.

Leah didn't have to help with the animals like everyone
else because she was tender-eyed. In bright sunlight she
squinted, even though she wore a fine black cloth over her
face to fend off the worst of the dazzle. And she couldn't see
anything at all that was far off. Bilhah had noticed it almost at
once, because when she first encountered Leah, she walked

right up to Bilhah and peered at her closely, her face only inches away, her head moving up and down as if she could see no more than a palm-size patch of Bilhah at a time.

But Leah was *not* blind. Bilhah had made the mistake of calling her "the blind girl" to one of the older servant women, and to Bilhah's shock, the woman slapped her, and not lightly, either. "The lady Leah is not blind," the woman said harshly. "Her eyes are tender, and this causes her great danger, for she cannot see things that might be approaching from far away. But she can see well enough to know who she's talking to, and to go wherever she wants in the camp, and to tend the garden. And she can *hear* words that are uttered half the camp away, including the words of stupid servant girls who call her blind, which makes her cry. And only the worst sort of person would ever make Leah cry."

The woman's lecture did the job—and to avoid the chance of giving offense to Leah, who could apparently hear like the gods, Bilhah didn't mention Leah at all after that, to anyone. She also avoided her, because it was so strange to know that Leah could see her and not see her at the same time. Once, though, when Bilhah was alone out at the women's private booth, she tied a scarf across her eyes and tried to do every-thing just by the feel of it. She found she made a tangle of her clothing and kept fearing that she'd step in something awful and after only a few minutes she took off the scarf and looked around gratefully and vowed never to be envious of Leah, even if she was the daughter of Lord Laban, and a lady.

Big as the camp was, however, there was no way to avoid someone forever, and on a particular day in the rainy season, almost half a year after Bilhah arrived, she was in the garden plucking beans when Leah started up another row, pulling weeds from the pepper plants.

Even though she wore her veil and was far at the other side of the field, Leah waved to her. "I know you," she said. "You're the mysterious cousin."

Cousin? Not *Leah's* cousin. And there was nothing mysterious about Bilhah.

"Noam used to talk about how his cousin was a great artist in colored tiles," said Leah loudly.

Bilhah did not know what to say to this, especially with Leah shouting it over such a distance. Well, not shouting, really, but her voice was pitched so that it carried, and Bilhah was sure that she could not answer without her words being heard all over the Padan-aram.

"It's all right that you don't want to talk about it," said Leah. Then she rose up and walked down the row until she was parallel with Bilhah, and only a few steps away. "I can weed beside you as easily as I can weed across the field from you."

"Yes, Lady," said Bilhah.

"Please call me Leah."

"I'm Bilhah."

"I know," said Leah. "And you're a free girl, not a servant."

"I can't tell that it makes any difference," said Bilhah. "Without money, there's no freedom anyway."

"God will punish Noam for what he did," said Leah matter-of-factly. "So you don't have to worry about that."

"I don't care about punishing him," said Bilhah. "I just wish I had my papa's money back. He didn't save it all those years to give it to Uncle No."

"Well, if it's any comfort, you can be sure that Uncle No doesn't have it any more, either," said Leah. "The reason he had to sell himself to my father was because he's the worst gambler who ever lived, and what he doesn't lose at gaming he gives to bad women." Then Leah giggled. "I've never met a bad woman, so I don't know why men give them money."

"I saw a lot of them," said Bilhah. "They paint their faces and call out rudely to farmers and travelers."

"What do they say?" asked Leah.

Bilhah blushed and said nothing.

"You're blushing," said Leah.

"I thought you couldn't see," Bilhah blurted. And then, mortified, she said, "I'm sorry, Lady."

"I can't see very *well*," said Leah. "But I know that when people blush, they hold still and sort of dip their heads in a certain way, and you did that, even though you're plucking beans."

"So you didn't see me blush," said Bilhah.

"I see more than I see, if you know what I mean," said Leah. "Most people don't see the things I see, because they don't have to. And call me Leah, please."

"Nobody calls you by name, Lady," said Bilhah.

"I know, and that's why I wish you would."

"But if one of the older women hears me, she'll slap my face, and if one of the girls hears me, she'll tell."

"Then call me Leah when nobody else can hear."

"Yes, Lady."

Leah giggled. Bilhah realized that Leah's giggle was more about embarrassment or frustration than about amusement. So she decided not to be offended, because Leah wasn't actually laughing at her.

"I came out here to see if I would like you," said Leah, "and I do."

"Thank you . . . Leah."

"Because I was talking to Father and I said, If the tile-setter's daughter can't work with the animals, then let me have her, and he said, Be sure you like her well enough to have her with you day after day."

Bilhah had nothing to say. The whole idea of this girl saying to her father, "Let me have her," as if Bilhah were a puppy or a lamb—no one would have spoken of her that way in Byblos. And even here, that's how they talked about servants, not about free women. So even though Leah remembered that Bilhah was free, she still thought of her as someone she could ask her father for.

"You don't want to stay with me," said Leah.

"I didn't say anything," said Bilhah.

"I know," said Leah. "You caught your breath and held very still, and now your heart is beating fast and I think you're angry with me, but I don't know why."

"I'm not angry, Mistress," said Bilhah.

"I'm not your mistress," said Leah. "You're free."

"But you can ask your father to let you 'have' me." The words escaped before she could stop them.

Leah was quiet for a moment. "I'm sorry, I didn't think. I meant only that I need help, and since you aren't good with animals, you'd be the best choice to help me, since I can't work with them either."

"What do you need help with?" asked Bilhah.

"My eyes aren't getting better. It hurts to read. If you could read aloud to me."

Bilhah laughed. "I can't read," she said.

"But I thought you kept the counts for your father."

"I kept them, yes," said Bilhah. "In my head. It's not as if we had all that many customers."

"Well, then," said Leah, "we'll begin with me teaching you how to read."

"But that's for priests and priestesses, and scribes in the market," said Bilhah.

"And it's for the girl who stays beside me all the time, reading for me, and being my helper for any task that needs good eyes."

"If that's what Lord Laban wants me to do," said Bilhah, "then I'll do it, because I want to earn my place here, and it's shameful that I can't help with the animals as the other girls do."

"Everyone knows you're not lazy," said Leah. "You can't help it that you never feel sure around the beasts. They *do* keep moving and when they step on you, it isn't funny."

"I'll work hard at learning to read," said Bilhah.

"I want you to learn very quickly, because it's almost time for my sister to come home."

"Your sister?"

"Rachel," said Leah with a sigh.

"I didn't know you had a sister." But then Bilhah realized that she *did* know, without realizing it. Because there had been comments one time about how beautiful Laban's daughter was. Leah didn't seem particularly beautiful to Bilhah, but she had assumed that was just the way people talked about the daughter of the lord of Padan-aram. But if there was a sister, then . . .

"Oh, *she* must be the beautiful one," said Bilhah.

And now, because it had been pointed out to her, Bilhah

noticed how Leah didn't just blush, she also froze and her head sank down a bit into her shoulders.

"Not that you aren't pretty," said Bilhah.

"Oh, Bilhah," said Leah. "That's what everyone always says. 'Not that you aren't pretty.'"

"You *are* pretty," said Bilhah. "You have a nice face. And you smile very sweetly, and your teeth are good."

"But Rachel is beautiful," said Leah.

"I don't know," said Bilhah. "I heard them talking one time about how beautiful Laban's daughter was, and it was only when you mentioned having a sister that I realized . . ."

She realized there was no good way to finish that sentence.

"You only *heard* about my sister and you knew that I couldn't possibly be the beautiful one."

"I'm sorry," said Bilhah. "I keep giving offense but I don't mean to. I just . . ."

"You just can't help seeing what you see."

"It's your eyes," said Bilhah. "You squint when the veil is off, and even when it's on, you cock your head oddly to see, and you lean in close to look, and it doesn't make you pretty, it makes you . . ."

"Strange," said Leah.

"Tender-eyed," said Bilhah.

"And my nose is too big," said Leah.

"No it's not," said Bilhah.

"Everyone always talks about how perfect and tiny Rachel's nose is. And when they praise something about Rachel, they always mean 'compared to Leah.' So my nose must be big or misshapen. Or both."

"Your nose isn't unusually big," said Bilhah. "I mean, nobody would stand you on your head to catch rain with it."

"Tell me the truth," said Leah.

"You look like your father," said Bilhah. "He's a handsome man. And you're a handsome girl. And he has a nose that is as strong as his face."

Leah covered her face with her hands. "Oh why did God have to make me so ugly!"

"I swear, Lady, you aren't. You really are pretty, and strong, and good, and you can't help it that you have to squint."

"You're the first person who ever admitted to me that my nose was big."

"I didn't!" cried Bilhah. "I said it was strong."

"You said I looked like my father and he has a *beak*."

"It doesn't hook under his chin, if that's what you mean!" said Bilhah. "And yours isn't as big as his. Yours is proportioned to your face. Noses aren't beautiful on anybody. They always stick out in front no matter what you do. Oh, Lady, I didn't mean to make you unhappy."

"I know. I told you to tell the truth."

"But I always say things too . . ."

"Clearly."

"Rudely," said Bilhah. "I'm too blunt."

"Blunt as my nose," said Leah.

"I like your nose," said Bilhah. "It's the same size as mine, and I think I'm as cute as can be."

"Well, you aren't, you know," said Leah.

"My papa always said so, and so did his customers and the shopkeepers."

"But not recently," said Leah.

"So now you're getting even with me for what I said to you."

Leah laughed—only it wasn't that nervous giggle this time. "No, I'm just telling the truth! Because that's how it is with all of us. When we're little, we're all as cute as can be. Especially if we talk very well and we're clever beyond our years when we're still small. Oh, you're the cutest little girl! Oh, aren't you the smartest little child!"

It was a perfect imitation of the way older people had always talked to Bilhah, so she couldn't help but laugh.

"But then we turn ten," said Leah. "You're ten, aren't you?"

"Almost twelve now," said Bilhah.

"Ten is a very ugly age in girls," said Leah. "Girls all look like colts for about three years. Except Rachel, of course. She just got *cuter*."

"Colts are cute," said Bilhah. She refused to believe that her father had been lying to her. She was as beautiful as her mother.

"Colts are awkward and bony and it's not how a girl wants to look."

"So I'm awkward and bony?" asked Bilhah.

"I don't know," said Leah. "I can't see that well."

"You see everything."

"I see that you duck your head a little and slump when you walk, so you aren't used to being as tall as you are, and you trip sometimes just walking along, which means your feet are bigger than they used to be."

"I'm just clumsy."

"Not when you're picking beans you're not," said Leah.

What were they arguing about? Leah couldn't see very well, and yet she was insisting that Bilhah wasn't pretty. "So is this a test?" said Bilhah. "If I admit I'm ugly, you'll choose me to be your handmaiden?"

Leah giggled. "No, silly, I can't have a handmaiden till I'm married, or old enough to be married, and I'm *not*. I mean, I suppose in the city, rich girls might have handmaidens from the time they're born, but not here. Everybody works here, and so a girl doesn't need a handmaiden until she needs help dressing in very difficult clothing and needs somebody to carry away her rags and wash them."

"Is that what you want me to do?"

"No," said Leah quickly. "Well, I suppose so, but I'll carry *yours* away and wash them for *you* when you're in your time apart, so it'll be a fair trade."

"No you won't," said Bilhah. "Your father would never stand for that. And I won't mind. As long as *you* know that I'm a free woman, I won't mind acting the servant in the eyes of others."

"Don't you see?" said Leah. "I don't want a servant. I want a . . . a *friend!*"

An ugly friend, thought Bilhah. And the word Leah had been about to say was not *friend* at all. So she knew she wasn't being kind when she said, "Isn't your sister your friend?"

Leah giggled. It didn't sound as though she was amused. "Rachel is the chosen daughter of God."

"Is she a priestess then?" asked Bilhah.

"No," said Leah. "She just . . . doesn't have time for me. She's the queen of the shepherds now. She talks to Father about the animals practically all by name, she knows the herds so well. And I'm completely cut off from all that. Everybody always has things to say to Rachel, and Rachel always has things to say to them—and she's funny and smart, too, so they laugh and nod and pay attention to her as if she were a visiting angel. But when I talk, everybody's *patient* and they can hardly wait till I'm done because nothing I have to say is ever interesting."

"At least they listen," said Bilhah. "You should try being the new servant girl."

Leah fell silent a moment. "You're right," said Leah. "What am I complaining about? My mother's dead, like yours, but I still have my father, and he's lord of Padan-aram, and I'm living in my home as I always have, and here you are an orphan, among strangers."

"But I might be starving on the street, and instead I have a home here, so I'm well off, too."

"We're the two luckiest girls in the world," said Leah.

"No," said Bilhah. "But we're not without hope."

Leah laughed at that. "All right, that's true enough. Not without hope." Leah leaned in close so she was almost eye to eye with Bilhah. "You have beautiful eyes," she said. "I need someone to read to me so I can study and become wise. And I need someone to talk to me and tell the truth about everything I can't see—even if it's about how my nose is a beak and I walk like a hoopoe bird."

"I didn't say that!"

"But you could, if it's true! We'll always tell each other the truth, promise me!"

"No," said Bilhah. "The truth is mean and cruel, and besides, nobody ever knows the truth anyway."

"Of course they do."

"I knew a woman that wanted to marry Papa after Mama died, and she always told the 'truth' to everybody—but it was just meanness, because she always said the ugliest thing anybody could imagine, and then she'd say, 'If you can't face the truth, then you remain forever a child.' And Papa finally said, 'The truth is beautiful. Only ugly people make it harsh and unkind,' and she was so offended she went away without another word."

Leah laughed. "I like your papa!"

"I liked him too," said Bilhah.

And then, to her horror, she burst into tears and bent over there in the garden and wept into the basket of beans. "I miss him so much," she said. "I want my papa back. I want to go home."

She felt Leah's hand on her back, stroking her shoulders, stroking her hair. "Oh, Bilhah, I miss your papa too, and I didn't even know him. Think about that! You're luckier than I am, because you *knew* him, and he was so *good* to you for all those years, and I'll never know him."

"But you still have your father," whispered Bilhah.

"No," said Leah sadly. "Rachel has my father."

Bilhah could hardly grasp what such a thing might mean. But then, she had never had a sister to be compared to. She had never had even a brother for her father to love more than her.

"So could I borrow your memories of your father sometimes?" said Leah. "Could you tell me about him and let me pretend that we grew up sisters, and that he liked me as well as you, and always treated us both the same?"

Bilhah nodded. "I'll share him," she said. And then she thought of something funny. "It's always easier to share what you don't actually have," she said.

They laughed and cried together for another moment, there in the garden, and then they picked beans together till the job was done, and then weeded together till *that* job was done, and that night Bilhah went to sleep in Leah's tent, at the foot of her bed, the way the harness maker had once slept at her feet, to be her true friend and protector in the dark of night.

PART II

THE GIRL WHO COULD SEE

CHAPTER 3

Rachel could see two things at once. Not all the time. Not when she was talking to someone face to face, or pulling a thorn from a lamb's foot, or trying to herd a he-goat without getting butted for her pains. At times like that, she saw only the thing she needed to see.

But other times, sitting on a grassy slope on a sunny day, or huddling by a fire on a cold night, or staring up into darkness inside her tent, then other visions would come to her mind. To her *eyes* is how it seemed to her, but she knew that what she saw wasn't really there. If she moved her hand, then the vision would vanish and all that would be left was the nothing-in-particular she had been looking at before.

Sometimes the visions were meaningless, just strange shapes in the air, constantly shifting. There was a beauty to it, but if she tried to concentrate on any part of the shifting pattern, it would disappear.

Sometimes the visions were like dreams, with people doing things, events happening, but this kind of vision always ended with waking. Then she would know that she had merely dozed off, and the dream meant nothing. For a time it worried her that she was able to fall asleep with her eyes open, sitting up, but now she was used to it.

There was another kind of vision, though, which did not end with waking. There was always a voice—though not always the same voice. Sometimes it was a woman, and Rachel used to think it was her mother, though she would have no way of being sure. Usually it was a man, and the voice didn't belong to any man she knew.

The voice would start talking to her without her even noticing. She'd be looking at the sheep or the stars or a fire or the darkness and she'd realize that she was hearing someone saying things to her.

The first time she remembered this happening, she was five years old, and she thought someone was calling her. "Who is it?" she said, and when no one answered, she went looking for the man, but she found no one. A few weeks later it happened again, and she looked again, but eventually she learned that there wasn't anybody real talking to her, and instead she tried to listen to the voice.

It was hard, because the voice was usually just out of reach, like overhearing somebody in a brisk wind, with words being snatched away so that you could catch phrases but never understand anything.

But when she *could* understand, then visions would come with the words. She would see things.

When she was eight years old, she was lying in the dark of the tent, Leah asleep beside her—they shared a bed in those days. The voice was calling a name, but it wasn't hers. It was saying, "Rebekah" and then something about "drawing water from the well" and then "Rebekah" again and something about the household of Abraham.

Of course she knew the story of Aunt Rebekah, how she had gone to draw water and found a stranger there, and shared her water with him—and he turned out to be the servant of the great Abraham, who had come looking for a wife for Isaac. The way the story got told, Rebekah was so beautiful that the servant fell in love with her, but because he was only a servant and had given a most solemn oath, he could not woo her for himself, and instead he faithfully discharged his office and led her home to marry Isaac. Some people said the servant killed himself out of grief; others said he went mad; others said he continued to serve Abraham and then Isaac all his life, but he never married because he always loved Rebekah in his heart. Father said these tales were all nonsense, and he should know, because he had carried out the negotiations, and the servant was never in love with Rebekah.

But Rachel loved the story anyway, every version. Her favorite, though, was the one where the servant kept working in the same household with the woman he loved, never able to speak of his longing. It was a very lovely story, tragic and beautiful, and she cried now and then thinking of it.

So when she heard those words, of course she began to see the story in her mind as she had always imagined it.

But it wouldn't stay. It kept changing. The woman kept not being the beautiful Aunt Rebekah but instead was a gawky girl of twelve or so, and the man was no servant bearing noble gifts, but a lone traveler on foot. And instead of the girl fetching water for the man, it was the other way around. It made no sense. Could it possibly be that everyone had told the story wrong for all these years?

The voice made no sense to her, the vision made no sense, and yet it was very real to her. So of course she told Leah about it, because Leah was older and understood many things.

"I don't know," said Leah. "It could be a vision from God, or it could be a dream—"

"I wasn't asleep," insisted Rachel.

"Or you could be crazy," said Leah. "Probably that."

So Rachel went to her father, and of course Leah tagged along, because Leah couldn't *stand* to be left out of anything, though of course with her weak eyes she was left out of a lot of things just because she couldn't see well enough to stay out of the way and not get hurt, which made her furious, and Rachel could understand that, but she hated the way Father always made her stay with Leah, until the day she got furious and said, "Why should I always stay with Leah? *I'm* not blind!"

That had been a very bad thing to say—Father gave her a sharp swat and angrily forbade her ever to call her sister "blind" again, and Leah didn't speak to her for weeks. But from then on, Father no longer insisted that Rachel stay with Leah. However, *Leah* continued to insist on staying with Rachel, including this time, when Rachel wanted to tell Father about the vision.

"Girls dream of romance," said Father. "My sister's story has become very romantic, the way people tell it. But it wasn't. It was very complicated. Delicate negotiations. Businesslike, that's what it was. So of course you have dreams about it."

"It wasn't a dream," insisted Rachel. "I was awake."

"I often have dreams like that," said Father, and then he went on to talk about dreams so real he didn't realize he wasn't awake until he woke up—but the more he talked, the clearer it became that Father had no idea of the kind of dream Rachel had.

Finally, frustrated that he thought he knew everything when obviously he understood nothing, she stamped her foot and shouted at him—though she was only a few steps away. "I didn't wake up at the end because I was never asleep!"

He looked at her, quite startled. Then he replied, softly, "You mustn't yell at me like that."

"I never yell at people," said Leah.

Which was such a lie, thought Rachel. But it did no good to argue with Leah, because everybody took her side because they pitied her blindness. Let her say what she wants, and just remember that *you* can see.

Why doesn't anybody ever tell *Leah* to remember that Rachel can see, and therefore maybe she might know some things that Leah didn't know!

"When you yell at me, then I have to punish you," said Father, "or there'll be rebellion in the camp."

"Father," said Rachel, "I yelled because you weren't listening to me. You decided you knew what my vision was, only you were wrong, my vision was nothing like what you were saying. And it wasn't like the romantic stories of Rebekah, either, because the girl in my vision was too young, about twelve years old maybe, and the man was on foot, carrying a bundle on his back, and *he* drew water for the girl. So it was nothing like Rebekah."

"Then why did you tell me you had a vision of Rebekah?" said Father impatiently.

"Because the voice said her name," said Rachel. "At least that's all that I caught."

"What voice?"

"The man."

"What man?"

"The man who talks when I have this kind of vision."

Father got very serious. He led her to the table where the two images of the gods always stood and made her place one hand on each of them. "You're speaking before God now," he said. "Who was this man?"

"I don't know," said Rachel. She tried to take her hands off the little stone statues. Father held them there.

"It's a terrible sin to pretend that God is talking to you when he isn't," said Father.

"I never said it was God!" said Rachel.

"She said it was a man," said Leah helpfully.

"I know what she said," said Father. "It's exactly what a child might say if she wanted people to think that she was getting visions from . . ."

He let his words trail off and relaxed his hold on Rachel's hands. She pulled away from the statues. She didn't like the statues. They didn't look anything like God, she was sure of that. God had to be tall and strong, not little and stumpy and rather badly sculpted.

"Listen to me, Rachel. You must tell me. Was the girl in the dream *you?*"

Rachel wondered if he ever listened to her at all. "I said she was older than me. How could she be me if she's eleven or twelve years old?"

"But did she look like you?" he asked.

Rachel rolled her eyes. "How would I know? I've never seen myself."

"You're very beautiful," said Leah. Rachel hated when she said things like that, because of course Leah couldn't see her all that well, so she was really repeating what everybody else said, and Rachel was sick of hearing it, especially because she knew it hurt Leah's feelings.

"I don't know what beautiful looks like," said Rachel. "Or what I look like."

"Haven't you ever looked into a still pool of water and seen your face?"

"The girl in my vision wasn't all ripply and dark with stones and moss in the middle of her face."

Father glowered. "Don't get bratty with me, Rachel. I won't take it from you."

Leah murmured, "You always do." Naturally, Father didn't hear what she said—and Rachel did. Leah was very good at pitching her voice exactly right.

"What?" said Father.

"I don't think it was a vision," said Leah.

Rachel turned and glared at her sister, but they were standing too far apart, so Leah couldn't possibly see the expression on her face.

"What do you think it was?" said Father.

"I think it was a wish," said Leah. "I think Rachel is wishing it would happen to her like it happened to Aunt Rebekah."

"Then why was everything different in my vision?" insisted Rachel.

"What kind of blessing is this?" said Father. "Two beautiful daughters, one who can only see half of what's there, and now the other sees more than what's there."

Neither Rachel nor Leah thought this was a very funny comparison, but Father did, and he chuckled at it for so long that he ended up brushing tears of mirth from his eyes. "Sorry, sorry, I keep forgetting that neither of you has a sense of humor."

Rachel knew perfectly well that both she and Leah had very good senses of humor—they laughed a lot. They just didn't think Father's joking was very funny. Usually, in fact, his jokes were just a little bit cruel, though he probably never meant them to be hurtful.

"Listen, Rachel," said Father. "I won't have you telling people you see things and hear voices. Either they'll think you're some kind of priestess and you'll start getting pilgrims and petitioners—and I won't stand for that!—or they'll think you're crazy—"

Leah gave a tiny hiccup of a laugh at that, which of course Father didn't hear but Rachel did.

"And I don't think," said Father, "you'd like to be known as Laban's crazy daughter."

"But what if it *is* from God?" said Rachel.

"It isn't," said Father.

"How do you know?"

"It's obvious. First, when God wants to tell somebody something, he speaks clearly. There's never any doubt. Second, you're a woman. There's no reason God can't talk to a woman, but who would listen to her? So God gives visions to men so that others will pay attention to his message. Third, you even said it yourself, the vision was all wrong. Visions from God don't *lie,* so if it wasn't like what happened with Rebekah, then your dream wasn't from God."

Father was very convincing.

"Was her vision from the Evil One?" asked Leah.

"Her vision was from her own imagination," said Father. "She thinks she hears the name of Rebekah, she dreams but the dream gets it all wrong, the way dreams do. It means nothing, but if she blabs about it to everybody it will damage her reputation and mine as well. So, Rachel, you will not tell anyone about this dream or any other dream you get. Except me. If there's ever a clear message of some kind, then tell me at once."

Later, Leah reassured Rachel that this meant Father secretly believed in her vision. "Why would he want you to tell him, except that he believes?"

"I never get clear messages," said Rachel. "So I'll never tell Father about it. So that's all over. I hope I don't have any more visions like that, now that Father has commanded me not to tell anybody."

"You can tell me."

"Father said not."

"I already think you're crazy," said Leah. "So what harm can it do?"

But Rachel never told Leah another vision, because the next day when Leah was irritated that she couldn't go along to watch the shearing of the sheep—too many knives flashing for a weak-eyed girl to be leaning in for a closer look, Father said—Leah's retort was, "I may not see everything, but at least what I *do* see is *real*."

That's how Rachel knew that Leah hated her visions. So as far as Leah heard of it, Rachel never had another.

And she didn't have many. Most of the time, the visions she saw were empty nothings. The voice only came now and then, and she only understood bits and snatches, and she never saw that particular dream again. She rarely thought of it, and when she did, she couldn't even remember what anybody looked like, so what was the point? Mostly she tried to ignore the things she saw that weren't actually real, and when she did see the patterns she'd dispel them as quickly as possible, and when she did hear that voice—the man or the woman, either one—she'd look for somebody to talk to.

But on this day, returning with the flock she and four older boys and Old Jaw had been grazing up in the southwestern hills, the voice came back to her and would not go away.

She was leading the way—nobody remembered paths better than Rachel, and Old Jaw was always content to lag behind, "watching for strays," as he said. The dogs knew their business—they were keeping the flock together, right behind Rachel. So there was nothing in front of her except grassy hills and the unmarked path that she knew from childhood on, leading to the little well about four miles south of Father's settlement.

"What's the hurry?" called one of the boys—a particularly stupid one who was always showing off for her, even though she made it clear she had nothing but contempt for his stupid acrobatics and races and clowning. She refused even to remember his name.

Only when he spoke to her did she realize that she had quickened her pace and had led the flock at least a hundred paces ahead of Old Jaw and the boys.

"I'm not hurrying," she called back. "You're just slow."

"Doesn't do any good to hurry!" shouted Old Jaw. "We don't water the flock in the heat of the day!"

"It isn't summer yet," said Rachel. "It won't hurt them!"

"Well, if you get there ahead of us, who's going to get the cover off the well?" shouted Old Jaw.

The boys whooped at that. "Rachel's going to get the dogs to do it!" said one.

"She's going to give it her prettiest smile and it will open up for her by itself!" shouted another.

Rachel detested boys. They were all despicable. Why the Lord had bothered to make them, Rachel couldn't guess. They were created in the image of God. But couldn't he have gone all the way and given them some wits, too?

So she forged ahead even faster, to put their jeers behind her.

And when their voices fell away, she was aware that there was another voice that had been with her for some time, perhaps since they had set out that morning. It was the man's voice, and it was murmuring, or perhaps chanting, and the one phrase that kept emerging in rhythm with her steps was "to the well."

By now, she had convinced herself that Father was right and the voice came out of her own imagination. She knew she was heading for the well, so the voice was chanting about it, pushing her along. She wished it would go away. After all, she wasn't sitting around staring off into space. Why would the voice bother her now?

She followed the pace it set, however, walking so quickly that the sheep seemed to catch some kind of excitement from her. They became noisier, bleating more often, and the dogs yipped and snapped more than usual, until as they crested the last hill and started down into the little vale where the well was, she was almost running.

I don't want to be late, she thought.

Or had the voice said that?

There were already quite a few sheep in the valley, two separate flocks, but down at the bottom end, almost to where it debouched from the hills. She didn't recognize the shepherds, but that was no surprise—she knew all the major herdsmen in the area, but this close to Haran, the great houses would tend to send boys and new men . . . and their daughters.

Still, strangers meant that they might not know who she was, and that she was under the protection of a great house. There might be some danger here. How far behind her were Old Jaw and the boys? Not that they would be much in the way of protectors, but they could convincingly invoke Father's name and reputation. No one would dare to lift a hand against the flocks of Laban, still less against his daughter.

The last thing she should do, she knew, was to show timidity. So she continued at the same pace until her flock was gathered around the well and the troughs.

One of the strange shepherds called out to her. "It's the heat of the day!"

She ignored him.

"You going to lift off the cover yourself?" The others thought this was very funny.

But of course it was not funny. She was still too small to lift or even slide the heavy stone that covered the mouth of the well. So she sat on top of it, her back to the strangers, while her sheep milled around the well and tried to lap water from the wet spots in the troughs.

Some of the men in the nearer herd soon began to speculate loudly upon why she had been in such a hurry to get to the well, and what it was she actually intended to do; and as the men began to get more and more amused at their own wit, their speculations became more and more obnoxious. What was keeping Old Jaw and the boys?

Why doesn't the voice come now and tell me what to do?

Then, suddenly, the men fell silent.

She turned and saw that one of the men from the farther herd was approaching her.

She murmured a prayer for protection.

As if in answer, the dogs ran toward him, barking, warning him away. *Loyal dogs!*

Then he bent down and spoke to them, in a voice too soft and distant for her to hear. They sniffed his hands; he stroked them, scratched them, and when he arose they were *his* dogs, scampering around him like puppies as he again walked boldly toward her. *Treacherous curs!*

Then she studied the man a little, and realized that he wasn't one of the shepherds. The bundle he carried on his back was far more than any shepherd would willingly carry, since you never knew when you'd have to lift a lamb onto your shoulders and carry it. And he wasn't dressed right. His clothes were too fine for a shepherd—and too dusty. He hadn't spent the morning on grassy hills, he had been walking along a dry road. *A traveler.*

"Don't be afraid, Rachel," he said. "Be at peace. I won't come any nearer than this."

"Who are you, sir? How do you know my name?"

"When I saw you and your sheep coming down the hill, I asked the other men who you were."

"I don't know those men."

"Neither do I," said the stranger. "But they know *you.* They said you were Rachel, the daughter of Laban. Or rather,

I asked them if they knew Laban of Haran, and they said that of course they did, he's a great man and his camp is not five miles away, and look, there's his daughter, Rachel, the . . . coming down the hill with Laban's sheep."

Rachel the what? She knew very well, and she pursed her lips. Rachel the Beautiful. That's why they knew of her. The one aspect of herself that *she* never saw was the only one that anyone else cared about, while all the things that made up who she was in her own mind, nobody knew. I am surrounded by strangers, and the more well-known I am by reputation, the more alone I am.

"If you get off the stone," said the traveler, "I can uncover the well."

"I'm not so very heavy," said Rachel. "If you can move the stone without me, surely you're strong enough to move it with me on top."

"With you and three sheep, if you can balance them all there," said the traveler. "But I don't believe in making foolish displays of strength. It makes other men jealous and their wives covetous, and then I have no peace."

Rachel refused to laugh, and she hoped he did not notice the twitch of a smile that crept to her face before she could stop it.

She got up and lightly leapt to the ground. "I can help," she said.

"But what if, with my massive strength, I accidently tossed the stone onto your foot? Then you'd be Rachel the cripple, and your father would have to kill me, or at least cut off my leg."

"My father would never do that."

"Then you don't know fathers."

46

"He's never done anything like that before."

"Only because no traveler has ever cast a huge stone onto his daughter's dainty foot."

Rachel looked down at her calloused, toughened feet. "I'm a shepherd, sir. My feet are not dainty."

"I thought it was a nicer word than 'dingy,'" said the stranger. "And 'dung-covered' would have been rude." Now he began pushing the stone in earnest, and there was no breath for speech. His word was true: he slid the stone off with no one's help, and in one continuous movement, too, no pausing to rest.

"That's a useful skill to have," said Rachel. "Most wells are covered so heavily that travelers could die of thirst trying to find a well they could open by themselves between here and Salem."

"Have you been to Salem?" asked the traveler.

"No," said Rachel. "Father only lets me tend the flocks close to home. But that's all right. I work with the lambs and kids especially, and I know them better than any of the other herdsmen. Are you going to take the first drink or not?"

"I opened the well for you, Lady Rachel."

"You look drier than the sheep," she said. "Go ahead."

He grinned. "You saw the test of my strength," he said. "What about the test of yours?"

She glared at him. "I'm just a child, but I can draw water well enough." She lowered the bag into the well, then braced herself and drew it up, full, and without letting the rope rub against the sides of the well, either.

"Done like a shepherd who knows the value of rope," said the traveler.

"Done like a shepherd who has plaited many a rope and

has better things to do with her time," said Rachel. "Now will you dip into the water bag or do I have to do that for you, too?" She tried to conceal how much she was panting from the exertion of lifting the water straight up.

The stranger took his own cup—a rather fine one of bronze—and dipped, and drank. He did not tip his head back and pour the water over his face, the way some did, to show off how thirsty they were. Instead he sipped carefully, husbanding the water, swishing it in his mouth several times before swallowing.

She watched him and thought, Is this the man from my vision? She couldn't remember what that one had looked like—it had been too long ago, and maybe she had never actually seen him, in that peculiar way of dreams, where you know that a man is standing there, but you don't actually see any part of him. And what if it *was* the man? This was no servant of Abraham, come to woo, for there was no chance that his bundle contained enough presents to impress a man like her father; and besides, Rachel was too young to wed, and she knew her father would never allow it.

Then she realized that she had been thinking of this man as someone who might marry her—an attitude she never took toward any of the men who came to visit Father, even the ones who *were* sizing her up as a mate for themselves or one of their sons. And she wondered if that was the point of the vision, to make her think of strangers at wells as having something to do with her future.

Having drunk his fill, he put his hands into the water and, bowing over the waterbag, brought two cupped handsful to his face, to wash. And then, before she could suggest doing it, he carried the bag to the trough and emptied it.

The sheep, of course, were quite interested in this, and crowded around the trough. The traveler laughed. "Sheep don't bother to hide their passions, do they. Water! Grass! That's why God didn't give them speech. They would only need a couple of words to cover the entire range of their desires."

He lowered the bag into the well himself this time, and drew it up far more quickly than she had. But she saw how he was careful to spill nothing between the well and the trough— what he drew was to be used, not wasted on the ground. He poured it out into a second trough—but the two of them had to drag sheep from the crowd milling around the first trough, because they were too intent on the water there to notice water that was much more easily reached.

She saw how he handled sheep, and knew that though he might be dressed as a traveler, he *was* a shepherd after all, and a good one. He used just the right amount of strength to bring the sheep, murmuring peaceably to them as he turned them smoothly and pulled them toward where he wanted them to go. And once a few of the sheep were drinking from the second trough, it was enough simply to turn the other sheep that were not already drinking.

He left Rachel to that task while he fetched yet another skin of water and filled the third trough. When the flock was evenly divided among the three, he continued drawing and pouring, ignoring Rachel when she said, "Surely you've done enough now. The work *is* mine."

"The work is Laban's," said the traveler, "and I want it to be seen how readily I labor in his service."

"Have you traveled so far, without knowing whether my father needed another servant in his household? And you're a free man, sir, one accustomed to wealth, from your clothing. Surely you can do better than the poor wage that a free man makes from my father, even if he were to hire you."

He smiled and continued watering the sheep. Rachel took her turn at last, dipping with her own cup from the waterbag. When she had drunk her fill, she fastened the cup again at her waist.

"Do you know my father, sir?" she asked.

"We've never met," said the man.

"And yet you traveled all this way to serve him? Why should the fame of my father be known so far abroad?"

He laughed then. "You don't know how far I've traveled."

"Of course I do," she said. "We had rain three days ago, and yet your clothes are heavy and white with dust. So you come from a place where the roads are dry and where the rain did not fall. That means you come from the south, because the paths are grassy to the north and east."

"What about the west?"

"A man who knows animals as you do is no sailor, sir."

The watering was done; they both knew when there was enough in each trough to satisfy the whole flock, and now Rachel's work was to pull off the ones who she knew tended to drink more than was good for them, while the stranger slid the stone back in place. This was harder than uncovering the well, Rachel knew, because there was some lifting, not just sliding, but he did it with no more strain than he had shown before. She hoped her father *would* hire the man. She would try to get home early, to tell her father what she had seen of him, how hard he worked, how strong he was, how good with the animals. And if he didn't have skill with weapons, too, she'd be surprised. A man who dared to travel alone, armed only with a heavy walking staff, had great confidence in his ability to wield that staff to keep better-armed robbers at bay.

"Did you have to fight anyone on the way here?"

"No, thanks be to the Lord," said the traveler. "But I don't look like someone worth robbing, do I? No pack animals laden with goods to sell."

She laughed. "I've heard of robbers setting on a half-naked beggar, stealing his loin cloth, and beating him for not having had more to take."

"Ah, but there you are, a half-naked beggar isn't likely to put up much of a fight. Men don't go into the robbery business because they're brave."

So he did think of himself as a formidable fighter.

It was only now that Old Jaw and the boys appeared over the crest of the hill. Apparently once she had gone on ahead, they had taken their own lazy time about sauntering along.

But when they saw her with a stranger, Old Jaw began to hurry down the hill, coming as close to a run as a man that old was capable of. Rachel smiled at that. Oh, yes, Father would hear—from the other herdsmen, not from her—about how his daughter had come to the well alone, and took up with a stranger for fifteen minutes before Old Jaw could be bothered to show up, and him entrusted with the safety of Laban's daughter! As if hurrying *now* would change any part of *that* story. Of course, Rachel would assure her father that she had deliberately outpaced the old man and was never in danger. And she would jolly him out of whatever anger he might feel toward the old man, and deny that it had been any time at all before he came.

Old Jaw was full of challenge when he got near enough to

speak. "Who are you, stranger! Why are you bothering this child?"

Anger flashed in the stranger's eyes. "What do you accuse me of, sir!" he said. "Have I bothered her? Have I laid hands upon her?"

Whereupon he *did* take her by the shoulders. His hands were huge on her, and yet his touch was even gentler than it had seemed upon the sheep.

She remembered again the man in the vision, and the girl of eleven or twelve. She had seemed so big to her then, when she had the vision, but now she *was* eleven.

"When you came over the hill, did you see me watering the sheep? Or was I kissing her?"

And as he bent toward her, and she realized that he was, in fact, going to kiss her, she remembered the voice that had chanted to her all the way to the well today, urging her on, faster, so she wouldn't be late. If her vision meant anything at all, it meant *this*, that she was supposed to be here.

She did not have to let him kiss her. His hold was gentle and she could break away at any time, without effort. And he had not tried to touch her until he was accused falsely. It was so perverse, to be defiant like this and actually do the thing he was accused of. But she understood such impulses; hadn't she done the same to Leah, acting as she was accused of being, just to show how different things would be if the accusation were true?

And yet it was a dangerous thing for this man to do. There were more witnesses than Old Jaw and the boys. Those other herders, they'd have the story all over the land of Haran within days, and then how could Father keep his honor without hunting down this stranger and killing him? She should not let him kiss her.

All this flashed through her mind in the time that it took him to bend, deliberately, and kiss her, not upon the cheek, but on the lips, a bold, firm-lipped kiss like a father, like a brother.

"You are a dead man!" shouted Old Jaw. "You think because I'm old you can have your way, but her father is a mighty man in this country! You take your life in your hands, sir!"

The stranger pulled away from Rachel, and to her surprise, tears were streaming down his face. Yet they were not tears of grief—his smile was broad and his eyes were kindly as he looked at her. Nothing like the frown she wore on her own face.

"I know that her father is Laban," said the traveler, his tone amiable enough, "and this is his daughter Rachel. Which makes her my kinswoman, for I'm a son of Laban's sister, Rebekah. Laban and I are truly brothers, and like a brother I greet his quick-witted daughter with a brother's kiss. Do you dare to say I have no right?"

And in that moment, everything changed. This was one of the sons of Isaac. A prince, truly, for he was a grandson of Abraham. And as Rebekah's son, he had claim upon that story, too—the tale of the woman who met a stranger at a well.

Meanwhile, Old Jaw was about to continue his bluster. "Any man can claim to be a kinsman, but how do I know—"

"I know you, sir," said Rachel. "For Aunt Rebekah has two sons, one who is known to be red and hairy, which is not you, so you must be the other one."

"Yes," said the man, laughing. "I am, always and forever, the other one."

"How can this be true!" demanded Old Jaw. "The camp of Isaac is at Beersheba."

"And from Beersheba I have come," said the traveler. "I

am Jacob, son of Isaac and Rebekah, grandson of Abraham and Sarah, and I have come to ask the hospitality of my brother Laban."

"It's a strange thing, to ask it upon the lips of his favorite daughter!" said Old Jaw angrily.

Favorite daughter. It made Rachel shiver, to hear it said so baldly. Was it true? Father doted on Leah, constantly looked after her, made sure her every whim was catered to. While Rachel was expected to do a full share of work in the camp, learning all the work, and not just the work of women, either. It had always seemed to Rachel that it was Leah who was the most favored. Leah was pretty, wasn't she? And even though she couldn't see well, she wasn't *blind*. Father loved Leah dearly. Surely more than he loved Rachel, who was always getting into trouble and whom he constantly had to rebuke.

But if this was what everyone believed, then Leah must believe it, too. No wonder she is so angry at me for no reason. She thinks I'm Father's favorite! Such foolishness.

"My father," she said coldly to Old Jaw, "has no favorites among his children."

But it was Jacob who answered. "I'm glad to hear it. I've had enough of parents who have favorite children." Then he grinned at Old Jaw—not a friendly grin, a grin full of malice, like a baboon challenging a stranger. "And I've had enough of accusations. I am who I say, and my proof is that only a fool would have kissed this young woman if he were *not* who I say I am."

His hands were still upon her shoulders, but now they felt heavy to Rachel. Too big. She could be lost in those hands, powerless, swallowed up. This man who could move the well-stone by himself, this man who could turn sheep where he wanted, with his strength and his soft murmuring voice, she could be lost if he held her a moment longer.

She pulled away, and as she had thought at first, he held her so lightly that he barely had to move his hands to let her go.

"I have to go," she said. Or meant to say. The words came more like a gasp. "I *must* go. Must *run*. And tell my father." Old Jaw and the boys and the dogs could bring in the sheep. She turned her back on Old Jaw and found herself facing Jacob. Her cousin Jacob.

Isaac had been Rebekah's cousin.

He smiled at her. And laughed.

He had called her quick-witted. Not beautiful. Could a man be more perfect than that?

She turned and ran away from him then, because she had to tell her father that he was coming, and especially to tell him about the kiss before anyone else could, so she could turn away Father's wrath before Jacob came into the camp. And she also ran away from him because it frightened her to think that perhaps God had brought him to her, and had planned it since she was a little girl, or perhaps had planned it all her life. Perhaps she had always belonged to Jacob, and never knew it.

But could such a man as that ever belong to *me?* thought Rachel.

There was no voice in her head to answer her question. She didn't need one.

CHAPTER 4

Rachel told it in the wrong order, though she had thought it out carefully on the way. First tell Father that Rebekah's son Jacob had come to visit, *then* tell him about the kiss. She hadn't anticipated Father's reaction to the news. You would have thought the king of Byblos was coming to visit, the way he immediately began to run around giving orders. Slaughter this animal and that animal, pitch the best visitors' tent, clean this up, tidy that, make this place look respectable, don't you know a *prince* is coming?

There was not chance to say even so much as, By the way, Father, he kissed me, and then cried. But then, did she really have to? Father knew the important information—the visitor was his nephew, Rebekah's son. When he heard about the kiss—and he would—he would already know that it was a kinsman's kiss and nothing more.

The sudden uproar in the camp brought Leah out of her

tent, of course, and she was holding lightly to the arm of a new girl that Rachel hadn't seen before. Had Father bought someone? Not likely. Probably someone's relative, or an orphan he had taken in. She was a comely girl and didn't carry herself like a slave, so perhaps she had not been bought.

"What's going on?" asked Leah. "Is that you, Rachel?"

"You know it is," said Rachel. She knew perfectly well that Leah could recognize most people from a distance, just by their gait and voice, their posture and general coloring. "Who's the new girl?"

"Bilhah," said Leah, just as the girl herself said, "I am Bilhah of Byblos, and I'm a free girl."

Leah smiled. "She's Noam's cousin. He stole her dowry money and ran away, and now she serves in his place."

Bilhah turned red. "I do not," she said. "Your father refused me as a servant, and said *he* was my cousin now."

"I'm sorry," said Leah. "How could I forget? That's very important."

"I'm a free girl."

But Rachel could see that Bilhah was sizing her up, and she wanted to scream at her, Yes, I'm the pretty one, whatever that's worth, but if you say it in front of Leah then you're not a very good person, are you.

Instead Bilhah said, "I don't think I've ever seen anyone as dirty as you are right now."

Leah spoke up at once, as if to cover the girl's excessive directness. "She has city manners."

Rachel at once answered with the family joke, "Which is even worse than no manners at all!" She and Leah burst into laughter.

Bilhah smiled thinly. Rachel decided she didn't like the

girl. All she seemed to be able to think about was how *free* she was, as if that made much difference in the life of the camp. Everybody did what Father said, and that was that. The only distinction that mattered was whether you were a member of the household or a guest or an intruder. Either you owed Father service, or he owed you hospitality, or you were driven away. Bilhah was under Laban's protection, and she obeyed him, and what difference, then, whether you were a daughter or a servant or a free girl from Byblos? As if there were some great honor in being from that filthy city by the sea.

"You still haven't told me what's happening," said Leah. "Is someone invading the camp?"

"Yes," said Rachel.

Bilhah looked alarmed and Leah must have felt her stiffen, because she said, "That's just Rachel's joke, Bilhah. Everything's a story and full of far too much excitement."

"So it's only one man," said Rachel, "and it's not exactly an invasion. Everything else is true!"

"But that's all you said," answered Bilhah, looking puzzled.

Rachel and Leah laughed again. "That's the joke," said Leah.

Bilhah looked at them as if they were possessed by some spirit.

"It's a visitor," said Rachel. "I met him at the well, and he kissed me."

Now it was Leah's turn to stiffen and look alarmed. "Then Father will have him killed, you know that."

"No, Father has decided to kill two kids and a calf and set them a-roasting so they'll be ready for supper at nightfall."

"He's giving hospitality to a man who filthied you?" said Leah.

"Well, he doesn't know about the kiss."

"You didn't *tell* him?"

"I thought it was the right thing to do at the time. And besides, the man cried when he did it."

Leah's consternation was growing, which was, of course, the goal. "Whatever you're not telling me that will make it all seem sensible, tell me now!"

"He's our cousin, that's why he could kiss me and not be killed. Aunt Rebekah's boy."

"Boy? She only has the two sons, and they're grown men."

"Well, he certainly wasn't a man when Rebekah gave birth to him!"

"So which son is he? The hairy one or the sneak?"

"He's not a sneak," said Rachel.

It was Leah's turn to laugh. "Didn't he grab his brother by the heel as he followed him from the womb? That's the story they tell. Anyway, you've told me which one it was who kissed you, because if it was the hairy one, you wouldn't have minded my calling the other a sneak."

"His name is Jacob," said Rachel.

"The son who will *not* inherit," Leah pointed out.

Rachel hadn't thought of that. "They're twins, aren't they?"

"Great houses aren't divided among the sons, or within three generations they're not great houses anymore."

"So Nahor will get *everything*? Just because he's oldest?"

"Don't you know anything?" said Leah.

"I never thought Father would choose among our brothers and give it all to one."

"He doesn't choose. The birthright goes to the oldest, unless he does something really terrible and gets cut off from the family."

"What happens to Terah and Choraz? They starve?"

"No, Father gives them something, enough to show they're worthy men. Then they go into service to a king, or set up a small herd and do their best to make it a great one. That's why Choraz went off in the service of Kedar ben Ishmael, to see if he could win a place for himself at the table of the prince. Honestly, Rachel, what do you and the shepherds talk about out there in the hills, if you don't know anything about how your own family inheritances go?"

"Why would we talk about inheritances? They won't get anything, and neither will I, and besides, it's awful thinking about what will happen after Father dies, he's not even old yet, is he?"

"So the man who kissed you, O Lady of the Visions, is just a second son after all."

"He kissed me as a cousin. If you had been there, he would have kissed *you* just that way."

"Oh, yes, men are always kissing me. Father buries them in the garden, to help the crops grow"

"Well, they're not always kissing *me*, either."

"I wonder why Jacob would come here," said Leah. "Did he bring a great many men with him?"

"Not any, and no animals, either."

"Alone?"

"With a bundle and the clothes on his back."

"So he really is *poor?*" said Leah.

"I don't know. Maybe he's bringing a message from his mother."

"Isaac would send gifts," said Leah.

"Why?"

"You don't know anything about good manners," said Leah. "You'll make someone a perfectly awful wife."

Leah was always saying things like that, and Rachel couldn't answer with the obvious retort that at least she could *see*. It would be wrong to taunt Leah about her frailty. But it was also unfair for Leah to taunt *her* when she knew Rachel couldn't answer. "I don't want to marry anybody," said Rachel.

"Oh, right," said Leah, "that's why you keep them all staring at you like a prize heifer."

"I don't *do* that," said Rachel angrily. "I can't help what people look at."

"But you like it," said Leah.

"No I don't," said Rachel. "You only say that because you want the men to look at you, but I don't want them to."

"I don't want them to, either," said Leah, "but I think you like it."

Rachel turned to Bilhah. "She thinks she knows my heart better than I do myself."

"Yes," said Leah, "I do. For instance, I know that you let him kiss you because you were hoping that he was your vision coming true. I bet you let him kiss you before you even knew who he was."

There it was—her secret. The thing she planned to deny if Father asked her. How could Leah guess it?

"I did not," said Rachel.

"Did you hear that?" said Leah to Bilhah. "That's how you know when Rachel's lying. There's that little pause, and when she tells her lie there's that little whine in her voice."

Bilhah clearly did not want to play the Quarreling Sisters game. She looked away, making no response to Leah's words.

"I'm not lying," said Rachel.

"There it was again—the pause, the whine."

"She can mock me like this," said Rachel to Bilhah, "because she knows that if I ever complain to Father, he'll tell me that I should just be grateful that I have two good eyes and be patient with Leah."

But the moment she spoke, she knew that she had done it—used Leah's tender eyes as a strike against her in a quarrel. Never mind that she was quoting what Father said—in fact, that made it worse.

Leah did not burst into tears the way she used to do when such things were said. She simply turned and walked back to her tent.

"I'm sorry," said Rachel softly. But she knew Leah could hear her. Leah could hear everything.

Naturally, though, Bilhah would think she was talking to her. "I never had a sister," said Bilhah, "but I hope if I did we would never have been so hateful to each other."

"We love each other," said Rachel. "You don't know anything."

"You don't love each other," said Bilhah. "You hate each other. Every time something good happens to you, Leah thinks it was stolen from her, and whenever somebody treats Leah kindly, you think they're giving you a slap."

"You never saw me before this moment," said Rachel. "And you're very rude."

"I didn't ask to be part of all that nastiness," said Bilhah. "If you don't want other people to judge you, keep your spite to yourself." She stalked away.

Now, though, Rachel understood what difference it made to be a free girl. No slave who could be whipped would ever have said that to the daughter of Laban. And if Rachel wanted to go to Father and complain about Bilhah being cruel to her and saying ugly things, what would Bilhah think *then,* as she found herself getting thrown out of camp?

Rachel shook her head to drive out the ugly thought. Would I do that to a girl, just because she spoke boldly? Deprive her of the only home she had?

Besides, Bilhah was about half right. There were still times when Leah and Rachel laughed together at jokes that only they understood—hadn't they laughed like that only a few minutes ago? But quarrels came up more often now than ever before, and they were uglier and more spiteful. Why had Rachel said that, about Father insisting that Leah be forgiven for everything because of her eyes? That was low of her, and she was ashamed.

She stood there, staring off into the dim distance, thinking only of her shame, when suddenly the vision came to her again. The man at the well, and now it was Jacob. The girl, and now she knew it was herself. And he kissed her. That wasn't in the first dream she had, was it? She would have remembered. She would have told Father about it. No, this wasn't the vision returning, this was just her imagining it, only now the way she wanted it to have been. She wanted to have Jacob brought to her by God. Maybe he would marry her and take her away from Leah and her envy—and the constant temptation for Rachel to be meaner than she really was at heart.

"Rachel!" It was Father's voice, and he didn't sound happy. "Come here!"

Of course she went to him, but at a walk, not a run. It was

hard to run toward peril, and from his voice, she was in danger.

"Why didn't you tell me this man kissed you?"

"I was about to, but you started telling everybody what animals to kill and how to roast them and I couldn't say *anything* to you."

Father glared at her. "Don't blame *me* for your deception."

"Why would I lie?" said Rachel. "He's my cousin, he has a perfect right to kiss me."

"Old Jaw says he kissed you before he told anybody who he was. So as far as you knew, he was a complete stranger, and you didn't even try to stop him."

"Of course not," said Rachel. "I saw him kiss me in my vision."

Technically, it was true—not in the original vision, but in the vision she had had only a couple of minutes ago. So maybe it wasn't a lie, and if it wasn't, then maybe she hadn't done the things that made it so Leah could easily tell when she was lying.

Whether her pause and whine gave her away or not, Father didn't notice. He had stopped cold at the mention of her vision. He took her by the shoulders—far less gently than Jacob had—and in a fierce whisper he said, "Tell that to no one, do you understand?"

She knew then that Father feared her telling that story. So she could use it to end the suspicion of Jacob. "I will tell it to *everybody* who accuses Jacob of anything improper."

Father glared at her. "You think you're so clever, getting me to do whatever you want."

"I can't help what I'm shown in visions," said Rachel. "And none of the voices I hear ever told me not to tell." Which was a flat lie, the woman's voice especially was prone to whisper, Shhhhh, don't say it.

I lie too much, thought Rachel, but the thought soon fled, because it's not as if she started each day thinking, I'm going to tell a dozen big old lies today. She only lied when somebody *made* her do it. She had to protect Jacob, and if she could do it by pretending that God had shown her a vision of Jacob kissing her, well, it was worth the lie. If that made her wicked, then maybe God would punish her by stopping the visions, and if the truth be known, she could hardly think of anything she wanted more.

PART III

FATHERLESS CHILD

CHAPTER 5

Zilpah's mother had never actually *said* that Laban was the man who had sired her. When Zilpah was six, she asked outright where her father was. Mother hushed her immediately, with tight-lipped anger, and told her that there were some things she was too young to know.

Zilpah never asked again, but she knew her mother's answer was absurd. All the other children knew who and where their fathers were, even the ones who were younger than her, even the ones whose fathers were dead. So is my father *worse* than dead? Was he a criminal? Why should I keep still about him?

Then she heard the word *bastard*—hurled by one shepherd at another, in a quarrel—and asked one of the other children what it meant. "It's a man who doesn't know who his father is."

This set Zilpah to wondering: What about a girl who

didn't know who her father was? Was she a bastard, too? And was it an awful thing to be? The shepherd who had said the word was full of hate when he said it, and the word made the other shepherd fly at him, flailing about with his crook. Am I a thing so awful, that a man would attack a bigger fellow for having said he was one?

So once again she braved her mother's wrath, expecting to be rebuked even more sternly for asking, "Mama, can a girl be a bastard?"

Her mother was angry all right, but not at her. "Who called you such a thing? I'll kill him."

"Nobody," said Zilpah, frightened.

"Then how did you ever hear that word?"

Zilpah told about the quarrel between grown men, and Mother relaxed. "Well, it has nothing to do with *you*."

"But Amar said that—"

"Amar doesn't know his leg from his neck, so he scratches his knee when his head itches."

Miserably, Zilpah confessed her worry. "Other children younger than me know who their father is."

"That's because it's all right for them to know. Their father is nobody important, and so they don't have to keep the secret."

Ah. So her father was someone so important that his identity could not be known. That was better than any answer Zilpah could have imagined.

Of course, the most important man that Zilpah knew anything about at that age was Laban, the lord of the camp, who ruled over everyone and dispensed justice, food, and labor assignments every day. So for several years she believed Laban was her father.

But as she grew older and learned more about the world, she began to realize that this was not very likely. While Laban did not marry again after his wife died, he could easily have taken a concubine, or several concubines. Even if he had wanted to keep his liaison with Mother secret while his wife was alive—some women were jealous about their husband taking concubines among the women in the camp—there was nothing to stop him from recognizing Mother as a concubine after he was a widower.

She even asked one of the old women called Hobbler why Laban didn't take concubines the way other powerful men did, and Hobbler only laughed. "He's not the kind of man who can't live without a woman. His eye never wandered the whole time his wife was alive. She never had to shed a tear because he was sleeping in another woman's tent."

It dawned on Zilpah then that since there were no secrets in the camp—the old women knew even more stories than were true—it was almost impossible that Laban could have fathered her, not without some kind of rumor among the women.

So her important father must have been someone from outside the camp, and that made more sense anyway. Mother must have sneaked off to the city, or perhaps a visitor crept into her tent one night. Maybe he even forced himself on her, and she had to keep it secret to avoid a terrible war between great houses.

And then, by the time she was twelve, Zilpah came to the realization that her mother was probably lying. She had only been about fifteen when Zilpah was born, and in all likelihood the only reason Zilpah's father wasn't known was because there were too many candidates for the title to be certain.

What made Zilpah almost sure that this was the truth was the way her mother watched over her once she started turning into a woman, refusing to let her do anything that would leave her alone with any man or boy old enough to cause mischief. "A man's all full of talk about love," her mother said bitterly, "but he cares less for you than he does for a sheep. Don't trust them! Not a one of them! I want you to have a husband, a good man who'll stand by you."

That was as good as a confession, to Zilpah's mind. Only now she was old enough to know that she was indeed a bastard, and there would be no fine husband for *her*. The best she could hope for was to be a concubine—a woman taken under a man's protection, but whose children would not be heirs. A second-class wife, a wife who was a servant, a wife who might even be sold as a slave, if the man had no honor and he grew tired of her.

But better a concubine, Zilpah knew, than what her mother was. Zilpah was born into bondage because it was the only way for a fatherless child like her to have a place in the world, and with the taint of illegitimacy on her, there was no escaping her bondage. She'd be lucky if Laban didn't simply sell her off to someone, who could use her as her mother had been used.

Laban wouldn't do that, of course. He looked out for his people. He never sold any of his bondservants; he was a man who took in strangers and made a place for them, like that orphan cousin of Noam's, Bilhah. Of course, Bilhah had parents, Bilhah had a father, and even a dead father was better than the nothing Zilpah had. Oh, that galled her, to watch that girl come in from the city, knowing almost nothing, having no useful skills at all, and get preferred above *her*, who had faithfully performed all her tasks—even the absolute scutwork that was often assigned to her because, after all, she was only a fatherless girl and couldn't refuse to get up to her elbows in filth because how dare she think there was any job she was too good for?

Not that anybody ever said such a thing in so many words. Laban didn't tolerate unkindness to children in his household. But it was clear enough, when five children were assigned to Hobbler for cleaning, and she always chose Zilpah to bury the week's latrine—while the other children were assigned to dig the new latrine in clean ground.

Zilpah didn't actually mind. The smell wasn't pretty, but in a herding camp, there was nothing unusual about having dung smell of one kind or another in her nose. If she was careful, nothing ugly got on her—and it was a lot easier to scrape loose dirt over the latrine and tamp it down than to dig a new latrine in hard, unbroken earth. Let *them* get covered with dirt and streaked with sweat, while I stay cleaner doing the "filthy" bastard's work. It suggested that God had set up the world so even the lowest-born got a bit of mercy now and then.

When full womanhood came on her, though, Zilpah learned that a man's eyes saw only her body, not her illegitimacy. With her mother's fierce protection, the boys and men of the camp had learned not to attempt even a moment's solitary conversation with Zilpah—the tongue-lashing could be heard by eagles overhead and awoke the worms sleeping in the earth, as the saying had it. But that didn't stop Zilpah from toying with them a little, loosening her clothing a bit and bending over at her tasks so that some hapless male was afforded a lingering glimpse down her blouse. The ones who frankly stared at her, she would ignore; the ones who took only furtive glances, though, she would confront with her haughtiest glare, making sure they knew they had been caught. Let men covet her all they wanted, was her opinion, but don't let them get away with trying to hide their lust. It gave her a feeling of power, to control their thoughts that way, and to leave them shamefaced whenever she chose to let them know that she knew what they were about.

Zilpah didn't hate her life—she had many pleasures and amusements, and if some kept their distance from her because of who she wasn't, she still had her friends, and for all that her mother was so grimly protective of her, they were still close and Zilpah enjoyed her mother's company. It was not a bad life. It was her future that didn't bear examining. What if she never found a man who wanted her for anything other than a bondservant? Laban would never sell her without her consent, but what if that was the only way to have a man? What if she ended up like her mother, raising some man's baby without even concubinage to give the child a position in the world? No, I'll never do that, Zilpah resolved. I'd rather be one of the spinsters in Laban's camp, dried up and childless, than be trapped into a position of shame like my mother, or bring up a child in shame, as I have had to grow.

Even a future as a spinster was uncertain, though. Spinsters were well-treated in Laban's camp; no one was allowed to treat them with open contempt, despite their barrenness, their unwantedness. But Laban's two older sons, Nahor and Terah, showed no sign of growing into kindly men like their father. They were thick as thieves, those two, always thinking of mischief and goading each other on when they were young, and now that they were adults and married, they still took more pleasure from going off to town together than from their wives or the new babies that both of them had. It was Laban who doted on their babies—daughters, both of them—and looked after his sons' wives while his boys went off to play. No doubt visiting prostitutes in the city, though they swore to Laban that they were there on business and were full of talk about merchants taking caravans who might bring them exotic dyes or to whom they might sell one of the young camels, if things worked out right.

What would happen when they were masters of the camp? For they had already hinted that instead of Nahor inheriting alone, the way they would avoid dividing the inheritance was to rule it together. "We share everything as it is, so why should that change?" Zilpah figured *that* arrangement would last until the first disagreement, whereupon Terah would find out just what it meant not to be the eldest son. The third boy, Choraz, who was still just a boy, was wiser than his older brothers—he was off in the service of some desert lord, preparing to make a place for himself without counting on the mercy of Nahor.

But the brothers' future hardly mattered to Zilpah. All that she cared about was what they might have in mind for her, when she belonged to them. By then she'd probably be an old woman. But what if Laban died suddenly? Men did. And she had seen both of them look at her from time to time, not with the hopeless longing that some of the young men showed, but with cocky certainty. She did not bend over toward *them*; that was no sport at all, when she knew that someday they would own her more certainly than she owned herself.

Then Laban's nephew Jacob came to camp.

There had been many visitors before, and some so important

that young he-goats were slaughtered and roasted. But all those other visitors had been men of business, or suitors trying to ingratiate themselves with Laban in advance of his daughters' maturity. None of them got much encouragement from Laban; he put on a good feast because that was one way a man showed his wealth and power, but he was just as happy when they went their way.

With Jacob, it was obviously different. Instead of leaving matters to his steward as he usually did, Laban was hurrying from place to place giving needless and sometimes wrong advice to people who knew their work better than he did. And he sent two riders to the city to fetch his sons home before nightfall—two, so they might find them all the faster. Such extravagance was unheard of.

So this Jacob was important. Well, it didn't take much guessing as to why. He was the grandson of the legendary prince and prophet Abraham, who had once taught a Pharaoh of Egypt about the stars, and the son of Isaac, who held the birthright of Abraham. There were whispers about them being the true kings of the earth, who by right should rule over all nations, and that one day an heir of their line would make good on that claim. Laban was a kinsman, but the birthright went through another line—if a daughter of his married the heir of Isaac, then Laban's grandchildren would be part of that noble lineage.

Though Isaac had two sons, didn't he? And rumor had it that they didn't get along as nicely as Nahor and Terah. Was this Jacob the heir or not? There were stories that had it both ways. So Laban, no doubt, was playing it safe. Besides, elder sons sometimes died before they could inherit, and then it would all be Jacob's by any accounting. Maybe that's what

Terah was counting on: Nahor getting so drunk in the city that he would provoke the wrong man and find just how much of a blade could fit inside his body.

Maybe Jacob was here for the reason young Choraz served with Prince Kedar—hoping to make a place for himself.

Zilpah caught a couple of glimpses of the man during the afternoon. And then she was assigned to carry in heated water for him to wash himself. This was an opportunity not to be missed—his legs were grimy and he was tired. So she offered to wash his feet for him.

If Reuel the steward had someone else in mind to wash the visitor's feet, he gave no sign; maybe that was why she had been sent in with the water. Anyway, Jacob said yes, with thanks, and sat back leaning on one elbow as she put one of his feet, then the other, into a basin and scrubbed off the grime of the road.

And as Jacob and the steward talked, she loosened the neck of her garment as far as she dared. Because she was not stupid. She would never be more desirable than she was right now. And it was possible he might covet her, and ask Laban for her. Laban's daughters were both too young to marry— Laban said so to every would-be suitor who inquired—but Zilpah knew she was *not* too young for concubinage. Jacob seemed a kind man, gentlespoken and polite enough to thank a serving girl for offering to wash his feet. She could do no better than to be taken as the concubine of such a man; and even if he only bought her and used her for pleasure, he did not seem the kind of man who would cast out a fatherless child of his own loins. This was a chance, however slight, of a better future, if he only desired her.

No other man had been able to avoid looking at her with

desire, not once she made the decision to catch his eye. But Jacob was the exception. She might have been a five-year-old or an old crone for all the notice he gave her. She scrubbed hard, too, in the effort to draw his eye, but all he did was wince and say to the steward, "She's a hard scrubber, isn't she?"

When Reuel began remonstrating with her, Jacob only laughed. "I don't mind—I'd rather be clean when I dine with your master than be left dirty because I wasn't man enough to bear a little scraping from a little girl!"

Little girl indeed! Was he blind?

Or was he some sort of paragon among men, one who was above the power of women? Most men *thought* they were, so tall and strong, so fast at running, so powerful at gripping. How could a woman resist a man? And it was true of bad men, the kind who bullied and forced others to do their will. But most men tried to be civilized, or at least seem civilized in front of others, so they wouldn't show themselves to be bullies. And over such men, women had enormous power. Zilpah had watched them enough, the wives of the shepherds and weavers and tentmakers, how some of them scolded so their husbands cowered in terror of their tongues; how others never raised their voice, but had trained their men to be alert to every nuance of their mood. Those quiet ones, it was amazing to watch them. It took only a hint of disappointment and their man would be all over himself trying to find out what was wrong, how had he disappointed her.

Even the bullies were often under some woman's control. Some of them struck their wives and even beat them, as the law allowed, but they had Laban to keep them from going too far, and between beatings, those same women still got their way about a lot of things. Though Zilpah still had contempt for them—why would they let a man hit them a second time? Didn't they have any knowledge of the herbs that would put a stop to that at once? She said this to her mother once, and got a slap for her trouble.

"Or will you poison me now because I hit you?" whispered her mother.

"Why did you slap me?" Zilpah asked.

"Because even to think of murder is wicked. An offense to God!"

"If a man beats another man, then it's honorable for the beaten man to get his friends together and kill the man who humiliated him. But if a man beats a woman, it's wicked for her to take the vengeance that is within *her* reach?"

"Poison is vile and sneaky, and it's done cold, not in the heat of anger."

"Oh, if a man ever beat me like Chadek beats Tamaleh, I'd keep my anger hot enough."

"And how would you keep from poisoning the whole camp?"

"I wouldn't," said Zilpah. "I'd make sure to eat a little of it myself, enough to get very sick."

Her mother looked at her in horror. "Have you thought so much about it? What kind of monster have I raised?"

"God made women smaller than men, so we can't fight them as equals. We can't divorce them and send them away; we can't even leave them, because where would a runaway woman go, except to be a prostitute or a priestess? But we're just as much alive as any man. We have our honor, too."

"The honor of a woman comes from the love and respect of her husband."

"Exactly," said Zilpah. "Tamaleh gets *none* from her husband, so he deserves none from her." She did not add, What love and respect do you get from yours?

Oh, Zilpah was sure she knew all about men, despite her mother's assurance that she had "no idea of what goes on between a woman and a man, and I mean to *keep* it that way until you're married."

Except this Jacob. He did not seem to be a brutal, bragging man, though he was obviously strong and tall. The kind of man who didn't have to fight because few would dare to fight him; the kind who didn't love to fight, and so if he was left alone, he left others alone as well. That much could be told from the way he talked to Reuel, a mere steward—so simply and quietly, explaining how he came from his mother's house after being blessed by his father with the birthright blessing.

"It was bound to provoke Esau," said Jacob. "Better not to stay where he might look for vengeance."

"But if you don't stay there," said Reuel, "won't your father's men follow Esau, taking all your father's flocks and herds, the moment the great Isaac dies?—may God delay the day."

"If God wants me to have flocks and herds, and men also," said Jacob, "then I'll have them."

Reuel nodded wisely, but Zilpah knew enough about the man to guess that he was thinking that this Jacob was insane.

"The birthright that I have is the one that matters," said Jacob. "Tell Laban that I have the holy books."

Reuel nodded wisely. Clearly he had no idea what Jacob was talking about.

"Tell Laban that I inherit the blessings of Abraham and Isaac."

Reuel finally had to admit his ignorance. "And which of their blessings might these be?" Zilpah could almost hear what he must be thinking: It's certain that these "blessings" don't include flocks, herds, lands, servants, tents, or worldly goods of any kind.

Jacob smiled slightly. "I'm glad that Laban has kept such matters sacred. It means he treasures them as I do."

Zilpah almost laughed—Jacob understood that Reuel was being haughty with him, even though it was hidden behind a mask of courtesy; and so Jacob answered with a reminder that the things that really matter would be between Jacob and Laban, and need not be justified to a servant, however lofty Reuel's role in the camp might be.

I *must* make this man notice me, she thought.

Though it had never been part of her plan, she washed higher on Jacob's leg. At once he turned his body so his legs withdrew from her reach, as he bent to her, smiled kindly, and said, "You've done well to wash my feet so thoroughly. I was truly filthy. But another minute and I'll have no skin left on my bones, and that's cleaner than I want to be!"

She had gone too far, reached too high, but instead of rebuking her—which, in most camps, would have led to a beating later, at the steward's order—he merely put an end to her service by thanking her, so now she had to go away. If only I hadn't overreached!

When she carried the basin out of the tent and poured it out over the beans in the garden, she had several older women following after her. "What did he say?" "What is he like?" "Is he here for one of the daughters?"

"He's a kind and gracious man," said Zilpah, "worthy of all honor."

They groaned at the correctness—and emptiness—of her reply.

Old Hobbler chuckled nastily. "Did you show him your breasts?"

Zilpah smiled faintly. "A man like that doesn't care about such things."

One of the others laughed. "He would if they were bigger! Little figs like yours aren't worth searching out."

Zilpah smiled and pretended to think this was amusing. Life would become altogether intolerable if these old biddies thought they had cause to dislike her, so she did not answer by comparing their sagging old dugs with her own bosom, which might not be as big, but attracted the gaze of a lot more men.

"Is he here for Rachel or Leah?" asked an old woman.

"He came for me," said Zilpah saucily, but with a flip of her head that made it clear that she was joking. They laughed, of course. What could be funnier than a fatherless girl thinking she would be courted by the son of Isaac?

But she wasn't joking. Without consciously deciding it, she knew that she would only consider her life happy if she left Laban's household when Jacob did, as his wife or concubine, with his child in her belly or her arms. This is the man that Mother has been saving me for, even if she doesn't know it. Even if she would beat me for daring to suggest it. Why should one of Laban's miserably selfish arrogant daughters get this man as her own? God brought him here for the woman who needed him to save her from a life of slavery and other degradations.

Her mother would tell her—while thrashing her with a stick—that there was no way that a decent girl could get in the bed of a man like that, or an indecent girl either, and she was insane to even imagine it.

And then, when the thrashing was over, her mother would tell her she was crazy to *want* to. "He's not the one with the flocks and herds, the servants and the mighty men of war! He'll be poor, a man who fled out of fear of his brother's wrath! He'll be lucky to afford one wife, he'll be taking no concubines!" Her mother would not say, though Zilpah would hear, the final condemnation: He's too poor to take you on as a slave, and too respectable to link himself with someone so lowborn.

But Zilpah was not insane. She knew perfectly well how improbable it would be for her to end up in this man's tent, and as for his prospects, she knew as she washed his legs that this was not a man who would remain poor. He did not act toward Laban as a supplicant would act. He knew he was a prince, and had a prince's birthright. How could he fail? Weaker men looked for chances to bow to a man like that—or tried to destroy him. There would be no life of obscurity or poverty for Jacob son of Isaac. He would have great possessions to pass on to his sons. And she would be the mother of at least one of them, or die trying.

Her mother's only child had no father, but her children would be princes, and there'd be many of them, if she had her way.

CHAPTER 6

S till, wishes were only dreams if she didn't think of something to do to catch his eye. The trick with the loosened neck of her gown had done nothing. Nor had her awkward attempt at washing more of his legs than a traveler might decently expect.

What was left? She knew she was pretty, but he hadn't cared about that so far. What else could she show him? How hard she worked? How graceful she was? How much smarter she was than the stupid ordinary girls of this camp?

How could he ever even hear her speak, unless she also showed herself to be outrageously rude and unmaidenly by speaking to him unbidden?

Well, whatever he ended up noticing about her, it couldn't happen if she wasn't in front of his face. So she headed for Reuel, who was making the arrangements for the feast in Jacob's honor.

"Let me serve at dinner," she said.

He looked at her coldly; then his expression softened. "It was generous of you to offer what you offered him today in the tent. I know of no other man who would have refused you. Did your mother tell you to honor your master by giving yourself to the greatest guest his tents have ever known?"

Giving herself? Was that what Reuel assumed was going on? She wanted to rebuke him coldly—I'll be married to the man who has me first. But then she realized that to his eyes, maybe her self-display, her aggressive washing, they might have looked like a more generous offer than she intended. And since he thought it was done as a generous sacrifice for her master's sake, he might feel that he owed her a favor.

"My mother did not suggest such a thing," she said quietly. "But I saw how my master wanted to please his guest. My mother would probably beat me if she knew."

Reuel nodded. "Well, you were wise to make the offer where only he and I could see. Other men in this camp might have thought your offer was more . . . general. I make no such mistake."

Which made her see the steward in a new light. He was one of the men who pretended that he didn't look at her body, and she had put him in his place once with a cold glare. He might have held it against her, might have taunted her. Instead he respected her. Good.

"If I can't serve my master another way, might I carry in and carry away?"

"Not in that dress, you can't."

"I have no better."

"There are better gowns in camp. Let's see if we can get you looking more like the kind of girl who serves food than the kind that washes feet." He strode away from her. She started to follow him, but in moments he was back with Derkah, the old woman who had once attended to Laban's wife. "Make her look worthy to serve a prince," said Reuel. He walked away.

Derkah looked down her nose at Zilpah. "What kind of favors have you been doing for that man, that he offers you such an honor as this? There are girls far better born than you who are being passed over."

"Every girl and every woman in this camp and half the dogs are better born than me," said Zilpah defiantly. "But the only favor I have done for my master's steward is to give him my obedience, my respect, and my earnest labor, like every other good servant in this household."

Derkah smiled, but there was still something hard in her eyes. "You're a good listener. You've got the elegant speech down—something your mother never mastered."

Zilpah curbed her resentment of the slur against her mother and smiled. "Thank you for helping me to do honor to our master's guest tonight."

"The effect must be one of chastity," said Derkah. "And cleanliness."

"I could bathe."

"There's no time for that. But your face could use a washing. And I'll get a girl to work on your hair while I choose your clothing. You're young, we want your hair to swing free but stay out of your face and out of the food. We'll braid here and here and bind the braids behind."

It all went very quickly then—hands working on her hair doing things her mother had never done, and so firmly and deftly. And the dress was a beautiful one; she wondered why no one had ever worn it before. But of course it would have been stored up against such an occasion as this—the arrival of the greatest guest these tents had known.

When she pulled it on, though, the fit was wrong—the neckline was low enough to shock even Zilpah. She would never be able to raise her arms while wearing this. Whomever the dress had been made for, she must have been older, with a bosom that had already settled into a much lower position on her chest.

But Derkah didn't seem to notice the problem. "Very nice," she said. "Yes, yes, he chose well, having you serve. Can you manage to bring in all the food and carry it away without spilling?"

"I never spill," said Zilpah. "I never trip. I'm surefooted and my grip is strong."

"Well, make sure you *kneel* to serve. If you bend over in that dress somebody might try to take two melons from the top of the bowl and put them on his own plate."

Zilpah blushed. Derkah *did* know how revealing the dress was. So much for an air of chastity! All these years of trying to conceal from other women how she teased the men, and it turned out that when they dressed her up to make the best possible impression, they openly used her body the way she had used it on the sly!

Or were they, perhaps, using this gown to repeat the same offer Reuel had thought she was making earlier in the day?

No matter. They were giving her the best chance of any girl in the camp to catch this man's eye.

And despite her confidence, she practiced kneeling and rising from her knees several times, holding heavy objects as she did, to make sure she knew how to balance in the gown and not trip over the hem or bow too low. It took great strength to keep her back vertical as she sank to her knees, and a great deal of balance to keep from falling over backward as she rose again to her feet.

While she had been footwashing and plotting and getting dressed, apparently Reuel had been able to get word to the village of Haran, for the dinner included four of the great men of the town—though Haran *was* just a village, and not a city. Also, Laban's older sons, Nahor and Terah, had arrived home without even the time to change clothes—and that was unfortunate, because Terah had apparently spilled something down the front of his tunic. Clearly he resented being put on display before this guest in something other than his best clothes. Whatever quarrel there had been over it, though, Zilpah would have to find out later—there had been nothing of it in the tent where she was being dressed.

As the chief cook put the first bowl into her hands, Zilpah said, "This is not enough for all the men at dinner."

She looked at Zilpah like she was crazy. "Ignorant girl, do you think you're wearing that dress in order to serve villagers and those rowdy boys? You will serve only the master and his great and honored guest. You kneel between them, and offer it first to the master. He will make a great show of directing you to serve Jacob first, which you will do. Then you offer it to the master again, and when they've taken what they want from the bowl, you bring it back to me and don't you *dare* offer it to anyone else on the way in or out, even if there's plenty left. Do you understand? One of those boys is perfectly capable of trying to trick you into humiliating their father by serving them from the same bowl as the honored guest, but don't you do it, or I'll stripe your back for you!"

Why hadn't Reuel mentioned *that?* Did he think that Zilpah already knew it? Or was he hoping that she'd make some gross mistake and get a beating?

But she drove her annoyance out of her mind. Grace, chastity, beauty, modest manners, and just under half of her bosom—that was what she was to show tonight, not pique at the foolishness of people who don't tell you all that you must know to do your job properly.

From the first bowl she carried in, the dinner went perfectly—or at least her part of it. She sank straight down to her knees with each bowl and platter, offered it to each man as she was instructed, and held it firmly and steadily. When they jabbed with a knife to pierce some choice piece of meat, she offered just enough upward resistance that it was as smooth as if the platter were resting on a table. When they ladled soup from a bowl, she followed under the ladle just far enough to keep anything from dripping onto the carpet or their clothes— but never so far as to bump into their bowl.

She behaved with perfect modesty, and when—as predicted—Nahor called out for her to bring the plate of cheese to him, she did not so much as hesitate in her path. It was as if he had not spoken. Though she was not so intent on her task as not to notice the way Laban glowered at his son's rudeness.

By halfway through the meal she was so sure of her perfection that she allowed herself to listen to their conversation. At first it had all been about their mutual ancestors and reports of Rebekah's and Isaac's health, so it's not as if Zilpah much cared what they were saying anyway. Later, though, as they grew more sated and the winebibbers from the village of Haran—not to mention the winebibbing Nahor and his wine-spilling brother Terah—began to doze in their places, the master began the serious conversation.

"To journey all this way, surely you will live with me now as my brother. All that I have is yours!"

This of course was merely courtesy, Zilpah knew, but it was wonderful how sincere Laban sounded as he said it.

"And I am ashamed to have brought no gift better than my service among your flocks and herds."

"Does a beggar ask a prince to hold his cup?" said Laban. "It is I who should serve *you*."

And so on and so on. But when it came down to it, Laban insisted that Jacob would only serve him so as to teach him and his men the herding lore of Isaac's house, so that he was bestowing a great favor on Laban's house. While Jacob insisted that he was here only to learn from Laban's mastery of the husbandry of beasts, so he could one day bring this wisdom back to his father's house.

Then there were the compliments about the meal—Jacob insisting that such a feast had never been seen at his father's house, and Laban insisting just as firmly that he was sure that this feast would seem inconsequential.

"But my dear brother Laban," said Jacob, "I can never learn from you properly if you put on feasts like this for me every night! I must eat a shepherd's simple fare, or I'll become so languid that a pregnant ewe could outrun me."

Laban laughed at that, and then went into a fit of choking and hiccupping that was funny at first but quickly became alarming.

Laban's face turned red. Zilpah was frightened. Should she set down her bowl and run for help? Or was Reuel watching from the tent door? Would he rush in and . . .

Yes, the steward rushed in, but before he could get to his master, Jacob had reached over, seized Laban by the shoulder with his left hand, and driven his right palm forcefully into the older man's stomach.

A chunk of meat popped out of Laban's mouth and flew into the bowl that Zilpah was holding.

Jacob looked at her and winked.

Somehow she understood immediately what his wink was meant to convey. Holding the bowl against her chest with one arm, she quickly moved the fruits around so that the chunk of meat could drop down out of sight deep in the bowl.

Meanwhile, as Reuel started slapping Laban on the back, Jacob sat back down on his rugs as calmly as if he had never moved. Laban looked up at the steward and irritably said, "What are you doing, you madman? My brother already saved my life, and now you seem to be trying to undo his work by killing me!"

"But I did nothing," said Jacob. "I was only reaching out to ask if I could help you when your steward arrived. I believe he was the one who dislodged whatever was in your throat."

"I could breathe clearly again before he ever started beating me," said Laban, puzzled. "And didn't I feel you . . . or somebody, anyway . . . didn't I—"

"Look," said Jacob, "this pretty girl has brought us dates, for digestion."

Zilpah dutifully offered the bowl to Laban, who took one. Then he remembered his manners and almost put it back, before saying, "Look how distracted I am, I took a date myself before offering any to my guest."

"You already offered me dates before you had that moment of choking, Brother Laban, and I took one. But now that you offer it again, how can I refuse? And from such lovely hands. I thought earlier today that it was astonishing that you would send your prettiest girl to wash my feet, instead of your most miserable wench; and now I see that you have a damsel even more beautiful to serve at dinner."

Laban obviously had no idea that the girl who washed Jacob's feet earlier had been the very one now kneeling before them with a bowl. "Oh, well, there are many pretty girls in our household. But none so beautiful as my . . . as my daughters."

Zilpah rose smoothly to her feet and as she carried the bowl of dates out of the tent, she heard Jacob telling him that he had been blessed by God with the chance to behold his younger daughter at the well, and had to agree that she was lovelier than the moon in its fullness and other such nonsense.

"Quick," Zilpah said to the cook. "What's the next platter? They're finally talking about our master's daughters."

"But that was the last," said the cook. "Don't you know anything? The digestives come last. Now it's only wine."

"Well, that's just silly," said Zilpah, exasperated. "Then they'll get drunk. And we won't hear anything." She saw a basket of bread sitting near the door. Quickly she took out a couple of broken buns and rearranged the others into a nice mound so it didn't look like leftovers.

"What do you think you're doing?" demanded Reuel in a whisper.

"I'm going to kneel just to the side and have the bread ready in case they want it."

"You're going to eavesdrop," said Reuel.

"I'm going to tell you everything I hear," said Zilpah.

He let her pass.

But once she had knelt, bowing her head so as not to see

Laban's questioning glance, there was little left to the conversation. Apparently Laban had promised that sometime over the next few weeks, he hoped to be able to present his daughters to Jacob so he could tell Rebekah that his daughters were almost as beautiful as she had been in her youth, and Jacob had sworn that already the beauty of his daughters was legendary even as far away as Beersheba.

So much insincerity and formality was enough to wear out anyone, and if Jacob and therefore Laban had not been so sparing of the wine, they wouldn't have got even that far. But the time had come, and so Jacob turned away for a moment to conceal a yawn, which was Laban's cue to apologize for keeping a weary traveler up so late, while Jacob insisted that he longed to stay up all night in conversation with his new-met brother, and on and on, but not *too* long before they both arose and, quite steady on their feet, despite the wine and the long sitting, they made their way out of the tent.

But as he passed her, Jacob bent down and took a small loaf from her basket. "For the morning?" said Jacob. "I've rarely had loaves as sweet as these." And for a moment, Zilpah wondered if he was making an oblique reference to . . . but no, Jacob probably did not even notice the neckline on this gown any more than he had noticed earlier in the day.

Or maybe he noticed her perfectly well both times, but was merely too polite and disciplined to let it show.

Once the host and the honored guest were out of the dining tent, with torchbearers lighting their way to their sleeping tents, Reuel rushed in and helped her to her feet. "What did they say?"

"He's staying a month at least," said Zilpah. "And there's a promise to introduce him to Leah and Rachel. Also, he intends to help with the herds. I think the master intends him only to observe, but I think the honored guest intends to work with the animals and truly serve, with honest hard labor."

"He never said *that*, did he?" said the cook doubtfully—for she was in the dining tent now, looking across the sleeping villagers and sons.

"Not in those words. But what he says, he means, I think," said Zilpah.

"And no invitation to you?" asked Reuel.

"He had no invitation *from* me, sir," said Zilpah coldly.

The steward was nonplussed for a moment. But Zilpah did not leave him speechless for long—after all, he had let her have this place of honor, and she owed him a respite from the embarrassment she was so deft at causing.

"I think he truly is weary. And I also think he's not a man to please himself so casually. He might even be as chaste as our master."

They questioned her a little longer, but there was still much work to do, and soon they set about doing it.

As for Zilpah, she assumed that the gown would be taken back from her tonight, but apparently not. Derkah had gone to bed, and the woman who had done Zilpah's hair was not happy to be wakened. "Sleep in it, for all I care," she said, and went back inside the tent.

But of course she didn't mean that, and would deny having said it if Zilpah was so daft as to follow her suggestion. Instead Zilpah took it off inside the darkness of her mother's tent and laid it gently on the carpet beside where she would sleep, then snuggled down naked inside her light summer blankets.

"How did it go, you pushy girl?" asked her mother with sleepy affection.

"I didn't spill anything," said Zilpah. "Did you see me in the dress?"

"Oh, I know that dress well," said Mother. "The last person to wear it was the mistress."

"Laban's *wife* wore it?"

"It didn't look the same on her."

"But . . . to have me wear his wife's dress before him . . ."

"He knew it was the best dress in the camp, and since he couldn't very well have his daughters appear in it without looking like he was holding an auction . . ."

"But his *wife* wore it?"

"As I said, it didn't look the same on her. It . . . contained her much more completely."

"So you saw me."

"You were as beautiful as I ever saw my daughter in my happiest dreams," said Mother. "But in the morning, you'll still be Zilpah, and the dream will be over. So you need your sleep, my little hoopoe bird."

"You were proud of me?" asked Zilpah.

Her mother took her hand and kissed it in the darkness. Soon she was asleep.

But not Zilpah. She lay awake thinking back over the night's events. How Laban had been choking, and Jacob acting quick as a snake to punch the food right out of his throat. But then he denied having saved him, and gave the credit to the steward, and Laban, in his confusion, might well have believed him. Why was that? Why deny what he had done? It would have put Laban in his debt.

Here he was at dinner with a potential benefactor—for it

was plain that Jacob really did have nothing in the world except his bundle, which apparently contained nothing but books, and he would need help from Laban to reestablish himself in the world. While Laban's sons were sleeping off their wine, Laban's life is saved by Jacob—it's the sort of thing that could make a man's fortune. And yet Jacob turned down the opportunity, denied that it had happened, used the moment to enhance the steward in his master's eyes.

Why? Didn't he *want* to rise out of his poverty and restore himself to a princely state? If he had acted wisely, he might even have taken the place of Nahor and Terah, getting himself adopted as Laban's heir. It was so obvious how unworthy Laban's sons were, compared to Jacob.

Then it dawned on her. If he behaved that way, he would have to spend his life in fear of Nahor's and Terah's revenge. Eventually, he would either have to kill them or leave. And he had already proven himself to be the kind of man who would rather leave than join into a struggle over inheritance.

Did that mean he wouldn't fight for anything? Was he, after all, weak?

Or did he want his possessions to be his by undisputed right? No rivals, no one who could say that they had made him rich. No adoption by Laban as his heir—he already had the birthright of princes. Yes, that's what he is, a man of such honor that a fatherless girl like me can't even conceive of the loftiness of his thoughts.

And I will have him. Not for myself alone, but I will have him, and my sons will be his sons. Because I'm not as lofty as he is. I can scheme. One way or another, I'll find a way into his bed, and my sons will be recognized as his. I will be the mother of princes.

He definitely noticed me. He even joked with me about being prettier than the girl who washed his feet. And when he said that about never having had such sweet loaves—no matter what he meant, it was from my basket he took the bread. He saw me. And having seen, I'll make sure he doesn't forget.

PART IV

TENDER EYES

CHAPTER 7

Leah didn't like change. Didn't like the way all the patterns of life were subtly altered by the presence in this camp of a poverty-stricken prince who was also a cousin and also unmarried and also the kind of man that everyone wanted to please.

She knew that part of her irritation was at the way attention was drawn away from her. Until now she had not realized how spoiled she had been, how much her father had shaped the routines of the camp to minimize her inconvenience and embarrassment from being so limited in her vision. If she had thought about it, she would have realized that it took conscious effort on everyone's part to make sure things were left always in the same place, so she could always find them, and the smoothness of her paths was not an accident. Now that the people assigned to sweep the grounds were sometimes away on other work, she realized that in the

normal order of things, stones, sticks, brush, animal drop-
pings—many things found their way into the path and therefore onto her feet. Other people could see these objects and
avoid them. Leah could not.

But she did not complain to anyone, not even to Bilhah.
Leah was ashamed to think how much work others had
always gone to to shelter her from the normal accidents of life.
She was even more ashamed to know that her disability, far
from being "unnoticeable," as her father had always insisted,
was instead like a great lion constantly prowling the camp.
Everyone had to be aware of it at every moment, yet no one
had the power to do anything about it. So far it had not con-
sumed anyone, but it required relentless vigilance.

Perhaps none of them actually hates me, thought Leah, but
they have to resent me—a privileged child who, born with less
good fortune in her parentage, might have become a beggar,
or simply died young from the kind of accident that, with a
camp full of protectors, had never been a possibility for Leah,
daughter of Laban.

If Jacob had not come, I would not have known this—
about myself, about the care the whole camp has taken for me,
about my father. So it's a good thing; simply by being here, he
has been my teacher.

Yet even with this thought, she could not change the fact
that her gratitude was fleeting, while her annoyance at the
changes kept being revived with each thing she stepped on,
each stumble, each item out of place, and each fresh remembering that she really was good for little in this world, that the
tasks she was able to perform were generally those that little
children were given. She could not sew—her stitches would
all have to be taken out again. She could not even spin, for

even though you did not have to stare at the yarn you still had to be aware of it, and aware of how much fleece remained. And you had to know whether the spindle was still spinning from the distaff. All impossible for her. So even the most continuous occupation of women was barred to her.

She could weed, once a garden was well started—once the plants were big enough that she could tell a bean or radish or squash from the weeds that sprang up. She could carry water—if someone kept the path clear—which probably took more time than if they simply carried the water themselves. Was it even possible that her voice did *not* please Father, that he only said it did because singing was one of the few things she could actually do without the work having to be redone by others?

There is no more useless person on earth than I am, thought Leah. She did not say this to anyone because, first, they would certainly agree with her, and she could not bear the slight hesitation before they reassured her that it wasn't so. Second, she recognized that there was something very selfish and wicked about spending time moping about because of how limited she was, when instead she ought to be grateful every moment that she was so blessed by having a father who bent his whole household to taking care of her. And third, why should she complain to any living person when it was God who made her half-blind like this and therefore her tender eyes must somehow fulfil a purpose he had in mind for her?

Wouldn't it be nice, though, if God would send her a dream to explain everything—like those dreams he kept sending to Rachel, who had perfectly good eyes. Wasn't that just like God, to send the girl with good eyes the visions that assured her that God had a great purpose for her, while to

Leah, who could not see with her natural eyes, he sent only spiritual blindness as well?

Maybe that was why God had brought Jacob to their camp. Rachel got dreams, but perhaps Leah had been sent a prophet. An angel, even—to hear everyone speak of him, he was almost divine in all his attributes, as an angel would appear to be, among ordinary mortals. He had the holy books, didn't he? He had the words of God in a bundle he carried with him on the road, and he had the power to open them and wake up the sleeping words and speak them aloud. Could he not tell her what God meant her to make of her life?

That was why, along with her annoyance at the changes in the camp and her annoyance at herself for being annoyed, she also was filled with hope. For of course, when God wished to change your life, the change might not be comfortable in *every* way.

But what good did it do for God to send her an angel, or at least a cousin with God's word in a sack, if she never had a chance to speak to him? He had been here more than a week and she had not been in his presence. He was everywhere— the gossip of the camp was about nothing but him, how he had gone here, done that, said this, smiled at someone, laughed at someone's jest, noticed a problem with one of the animals, taught the cook how to make lamb taste like venison, and on and on. Everyone, it seemed, had had some encounter with him . . . except her.

Well, of course not Leah! Besides the natural modesty of women, which would keep her from meeting him casually in the camp, she was kept out of the way of the real work of the camp. And since he was endlessly working, and she was end- lessly kept from the work, how would they meet?

She mentioned this once to Rachel, who said, "I know, they don't let me see him either, except when I'm caring for the lambs and he comes to see the animals." Naturally, Rachel did not realize that she was, in effect, saying, You're right, Leah, everyone, including me, gets to spend time with him. Only you are excluded." No, Rachel actually thought that their situations were somehow alike!

Then one morning Bilhah came back to the tent with breakfast and could hardly keep from spilling everything, she was so excited. "You and Rachel are to be officially presented to him tomorrow night, before dinner," she said.

Leah knew whom she meant—to whom else would she be presented? Then again, why would *Rachel* be presented, since she and Jacob had seen each other almost every day, including that "cousinly" kiss at the well, which everyone thought was so sweet that they told the story over and over. Leah was the only one who needed to be presented. So maybe there was someone else who had met *neither* of them. "Presented to whom?" she said.

Bilhah laughed, one short titter, before she realized that Leah wasn't joking. "Jacob," she said. "He hasn't met you."

"But he's met Rachel."

"He wasn't presented by your father."

Presented by Father. As if he were a suitor.

"Do you think he means it like that?" asked Leah.

"Like what?"

"A presentation of his daughters to a man who might wish to marry one of them."

Bilhah was taken aback. "I don't know. Is that what's done here?"

"It's happened before, but Father never meant it. And it

was always to a father looking for a bride for his son. This would be the first time he presented us to the suitor himself."

"You're too young to marry," said Bilhah.

"But these things are often settled when you're young. So there's no uncertainty. And no delay when we reach child-bearing age. Wasn't it done that way in the city?"

"I wasn't at the age yet. To be presented, even."

"But your father had a dowry for you."

Bilhah nodded. Undoubtedly it was still a sore spot for her, to remember what happened to her father's savings, so carefully kept for her.

"It's what a father does for his daughters—tries to make sure that they have a good marriage. These things aren't left to the last moment."

"But he's not simply offering you, like fruit in a bowl, is he?"

"Of course not," said Leah. "Officially it's simply a cour-tesy, nothing about marriage at all. But men who really come on business, Father doesn't present us, he keeps us out of sight. Only the men who specifically ask about us, and then only the ones he thinks are even remotely eligible. But none of them were really to be considered, till now."

"Why not?"

"Because they're all Ba'al-worshippers."

Bilhah didn't understand. "But don't we worship the Lord in this camp, as well?"

"Not the Ba'al *they* teach about, those false priests. They make their statues of Ba'al, people pray to them, the priests take their offerings, but none of it gets to God."

"But your father has statues, too. He prays to them," said Bilhah.

"He doesn't pray *to* them," said Leah. "He keeps them because they belonged to his great-great grandfather, Terah. Abraham got the birthright, but our family got the statues."

Bilhah said nothing, but from her posture, Leah knew she wanted to. "What?" Leah asked.

"If he doesn't pray to them, why does he always have them in the tent with him when he says his prayers?"

"He keeps them in the inner room of his tent because they're a great treasure to the family. And he prays in that room because it's his most private place."

"And he faces them while he's praying because . . ."

"How do you know where he faces when he prays?" Leah was suddenly suspicious. Had Bilhah been spying?

"Don't you know that servants go everywhere and see everything?" said Bilhah.

"Oh, so you've *heard* this from others," said Leah.

"And seen it myself."

"Why would my handmaiden have occasion to enter my father's tent?" She had a sudden, horrible suspicion. "Oh, Bilhah, he couldn't be . . ."

It took Bilhah a moment to realize what Leah feared. "Oh, don't be silly," she said. "He's an old man and I'm just a girl."

"I've heard stories of what wicked masters do," said Leah. "But my father would never."

"He would never," said Bilhah. "And he *has* never, and even if he would, *I* would never, so it will never happen."

"Good," said Leah. "I'm sorry I even wondered. You think something is unthinkable simply because you never thought it, only then one day you do think it, and then you realize, this isn't unthinkable after all. But still it's a relief to know that I needn't have thought of it."

Bilhah's mind had already wandered to another subject, though—she never seemed to stay on the same topic for more than a few moments. "Leah, isn't your father presenting you to suitors—isn't that like, I don't know, offering a servant to someone who might want to buy their bond?"

"Nothing like," said Leah. "Nothing at all. Was the princess Sarah a bondwoman to Abraham? Did Rebekah go to Isaac to be his bondwoman?"

"Why are all your examples taken from Abraham's family instead of your own ancestors?"

That was the maddening thing about having Bilhah as your only companion—she kept jumping from thought to thought, and had no sense about which questions were just silly. "I'm not even going to answer that. Abraham's family is famous, that's all, with lots of stories, and our family is not famous and we have no stories except when we're part of Abraham's story."

"Why should that be?" said Bilhah. "Why should Abraham be famous? And even if he is, why should his sons and grandsons be famous? They've never done anything except when Isaac married Rebekah, and now maybe there'll be a story about Jacob because *he* came here—but it seems to me that the only stories that matter about Abraham's children and grandchildren don't even get interesting till they come here to *your* family, so who's the interesting one?"

"Abraham has the birthright, and then Isaac got it, and now Jacob, I suppose. They're chosen by God to be a mighty lineage. We're chosen by God to be shepherds and get along as best we can. Of course Abraham is famous and we're not. Let's not waste more time talking about obvious things like *that*."

Now that Bilhah had brought it up, however, Leah could not let go of the question. Why *had* God chosen Abraham and not one of *her* family? And how was Jacob chosen?

"I'm probably wrong," said Bilhah, in that tone of voice that she used whenever she wanted to argue but didn't want to seem to be arguing, "but it seems to me, if you don't mind my saying . . ."

"I wouldn't mind you saying if you'd just say it," said Leah.

"Isn't your family just as chosen? I mean, not *all* of Abraham's lineage got the birthright. Not Isaac's half-brother, whatever his name was—"

"Ishmael."

"Not him, and not Jacob's brother, either. And Abraham had brothers, because you're descended from them, so they didn't get the birthright either, so even in that line, the birthright picks one. Well, in your family, too, right? That servant came and picked Rebekah."

"Well he could hardly pick Father, could he?" said Leah.

"And now Jacob has come and he'll pick one of you and leave the rest behind. Just like happens in his own family. One out of each generation. Just as many from your family as from Abraham's."

"But our family only supplies the women, so it's not as if they have the birthright."

"Oh?" said Bilhah. "What was the promise . . . Abraham's and Isaac's descendants would be numerous as the sands of the sea? Well, won't that be true for Sarah, too? And if it's true for Isaac, won't it be just as true for Rebekah?"

It had never crossed Leah's mind to think that way. To her, always the outsider, the birthright was just one more thing that would never be hers. But it really did belong to Aunt Rebekah too, now, didn't it. And Sarah received it as surely as Abraham.

And in that moment she was filled with grief to realize that the choice had already been made in her generation. It was Rachel who had the vision of meeting a man at the well. Rachel who had his kiss when he arrived. Rachel who was the pretty one, the one he'd want, the one he certainly already wanted.

Tears came unbidden to her eyes. Something precious had been brought so near to her, but she could never have it. She had thought of him with hope only a few moments ago, because he would be the angel who could tell her what God meant her to make of her life. But Rachel wouldn't have to ask, and he wouldn't have to tell her God's purpose. He'd simply bestow her purpose on her. What Rachel was to make of her life was to be his wife and therefore the mother of a posterity as boundless in number as the stars in the sky. Question answered before it was ever asked.

While for Leah the question was an empty one, for she could not make anything of her life, and if she had progeny it would be because Father could give a good dowry or because the man was unpleasant in some way that would make him believe she was the best wife he could get; or, in the *best* case, because some man pitied her and mistook that sentiment for love. Such a man would be kind to her all her life, as Father had been kind to her. He'd take care of her, protect her. She might even bear him children. But she would be useless otherwise. Even raising her own children—how could she do it? How could she be a mother and rear children she couldn't see?

"I'm sorry if I made you cry," whispered Bilhah.

"No, no," said Leah, brushing the tears from her cheeks. "It wasn't you. My thoughts already left what you said, and went to another matter entirely, and besides, with my bad eyes I always shed tears more easily. It doesn't mean I'm sad, it just means my eyes are irritated."

"Dust? My eyes water when I get stung by dust."

"Yes, I'll bet that's it," said Leah. "Because I certainly have nothing to cry about! As you said, my family is as great a one as Abraham's!"

Bilhah was silent for a while. And then she said, "So, what are you going to do so you can arrange to meet Jacob before the official presentation?"

"What do you mean? Nothing. I'm going to do nothing. A well-bred girl doesn't throw herself at men."

"Rachel's life is such that she's there, where Jacob can see her," said Bilhah. "Not that she's like that horrible Zilpah, always flaunting her body to make the boys go insane, but still, there she is, and where are you? Here in your tent, or in the garden. It can't be helped, but it's still not fair."

"No," said Leah. "Not fair, but nothing is fair. You're as good a person as me, if not better, but your father is gone, while I still have mine. Is that fair?"

"And neither of us has a mother," said Bilhah, "while Zilpah has *hers,* and that's not fair either, but I wouldn't trade places with *her.*"

Leah chuckled. "I suppose I don't really know her, not well. They must not have her work near me very often."

"Nobody would let her do your hair, if that's what you mean. But she got Reuel to let her serve at dinner Jacob's first night here, and the things I hear about the dress they put on her—"

"Derkah told me it was my mother's dress," said Leah.

"Well, it must have been one she wore while nursing you or Rachel, because there was nothing to bar a baby from finding its food."

Leah had to laugh. Bilhah had a way with gossip.

"Still, Leah," said Bilhah, "there's no reason Rachel should have all the advantage in this. Why shouldn't you get to know Jacob, too?"

"Rachel didn't plan it," said Leah. "God led them to each other."

"So?" said Bilhah. "How do you know God didn't lead me to your father's camp in Padan-aram so I could sit here at this very moment and say to you, There must be some reason for you to seek to talk to Jacob."

"You almost make it seem possible," said Leah.

"It can't be forbidden, or Rachel would be kept from him."

"But for them it's natural. For me it would be contrived."

"Oh, yes," said Bilhah, "I'm sure Rachel *always* used to tend to the lambs every morning, at exactly the times Jacob's sure to pass by."

Leah had to giggle. Oh, it was good to have a friend. She *was* a friend, it seemed. Who could have guessed it? But God couldn't have been so cruel as to take her father's life *and* cause her dowry to be stolen just so she could be here to befriend Leah. If she started thinking that God was shaping the whole history of the world to make her life better, that would surely be the beginning of madness.

"How do you know God didn't put this idea into my head?" said Bilhah.

"Be careful," said Leah. "If you claim to be a prophetess, somebody will believe it and then they won't leave you alone."

"I never thought of that. A soothsayer! Some of them get very rich," said Bilhah.

"And some of them get stoned to death if they are accused of witchcraft, so I think you'd better not. They're all frauds anyway, Father says. God doesn't tell the future to people who charge money for it, and the devil doesn't know the future, so all he can tell are lies."

"I can watch," said Bilhah, "and tell you when he's coming, and then you can walk out into the path and get him to lead you somewhere."

Get him to lead her. Because she's *blind*.

Not a friend, after all. Just a servant girl with a lot of chatter in her. "I'm done with you for now," said Leah. "You can go."

"What did I say?"

"I'm tired. I need to rest."

But the girl didn't go. She lingered near the door. Even with her back to her, Leah could hear her—the breathing, the slight movement of fabric as she shifted weight.

"Is it because I said you might use your tender eyes to show that you need his help?" said Bilhah. "Well, if that makes you so angry that you send me away, then shame on you for a fool."

"I won't be talked to that way," said Leah.

"Maybe not, by servants, but I'm a free girl, and I tell the truth to my friends. How do you think Rachel got to know Jacob? He uncovered the well for her because she wasn't strong enough! Jacob is a man who helps, but it has to be something a woman really needs from him. I have to lead you through this camp because you can't see well enough. Did I make that up? Or am I supposed to pretend that you cling to my arm because we're such *close* friends? Well, close friends don't send each other away like slaves who've spilled something on the rug. Rachel really was too small to move the stone, and you really are too tender-eyed to walk safely without a guide. Or would you expect a man to marry you and spend the rest of his life pretending you can see like normal people? Whom do you think you're fooling? Only yourself."

"I don't ever want to see you again," said Leah.

Bilhah laughed harshly. "I'm a better friend than you think. But perhaps you prefer to live your life with people who go along with your pretenses."

"How long are you going to stay here? Until I hate you so much I have to beg my father to send you away from the camp?"

"Is that where it goes? A true friend tries to help you find a road to happiness, but because she says it *wrong*, you'll destroy her, just like that. What *are* people to you, Leah? Flies to be flicked away, without regard for whether it kills them?"

"I beg you to leave," whispered Leah.

"I never want to see *you* again, either. So I'll pack up the nothing that I own and find my way back to Byblos and find some tiler who will take me on as his assistant."

And then, finally, the torment ended. Bilhah was gone.

Yes, Bilhah. You can leave and become a tile sorter, arranging the bits by color and size. But what could I do? Where could I go? If someone hurts you, you can leave. But I can't leave. My only chance is to send them away from me, since I can't go away from them. Did you ever think of that?

It was a good thing that she had provoked Bilhah's temper like that. It was good to know that Bilhah was not her friend, no more than any of the other women in the camp. That was Leah's fate. To spend her life completely alone.

She cried in solitude, but not for long. Once the first rush of fury was gone, she controlled herself and lay there in the silence, thinking. Not about Bilhah—she refused to let herself think about the harsh things Bilhah had said.

Instead she thought about Jacob. And, following Bilhah's suggestion, she began to think about how she might contrive to meet him. Not so she could marry him—that thought was absurd. What she wanted was not to meet a husband, but to meet the keeper of the word of God.

She had been thinking about doing that already, before Bilhah said a thing. So it wasn't that cruel girl's idea, after all. Maybe it really did come from God.

CHAPTER 8

L eah made her way to Jacob's tent early next morning, when the sky was barely lighter than full darkness. When else could she be sure of finding him there? Except at night, of course, but she could not have gone to his tent in the darkness, or it would look as if she were trying to entice him. During the day, though, he would be out in the camp, among the animals, among the skilled workmen, the weavers, the dyers—he cast his attention on everything and showed that he knew all there was to know about tending a great herdsman's household.

But all of that was Rachel's world, and that was why he would marry her. Leah could only reach out to one part of him. Not as Bilhah had urged, as a ploy to try to compete with Rachel. What good would that do? No, Leah would do what she planned in the first place. She would come to him as the keeper of the birthright, and ask him to open the holy books and tell her what God had in mind for her.

Approaching his tent, though, her mind wandered for a moment, and suddenly she realized that she did not know precisely where she was. There wasn't light enough to show her the shadowy shapes of the tents. And she had lost count of her steps, and which turns she had made. It was infuriating—with eyes as weak as hers, with the whole world constantly blurred, why was she still so utterly dependent on what she could or couldn't see?

Well, she *wasn't*. She just had to remember to use her other sense. So she closed her eyes entirely and listened.

There was a shape to the sounds the breeze made among the tents. A certain snap to the doorfly of one tent, a whistling along the eave of another. And there were smells, and the sounds of animals stirring in the dawn, and after a few moments she could hear the sounds of a few people moving about in the camp. That faint thump would be the cook's assistant dropping the day's logs beside the fire. And the soft murmuring would be two girls going down to the well to bring the morning's water.

In moments, someone might come along and see her and insist on *helping* her.

No sooner had she thought this than she heard the faint sound of a man passing his first water of the morning. Few of the men liked to rise this early, and all of those that had to rise at this hour slept on the far side of the camp. So unless some bad dream had roused Father or Reuel or one of her brothers—oh, that was likely, one of those lazy boys rising early, if they were even in the camp tonight—she was hearing Jacob. She almost turned around and headed back to her tent.

She had to remind herself that no one but her could hear so well. There would be no embarrassment, as there would be if a woman happened to *see* him at such an indelicate moment. So instead of fleeing, she boldly walked toward his tent. For of course she knew now where she was, and where it was, and she made a point of walking boldly, with her longest stride—and she was long-legged, a good walker, what a pity it was wasted on someone who could never walk anywhere except the familiar paths of the camp.

She reached the door of his tent just before he did.

"Have you come to see me?" he said softly.

She turned toward him. "Are you already up and about? Then I can come another time. I hoped to talk to you before you had started on the day's work."

He stood in silence, and she wondered: Is he looking at me? Are his eyes so good that in this faint light, he can see something to look at?

"They told me your eyes were very tender, and you couldn't walk about alone," said Jacob.

"You know who I am?"

"I've met everyone in the camp but you, Cousin Leah," said Jacob. "I was beginning to think you were my brother Laban's dearest treasure, that he dared not let out where covetous eyes might see."

She couldn't stop herself from chuckling a bit, though she hoped the bitterness in her heart could not be heard in her voice.

"Too tender-eyed to walk in the day, but like a hunting cat, you prowl the darkness and find your way by scent and sound and the feel of the wind in your face."

She loved him in that moment. She had not meant to. She

was here to speak to the priest, not the prince, and certainly not the man. And yet it was the man's voice that stirred her. The voice of the poet who had found words to make her affliction seem like a mystery.

"Oh sir," she whispered.

"Jacob," he said. "I'm your cousin, not your master."

"I came to speak to you of the holy books."

He did not answer. Had she crossed some invisible line? Should she not have spoken of them? If only she could see his face!

In the continuing silence she flailed about for words to cover whatever misstep she had taken. "Shouldn't I have mentioned them? Is it forbidden to ask?"

"No, no," he said. "I was only waiting for you to tell me what you wanted."

"Can we . . . the camp is coming awake, and my question is . . . private."

"But it wouldn't be right for me to take you into my tent in the darkness," he said.

"That's not—of course I—"

He took her by the arm. "Here," he said. "Let's sit under the awning. People will see that we're in conversation and no one will disturb us. But it will still be in the open."

He was so careful, to care for her honor. Or was this a veiled rebuke to her for having been so careless of her own reputation?

"What did you want to know about the holy books?"

"I don't know enough even to know what to ask," she said. "My question is a hard one." And now that she loved him, loved his voice, the poetry of his words, she could hardly bear to bare her heart the way that she had planned. And yet if she could not speak to God's servant, how could she ever hear God's word to her? "Sir. Cousin Jacob. It's just that I . . . I don't know whether the holy books contain what I hope for, but I . . ."

"You have a question, and you want God's answer."

"It's not a matter of law, you see. My father teaches us the law, though I'm sure he doesn't know as much about it as you and your father and his father did."

"Your father is a wise and worthy man, and his camp is known as a place where the law is kept and justice and mercy are both well served."

"Yes, you see? It's not to know what's right or wrong. It's to know *why* something is the way it is. Why God has ordered the world a certain way, when . . ."

"When it seems so unfair to you."

She almost gasped at his wisdom. "Sir, do you already know my heart?"

"No," he said, chuckling. "Do you think I didn't have the same questions? Do you think you're the only one?"

"But how could you have questions like mine?" she asked.

He laughed again, more of a hiss than a laugh, really. "A boy who loved the holy books, with a father who loved them also, and the boy wanted nothing more than to sit at his father's feet and read the books aloud and hear how his father explained the word of God. Only the father loved his brother better, the brother who had the birthright but despised it, who lived only to ride out to hunt, to lead a band of men in pursuit of raiders and slaughter them all. The violent man, the hairy, bloody-handed man who thought that it was for old men to sit in a tent door and read and write. He was the one his father loved."

Leah could not believe how easily he spoke of it; and yet

now she saw that it must be that way, that the stories of Esau were true, only she had never stopped to imagine what it must be like to be Esau's younger brother. "Yet you have the birthright now," she whispered.

"I do," he said. "I tried to get it by bargaining, and Esau gave it to me with laughter, with contempt, because he knew that he could reach out and take it back from me whenever he wanted. I tried to get it my mother's way, by trickery. I could fool my father, but how could I imagine I might fool God? In the end, my father gave it to me as he should, not because I reached for it, nor even because I deserved it, but because he is a man of God, and God led him at the last moment to do his will. Like Abraham finding the ram in the thicket, and sparing his beloved son."

"So you know," said Leah. "What it means to be . . ."

"What it means to be alive when God seems to have no purpose for you," said Jacob.

"You knew before I even spoke," she said, tears on her cheeks, but not really weeping, was she? Her voice was still under her control. And in this dim light, perhaps he didn't even see her tears.

"No," he said. "Or yes, I did, but not by the gift of God. I heard your father speak of you, and Rachel, and others. Your father and sister love you, but they also speak of you like someone apart from the life of the camp. Like a painted clay cup among the carven bowls, fragile, not to be used. And even before I met you, I wondered what it was like for you, and whether you understood God's purpose for you."

"I don't," she said. "And I think sometimes that he has no purpose. That I'm here only to be a burden on my father. Until he can find a man willing to marry a wife who can barely see. Not that I'm blind. I found my way here, didn't I?"

"You didn't have to come to my tent to find your way to God," said Jacob. "Why didn't you ask him?"

"What makes you think I haven't? A thousand times. As many times as I've had days in my life."

"So you think he hasn't answered you."

"I think he *has*," said Leah. And she summoned enough courage to finish her thought. "I think he sent you to answer my question."

"But how can I know the answer?" said Jacob. "I've never seen you before this morning."

"You have the holy books," said Leah. "All of God's words are there, aren't they? Even his words to me, aren't they?"

"What do you think the holy books *are?*" asked Jacob.

"Father said—the way I understood it . . . aren't all of God's plans for humankind written there? Father says God knows the end from the beginning, and every soul who ever lived or will ever live. I thought . . . they say that Abraham knew the path of every star. And since everyone knows that the stars guide the lives of men and women in this world, then somewhere in the book he must have charted the course of my star."

To her embarrassment, Jacob laughed. Softly, but any laughter cut her to the heart.

"No, no," he said soothingly. "How could you know? Who teaches such things to girls? Or to boys, for that matter. Have patience with me. No one has ever come to me like this, asking for counsel. It's good that you want to know, and it's true that there are answers to be found in the holy books. I've found them there, but not the way you think."

"How then?" she said.

"To start with," said Jacob, "that idea about the stars telling the lives of every person—it's just not true. That's what they teach in Babylon and Sumer. What the false priests of Elkenah teach. They made it all up to gain power over people, by pretending to have the secrets of all knowledge. But the stars aren't tied to people that way."

"But then what are the stars *for?*" asked Leah.

"That's what Abraham taught us. The stars are really suns, like our sun, only far away. We don't see them in the daytime because our own star, the sun, shines so brightly. But they're there all the time, day and night, shining down on worlds of their own, like ours. God made them all, and he knows their times and seasons. All that we're given to know is our own world, and our own sun, and our own times and seasons. But to God it's all known."

"Abraham knew it, though?"

"He knew it but he didn't write it all. Every star? It wasn't important for us to know every star, so there was no reason to write it. There isn't papyrus enough in all the world to write all the creations of God, and if we could write it there isn't room enough to hold all the scrolls on the whole surface of the earth. No, what Abraham wrote was the same thing Noah wrote, and Enoch, and Adam when he first kept the book of remembrance as the Lord commanded at the very dawn of time."

"And what is that?"

"The covenants of God with men, and the doings of men in the eyes of God. His judgments and his mercy, his laws and his love, and how his children serve him sometimes, and fail him often, and rebel against him in every generation. His sorrow for us, and his punishment, and his generosity and atonement."

"But that's what I want to hear," she said.

"No," said Jacob. "What's written here is what God has done for others, and what you want is to learn what he has in mind for *you*."

"Yes," she said. "That's what I want. To know why God bothered to make me, to be a burden on everyone."

"Your eyes are lovely," said Jacob. "Dark and beautiful wells, deep with the promise of wisdom. But they don't serve you well, those eyes—lovely to look at, but hard to see out of, and it puts a high fence around your life, so you're a lamb that can never leave the fold and go out onto the grassy hills."

He knows my heart and yet he describes it in words that are not bitter but beautiful. Does he really see me this way?

"But the holy books don't have any passages addressed to Leah, daughter of Laban," he said. "There are words of God to prophets, and words of God to the people of each prophet's own time. And there are words of the prophets to the people, and stories of the prophets' lives, and stories of the lives of people who weren't prophets, some of them even the enemies of God."

"Then there would be no answers for me."

"Ah, but there you'd be wrong," said Jacob. "Here is how God speaks to us through the holy books. First, when I read the stories, I think, is this like my life? Can I learn from this how to live my life closer to God? Second, when I read the covenants and laws, I think, am I keeping these covenants? Am I breaking these laws?"

"But that's your own thinking, not the voice of God."

"It's me thinking *about* the voice of God. He has already

spoken. I have to use my ears to hear him. But then, when my own reading and thinking have taken me nowhere, and I still don't understand, then I pray and I read again, and this time Wisdom comes into my heart while I read, and now words and phrases come to life on the page, and things that I read before without understanding now say something new and clear, and my eyes are opened."

"*Your* eyes are open," said Leah. "But what about me? I don't have the holy books, and even if I did, how could I read them?"

"When I was born, I didn't know how to read. I learned."

"But you had eyes that could *see*."

"And you have servants that can learn and read aloud," said Jacob.

"You have these books as your birthright," said Leah. "Would you give them to a servant to read to me?"

"I would let you and your servant come into my tent during the day, and read. When I'm here, I will explain what I can, if you have questions. This birthright is not given to me to hoard, but to share."

Leah could hardly breathe.

"Who is your handmaiden? Bilhah? The mosaic-maker's daughter?"

Had he learned the story of *every* man and woman and child in Laban's camp?

"I think she can learn to read to you," said Jacob. "I think she already knows a kind of writing, so it will be easier to learn another."

Now it seemed silly to her, that quarrel with Bilhah. The girl had meant well. It's not as if she said anything untrue. Bilhah was young and tainted by the city; of course she could only think of a woman's life as leading to marriage. But it wasn't marriage Leah would get from Jacob. It was the path that would lead her to Wisdom. Marriage to a man whose affection was nothing but pity would not make her happy, but Wisdom would.

Bilhah would bring Wisdom to Leah, not out of her extravagant imaginings of the stranger from the southern desert who falls in love with the half-blind girl, ignoring her beautiful sister, but from Bilhah's learning to read aloud the words of God and the prophets out of Jacob's holy books.

Bringing the birthright of Abraham into her life.

PART V

BARGAINS

CHAPTER 9

Bilhah crested a hill and stopped, for there on the plain below her she could see, for the first time, the great city of Byblos. For a moment she forgot to breathe, and then took in great gasps of air, to keep herself from sobbing in relief. In her year in a herdsman's camp, had she forgotten how much she loved the city? No, she had never known how much she loved it, because until her father died the city had surrounded her like water around a fish. And when she left, she had been grieving for her father, and hardly thought of the city itself.

She had even imagined that she hated those crowded streets—after all, it was precisely that crowding that had crushed the life out of her father.

But now, seeing the walls of the buildings, white or brown or grey, yet all bright in the bright sun of early afternoon, and the roofs of thatch or tile, she was filled with a sudden longing for all that she had lost when she left the city behind. To live in a place where she didn't know everyone and exactly what their business was, where life was never the same two days in a row, where sheep and goats did not outnumber people, where you might catch bits of a hundred different songs and conversations during a five minute walk . . . how had she stayed away so long? Leah had done her such a favor by ordering her to go.

Just because she could see the city, though, did not mean she was close to it. She had a long way to go on this winding road, and she would not get there before dark unless she quickened her pace. She was hungry and thirsty, having brought only one small water sack and nothing but her breakfast bread and cheese, which had not even lasted her till noon. She knew that she was probably hungry precisely because she knew there was nothing she could do about it. And it might get worse before it got better, for no one in the city would be expecting her. But certainly one of her father's friends would take her in, if only for a night or two, and then she would go to the men who followed her father's art and offer herself as an assistant, a skilled sorter of tile shards. She could earn a living for herself and not be dependent upon the whims of a spoiled, angry, self-pitying child.

"Are you already a harlot, or merely planning to become one?"

The voice startled her, for she had not heard anyone approach; and then, when she realized what the man had said, she responded with all the venom she could put into her voice, "What kind of man looks at a girl my age and thinks such a vile thought?"

The man—who was not tall, and not old, and scruffy-bearded—merely laughed. "Hundreds of men on this road would look at a girl like you, walking alone, and wonder what her master charges for her services. The men who are more fatherly than lustful will shake their heads and wonder what vile turn of life left you without protection. While the truly evil men—who are, fortunately, rare in this world, will say to themselves, this girl has been walking alone for miles, and carries no burden. Perhaps she has no master, or has run away, and no one will miss her. So I can take her by force, and use her up, and leave her so that no other will ever have her except for the wild scavenging animals of these mountains, and for those few minutes I'll have the power of a savage god over her, and no one will hear her scream."

He said this so pleasantly that the sense of his words almost failed to register with her. "Are you trying to frighten me, sir?"

"Why would I want to do that?" he said. "Any girl who wanders this road alone must fear nothing at all. The only surprise is that you got this far without meeting one kind of man or another."

"I have met many men and women on this road today," she said, "but none spoke to me except to offer me peace." She turned away and continued walking down the road. The city fell out of sight below the next hill.

He walked behind her. "A girl who is determined on harlotry must choose her master carefully. For she *will* have a master, one way or another—if she lives at all."

Now she was frightened, for it was obvious that he had something in mind for her.

"A kind master can make sure you are offered only to the gentlest of clients, the kind who pretend they want their young girls to feel pleasure rather than pain. A kind master will teach a girl patiently and well how to ply her trade, and dress her richly in fine clothing instead of a scrap of a rag. A kind master will keep her well fed, with plenty of drink to help her forget what she has become."

The road widened, and she darted to the left, then ran back up the road, passing him. He did not reach out to try to stop her, but he did turn to follow.

"How far have you already walked? Will you make it back home before dark? If not, some mountain cat might find you. Some beast of prey whose heart knows nothing of beauty, but only hunger. One way or another, girl, you're bound to be devoured today, unless someone takes you under protection." She was back at the crest of the hill, but without even breaking into a run, he had nearly kept up with her, so she could not catch more than a glance at the city that now seemed infinitely out of reach.

"I'm a strong man," he said. "I offer my protection. My companionship. The shelter of my fine tent, not far from here, where I offer a bed to travelers, and all the comforts of home, only without the nagging."

She ran down the other side of the hill. The man behind her laughed. And why shouldn't he? For now, from behind an outcropping of rock, a young man who could have been his son stepped out into the road to block her way. "I'm the one he wants to protect you from," said the young man with a leer.

Bilhah realized that they must have counted on her turning back in order to trap her between the two of them. Unless there were others of their band even farther along the road.

"What do you think?" called out the man behind her. "Will

she be quick to learn and like her work, like a good little lamb, or must we tame a lioness?"

The young man in front of her laughed. "Look how she stands still in the road! I think we've got ourselves a ewe-hare, too frightened to move!"

Then, suddenly, he got a startled look on his face. A stone thudded to the ground behind him, between his legs. He fell over forward onto the ground.

The back of his head was bloody. He had been hit from behind by a well-aimed stone.

And now, emerging from the shadow of a cliff a ways farther up the road, came Jacob himself, lazily spinning a shepherd's sling that was obviously loaded with a good-sized stone. He did not look at Bilhah, but kept his eyes on the man behind her as he spoke to her. "Drop to the ground, Bilhah," he said, "or he'll hurt you."

She obeyed instantly, feeling the man's hands on her as she slumped. He tried to hold onto her dress but she slipped out of his grasp. And then the sharp snap of the sling being released and the stone striking flesh and the older man was also lying motionless on the ground.

"Are they dead?" she said softly.

"Whether they live or die is in God's hands," said Jacob. "We won't be here to see if they wake up or not. The only question that matters is, am I taking you down to Byblos, or back to Padan-aram?"

Bilhah, who had been so certain only a few moments ago, did not know now what she wanted. "There are men like this in the city, too, aren't there?"

"There's no shortage of such men in the world. A woman alone is their natural prey. You've been under a man's protection till now. Your father, and then the friend who led you to Padan-aram, and until this morning, my uncle Laban."

"I can't stay there," she said. "Leah sent me away."

"Leah sent you away from *her*," said Jacob. "She doesn't have the authority to send you away from your father's camp. And you're not stupid. You knew that. So you were using that as an excuse to try to go home."

She nodded miserably.

"Byblos was your father's home, not yours. Without his arm, his name, his house to protect you, it won't be the city you grew up in. Before long you'd be wishing for the sheep and goats and cows of Laban's camp."

"I think I already do."

"Leah looked for you this morning. She wanted you to learn to read the writing of the Holy Books, so you could read them to her."

"Is it the writing of Byblos?"

"Easier," said Jacob. "Only a couple of dozen signs to learn, instead of hundreds."

"I ran away. They won't trust me now."

"You're not a bondservant," said Jacob. "You're a free girl. Laban told me to ask you to return to help his daughter learn the word of God from the books I brought with me. For this he will pay you by adding a ewe lamb to your dowry year by year. By the time you come of age, there will surely be three or four lambs to give your husband, so he'll respect you as a bringer of wealth, and not just a servant and mate."

"But I agreed to serve him for my keep."

"He realized, when you left, that your service was more valuable than this. And when you learn to read, you'll be skilled in a trade. A ewe lamb each year, plus bed and board, are low pay for a scribe, but he hopes you'll accept the offer anyway."

"These men frightened me," said Bilhah. "I would go back to Laban just for his protection."

"At the moment," said Jacob, "the afternoon grows later, and if these men happen not to be dead, they're bound to wake up eventually. Though I think that you're entitled to whatever money they have on them, for the trouble they caused you."

"They caused me no trouble, thanks to you," said Bilhah, "and I don't want their money. Besides, I doubt they have anything of value with them, except perhaps a knife or two."

"Then I'll take those," said Jacob.

A few moments later, they were walking briskly back up the road toward Padan-aram. Jacob was balancing the two knives in his hand. "Most robbers use cudgels or javelins, and they strike from hiding. My guess is that these lads aren't robbers in the ordinary sense. I think they're slavers, and when they accost travelers, it's not to steal their goods, but themselves."

"He said terrible things to me."

"I think not," said Jacob. "I think he gave you a very clear and helpful warning about the dangers of traveling as a lone woman on this road."

"Just as *you* gave him a warning about the dangers of trying to capture lone women."

"Your lesson might have been less painful," said Jacob, "but I hope it is no less effective."

"Will Laban really take me back?"

"Your departure caused such an alarm in the camp, and half the men were ready to go in search of you, until I insisted that I could do it better on my own, being a fast runner and good with a sling. Leah wept in sorrow for having driven you away, though I think she didn't. I think it was an excuse for doing what was already in your heart to do."

"I miss the city."

"Maybe someday you'll live in a city again. Now that the years of drought are over, people are coming back into the land and building up many of the old places. There'll be a husband for you, and it doesn't have to be a wandering herdsman. But this world is an ugly place for the weak and defenseless, and against a strong and determined man, what defense would you have? Wait for your marriage to leave Laban's house. And I think you'll find a repentant Leah when you return. She wants to hear the word of God spoken to her. I think it will be a good thing that she hear Wisdom speak to her in your voice."

So Bilhah retraced the day's steps, but now in company with this man of the birthright, who knew her name, and had chosen himself to come and save her from the dangers of the road.

It was only when they got back to Laban's camp that Bilhah realized just how disruptive her attempted return to Byblos had been. It was well after dark when they got there, and Bilhah had expected to slip quietly to her tent—though she hoped for food.

What she found, however, were servants wide awake and sitting or walking around in the camp. When they saw her and Jacob, however, they immediately leaped into action, so a great busyness sprang up as they walked among the tents and pens. What most surprised Bilhah was the way the servants cheerfully waved to Jacob, but glared at her before resuming their business.

"Why are they all looking at me so hatefully?" she said to Jacob. "Why should *they* care whether I come or go?

"I think it's because of the feast."

"Feast?" said Bilhah. And then, after one long stupid moment, she remembered. "Why did *you* come to fetch me when you knew you couldn't be back in time to have Leah and Rachel presented to you? Lord Laban could have sent someone else."

"He intended to. In fact, he was irritated, I think, when I insisted on going. But, you see, I didn't expect that you would have got so far—you're a fast walker, and the brigands on the road are surprisingly inefficient, not to have taken you far sooner. So I thought I'd be back well before dark."

"I knew the roads were unsafe. That's why I hurried.'

"Whom would Laban have sent?" asked Jacob. "Someone he could spare? That would be someone much slower than I am. Or suppose he did send some of his strongest and fastest shepherds. There was still a good chance that you would already have been carried off. Which of Laban's servants could have been trusted to go looking for you? How many of them would have kept going right to Byblos, losing you and wasting the whole journey?"

"Would you have gone searching for me?"

"If I hadn't kept finding your track on the road, I would have gone searching for you long before. And think of this. What if the shepherds had arrived just when I did? Wouldn't they have tried to confront the men and talk to them, persuade them or threaten them into letting you go?"

"Probably."

"But that doesn't work with brigands like them. For one thing, they probably had a couple of other men lurking somewhere. As soon as there was a discussion, they would have come out into the open to try to scare your would-be rescuers. That's why the way I handled it is the only way. Let your first salute be a stone in the back of the head, and you have one less enemy to deal with. It also scared their lurking friends that maybe it wasn't such a good idea to emerge from hiding."

"What if they hadn't been brigands, though—what if I'd just been asking directions?"

"When you're asking direction, decent men don't get on both sides of you, blocking your escape in either direction, and laugh loudly at you."

"I see your point. I just don't know that they did anything bad enough to deserve killing."

"I wasn't punishing him, I was preventing him. You don't have to wait for a bad man to succeed in his wickedness before you're allowed to stop him. I'm not much of a fighter, so the only way I could deal with two men was to knock one down before the conversation started. If he had wanted not to die, he wouldn't have threatened a helpless young stupid girl that way."

The word *stupid* really stung.

"Don't take offense," said Jacob. "You have to admit that walking along that road was stupid."

"No it wasn't," said Bilhah. "I didn't know men like that would be on the road."

"I see," said Jacob. "You weren't stupid, you were ignorant."

"No," said Bilhah, with mock sadness. "It was stupid to

try to go to Byblos at all. But you have to admit that taking the road was smarter than trying to go over strange mountains."

"True. I never would have found you. So we're agreed: Stupid *and* ignorant."

Then, having reached the point where the route to his tent diverged from the route to hers, he walked briskly away from her without a word in parting.

"Jacob!" she cried, by reflex, really, only thinking afterward that she should probably have said Lord Jacob or at least Master Jacob.

He turned to face her.

"Thank you for saving me. Even if no one else is glad you did it, *I* am."

"And I'm glad you've decided to value your life more highly than you did this morning." He bowed and then headed on toward his tent.

When Bilhah entered Leah's tent, there were still more glares from the women helping Leah with last-minute primping for her presentation to Jacob.

"We *heard* Lord Jacob was back," said one of the women to the other, pointedly *not* speaking to Bilhah directly, but making sure she was hearing all that was said. "Imagine, making Lord Laban and his daughters wait just because some foolish ewe had gone astray."

"Anybody can fetch back a lost sheep."

Bilhah wanted to retort, Only a clever man would know what he had to do, and only a bold one would do it, and only a noble one would insist on doing it himself. But she said nothing, because she knew they were not criticizing Jacob, they were finding fault with her. And since she deserved the rebuke, there was no point in disputing the point.

Instead she stood before Leah and bowed her head. "Mistress, I'm sorry I caused such disruption on this important day."

"On your knees, girl," said the woman who was doing Leah's hair.

"She's not a bondservant," said Leah promptly. "She's a free girl, and she does not owe me her knee. She is free to come and go as she wishes."

This silenced the women completely, since they *were* both bondwomen. In fact, Bilhah knew perfectly well that they were women who helped with washing and dyeing cloth and other rough work; they were not particularly skilled with hair and clothing, and it struck her that it was a kind of insult to Leah that they had been assigned to prepare Leah. There was no doubt that the women with real skill and experience were occupied with preparing Rachel, who needed less help to be beautiful.

"How do I look?" asked Leah.

"You're beautiful," said Bilhah. And despite the inexperience of the women, it wasn't far from the truth. If Rachel had been standing beside her, of course, no one would give Leah a glance—and that was precisely what would happen when the two of them were presented to Jacob. But by herself, without her younger sister to distract from her, Leah was lovely, her face sweet, and her trembling shyness quite endearing.

"The truth," said Leah.

"That *is* the truth," said Bilhah. "Why would I lie? I'm still angry with you, and yet I have to say it."

The women were outraged. "How dare you be angry at your patient mistress!"

"If I were Laban I'd have you lashed for that!"

Again, Leah silenced them with a gesture. And Bilhah realized for the first time that there was something queenly about Leah, who did not have to shout or even turn to look at them; just a motion of her hand, and her intention was clear. The women knew to hold their peace, and yet knew also they were not being rebuked for having defended their master's daughter. Such poise and command—and yet she has never used this manner with me. She really *has* made a distinction between bond and free all along. And she really *might* be able to be mistress of a great man's house, even without far-seeing eyes.

"Good women," said Leah, "I must be alone with my sister now."

For a moment, Bilhah looked around to see whether Rachel had entered the tent. But she had not. The shock on the women's faces made it plain that Leah had been referring to Bilhah as her sister. Tears sprang unbidden to Bilhah's eyes at the generosity and forgiveness in Leah's treatment of her.

Alone with Leah in the tent, Bilhah did sink to her knees now, and would have pressed her weeping face into Leah's lap, except Leah stopped her. "Don't get tearstains on my gown, or father will think I've been clumsy and spilled something."

Bilhah looked up and saw her smiling. "Thank you for wanting me back."

"I always want you to speak the truth to me," said Leah. "I was wrong to take offense at what you said. But even if I had been right to send you away from me, I never meant you to be sent away from camp. You're Father's ward, not mine."

"I sent myself away, Mistress Leah," said Bilhah. "I thought that if I could no longer serve you, then I had no useful purpose in your father's camp, since I'm no good at anything else."

"Now you *will* be useful, and not just to me," said Leah. "Did Jacob tell you? You're to be taught to read the languages of the holy books, or at least some of them, so you can read them aloud to me. But once you have that skill, to read, I mean, then you'll have a trade that others might hire."

"Not if no one has anything in that kind of writing for me to read," said Bilhah. "If only Jacob has such writings, where else would I use my skill?"

"Father told me that when they used the holy writing to communicate with his deaf father, back when Rebekah still lived here at Padan-aram, many of the servants learned it, and the use of it spread. It's a more convenient way of writing than the cuneiform writing of Akkad, quicker to write and easier to learn. So there are many people in the cities of the coast who use that writing now. They've changed some of the shapes, but you'll be able to read them with only a little more learning."

"Who will teach me?" asked Bilhah.

"Father will," said Leah. "He said that Jacob is too good a man at the business of shepherding to waste his time teaching one foolish ridiculous girl how to read."

"So Lord Laban will do it himself?"

"He's a patient teacher," said Leah.

Bilhah doubted that he would treat *her* the way he treated his own daughter, but she said nothing; after all, it might be true, and the last thing she needed to do right now was contradict Leah. After the glares of the people in the camp, it was such a relief that Leah was treating her so generously. I was wrong to run away, thought Bilhah. I should have been more patient and understanding myself.

"I marvel to be so rewarded for my foolishness," said Bilhah.

"There are many foolish people in this camp," said Leah. "Including me. But you're not being rewarded for being one of us. I went to Jacob this morning, very early—while you were busy sneaking out of camp, I imagine."

"I'm glad you did," said Bilhah.

"Not for the reason you suggested. I'm perfectly content for him to marry my sister when she comes of age. No doubt Father will have found a husband for me well before he lets *her* go to another man's house. No, I went because I want to know the words of God. I want to know if there's something written in the holy books that will serve me the way Rachel's dreams have served her—to tell her what her life is for. Only I can't read them, and Jacob is too busy to read them to me. I had already forgotten *our* foolish quarrel, and so when he suggested teaching you to read so you could tell me all the words of God, I was so happy, I went in search of you at once to tell you the good news. That's when we found out you were gone."

"If you hadn't noticed until later in the day, it would have been too late for me."

"Really?" said Leah. "Did something bad happen on the road?"

Bilhah was about to tell the story, but at that moment the steward came to the tent door. "If the lady Leah is ready, your father wishes me to bring you and your sister to the banquet tent to be presented to his guest and brother, the lord Jacob."

"Tell me after," whispered Leah.

"And you tell *me* all that happens tonight!" whispered Bilhah back again.

Leah grimaced. "I won't *know* all that happens. Only what people *say*."

"You see everything," said Bilhah. "Just not with your eyes."

Leah laughed and rose to her feet. It hurt Bilhah's heart to see how, as soon as Leah stood, her poor posture and her squinting eyes defeated so much of the beauty of her gown and hair. But she said only, "Ah, Leah, you break my heart with your beauty."

"I break *something*," said Leah, chuckling. "But I appreciate your kindness. You're my dearest friend, Bilhah. I promise never to send you away from me again."

CHAPTER 10

If Rachel had to marry someone, then yes, it might as well be Jacob. And if her dreams meant anything—which she wasn't at all sure of—then they probably meant that God wanted her to marry him. Certainly Father did.

But as they led her across the dusty expanse between tents, her hair oppressively tight and heavy instead of loose and free—did they really think that would turn her from a shepherdess into a lady?—she felt afraid.

Of what? She couldn't name it. Not of Jacob. She was easy at heart whenever she was with him. And never of Father— even when he was angry with her, he wasn't *very* angry. Yet she was filled with dread. Maybe it was just the future that frightened her. Someday, instead of being free to care for the animals and stride boldly out under the sun, squinting to watch the flock in the bright day, she'd have a heavy belly and sit around in a stuffy dusty tent, listening to the nattering of the servants and getting ridiculously thrilled because the baby kicked.

Well of course babies kick. They're *trapped* in there.

Leah was waiting for her under the front awning of the dining tent when she got there. Usually they would be in the back, where the servants brought the food in and out. They would be brought into the tent by Reuel, the steward, who was hovering and fussing. Rachel treated him as if he were invisible, which usually made him stay away from her.

"I feel like I'm a sheep brought to market," said Rachel to Leah.

Leah smiled that irritating little half-smile of hers, as if she had some secret superior knowledge. "I don't think anybody's going to shear you," said Leah. "Or make you into mutton."

"No, they're going to breed me," said Rachel. And then, remembering how easily Leah could feel neglected, she added, "Or you."

"Don't condescend to me," said Leah.

Well, that's how it was with Leah. There was no pleasing her.

"Father is bringing me here out of courtesy," said Leah. "It's you that he wants, and don't pretend you don't know it."

"Nobody asks me what I want," said Rachel.

"Nobody has to," said Leah.

Rachel knew exactly where this argument led, but was powerless to turn from its inexorable course. "I suppose you're saying that I'm always asking for things."

"No," said Leah—and Rachel felt like she could say the words along with her—"little Rachel never has to *ask*."

"I'm sure that every sigh of mine brings rain from heaven or a bull from the river."

"Next best thing," said Leah. "A prophet from the well."

So Leah didn't want an argument after all. In fact, it was funny. Rachel laughed.

Leah smiled a little more broadly. "I just hope he doesn't marry you and go away at once."

"You've been praying for me to go away since the day I was born."

"Not until about five days after, and anyway, God never answers *my* prayers."

Did that half smile mean that Leah was joking? Or that she meant it, but wanted you to *think* she was joking so you wouldn't get mad? Or did she want you to know she meant it, and the smile was so she could tell Father, Rachel knew I was joking, I was *smiling* when I said it?

Rachel knew it was better to say nothing. "You mean I had five days when my sister was glad I was alive?"

"No, there were five days when I didn't know you existed. I was three. What does anyone tell a three-year-old?"

"So why don't you want him to take me away right off?"

"Because when he goes, he'll take the holy books with him," said Leah. "And I want to read them first."

"You can read?' asked Rachel.

"I can listen to someone else read."

This made Rachel very uncomfortable, though she wasn't sure why. "Jacob has a lot of work to do, he can't just sit there and read to you."

Leah openly smirked. "Oh, don't get jealous, my beloved and ever-watchful sister. *He'll* be gamboling with the lambs and you all day, I'm sure. Bilhah's the one who's going to read to me."

No wonder she ran away. Imagine being trapped all day, reading and reading. "Lucky Bilhah."

"She's excited about it. She already *can* read a little. A different kind of writing, but she'll learn this way easily, Jacob says. And I'm not *blind*. I expect I'll learn to read, too."

Reuel had been going in and out of the tent, but now he came out and walked right to them. "Your father has given me the signal to bring you in. Remember not to look the noble prince Jacob in the eye."

Rachel rolled her eyes and Leah laughed. "We've both talked to him face to face," said Leah.

"Don't shame your father by acting as if you don't know how to be modest young ladies," said Reuel.

"Someday," said Leah, "we'll be giving *him* the orders."

"No we won't," said Rachel. "Because one of our brothers will inherit him along with the whole camp." She stuck her tongue out at the steward, who ignored her.

"If I never get married," said Leah, "I plan to stay around camp and make his whole life miserable until he's eager to die."

The steward made a wry face. "You think you're irritating me, but you're not," he said. "Because you'll be some other man's problem."

"No I won't," said Leah.

"It's a world of wombs," said Reuel, "and men panting to have the use of them. You'll find a husband, you may be sure." He made one last fussy adjustment in Rachel's clothing, pulling the shoulders of her gown to be a bit more open, which made no sense to her, since she had absolutely nothing to make barer shoulders look attractive to a man.

"And speak only when your father speaks to you," said Reuel.

"We've been presented before," said Leah.

"But not to your Aunt Rebekah's son. Do you think your father wants him to go home with an ill report of you, and shame him in front of his sister?"

"He can't go home at all," said Rachel. "Or his brother will kill him."

"That's exactly what I'm talking about," hissed the steward. "Keep your pretty little mouths shut except to smile and show your good manners."

"Calling our mouths pretty," said Leah, "doesn't make it any nicer when you tell us to keep them shut."

"It makes it worse," said Rachel.

"When the two of you are together," said Reuel, "you're impossible."

"No," said Leah. "Just irritable."

Rachel beamed a big insincere smile at the steward. "How's that?"

"Repulsive," he said. "Only a crocodile could find that attractive."

"Good," said Rachel. "I'd rather have a crocodile than a husband."

"That's a good one," said Leah. "Mention that idea to Father and Jacob. They'll both laugh and think you're so cute."

"And then I'll make sure Rachel spends the next year carding wool in a tiny dark tent," said Reuel.

"That's how I spend my days already," said Leah. "I wonder what *I'm* being punished for."

Rachel sighed. It always came back to poor poor Leah and how she suffered.

Father's voice roared from inside the dining tent. "Where are my daughters, taking naps?"

"Poor Reuel," said Rachel, patting his hand. "We've gotten you in trouble, haven't we?"

Reuel pushed them toward the tent. "Fortunately, your father knows you both well enough that he doesn't blame me."

They had done this before, coming in through the front of the dining tent, stepping with bare feet onto the thick carpet, standing there with everyone's eyes on them. Usually Rachel looked only at Father—when she looked at anyone at all. For as soon as they started talking about her, praising her, commenting about her virtues, she could not look anywhere at all, but cast her eyes downward, forcing herself to say nothing, but longing to leave. What did they think they knew of her, just by looking? They praised her face, which Rachel herself had never seen, but they also spoke of her modesty and obedience, which was ridiculous, since they had no idea of how she behaved when she wasn't directly under her father's eye.

This time, though, she knew the man sitting beside Father, and liked him. He knew animals in general, and had come to know many of the animals in Father's herds individually. He was good with people, showing respect even to the shepherds who didn't deserve it, listening patiently to all advice but following only that which was wise. He was the kind of man who would insist on chasing after that stupid girl Bilhah because, as Jacob insisted, he was the only one who had no duties and so the only one who could be spared. No duties! He had been here so brief a time, and yet he was already nearly indispensable. Even some of the old shepherds counseled with him, and while Jacob was careful never to give orders to anyone, it was plain he knew how to run a camp at least as well as Reuel did.

He was an admirable man. Yet that would have made Rachel more nervous, less able to meet anyone's gaze, were it not for the fact that she also knew him to be kind to her. He was a man who listened patiently to her, who let her tell him her dreams, who took her concerns about the lambs seriously. She wondered sometimes whether this meant only that he was good with children—for he was, all the boys and girls in camp adored him and some of them followed him around as if they thought he was their mother. Or did it mean that he felt something special for her? She was sometimes sure that he did. But whatever he felt, it was not the leering possessiveness that she had seen in the eyes of some of the men who came looking for a wife for their son. He did not treat her as if he intended to own her. Nor did he coddle her as if she were injured or weak or a baby. He looked her in the eye as if she were his equal, a person that he respected, not gazing at her as a possession he was proud of.

So she met his gaze fearlessly and smiled at him, which of course she was not supposed to do, lest it make her look forward. But why shouldn't she? She knew this man. He was her cousin. They had spent hours together.

Jacob smiled back at her—and there was laughter in his eyes, as if he knew how artificial and silly this whole presentation ritual was.

Then he looked at Leah and seemed not to notice Rachel existed any more.

"Both your daughters are jewels, my brother," said Jacob. "But I suspect Leah sees better than anyone thinks she does."

"You wouldn't think that if you saw her stumbling around in the camp," said Laban.

Rachel could feel Leah stiffen beside her. She was so prickly. Why *shouldn't* Father say that? She did stumble, even with people leading her!

"My father's vision was fading. But his was the blindness of old age. He could see nothing near at hand, even when he could still see far-off things—a high bird, but not his own hand. And he talked about how the world closed down, how it felt as though he walked always in a tunnel, with darkness on every side."

"I'm sorry to hear of it. But God sends trials even to the best of men."

"Leah, though—she looked me in the eye and I know she saw me. Even the expressions on my face, and this was before dawn, when there wasn't much light at all. I think she has the kind of weak eyes that let a person see what's very close. I think she can do many things that you've placed out of her reach."

Rachel knew that Father didn't like hearing this. It would sound like criticism to him. She was also pretty sure that Leah wouldn't like having her tender eyes talked about. Well, too bad, Leah! This is Jacob's way, to speak plainly, and if you don't like it, I'm sorry, but it's better than the kind of person who sneaks around and never says what he's thinking.

"I think we know best what our daughter can and can't do," said Laban.

He must really be nervous, thought Rachel. To say "we" when Mother's been dead for so many years. It was the way he talked when supplicants came before him, or when he was administering a punishment to someone in the camp. Would Jacob recognize the rebuke that this implied?

"Oh, I know," said Jacob. "I'm like a child in this camp, compared to what everyone else knows. But sometimes a child can see what no one else notices, because everything is new to a child. I want to teach Leah to read, along with her servant. I know her eyes would get tired, but I think she can see the letters and could learn to write them. I think she could see well enough to spend time copying some of the books I have. Because that's part of the sacred duty of keeping the records. They fade with time and use, and they have to be copied out perfectly. If Leah can learn to write with a good hand, then I could use her help, and Bilhah's as well, of course."

"I don't know," said Laban. "Leah could never see well enough to spin yarn."

"But that's a different task, drawing the fleece, using the distaff. You can keep your eyes much closer to the book. It holds steady. And the ink is black on the white of the papyrus. Will you let me try?"

"Not if it makes her tired. She's fragile, and must be taken care of."

Again, Rachel felt Leah flinch. Silly girl, she wanted it both ways—to be coddled, but to have everyone treat her as if she were as useful as a regular person.

"She's a beautiful girl—quiet, not wild like that young lioness beside her."

"Yes, both my daughters look like their mother, thank the Lord."

But Father used the word *ba'al* for "the Lord," and now it was Jacob's turn to stiffen. "My father and mother taught me never to call the Lord by that name." Jacob used the word *Adonai* for "Lord."

"What does it matter?" said Father. "Neither one is his right name."

"But Ba'al is the name that is used by false priests to oppress the people and keep them in ignorance of the true and living God."

"Then with my friend and brother I will never say 'Ba'al.' Except when I need to say what word it is that I'm not saying!"

Father and Jacob both laughed at this.

"Well, I've met your daughters and I've met your sons," said Jacob. "They're all fine adornments to their father's house."

Laban laughed with some bitterness. "How kindly you put it. Adornments, yes, that's what my older sons are. Adornments. Which of them can take my place in this camp when I die? Here you are, the greatest guest this camp has ever known, and I could hardly get them to come home when you arrived, and now they're off doing some useless thing, wasting their time and, no doubt, their inheritance. Oh, I'm proud of those boys."

Rachel was stunned to hear Father speak so plainly about Nahor and Terah. While every word of what he said was true, Rachel had not known till now that Father knew it.

"I tell you, sometimes I'm tempted to give my flocks and herds to a son-in-law. A stranger would be better trusted with my household than my own sons!"

"You say this in frustration with them," said Jacob. "But they're young, and young men get older and learn wisdom. And your youngest son, Choraz, may be the wisest of all

154

when he comes home from the house of Kedar. Be patient. Don't even think of disinheriting them. Your daughters should go to a man who loves them for themselves, not to one who thinks that by marrying them, he'll inherit all that you have."

Laban grinned at Jacob. "Well said, loyally spoken. My sons have nothing to fear from you, is that it? No danger that you'll take their place? But what do *I* do about the fact that you own nothing and see no prospect of getting any part of your father's household? If you don't aspire to my fortune, and have none of your own, how do you plan to support a wife, and why would a loving father sentence one of his daughters to a life of want?"

"Perhaps you should measure me, not by what another man will give me—even my father—but by what I can earn with my own labor."

"And what can you earn?"

"Let me serve with you under a seven-year bond. What value would you place on such service?"

"You? A prince in the service of the Lord? Become a bond-servant to me, your uncle?"

"For a fixed term of years. But you would pay me no wage. Instead, I set a much higher value on my own service than mere money or possessions. The price of my seven years of service will be your daughter Rachel."

"But you'll still be a poor man, dependent upon others."

"But you'll be a richer one, having had my service all those years, and at no cost, for you will have given me what God gave to you and your wife for love alone."

"How will you support her?"

"If my labor for seven years is worth a daughter, what do

you think I will be able to earn after that, when I work for hire?"

"I've seen your labor," said Father. "The value is high. But the price you ask of me is higher yet. As you said, my daughters are gifts to me, from God and from my wife. And yet they are not mine the way that flocks and herds are mine. They belong to themselves more than to me, and to God more than to themselves." He turned to Rachel and spoke her name. "If this man serves me as a bondsman for seven years, obeying my commands and faithfully working to make my house greater, will you then consent to marry him?"

No discussion with a suitor had ever gone this far, or even close to it. Yet even without prior experience, Rachel knew that this was the telling moment. Father would not have put the question to her if his own answer was not yes, and he would have put the question privately if he had thought her answer might be no.

It was now that she would be giving her own oath, and binding herself as surely as Jacob was offering to bind himself to Laban. But Jacob's bondage would be only seven years, and hers would be for the rest of her life. His would involve labor, but hers would require the mysterious sharing of wife and husband, the bearing of babies, the passage into the borderlands of death to bring new life into the world.

Suddenly Leah's voice broke the silence. "Would she marry him at the beginning or the end of his seven years?"

Father looked at her in surprise, but since it was a sensible question, he did not rebuke her. Instead he looked at Jacob. "Of course the end of the seven years. She's far too young right now."

"I can wait seven years," said Jacob. "Every hour of service will be a happy one, knowing that I'm an hour closer to earning the right to be her husband."

Rachel felt the words as if they rushed like a blush into her face. In all their conversations, he had never spoken like that to her. Words of love—this was nothing like the bantering and bragging of the boys and men of the camp as they spoke to— or, worse, about—girls.

"I will also wait the seven years," said Rachel. "And at the end of that time, when you are free again, I will freely marry you."

She felt Leah's hand stroke her back. Comfort from her sister? But why should she need comfort? She had just promised her future to this man, but he was a good man, a prince that God had brought to her, first in dreams, and then in body. How could she not rejoice, to know she had set her feet upon God's path for her?

Yet if she did not need her sister's comfort, why was she crying, and why did her legs tremble as if they were cold? Why was her heart mourning the loss of her girlhood and the ending of her carefree days among the lambs and sheep, out in the sunlight and the rain? Why did she feel that her whole life now had closed behind her, and the future was strange and frightening? She should be feeling nothing but pure joy.

"Leah," said Father, "your sister trembles with joy, as you will tremble someday when you accept betrothal to a good man."

Rachel felt Leah's hand withdraw from her. Why did she have to take offense? Father was only reassuring her that Rachel would not shame her by marrying first. Why shouldn't he? Why did she always take it as an insult?

"Father," said Leah, "shouldn't Rachel remain to hear her

future husband swear his bond to you? At present she isn't sworn to any man, because Jacob remains unsworn to you."

Jacob laughed pleasantly. "And this from a girl who has never heard priests arguing the fine points of scripture."

"You're right, Leah," said Father. "Jacob, kneel before me, my brother, and become my son."

Rachel knew, of course, that what Jacob was becoming was not a son at all, but a slave. For a fixed term of years, yes, and with the promise of becoming a son-in-law when the time was done. But not a son. Yet those were the words. So many untrue things were part of such bargains, yet it seemed as if everyone agreed that if some parts of a covenant were lies, that was all right, but if other parts were lies, a man could be killed for it. Why not just tell the truth to everyone all the time? Why all the posing? Why did Leah have to be brought in to this presentation, when everyone knew it was for Rachel that Jacob was going to make his bargain? There was a pretense of trying to assuage Leah's feelings, but it only hurt her more; yet Leah pretended not to be hurt, at least in front of company, and Father pretended to believe that a husband just as good as Jacob would be found for her, even though everyone knew that there *was* no husband just as good to be had in all the world.

Jacob knelt and put his right hand on the inside of Father's thigh. Each swore an oath to the other. Jacob swore to be Laban's true and obedient servant for seven years, to labor for him and fight for him in battle, on the promise of Rachel's hand in marriage at the end of those years.

And Laban answered, "Rachel my daughter will be your wife when your seven years of service are complete, and during your service I will be your good master, providing for your wants and governing you wisely."

But *my* oath was given first, thought Rachel. Without my oath, there would be nothing between these men. As surely as if I stood between them, it was for love of me that this prince has humbled himself before my father.

It filled her with a rush of some heady emotion that she could not name. She was not trembling now. She felt light-footed, as if she could dance from the room, or float like a tuft of lambswool in a breeze.

"Can we go now, Father?" asked Leah.

Father looked at Rachel. "Come here, little one," he said.

Rachel went to him.

"Give me your hand," said Father.

She gave it to him.

"I dreaded the day I would promise you to your husband," he said. "I'm glad that seven years will pass before I give this hand to him. And I'm glad that when I do, I will be giving you to such a man as this. What man has ever married better?" Then he turned to Jacob. "Except perhaps your father Isaac, when he took my sister Rebekah for his wife."

"I am content to have a marriage that is the equal of my father's," said Jacob. "What contest can there be between youth and age? Each age has its beauties and wisdoms, and its own kind of love. May God bless us to be old together, as well as to be together in our youth."

"Amen!" cried Father.

"Amen," whispered Rachel.

Then Leah took her by the arm and led her kindly from the tent.

Outside, some of the women were gathered, openly

weeping and smiling, eager to hug Rachel and pat her and tell her how lucky and blessed she was and what a fine man she was getting. Even Reuel had tears in his eyes, Rachel saw.

Leah stood back apart from them all, not looking.

A hand gripped Rachel's arm tightly. Startled—because the older women had been so affectionate—she turned to find Zilpah holding her. "So it's done?" asked the girl.

Rachel nodded, wondering why Zilpah looked so fiercely happy about it. What was this to her? Why should she care?

"Let me be your servant when you marry him," said Zilpah.

Rachel shook her head. "That's not mine to promise," she said. "You don't belong to me."

"Your father will give you whomever you ask for," said Zilpah.

"But that will be seven years from now. You'll be married by then, with three fat babies."

"No I won't," said Zilpah.

Rachel couldn't help looking at the way the older girl was dressed, the way her body's curves cried out for men to notice her, her bright eyes and full lips and smooth and slithering hair as showy as the brightest fruit on a gray-green tree.

"Yes you will," said Rachel. "Or the boys in this camp will all run mad and marry sheep."

Zilpah laughed and winked, as if somehow in the past few minutes they had become great friends. Then she backed away and disappeared around the outside of the tent.

One of the old women leaned close. "Stay away from that one. Low born and low bred, there's a stain in her very breath, you can be sure."

That seemed unfair to Rachel. Zilpah couldn't help being

born fatherless. The things Rachel didn't like about Zilpah were those she chose herself—how she dressed, how she carried herself, and that grasping hand that had gripped Rachel's arm as tightly as someone falling from a cliff might hold to the one sapling that might save him.

Rachel smiled politely to the older women. "Thank you, it *is* a happy day. Thank you. Seven years is a long time, I'm still just a girl, but yes I'm glad."

Finally Reuel intervened. "Let the girl be. Her life has been decided tonight. Let her have some time by herself, or with her sister."

Please not with my sister. Let me not have to worry about what Leah's feeling.

And when she looked around, Rachel realized that her prayer had been granted before it was even thought of—Leah was not there. Leah had gone off by herself.

Reuel walked silently beside her to her tent and held the flap open for her. "Sleep in peace, little one," said Reuel. "If your father were not so rich and important, you wouldn't have had to think of things like this until you were old enough to want them."

"But I do want them," said Rachel.

Reuel smiled and shrugged. "Only because you don't yet understand what they are."

Annoyed, Rachel turned her back on him and went inside. What did he think she didn't understand? She knew all about marriage, all about men and women. She knew that men didn't butt heads together the way rams did, and the winner got the ewes. But then, wasn't the bargain between Father and Jacob just the human equivalent? I have the girl, you want her,

161

let's see who has the bigger, stronger set of horns, and the thicker head.

She undressed herself, laying out the dress for a servant to fold and put away, and then knelt to pray. If he's going to be a good husband to me, Lord, then please keep him safe, let no accident take him from me, no sudden disease, no assassin from an enemy, no terrible fall from a high place while he's tending sheep. And if he's going to be a hard man, a cruel husband—for some men are cruel, who seem to others to be good—then let me die before the seven years are up, so I don't have to be disappointed in him.

She thought she was done with her prayer, but then thought of something else that needed saying.

"Dear God," she whispered, "give my sister Leah a husband as good as mine, so she can be happy as I am happy."

PART VI

HOLY BOOKS

CHAPTER 11

At first Jacob took little time with their study. It was Reuel who taught Leah and Bilhah the shapes and sounds of the letters. It made little sense to Leah. "So when I see this shape, I say 'ba.'"

"No," Reuel explained patiently. "You say 'buh.'"

"So how do I write 'ba'?"

"With this letter," said Reuel. "But it could be 'ba' or 'buh' or 'beh' or 'bi.'"

"Then how do I know anything? A letter to say just 'b' makes no sense. You can't even *say* 'b' without *some* sound after it."

"Look, we don't *have* to have all the sounds on the papyrus. Just the hard sounds, and let the singing sounds be whatever they are."

Leah simply hated the thought that words could be broken into pieces like that, and only some of the pieces be written down. It made reading so hard, to have to guess what went between, and where words stopped and started.

But finally the conceptual battle was won, and Leah could kneel down and scratch the letters in the dirt, and read the letters Bilhah scratched, and they could make words and sentences out of them, and read them readily enough. Of course, Bilhah could read them standing up, while Leah had to bow down and put her face close to the earth to see what was written. But when Jacob came and saw them working at their reading, he said, "It's good to bow down when you prepare to read the words of God." So from then on, Leah did not mind her humble posture.

Of course, Bilhah also began to kneel when she wrote and read, even though she didn't have to. Which might not have been what Jacob intended, but Leah rather liked the effect, the both of them kneeling together; and if Leah bowed lower, then that only made her closer to God, and that's what all this was for, wasn't it? To find God's will for her?

When they could read and write with some ease, Jacob began to spend more time with them—but still he did not bring out a single holy book. Instead he gave them brushes and taught them to write with ink on stones. "Papyrus is expensive and has to be brought from Egypt," said Jacob. "But ink I make myself, and stones are free. So now you will learn to write on stones and read from rocks. The Lord made them all, didn't he?"

Leah laughed, for she could hear in his voice that he was smiling when he said it. A jest—because it didn't matter what they wrote *on*. Holy books were holy because the words spoke of God and the men and women who served him. If they were scratched in dirt, it made the dirt holy; if the words were swept away, then it would just be dirt again.

There came a point in every session, though, when Leah's head would hurt and her eyes would be too tired to work any more. That was when she would lie back and cover her eyes and Bilhah would continue her practice alone. Sometimes Leah would say words and Bilhah would write them down; later, when Reuel or Jacob came by, they would read what Bilhah had written and Leah would tell them whether that was what she said. Bilhah became very skilled at it—more so than Leah, but that was to be expected. She had more practice at it, and she could see better to start with.

Gradually, Bilhah's handwriting became quick and graceful and small—so small that if Leah held it close enough to her eyes to read it, she cast a shadow on the stone and then could not read anything at all. "Don't worry, Leah," Bilhah said. "You'll be able to read the holy books. The stones are grey, but papyrus is white."

"You could also write larger," said Leah pointedly.

"But this is the size that Jacob told me I had to be able to read and write. If you write too large, you can use up whole scrolls on just a tiny portion of a book. So the writing is small, to fit whole books on as few scrolls as possible."

"I was there," said Leah testily. "I heard."

"But your eyes were closed," said Bilhah. "You were resting. You didn't see the size of the writing he showed me."

Leah sighed. She didn't understand why Bilhah always had to taunt her with her blindness. What Bilhah could do easily, and for hours at a time, Leah could do only for a little while, and it remained a struggle. Yet Bilhah could not resist using her superior vision to clinch a point in an argument. I've seen, you haven't.

Well, with my ears I "see" more than most people do with their eyes. I hear in your voice how you brighten whenever Jacob is near, how your voice sings with a music that is never there for Reuel, or for me. That's my sister's husband you're falling in love with, foolish girl. You may be free, but you're not free to do *that*.

At last came the day when Jacob and Reuel both agreed that Leah and Bilhah were as ready as they were going to be. It was time to bring out the holy books, or at least one of them, and begin to hear the words of God.

They would need bright sunlight to read by—or at least Leah would—so Jacob had several men help him stretch a fence of cloth to make a dooryard around the entrance to his tent. This would keep the eyes of curiosity away from the scrolls.

Leah and Bilhah sat on rugs facing the tent flap. Jacob emerged with a low table, which he laid where it would be close to both girls and to him, once he sat down. Then he returned to the tent and came back a few moments later with a cloth-wrapped bundle. This he set on the table, and when he had sat behind it, he unwrapped a scroll which was tied with a thong of soft leather. He untied it, and pried up the leading edge of the papyrus, and at last the words of God unrolled on the table before them.

Jacob turned the scroll so the writing faced the girls.

The trouble was, Leah could see nothing on the scrolls at all.

"Lean down close to it," said Bilhah softly. "The writing is there."

But even though she put her face so close her nose brushed against the papyrus, the writing was never more than a set of grey smudges to her. She could tell that in the midst of the vertical bands of grey there were letters, but when she put her face close enough to read, her head cast a shadow on the papyrus.

She felt tears coming to her eyes and sat up quickly, to keep them from falling on the book and smearing the ink. "I can't read it," she said.

"We always knew that was possible," said Jacob. "That's why we made sure Bilhah learned beside you."

"But I hoped," said Leah.

"We all hoped."

"I prayed," she murmured.

"God's answer seems to be that you can hear his word, but in the voice of Bilhah."

"Then I'm glad I have this friend to help me," said Leah.

"Thank you for letting me be that friend," said Bilhah.

Jacob slid the papyrus slightly on the table, so now it faced Bilhah completely.

"I don't know this word," said Bilhah.

"It's a name," said Jacob. "Enoch."

"I don't know who that is," said Bilhah.

"He was the grandfather of Noah," said Leah. "He was taken up by God, he and the whole city of Zion, because they were so holy." She turned to Jacob. "Is this where that story is written?"

"One of the places. But not till the very end. This is the book of the revelations of Enoch. An account of his warnings to the wicked, and then of his promises to the righteous, and then his great hymn of praise to God, who walked among the people of Zion like any man, and they gathered at his feet to be taught wisdom."

The way we gather at *your* feet, thought Leah.

"Go ahead," said Jacob. "Read it! But don't expect it to be easy. It uses many strange words that my father had to teach me. I'll teach them to you, as well. Except that there are a few whose meaning is entirely lost. It's as if God has chosen to make us forget some of his secrets, that once our holy ancestor Enoch knew."

"If Enoch could know it, why can't we?" said Leah.

"These things are controlled by God, not men, and so the reasons can only be discovered by asking him, not me."

Leah smiled. "So to have the holy books does not necessarily mean you understand them."

"If I understood them perfectly," said Jacob, "I wouldn't need holy books, I'd be a holy *man*."

"I thought you *were* a holy man," said Bilhah.

Leah silently sighed at the worship in the girl's voice.

"I'm a man who loves holiness and strives for it," said Jacob. "But that doesn't make me holy. Not like Enoch. God spoke to him face to face. Like a man to his brother. Enoch walked with God, the way Adam and Eve did in the garden."

A question occurred to Leah and she blurted it out. "Did his wife, too?"

"Did whose wife do what?"

"If Enoch walked with God, did God also walk with Enoch's wife? Or did she have to stay away, like when men are eating? Was she unworthy?"

Jacob spun the scroll around to face himself and began reading quickly, moving his lips a little in a sort of whispered commentary but saying no clear words out loud. "I don't know," he finally said. "But it never says that when Zion was taken up to heaven, Enoch's wife was unworthy and got left behind. So I imagine she must have walked with God, too."

"So she was holy?" said Leah.

"She might have been," said Jacob. "She must have been. All the people of Zion were."

"So a woman can be holy," Leah insisted.

"Righteous women are taken into heaven," said Jacob, "to dwell with the Lord, as are righteous men. So of course a woman can be holy."

"And the Lord can speak to her, and she can write down his words, the way Enoch did, and her book will be preserved as part of the birthright?"

Jacob looked nonplussed. "I've read the scrolls, and there aren't any written by a woman."

At this, Bilhah chimed in. "So if I copy over this book onto a new scroll, I'll be the first woman to write a holy book?"

Why couldn't Bilhah stay out of conversations she clearly didn't understand?

But Jacob answered her patiently. "You might be the first to copy it, though I don't know that for certain. Copying a book isn't the same as writing one."

"But can I try?" asked Bilhah. "If I learn to write neatly enough?"

"Perhaps you'd best *read* the words of this book, before you begin to write a copy of your own."

Leah's patience with Bilhah's digression ran out. "This isn't for you to become a scribe or a holy woman. It's so I can learn the words of God."

"Learning the words of God," said Jacob, "is the beginning of holiness, and the desire to hear his words shows that there's already a love of holiness in your heart." He turned the scroll back around. "Read to us, Bilhah."

She began to read. If she was slower at reading than Jacob, Leah couldn't tell. She tried not to be irritated at how easily and well Bilhah could read, when just making out the letters was still so hard for Leah.

But this was the word of God. This was what Leah had worked so hard to be able to hear. What was the Lord going to say to her? It might be Bilhah's voice, and Bilhah's skill, but what she read was God's word to Leah.

It was the story of how Enoch was taking a journey, and Wisdom came suddenly upon him, and he heard a voice from heaven, calling him by name, saying, "My son," and commanding him to prophesy to the people and call them to repentance, "For my fierce anger is kindled against them."

Leah knew at once that this was why her life was so hard: The fierce anger of the Lord was kindled against her. She couldn't keep a tear from spilling from one eye.

"Leah," said Jacob. "Why are you crying?"

She knew he would insist that this was not what the scripture was saying—that it wasn't talking to her specifically. She didn't want to waste time listening to him reassure her. "My eye hurts."

"You're not a good liar," said Jacob, "so you shouldn't try."

"I'm crying because I realize the Lord's anger is kindled against me."

"It was the people of Enoch's day who were wicked, not you."

"But this is what the voice of God says," said Leah.

"Not to *you*," said Jacob. "The Lord was talking to Enoch."

"He was talking about the people who needed to repent. That includes me."

Jacob hesitated.

Bilhah began her chirpy answer. "It's about what God said to the prophets, and then what they did—"

But Leah wasn't going to get her instruction in the word of God from a girl who was only hearing the words herself for the first time today. "Bilhah," she said, "when you write your own book, you can explain it to people. I'm saying that when I heard those words, I knew that this was what God wanted me to hear."

"I can't argue with that," said Jacob. "Though I don't know just what sin might be so terrible as to kindle God's anger against you. *These* people were so wicked that in the time of Enoch's great-grandson, Noah, the Lord drowned most of them in a great flood."

"I'm not that wicked," said Leah. "So all the Lord has done to me, in his anger, was make me blind."

"You're not blind," said Jacob. "You're tender-eyed. And you were born that way. Exactly what sin do you think you committed in the womb?"

"The Lord knew what a wicked, selfish girl I would be."

"So you think all the blind and crippled and deaf people are sinful and God is angry at them, and all the people with perfectly good arms and legs and eyes and ears are righteous? Let me tell you a secret, Leah. Most of the strong and healthy people in the world are sinners, too, and some of them are far greater sinners than you."

Again tears slipped out of Leah's eyes despite her keeping them tightly shut. "How do you know that?" she whispered. "How do you know my sins aren't as great as anyone's?"

"Well, for one thing, you haven't killed anybody," said Jacob. "That's the worst sin there is, to murder somebody, and you've never done that, and a lot of the people who have are completely sound of body."

"Maybe the only reason I haven't killed anybody is because I can't see well enough to do it," said Leah. "Maybe the Lord made me this way to keep me from sinning."

Jacob shook his head. "Then if he were merciful he'd make us all blind, to keep us from sin."

Did he have to have an answer for everything? It made her so angry that she couldn't just say something and not have it contradicted so quickly and easily.

And then she realized that her anger was unfair. And that was precisely the sin that her blindness caused her to commit.

"No, you're right," said Leah. "I've sinned against God many times. I'm selfish and resentful and angry all the time, even against people who haven't done me any harm. And when I'm irritated, I snap at people and make them feel bad when they don't deserve it. I know that all the women in camp think I'm awful and they have as little to do with me as they can. That's why Bilhah got stuck with me—she was the new girl, and didn't know how awful it is to be with me."

"It's not awful," said Bilhah.

"Oh, you ran away that time because you loved me so much."

"I didn't run away," said Bilhah. "I'm not a slave. I'm a free girl, and I decided to go home."

"You know," said Jacob, "We've only just begun to read together. At this rate you'll never even hear the end of Enoch's book, let alone read any of the others."

"See?" said Leah. "I'm so selfish I'd rather talk about my

selfishness than to hear the word of God. I might as well give up right now."

"But let's not give up," said Jacob.

"You still haven't answered Leah's question," said Bilhah. "About why she's tender-eyed, if it's not because God is angry with her. And then what *you* said, about all the people who commit terrible sins and God doesn't punish them at all. You'd think he'd make them all lepers, at least."

This time Bilhah's question was one Leah wanted to hear the answer to.

"We don't see the Lord punish people, most of the time," said Jacob.

"Well, what kind of parent is he, then?" said Leah. "How do children learn, if they aren't punished when they do wrong?"

"They *are* punished," said Jacob. "Just not always in obvious ways. When you're wicked, then Wisdom departs from you. You become more and more like an animal—like the baboons of the wilderness, or like a jackal. But when you're righteous, Wisdom dwells with you like a dear friend, and whispers always in your ear."

"Is that how it is with you?" asked Leah.

"I sometimes hear the voice of Wisdom," said Jacob. "Like right now, with your questions, and Bilhah's. I didn't know the answer when you asked. But because you needed to know the answer, I think the words I said were given to me by the Wisdom of the Lord. Because even though I never thought of them before, when I said them aloud to you I knew that they were true, and I knew that *you* knew they were true."

"But I don't really understand them."

"But you know they came from God."

"I don't even know that," said Leah. "How would I know? But if you say they did, then I'll trust your word."

Bilhah spoke up again. "So what about the bad things that happen to people? If they aren't the punishment of God, what are they?"

"They're just . . . life. Things happen in life. A child is born with tender eyes. A man is crushed to death against a wall. While another man has to flee from his home because he's been given the birthright blessing that his older brother expected to receive, and he doesn't want to fight with his brother. Are these things all the plan of God? Maybe. But they don't happen because God is angry with us. They happen because God wants us to find out what kind of people we are. When everything is going well, then it's easy to be nice to people and obey the commandments of God. When things are hard to bear, that's when we're tested."

"So people who are leading happy lives, God doesn't love them enough to test them?" Leah couldn't keep the skepticism out of her voice.

"For some people, a happy life *is* the test. They think they're powerful and important and they begin to mistreat their servants and force other people to do what they want. Maybe no matter *what* kind of life you have, you still have plenty of chances to show how righteous or unrighteous you are."

"Are these words the Wisdom of the Lord again?" asked Leah.

"No, they're just the foolishness of Jacob, telling you what I've figured out on my own as best I can."

"Good," said Leah, "because I think that would make life meaningless. Sometimes the only thing that makes me feel like it's worth going on with my life is the thought that God is master of everything. If he just lets things happen willy nilly, and none of it means anything, then why should I care anymore what I do?"

"But it means *everything*," said Jacob. "He cares what *we* do, even if he doesn't decide what things happen to us from day to day."

"Maybe Bilhah had better read some more," said Leah.

Jacob waited a moment before answering, and with Leah's ability to notice tiny details of breathing and posture and intonation, she knew that he was frustrated with her; his exasperation was obvious to her in his voice, as he asked Bilhah to read again.

The words she read told how Enoch at first tried to get out of crying repentance to the people, because he was young and stammered when he talked. "Nobody has the patience to hear me say anything," Enoch said.

But the Lord knew his real fear—that he'd be killed for offending the rich and powerful sinners of the world. They already killed people all the time—what would stop them from killing him, especially when his words would be so offensive to them?

So the Lord assured him that they wouldn't have the power to kill him, *and* God would give him the words to say. "Open your mouth, and it will be filled," the Lord told him. "For all flesh is in my hands and I will do whatever I see is good."

"There," said Leah. "All flesh is in my hands. You were wrong."

Bilhah stopped reading.

Jacob's exasperation was obvious. "I never said we weren't all in God's hands."

"You said that he didn't decide what was going to happen to us from day to day, but *he* says we're in his hands."

"You take that to mean one thing, and I take it to mean another."

"But what it says is perfectly plain," said Leah.

"That's what I think, too," said Jacob. "And yet for all its plainness, we disagree completely about what he means when he says we're in his hands."

"Jacob's a holy man," Bilhah whispered. "God gave him the books."

"I'm listening to the words of God," said Leah. "God is holier than any man."

Jacob laughed. "Well, this is good. I think I'm right, and you think you're right, but the main thing is, we both trust that the *Lord* is right."

Leah thought that it mattered a great deal which of them was right, but she held her tongue.

Jacob nodded to Bilhah. She read aloud the great promise the Lord made to Enoch: "My Wisdom is upon you, and so I will make all your words come true. The mountains will flee before you, the rivers will turn from their course. You will dwell in me, and I in you. So walk with me."

As she listened, the promises at first sounded very remote to Leah. What *good* would it actually do to go around moving mountains and shifting rivers? And what about the sheep grazing on the mountain? Or the fish in the river? Would they get moved, too?

But those last four words—"So walk with me"—rang in her heart as if Bilhah had shouted them.

She realized that *this* must be what it felt like to have Wisdom tell her that certain words in the scripture were meant for her.

Walk with me. But God wasn't here. She couldn't walk with him anywhere. She had to walk with Bilhah or some other person leading her. What did God mean by making these words stand out to her? How could she obey him, if he was commanding her to do something impossible?

She realized that Bilhah had stopped reading. "Go on," she said.

Bilhah glanced at Jacob.

"I asked her to stop," said Jacob. "When you suddenly knelt upright and held your breath for a moment. I thought you meant to speak."

"No, no," said Leah. "I just . . . for a moment I had to think." She didn't know why she was so reluctant to tell him what had just happened.

"Should we go on now?" asked Jacob.

"Please."

"Read again, fair Bilhah," said Jacob.

Bilhah read the next thing that the Lord said to Enoch. "Smear your eyes with clay, and wash them, and you will see."

Leah almost gasped at the shock of these words. You will see! Smear clay on your eyes, and wash them, and you'll be able to see!

"Wait," said Jacob. "Leah, the Lord doesn't mean . . . Enoch could *already* see as men see. He was commanded to anoint his eyes in preparation for seeing visions of all the creations that God had made."

"But it's what I was looking for!" cried Leah.

"I thought you wanted to hear the words of the Lord," said Jacob. "Not a magical cure for your eyes."

"Why shouldn't the Lord's words *be* a cure for me?"

"The Lord's word is meant to cure us all—but cure our souls, not our bodies."

"Are you saying you don't think God can heal me?" said Leah.

"I don't want you to be disappointed if it doesn't work."

"Why are the holy books entrusted to a man who doesn't even believe in them?"

Bilhah was shocked. "Leah!"

Jacob was very solemn as he began rolling up the book. "I think we're done for today."

"So because I don't accept your interpretation of everything, you won't let me hear any more of the book?" said Leah.

"I think that your anger and pride make it impossible for us to read any more today," said Jacob. "When you're ready to accept that not every word of scripture applies to you in exactly the way you desire it to, we'll open up the books again."

"In other words, when I agree to pretend to think you're the only one wise enough to understand."

"I don't know what I've done or said that makes you think I deserve to have you speak to me so arrogantly," said Jacob. "I've never spoken to you as proudly as you've just spoken to me. I ask only that you show me as much respect as I show you."

"I haven't shown you disrespect," said Leah. "You've shown *me* disrespect!"

Jacob had an answer ready to his lips, but he stopped

himself from speaking for a long moment. Then he put the scroll back into its bag. "Please forgive me for my disrespect. It was unintentional."

He got up and went back inside his tent.

Leah could not believe that he had walked away from her like that. "I didn't want him to leave," she said softly.

Bilhah said nothing.

Leah turned to her. "I should warn Rachel about the unreasonable husband she's going to get."

Bilhah looked at her steadily, and said nothing.

"Oh, I see, you think *I* was in the wrong, because women aren't supposed to have opinions of their own and I should have given in immediately when he so *rudely* told me I couldn't understand the scriptures even when the spirit of Wisdom told me that these words were meant for my ears!"

Bilhah smiled slightly.

"So you don't believe me," said Leah. "You think I'm lying, that God didn't really speak to me in my heart."

"I don't think you're lying," said Bilhah.

"Then why didn't you speak in my defense!"

Bilhah did not answer.

"Why don't you answer me?"

"Because you'll be angry."

"I'm angry when you don't answer me."

"But at least then you have no words to hurl back at me."

"Hurl back at you! You make me sound like a screaming nag!"

"You just hurled back at me the words 'hurl back at me,'" Bilhah pointed out.

"And now you mock me."

"No, I just answered your question."

"What question?"

"Why I didn't speak in your defense."

"Because you're disloyal and disrespectful!"

"Because when you're angry no one can say even the mildest thing to you without your flying into a rage, like this one, for no reason that anyone else can figure out."

"You call this no reason!"

"Hurling back the words 'no reason.'"

Leah roared with rage and might have gotten up and stalked away, but at that moment Jacob came back out of the tent.

He paid no attention to them at all, though Leah had *not* been quiet. Instead he began gathering up the cloth that marked the dooryard, signifying to the rest of the camp that privacy was no longer desired here. Leah watched him, growing angrier and more hurt by the moment that he could treat her so despitefully.

"Am I nothing to you?" she said.

He ignored her.

"You disdain me as if I didn't exist."

Jacob chuckled. "God be with you, daughter of my brother Laban," he said.

"Now you laugh at me."

"May the Lord fill your heart with peace."

"Don't ignore me like this!"

Bilhah extended a hand, but did not quite touch Leah. "He's not ignoring you, he's praying for you."

Jacob finished folding up the lightweight cloth. "May the spirit of Wisdom help you hear what has been spoken to your heart."

Then he went off, no doubt to return the cloth to wherever

it was kept, as if Leah didn't exist, as if he hadn't lashed out at her and wounded her to the heart by his contempt for her.

"Rejoice, Leah," said Bilhah. "The spirit of Wisdom spoke to you today. Let the words rest gently in your heart, and think no more about the injuries done to you."

"And now you mock me too, by talking to me like a baby," said Leah. "I have no one in this camp who thinks of me as having any worth at all."

Bilhah got up.

"I haven't dismissed you," said Leah.

"I'm a free girl," said Bilhah. "You can ask your father to drive me away from his camp, and see if he does. But I don't come and go at your command."

"I thought you were my friend."

"Do you *have* any friends who aren't hired or enslaved?" asked Bilhah.

"My sister Rachel!"

"Then go and tell her what happened here today, and see what she thinks."

That was the vilest mockery of all, because, first of all, Rachel wasn't *in* camp by this time of day, so there was no way that Leah could go to her without help, and second, because Bilhah knew perfectly well that Rachel was the person in camp who treated Leah the very worst. It made Leah ashamed that she had ever thought of Bilhah as her friend. They were all against her, every one. They had no compassion. They all thought that because she couldn't see with her eyes, she didn't understand anything, she was stupid, her ideas counted for nothing. But she was clever, she knew she was. She had not misunderstood the holy words of God. She knew what she was meant to do.

If they loved her, if they even had as much compassion for her as they would certainly have had to a lost lamb, then the moment she told them that the spirit of Wisdom had whispered that these words were for *her,* they would have smeared clay on her eyes and brought her water to wash them with, so she could see like Enoch saw.

And if Jacob was right and the "seeing" Enoch was supposed to do was the vision of a seer rather than mere eyesight, would that be so awful, to let Leah receive a gift like that from God?

Now here she was in the dooryard, displayed to everyone's eyes. They could see her, but she couldn't see them. They could all be watching her and she'd never even know it. The only time she knew she was alone was in the dark, because then nobody could see. And in the dark, she could hear things they didn't hear, she could tell where smells were coming from, she could know things just by the feel of them. In the dark, she would have the advantage over any of them.

But it wasn't dark, it was broad day, and she had been shamed.

CHAPTER 12

L eah rose to her feet and, remembering where her own tent was relative to Jacob's, she began making her slow progress through the camp.

As she walked, she remembered the words that had stood out as if they had been written in the air in shining gold, or burned with fire into her heart: "So walk with me." She had been invited by God to walk with him, as Enoch had done, as Enoch's *wife* had done. And yet in the camp of Padan-aram, her father's own household, she had to walk alone.

Walk with me, the Lord had said. But even God's words were a mockery. How could she walk with him? Where was his arm, so she could lean on him and he could guide her through the blur? Even *God's* promises were not kept.

She wept bitterly.

"Mistress," murmured a voice from not far off. Leah

ignored it. "Mistress," said the voice again. "May I walk with you to your tent?"

She knew the voice now—there was no one in the camp whose voice she did not know, if they spoke enough words. It was Zilpah, the one who had such an awful reputation.

Ordinarily, Leah would have thanked her and refused. But then she thought: Wisdom told me that God was saying "walk with me" to *me*, and then I wept because he wasn't walking with me. Well, maybe this is how his word will be fulfilled. Maybe he has sent someone to walk with her in his place.

So she reached out her hand, and Zilpah tucked it under her arm and walked so close to her their thighs, not just their dresses, brushed together at every step. "Are you sad?"

"What does it look like?" said Leah. "I thought *I* was the one with tender eyes."

"You could be crying for joy. Or the tears could mean your eyes hurt."

"Crying for joy," said Leah scornfully. "What do I have to be joyful about?"

"I'm always happy," said Zilpah.

"That's ridiculous," said Leah. "Nobody's always happy."

"I am."

"You have nothing to be happy about," said Leah. The girl was fatherless! She had no hope of a decent marriage.

"True," said Zilpah, "but I have dreams that make me happy. And besides, I don't have to have a reason. Being sad or angry won't make my situation any better, so I might as well be happy."

"You can't just decide to be happy."

"Why not? You decide to be angry whenever you want."

"I don't *decide*," said Leah, letting go of her arm.

Zilpah laughed.

"And now you laugh at me, you nasty little . . ."

"Go ahead and say it," said Zilpah, chuckling. "I know the word. I've heard it before."

"I don't know what word you mean," said Leah.

Zilpah laughed even louder.

"I don't need your scorn," said Leah, walking away.

But the servant girl stayed with her. "When I said that you decide to be angry whenever you want, this is what I meant. You *could* have laughed at me and said, 'Be careful or I might decide to get angry at *you*.'"

"I could have but I didn't."

"No, because you decided to get angry. But if you had decided to enjoy the silly thing I said, then you would have been deciding to be *happy*."

"But I wasn't happy."

"And that was your decision." Zilpah laughed again. "You must enjoy being miserable, since you choose it all the time."

And with that, Zilpah was gone, dancing away, her feet scuffing lightly on the dirt of the path.

Leah should have been furious with her for such an outrageous—and uninvited—judgment of her.

But she remembered that when she had thought of God's words—so walk with me—that was the moment Zilpah appeared. Did that mean that whatever Zilpah said to her came from God? But that was ludicrous. God couldn't speak to her from the mouth of a . . .

God *couldn't*? What was she thinking? There was nothing God couldn't do. He could use a fatherless bondservant as his messenger, if it pleased him to do so.

Was it possible that she *chose* to be angry?

No, that was stupid. The anger just *came*. Unbidden. Unwanted. Why would she choose such a terrible feeling?

Zilpah's coming had nothing to do with the words of God. The Lord's message to her had been in the book, not in a servant's mouth.

But Zilpah still had to be near. So Leah called to her. "Zilpah! Zilpah, I need you!"

"Zilpah's not here anymore," said Bilhah.

"Go away," said Leah.

"I'm sorry I spoke so disrespectfully to you," said Bilhah. "I was angry."

"You had no right to be angry."

"I see that now," said Bilhah. "You needed something—you called to Zilpah. Please let me do whatever it is you wanted her to do."

Leah's first thought was to say, No, you hate me and I don't have to associate with people who hate me.

Then she thought, I don't have to be angry.

And in just the moment it took her to think of it, the first hot spark of anger faded.

"I'm not angry now," Leah said, a little surprised.

"Thank you," said Bilhah. "Let me serve you."

"I need a basin of water," said Leah. "I'm going to wash my eyes."

"I'll bring it to you. In your tent?"

"Outside. Where there's clay."

"Won't any dirt do to make a kind of mud?"

"Clay, the Lord said."

"Let me bring that to you, then, from the potmaking shed."

Leah almost snapped at her, can't you just do what I

asked? But she realized that it would be much faster if Bilhah fetched both the water *and* the clay. "Yes, please," said Leah.

Was this what Zilpah meant? To choose not to be angry?

It was certainly true that by not *acting* angry, Leah was going to get both water and clay much faster. But that was different from not *being* angry.

I'm *not* angry, though. I acted as if I weren't angry, and now I'm not angry.

But that's just being a hypocrite.

Or maybe that's what it means to be kind—to treat someone well even when they make you angry.

Am I unkind?

The thought was an uncomfortable one. She wouldn't think it any more.

Having decided that, it was inevitable that she kept remembering recent moments when she had been angry, and had said things that were definitely unkind. To people who probably didn't deserve it.

Like Jacob. Maybe he really was just trying to tell what he thought, and not telling her that she didn't have any right to understand the scriptures her own way. Maybe she had just made herself look like a fool in front of him.

Bilhah returned with a basin and a small basket of clay.

"I'll bet they told you to make sure I didn't try to make any pots," said Leah.

"No, they didn't," said Bilhah.

"I know they did," said Leah, anger once again bubbling to the surface. "They think I'm ridiculous down at the pot-making shed. The women there thought it was so funny the time I tried to make a pot."

"There wasn't anyone there," said Bilhah. "I just took the clay, so nobody said anything because nobody even knew."

Leah found herself growing even angrier because Bilhah had made her look ridiculous for having been so sure the women talked hatefully about her. But she stopped herself long enough to realize that there was no reason to be angry. Leah was getting angry because Bilhah had said that no one ridiculed her at the potmaking shed, yet they couldn't have mocked her because they weren't even there. So instead of getting angrier, Leah should have gotten *less* angry.

And now I *am* less angry, just by thinking that I should be.

"I'm sorry," said Leah.

"For what?"

"I really do get angry over nothing, don't I," said Leah.

"Never over *nothing*," said Bilhah.

"But small things."

"Don't we all, sometimes?"

"I do it all the time," said Leah, with awe.

Bilhah said nothing.

"And you're silent now because you're afraid that anything you say will set me off."

Still she said nothing.

"Give me the clay," Leah said. "Let me dilute it in water and smear it on my eyes."

"I can do that for you."

"The Lord told Enoch to do it himself," said Leah. "So I'll do it, too."

She dribbled water onto the clay and kneaded the dampest part of it, then dribbled on a little more water until here fingers were covered with a thick, gloppy mixture.

Then she closed her eyes and smeared the wet clay so it

completely covered her closed eyelids, right up to the eyebrows and down onto the cheeks.

"Have I covered everything?" asked Leah. "Is there any skin showing?"

"Left eye," said Bilhah. "Upper eyelid, near the outside corner."

Leah daubed again.

"That's it."

Leah sat there for a moment. "I wonder how long before I should wash it off."

"The book of Enoch didn't say."

"The Lord just said, smear clay on your eyes and wash them, and you'll be able to see."

"That doesn't sound like there's any waiting time at all."

"Do you think I already waited too long?"

"If it mattered, the Lord would have said," Bilhah reassured her. "I don't think the Lord plays tricks on people."

Leah almost answered, You think not? Well, just look at my life!

But this wouldn't be a good time to say bitter things about the way the Lord had treated her. What if even *thinking* such a negative thought drove away the Lord's promise to her? No, no, as Bilhah said, he wouldn't have given her this promise just to punish her.

She washed it off, and again asked Bilhah to check that it was done completely.

Then Leah opened up her eyes.

Nothing was changed. Bilhah was still nothing but a nearby blur. Faroff things were completely invisible.

"I shouldn't have waited before I washed," said Leah.

"We can try it again."

"Maybe I only get one try," said Leah. And now tears began to flow. "Maybe I already proved that I'm not worthy."

"Try again," said Bilhah. "It can't hurt."

Leah tried again, and this time washed immediately. But to no avail.

She cried in earnest now. "I'm a wicked girl," she said, "and God is showing me just what I deserve."

"I think you're *not* wicked," said Bilhah. "I think the Lord loves you as much as he loves anybody."

"As much as he loves the girl whose father was crushed against a wall in Byblos?" said Leah.

"At least that much," said Bilhah.

"As much as a fatherless girl who has nothing to offer a husband except her own body?" asked Leah.

"Maybe a little more than that one," said Bilhah.

"As much as a beautiful shepherd girl that dreams of a prince coming to her and kissing her at the well, and the dream comes true, and now he has made himself a bondservant in order to earn the right to marry her? Does God love me as much as that?"

Bilhah had no answer.

"I want to be alone now," said Leah. "I'm not angry. I'm just very sad."

"Please let me stay with you," said Bilhah. "Please let me be your friend."

"You are my friend," said Leah. "You keep coming back to me after I drive you away. You keep forgiving me after I'm wicked." And then, because she couldn't help but say what was in her heart, she added, "You must love me more than God does."

"Nobody loves you more than God," said Bilhah, her voice sounding just a little shocked.

"That's what I was afraid of," said Leah. "Please. Go."

"Don't sit outside here, Leah. Let me help you back inside your tent."

"Just take away the basin and the clay," said Leah. "I can find my way inside from here. I'm not helpless at everything."

Leah got up as Bilhah gathered up the basin and the basket and started off toward the potmaking shed. But as Leah made her way around to the door of the tent, she heard Bilhah stop and then return.

"What is it?" Leah asked.

"I just thought," said Bilhah. "The thought just came into my mind, and it was so clear I just had to, I just had to come and say it."

"Say it then," said Leah. "I won't be angry."

"Are you sure that the thing about Enoch smearing clay on his eyes was the part that Wisdom told you was meant for you? That's all. I just wondered."

Leah felt her temper flare up. And she was so sad, she wanted to lash out, to scream her disappointment and grief. But she had given Bilhah permission to say it. And the moment's pause in which she thought of that was enough to remove the desire from her heart.

"I don't remember," said Leah honestly. "Maybe all that the Lord ever meant me to hear as his message to me was . . . Walk with me."

"But I say that to you every day," said Bilhah. "Walk with me."

"And I say the same to you," said Leah. "It isn't much of

a message from God, is it? Just something ordinary that we do every day."

"I guess what matters is that it's God saying it," said Bilhah.

"Maybe so," said Leah. Then she went inside the tent and Bilhah did not follow.

Maybe so, she murmured to herself again, but she did not believe it. She did not believe that Wisdom had whispered anything at all. What she heard was her own intense desire to know that God noticed her. But God did not notice her. She was as overlooked by God as she had been ignored by Father and Jacob when she and Rachel were presented. God, like Jacob, sees only Rachel, and loves only Rachel, and why not? I'm an angry, selfish, wicked blind girl. Which part of that would make me a woman to desire, or a child that God could love?

PART VII

BROTHERS

CHAPTER 13

The last assignment Zilpah wanted was to tend babies. They were filthy and demanding and when you were done, the best you could say was that you hadn't actually killed it, and no one thanked you for it.

Why *should* she be given such work, when there were plenty of old women in the camp who weren't good for anything else? It's not as if she could wetnurse a baby, and why else would a *young* woman be wasted on such work?

Yet that's what Reuel told her that morning. "You, Zilpah. You'll be needed in Asta's tent, to take care of the baby."

Zilpah wasn't one of those whiners who always wasted Reuel's time with all their reasons why they should get a different assignment. Sometimes it worked—but the cost was that Reuel thought of them with scorn and kept using them for the most distasteful work. Which provoked more whining, so he simply assigned someone else to tell them their work, thus moving them even lower down the social scale of the camp.

Zilpah was perfectly happy to have Reuel telling her personally what work he had for her to do. And if on a particular day, it was a nasty job like tending to Terah's and Asta's nasty puking crying little girl, she would take the assignment with a smile. For all Zilpah knew, this might mean she was now a particularly trusted woman. Or it might mean Reuel was trying to humble her, in which case she would bear it cheerfully—he was going to rule over her for a long, long time. Unless she could make something happen. And it was a sure thing she would *never* improve her lot if people in camp looked on her as a complainer or, worse yet, a rebellious servant.

So at the time of day when she would ordinarily be laundering or carding or spinning or hauling water or hauling slops, she found herself inside Asta's tent, trying to keep a smile on her face.

It began so well, with Asta glaring at her when she came through the tent door and saying, "What are *you* doing here?"

"Reuel sent me. To tend the baby today."

"You! To tend my baby!"

"I only do what I'm told, Mistress."

"You can tell him that . . ." But apparently Asta thought better of it and hissed out a long sigh. "Just because my husband is a younger son, Reuel goes out of his way to treat us with contempt."

Zilpah knew she was being insulted—because to Asta, merely sending someone as lowborn as Zilpah to tend to the baby between visits from the wet nurse was regarded as "contempt." But she was used to being treated that way, especially by Nahor's and Terah's wives. Nahor's wife Deloch was even worse than Asta—at least Asta spoke directly to Zilpah, however rudely, instead of acting as if she thought Zilpah had been spawned by a troop of baboons and spoke an unlearnable animal tongue.

"I will do my best, Mistress," said Zilpah.

"I'm *sure* you will," said Asta dryly. "Because if I hear you neglected my little Lisset, just because she's not a *son*, then you'll wish Reuel had never sent you to this tent!"

I already wish it, thought Zilpah, but of course what she said was, "I will be with her every moment."

"Don't just set her down and walk away because she crawls fast as a roach."

"Where is she?" asked Zilpah.

"In the inner room somewhere," said Asta, clearly wishing not to be bothered. Zilpah went there immediately, expecting to find the baby being cared for by one of the old women or perhaps the wet nurse. But no, little Lisset was crawling over a low pile of rugs. Just as Zilpah entered, the baby slid off the pile and rolled onto her back, whereupon she burst into tears, loudly.

Asta charged into the room at once. "What did you do to her!" demanded Asta.

"In the dark I couldn't even see her at first," said Zilpah.

"So you stepped on her? What an oaf!"

"I never came near her. I saw her just as she slipped off the pile of rugs she was crawling on."

And perhaps because Zilpah was still in the doorway and the room was dark and the baby was already calming down again, Asta apparently decided to stop being angry. "You just have to watch them *every* second," said Asta.

Zilpah refrained from pointing out that Asta herself wasn't very reliable at baby-tending.

Annoying as the baby was bound to be, it was nothing compared to having to keep smiling for Asta, so it was a relief when she finally was satisfied that Zilpah wasn't going to let the baby smother or choke and left the inner room. Moments later, Asta was out of the tent entirely, and Zilpah could settle down to her long, tedious day, with only the wet nurse from time to time for company.

"Good morning, baby Lisset," Zilpah said softly, in a voice that imitated the baby-voices she'd heard other women use with their little ones. "You're going to spit on me when you grow up, so you might as well start today."

The baby gazed at her like she was crazy and then started looking around frantically.

"Now you're going to start crying and everybody's going to think I was pinching you," said Zilpah.

Sure enough, Lisset began to squall. And picking her up didn't help. She was crying precisely because her mother wasn't there, so this horrible stranger wasn't likely to be much comfort.

If someone came into the tent to find out who was torturing the baby, Zilpah needed them to find her actively trying to comfort the creature rather than doing what she really wanted to do—curl up under a mound of blankets to block out the sound and sleep through the day.

"There, there, now, little whining lovely brat of a baby," cooed Zilpah to the baby whom she now held at her shoulder. "Please don't get me whipped."

A man's voice came from behind her. "Nobody's going to whip you."

She whirled around to see Terah standing in the doorway separating the inner room from the outer.

And right behind him was Nahor.

It took only a moment to realize that Reuel did not assign her this task because he suddenly thought she was the perfect one to tend a baby. Nahor and Terah must have been watching for Asta to leave, they had come so quickly to the tent where Zilpah was by herself.

"What do you want?" she said.

"Listen to the coldness," said Terah to Nahor, chuckling. "She speaks to us as if she were the lady and *we* were the low-born illegitimate children of some tribe of nomads who had enough coin to pay her mother."

Zilpah had heard worse. She was busy calculating. Was holding the baby a protection for her? Or did she need to set down the baby to try to fight them off? If she screamed, would someone come to help her? Or was everything so perfectly arranged that no one would be in earshot.

"Oh, sit down and relax," said Nahor impatiently. "Nobody's going to lay a hand on you, if that's what you're thinking."

It was precisely what she had been thinking, but telling her to relax only made her all the more tense.

"If we wanted you," said Terah, laughing, "we'd have taken you without any subterfuge. *That* would simply be our right."

As it would be my right to claw out your eyes like any cornered animal, thought Zilpah.

"We want to talk to you," said Nahor. "And we didn't want anyone to know we had talked."

"Except Reuel," said Zilpah.

"Reuel can think what he wants," said Terah. Still that nasty smile didn't leave his face.

So apparently they had implied to Reuel that they had decided to form a little troop to force Zilpah to fulfil all her teasing of the men in camp. And Reuel had gone along. Not that he had a choice. But he could have warned her!

"We're used to women who wash themselves occasionally," said Terah.

And since that category didn't include either of their wives, Zilpah could only conclude that well-washed women was at least one of the pleasures of the city that they couldn't keep away from.

"We want you to tell us," said Nahor, "about Jacob."

"What do you think *I* know?" she asked. "You were there when he dined with your father, just as I was."

"And placed far enough away that we heard almost nothing, whenever they spoke quietly," said Nahor.

"You were right in their laps," said Terah.

"Not to mention washing his feet," said Nahor.

"If it was just his feet you washed," said Terah.

"Reuel was there. Ask him."

"We're asking you," said Nahor. "Not just for what you've already seen, but for what you might see in the future. Reuel is going to assign you to attend to Rachel, so you'll have plenty of opportunity to learn what Jacob is planning."

"He's planning to marry Rachel," said Zilpah. "Surely someone already told you that."

Terah reached out and casually slapped her. Not hard, but it was humiliating, and something that Laban would not have tolerated if he had been there. So this was what camp life would be like when Laban died.

"He's a younger son," said Terah. "And he earned his brother's hatred. Why? Because he stole his birthright. You don't think we've heard stories? They fly like birds across the miles. There's a reason his name is Jacob, 'supplanter.' He steals things that belong to others."

"How can marrying Rachel deprive you of your inheritance? He's entering into service with your father, not getting adopted by him."

"Yes, very humble of him," said Nahor. "But he's full of tricks, this one. We know friends of his brother Esau's. And we want to make sure he doesn't take us by surprise."

"Rachel's so besotted with him," said Terah, "that I think if he wanted her to, she'd poison us."

Which just showed how little they knew their own sister. Rachel liked Jacob, but she wasn't possessed by him. If anything, it was the other way around.

"So you want me to watch them and see if they're plotting something?" asked Zilpah. "What if they're not? Or what if they are, but they never show a sign of it in front of me?"

"You're not the only friend we have," said Nahor.

Good thing, thought Zilpah, because if I were, the total of your friends would be zero.

"Just watch, that's all," said Terah. "And if you get a chance, you might, you know, earn his trust yourself."

"His trust?" she asked.

"His *intimate* trust," Terah explained.

"He doesn't look at me that way."

"Do you think we're stupid?" said Nahor. "Every man looks at you that way. You make it impossible for them to do anything else."

"Then Jacob does the impossible," said Zilpah.

"If the opportunity arises," said Nahor.

"No man can wait seven years without finding *some* woman," said Terah. "Unless there's something wrong with him."

"And when he looks for a woman," said Nahor, "and you're right there, let's not have any foolishness about your virtue being saved for your husband."

"The best you can hope for is to be some man's concubine," said Terah.

"We can promise you decent treatment, if you serve us in this," said Nahor.

And, therefore, the opposite of decent treatment if she refused.

"I am your humble and obedient servant in all things," said Zilpah.

"You *are* still a virgin, aren't you?" said Nahor.

"Don't be ridiculous," said Terah. "Do you expect her to tell you the truth, either way?"

"I am," whispered Zilpah.

"You see?" said Terah.

"All I'm saying is, keep it that way," said Nahor. "A man like this Jacob, who casts his eye on children like Rachel, he may only want virgins."

"Yes," said Zilpah. "I plan to keep it that way." I plan to give my virginity only to the man who takes me away from this camp and out of your power.

"Well, good, then," said Nahor. "That's all we wanted."

"Not quite all," said Terah.

He leaned close to her. She shuddered, thinking he meant to kiss her, with his own baby on her shoulder, drooling on her neck.

"When you want to tell us something, go to Reuel and tell him you miss my baby and want to tend her again. Just try to do it on a day when one of us is in camp. Reuel will get word to us."

"That's just stupid," said Zilpah.

Terah stiffened, and Nahor frowned.

"If *I* ask, then Reuel will know that I'm a spy, not a woman you make use of. Unless you want him to know."

"She's right," said Nahor. "It only makes sense if *we* ask for her to tend the baby—so he'll think we're in the mood to have use of her."

"Can he really think we're so desperate as to want to soil ourselves with this unwashed she-goat?" asked Terah.

"That's what we're counting on," said Nahor. "If anyone in the camp suspects that she's anything more than that to us, that she's actually in our confidence, then he'll make sure she's nowhere near him and Rachel, and we'll have to find someone else."

"All right," said Terah. "Besides, maybe one day she'll get caught in the rain and the dirt will get washed away and who knows? Maybe she'll be worth the trouble of peeling off all those rags."

To have them talk of her like this made her feel unclean in so many ways. She had always disliked them. Now she truly hated them, and feared them, too. This was the kind of men they were, the kind who enlist spies in their father's own camp.

"He's a clever one, this Jacob," Nahor said. "You have to listen carefully because his plans might be well disguised. And men like him are suspicious, expecting other people to have secrets of their own."

She almost laughed. They knew nothing of Jacob, with his almost childlike lack of deceit. They were describing themselves. Not that they were clever. But they thought they were. They suspected Jacob, not because of stories they heard, but because of what they knew they themselves would do.

In fact, it occurred to her for the first time that maybe the much-vaunted closeness between Nahor and his younger brother Terah wasn't really more of the same. Love between brothers as a mask for something darker—Terah plotting that when Laban died, there would be only one son to inherit; and Nahor keeping him close so that he could act first, when the time came. Maybe Choraz had guessed this about his brothers, and that's why he had begged his father to send him into service with a prince who made war instead of only tending sheep. So he'd be far away—or, if he came home, so he'd be trained as a warrior to fight and defend himself.

Once she knew that besides being drunkards and wastrels, they were also sly conspirators, she had to believe them capable of almost anything. The things they suspected Jacob of were a list of the kinds of things they thought of doing themselves.

So when Terah added, "The thing to watch for most is if he seems to be plotting against our father," Zilpah's blood ran cold.

"I'll watch indeed," she thought. I'll watch *you*, and warn your father or Jacob or Rachel or *someone* if I think you're actually readying yourselves to carry out such a plot as these you think Jacob capable of.

At least this one good thing: Neither of them kissed her

before leaving. Nor did they insult her intelligence by trying to pay her in city money. She could never spend it, after all—and if she tried, everyone would wonder how she got it. No, all they could offer her by way of enticement was a promise of good treatment later, and since their idea of good treatment was bound to be different from hers, they were promising her essentially nothing.

This was such a precarious situation—so much could go wrong—that for the first time in years she desperately wanted an ally. A protector. Not since she had first realized that her mother was as powerless as she was had she allowed herself to wish there were somewhere she could run for safety, for comfort, for advice.

Who? Could she tell Laban? If he believed her—and there was small chance of that, her word against his sons, with the two of them united as witnesses against her!—what could he do? What *would* he do even if he could?

Rachel? She was powerless herself, compared to her brothers. Not till Jacob was fully and truly her husband would he be able to act on her behalf.

Jacob himself?

Now, that would be a gamble, wouldn't it? He seemed smart enough, but would he have the cleverness to hear her warning and bide his time, doing nothing that would indicate he had learned of the brothers' plotting from her? She knew enough about the ways of powerful people to know that most such folk wouldn't spare a thought for keeping *her* from harm. If Jacob confronted them with what she had said, it would end her life in this camp—either she would be expelled or so mistreated she'd have to run away.

But Jacob didn't seem to be a confronter. He was a protector.

Hadn't he gone after Bilhah, to protect her, to bring her back? And Bilhah was a nothing, a stranger, not even beautiful.

Did she dare to trust Jacob?

Did she dare *not* to?

CHAPTER 14

Bilhah brought the comb to Leah's inner room, expecting to prepare her hair before they went to study with Jacob this morning. But Leah was still lying in bed. "My eyes hurt from yesterday's reading," she said.

"That's why you should stop trying to read for yourself," said Bilhah. "I was taught to read so you wouldn't have to."

"I like to see the words with my own eyes."

"They're written so small," said Bilhah. "They're not easy even for me."

Leah sighed. "I don't want to go today."

"But Jacob is waiting," said Bilhah.

Leah rolled over, turning her back to Bilhah. "Go and tell him not to wait," said Leah.

Bilhah couldn't understand why Leah was acting this way. "What about the word of God?"

"It will still be there tomorrow, won't it? The books won't

vanish in the night, will they? Can't anybody ever just do what I ask, for *once?*"

For once? People do what you ask all the time. Or rather, they do what you demand—and wish that you would ask, so they could do it freely.

But Bilhah said nothing. It wouldn't do to provoke an argument with Leah. When Leah was in a good mood, she was sweet and they could almost be friends. But when she was feeling sorry for herself, she would say the nastiest things and then, later, not even realize that she had been hurtful. Maybe, thought Bilhah, it was because Leah couldn't see the expressions on people's faces. If they didn't tell her in words what they were feeling, maybe she simply didn't know they were hurt or irritated by the things she said.

"Do you want me to comb your hair anyway?" asked Bilhah.

"I don't know why I should take special pains just to go see my sister's husband anyway," said Leah.

"I didn't think you combed your hair for Jacob," said Bilhah. "I thought you prepared yourself to go before the Lord."

"God sees me all the time anyway," said Leah. "So that's just stupid. He sees me when I'm dirty and sweating and stinking hot. He sees me at my very worst."

Bilhah knew this was a silly argument. But if Leah wanted to pretend she didn't know the difference between ordinary life and going to read the words of God, it wasn't worth arguing with her.

"I'll go tell Jacob you aren't coming," said Bilhah.

"I'm going to sleep again," said Leah. "My eyes are so tired."

Yes, you said that already, and I haven't forgotten, even if I am just the stupid girl who learned to read so that your eyes wouldn't *have* to be tired.

Of course Bilhah knew that this wasn't about tired eyes, or not entirely, anyway. Leah was disappointed in the word of God. She had expected to have the meaning of her whole life spelled out for her, apparently, and was bitterly disappointed that most of the writing was about Enoch and his teachings and experiences. Leah kept trying to turn the meaning of every line of the scripture into some specific reference to her own life, and Jacob kept saying, No, this is the message Enoch gave to the people from God. Now that Leah finally understood that not everything in the books was a private revelation for her, she was apparently getting bored with the whole enterprise.

On her way through camp, Bilhah greeted everyone she passed. When she first arrived, she had thought she could never learn who all these strangers were. Now she knew them all—at least the people who spent their days here in the camp, working. And she even knew some of the shepherds who roamed the hills, because their wives and children were in the camp.

Zilpah detached herself from a group preparing to dye some unusually fine yarn. "Bilhah," she said.

Bilhah had no use for Zilpah, but she was courteous to everyone. "Peace to you, sister," she said.

Zilpah smiled—and, as always, the smile seemed to be a thin mask for malice or contempt. "Nice of you to call me sister," she said.

"I'm on my way to Jacob's tent on Leah's errand," said Bilhah. "So if you have something to say—"

"I do," said Zilpah. "But not to you. To him."

"Who?"

"Jacob."

Bilhah noticed something furtive now in the way Zilpah's eyes avoided looking directly into hers.

"Then talking to me won't do the job, will it?"

"I need to talk to him alone," said Zilpah.

Bilhah didn't like this. "He's promised to Rachel."

Zilpah looked at her like she was stupid. "Don't you know the meaning of the word *talk*?" she asked.

"I just wasn't sure you did."

"Listen, Bilhah, I didn't get to choose being born into bondage, or being fatherless, or even having breasts like these when someone like you barely has anything to rub against her shirt. So whichever of those things you hate me for, remember that I can't help it."

You can help the way you dress, and that smirk you wear, thought Bilhah. "You're the only one who thinks of your bosom all the time," she said.

"Oh, yes, I'm sure I'm the *only* one who even notices," said Zilpah, and this time she gave that nasty little laugh of hers.

"Of course we all notice," said Bilhah. "The way we notice the udders on a nanny goat."

"You're such a lovely girl," said Zilpah. "Everybody's friend."

"I'm on my mistress's errand," said Bilhah.

"I thought you were a free girl."

Bilhah felt her cheeks go red. "I used language I thought *you* would understand."

Zilpah's face flushed in turn. "I don't know why you've

decided to hate me," said Zilpah. "I haven't done anything to you."

"I don't hate you," said Bilhah. "I never think of you." She started to walk again toward Jacob's tent.

"Bilhah," said Zilpah. "Please. Not for my sake, but for Jacob's and Rachel's."

Bilhah waited.

"I need to talk to him. That's all. But at a time when nobody will notice. While you're reading."

"But I won't be reading today. Leah has a headache. Or her eyes hurt. Something like that. There'll be no reading."

"Well . . . can't you stay and read anyway? At least long enough that I can talk to Jacob?"

"What's this about?"

"If I dared tell you I would," said Zilpah. "Please, Bilhah, do you think I like begging for your help? I can only tell you that it's not for myself, or at least not entirely. Be my friend today. Be Jacob's and Rachel's friend."

"I'll tell him you want to see him."

"Tell him I'll be coming into the dooryard while you read."

"Yes, I'll tell him that," said Bilhah. "*If* I read."

"Please," said Zilpah. "Read awhile."

"It's up to him," said Bilhah. "He keeps the books."

Zilpah seemed satisfied with that, and ran back to join the other dyers. Bilhah went on her way, wondering what strange dream Zilpah wanted interpreted. Everybody expected Jacob to be their personal prophet. Bilhah probably would too, if she ever had interesting dreams. But she didn't, and wasn't all that interested in her future. The future had stopped being all that interesting to her when she finally realized that girls without parents or possessions had no future.

At Jacob's tent, the dooryard had already been fenced off. She clapped hands twice to let him know she was there. He came out of the tent and greeted her. "But where's Leah?" he asked.

"Her eyes hurt her today," said Bilhah—not adding "she *says*" because that would be petty and snide.

"I'm sorry to hear that," said Jacob. "I wish she'd simply let you do all the reading. Or me."

"I think she believes that God can only speak to her if she's doing the reading herself."

"God speaks to all of us all the time. Even when he's saying something very specific to somebody long ago, it's important for us to know that he spoke then, even if the words don't apply to us exactly in our day."

Bilhah smiled at that. "Yes, well, you try telling Leah that."

"I have tried."

"I know," said Bilhah. "When she doesn't want to know something, she really, really doesn't know it."

"She carries a heavy burden," said Jacob, "and she doesn't understand why God put it on her shoulders."

His compassionate words made Bilhah feel churlish for having thought so ill of Leah. "I wouldn't trade my place for hers," said Bilhah, "even though she's so pretty and her father is a great man."

Jacob looked at her oddly. "Pretty?"

"She *is*," said Bilhah. "When she smiles. When she isn't squinting."

Jacob chuckled dryly. "Ah. I've never seen that, so I wouldn't know."

"Now who's being mean?" she said.

He shook his head. "She's the sister of my wife-to-be. I try to love her, but she makes it hard. I imagine that you know that. So I'm glad you've found a way to find beauty in her."

"And I was just admiring the way you show her such compassion," said Bilhah.

"She's young," said Jacob. "Young people don't see everything from a perspective of wisdom."

"Neither do old people," said Bilhah contentiously.

"There are different kinds of foolishness reserved for every age," said Jacob. "But part of foolishness is not recognizing your own."

Bilhah remembered what Zilpah had said. And in truth she liked the idea anyway. To read the holy book *without* Leah to slow everything down. It sounded nice. And far better than any of the other labor in the camp.

"May I read today, anyway, sir?" she said. "Even without Leah?"

"It wouldn't do for us to get ahead of her," said Jacob. "I think she might become annoyed with us if we did that."

That was that. Leah could block things without even being here.

"So," said Jacob, "I'll be happy to let you read a different book. In fact, I wonder if you'd like to work on copying one. To let me see how accurate you can be, and whether you can write a good enough hand."

"You would trust me?"

"No, I wouldn't," said Jacob. "That's why I want to *test* you first." He grinned.

She had to smile back. "All right," she said.

It wasn't until he came back out and had spread out a book and a scrap of papyrus on a low table that she remembered to tell him, "Zilpah will be coming to talk to you. She doesn't want anyone to see."

"Which means it's very important that you be right here, watching," said Jacob.

Bilhah looked up at him. He wasn't smiling. It wasn't a joke. So he had no illusions about Zilpah. That was good.

She set to her work, forming letters as carefully as she could. But for all her trying, she could not make them as small as the ones on the scroll.

Jacob was patient with her. "You're working too slowly. You're trying to draw each one like a picture. If you work a little more quickly, the letters become marks, not drawings. Little twists of ink on the papyrus." He sat down beside her and demonstrated.

But she could not understand the difference between what he did and what she did—though the difference in the result was obvious. He might as well have been saying, Don't do it badly, do it well, without conveying the slightest idea about how this was done.

"Don't worry," he said. "As you get more practice, you'll find that it comes naturally to you."

She looked back over what she had already copied and was dismayed to see that the ink had already faded. "It's disappearing!" she cried.

"No, I merely thinned the ink. This is for practice, remember? You'll write over and over again on the same papyrus, so we don't have to waste any more of it than this while you acquire the skill."

She understood and agreed that this was wise, but it was still quite disturbing to work so carefully on these letters, only to have them almost vanish.

Bilhah almost didn't notice when Jacob walked away. She only looked up in time to see Zilpah slipping in between the tent and the dooryard fencecloth. The two of them sat down in the shade of the awning, and for a moment Bilhah was envious—she had to sit out in the bright sun, with only the hood she wore on her head for shade. But that was the price of learning to write small—you had to have excellent light. And instead of straining to overhear their conversation, she redoubled her efforts at copying the text.

And yet she *was* alert to every sound, and did hear a few snatches of conversation, enough to know that it had something to do with Leah's brothers and spying.

And because of her heightened awareness, she also knew when someone's soft footsteps came to a stop at the dooryard fence.

Bilhah looked over her shoulder to see Leah standing there, looking into the dooryard at her, then at Jacob conferring with Zilpah. Bilhah immediately knew from the stricken look on Leah's face how this must appear to her—that Bilhah had taken advantage of Leah's absence to study without her. Or perhaps Leah was hurt because Bilhah was doing something that Leah's eyes would never allow her to do, copy the scriptures.

Either way, Bilhah knew that she had done no wrong; but she also knew that this would not count for much in Leah's feelings. She was bound to feel betrayed and mocked; and yet what else should Bilhah have done? She was a free girl—why should she spend her life bound by the limitations God had placed on Leah, when she had no such physical limitations herself? It would be unjust; God could not expect that of her; but Leah expected it.

Bilhah thought Leah would fly into a rage, but she didn't. She lingered only a little while longer, her eyes full of tears, and then she backed away from the fencecloth. To her surprise, Bilhah heard Leah's footsteps break into a run, and then—as anyone might have expected—she heard her fall and skid on the fine-stoned dirt, uttering a low cry as she did.

At once Bilhah was on her feet, rushing for a gap between cloth and fencepost. She saw Jacob look up in surprise— apparently he had been unaware of Leah's coming and going. Bilhah ducked through and reached Leah before she could rise.

Leah's sleeves were torn and blood streaked—her elbows and the heels of her hands had taken a vicious scrape. Her nose was bleeding—she must have fallen so unbrokenly that her face struck the ground with full force. That was hardly a surprise, once Bilhah gave it a thought. Because she never ran, Leah had no experience with falling hard since she was a baby. She would not have quick enough reflexes to catch herself, or strength enough to break her own fall.

Bilhah tried to help her up, but Leah shrugged her away, and then a second time, too. "Get away from me," she whispered.

"Please, let me help."

"You've helped me for the last time," said Leah, her voice husky.

She was crying. From pain, of course. But also from grief.

"We only thought not to waste the time or the skill I've learned. I wasn't copying the part we were reading. I wasn't getting ahead of you."

"I don't care what you do," said Leah. "Get away from me."

And now Jacob was with them, and Leah did not shrug away his hands as he helped her to her feet. "Let me tend to those scrapes," he said gently. "Come with me into my tent. I have balm for that—it doesn't hurt. Bilhah, fetch me some wine, would you? We need to wash this, and wine is better for washing a scrape than water."

Bilhah immediately rose to her feet and started for Reuel's tent—the steward kept a close eye on the wine, lest some servant be tempted to seek cheer or oblivion in drink. But she did not move too quickly to hear Jacob say, "When Bilhah gets back, she can fetch new clothing for you and help you change."

"I don't want her," said Leah.

And then, because Zilpah was loitering near the gap in the dooryard fence, Leah pointed. "She can go and get a dress for me from my tent."

Bilhah got the wine from Reuel, who was suspicious—it was his nature *and* his job to be so. When she came back and called out softly from outside the door of Jacob's tent, it was Zilpah who emerged and took the flagon from her.

"How is she?" asked Bilhah.

"How would she be?" said Zilpah. "In pain."

"I can fetch a dress for her."

"She said for me to do it, once the wine was here."

"But you don't know which one to bring."

Zilpah shook her head. "How many does she have? How hard is it to choose?"

Bilhah heard the scorn in Zilpah's voice and it rankled. "I helped you when you asked," said Bilhah.

"You helped Jacob," said Zilpah. "As for Leah, her ears are keen. She hears everything we're saying. I won't try to deceive her. I'll fetch her dress myself, even if I bring the wrong one by mistake."

Then Bilhah understood how it was. Zilpah had seen an opportunity. Leah was angry with Bilhah, so now she would want a new handmaiden. Zilpah was determined to get the job.

Well, you can have it, Zilpah-of-the-flagrant-bosom. I don't want it. I'm relieved not to have it.

"So I think that means you should go," said Zilpah.

"I have work to finish," said Bilhah. Whereupon she walked back to the low table and resumed the copying. Though she suspected that once she was no longer Leah's handmaiden—and that was surely what would happen—no one would think it a worthwhile use of her time, to come to Jacob and write for him.

But if I can make my writing small enough, I might be able to get work in the city, helping some scribe with his copywork. Of course he'd have to hide me indoors, so no one would imagine that he was using a woman to do a man's work. But it would be honorable work. I could earn enough to pay my way. I wouldn't be dependent on the whims of some desert lord's daughter.

She knew, even as she planned her plans, that it would never work out that way. Hadn't she already seen how impossible it was to go back to the city alone? And the letters she was learning to write so small were not the kind they used in the city, where it was cuneiform or the Egyptian syllables that the scribes all used. She would have to start learning all over again. No one would hire her for *that*.

I'm trapped here, where I have no useful skill even now. This is the only one I had, and now Leah will see to it that I never have a chance to write again. It will be Zilpah who helps her with her studies. And I'll be hauling water or weeding the garden and probably doing even *that* work so badly that Reuel will urge Laban to send me away, and Laban will only keep me on out of pity.

It was a bleak vision, but Bilhah did not let herself cry. Tears would keep her from seeing the letters she was making, and that would not do. This might be her last hour of writing for Jacob, and she was determined that he see that she would have been able to do the work.

She did not even look up when she heard them emerge from the tent, Zilpah helping Leah limp to the opening in the dooryard. No one said anything and soon they were gone.

Bilhah expected then that Jacob would come to her, take away the papyrus, the book, the table, the brush, the ink.

Instead he went back into his tent and she was able to keep working for another hour, and then another, until at last he came back out and looked at her work and said, "Better."

"Thank you."

"Now it's time for me to go, and I can't leave the book out here in the open."

"I'll be careful with it," said Bilhah.

"It's not you I fear," said Jacob. "There are those who might think it worth stealing something as precious as this book. Do you have strength to prevent them?"

"No one in this camp," said Bilhah. "They're all honest."

"Like your cousin was?" said Jacob.

She couldn't argue with that. She watched him reroll the book with despair. This is the last time, she said silently. Farewell, O holy words of God.

It was only then that she realized that she hadn't the

faintest idea what were the words she had spent the morning copying. They had gone from her eyes to her hand without imprinting themselves on her memory. It was as if even this morning's work had been taken from her, like the ink that faded so the papyrus could be written on again.

Maybe it's a sign from God, she thought. Proof that he doesn't think me worthy of this work. His words can't be held in a mind so small and poor as mine.

Only then did she let herself shed tears, and by that time Jacob was carrying the scroll and the table back inside his tent; so he didn't see, and she wasn't shamed.

PART VIII

JEALOUSY

CHAPTER 15

Jacob was troubled, Rachel could see that. He still did his work well among the animals—his hands seemed to know how to untangle wool, where to find a burr or a thorn, the tendon whose soreness caused a young ewe to limp. She tried to learn from watching him, but after all these months she could only conclude that there were things God whispered to him. Or maybe it wasn't God, maybe it was just the animals themselves whose secret inner voices were revealed to him. This is my complaint, touch me just there and I'll be healed.

But today he paused between animals instead of briskly moving on to the next. And instead of bantering with her, he was silent.

Rachel didn't mind his silences. He was a man of thought, and she knew that if she jabbered into his stillness she might break something, some inner thread that he was weaving into an idea. She had her own stillnesses, didn't she? And alone among men, he seemed to be untroubled by the silence of women.

So she showed him the same respect and said nothing. She did not even sing, as she usually did when alone with the lambs—her voice stilled them, but Jacob's hands did the same, and so her songs were not needed.

Only when it was noon and time to eat did he seem willing to talk. He had long since established the idea that when they ate out in the open, in the midst of work, he had no qualms about eating with a woman. Rachel dealt with this by sitting with him and conversing, but claiming not to be hungry until his meal was over. She would not let him be criticized for eating with a woman, even if the line she drew was a pretty fine one—for when his food was put away, she would bring out her own and eat in front of him, utterly without modesty. Let them talk about that, if they must, those gossipy shepherds! He would be her husband, she was betrothed to him, and so his word would be her law, not their sense of scandal!

Jacob gave thanks to God for the bread and cheese and wine, but then, instead of slicing off a wedge of tart ewe-cheese, he looked at Rachel and said, "What do I do about Leah?"

"I don't know," said Rachel. "Has God given you the power to restore her sight?"

"No," said Jacob. "And don't think I haven't asked."

"Then has God given you the power to soften her temper and make her more patient in her affliction?"

"That's the kind of thing that God lets us do for ourselves."

"Then what you can do about Leah is the same thing all

the rest of us do—avoid her when we can, and tread lightly when we must go near."

"But that breaks my heart. She wants so desperately to be a good person."

"I'm not stopping her," said Rachel.

"But am I helping her?" said Jacob.

Rachel appreciated the way he took the burden back on himself, instead of asking if *she* was helping her sister. Still, Rachel would not accept his generosity. "I'm *not* helping her," said Rachel. "We used to be great friends, but once people started talking about how 'beautiful' I am, it soured things between us. I can't help what other people say, can I? I think *she's* beautiful, but if I say so, she thinks I'm speaking out of pity. There's really nothing I can say at all, most of the time, so . . . we barely speak."

"She *is* lovely, when she isn't sullen," said Jacob.

"How would you know?" said Rachel.

He looked at her, startled.

"Oh, that *is* wretched of me, to say such a thing, but honestly, who *ever* sees her anymore when she's not sullen?"

"There were times, as she was learning to read, as she was first hearing the words of the books, that she was not sullen. And other times, too. When I can see in her face that she is, truly, the sister of the woman I love."

"I'm not a woman, I'm a girl," said Rachel. "I don't have to be a woman for seven more years."

"You sound as though it's something to be postponed as long as possible."

"Isn't it? Will a great prince of the desert allow his wife to go out among the shepherds and look after the lambs? No one lets a wife have the kind of freedom I have here, as a daughter."

"No one lets a daughter have the kind of freedom you have here, either. And while we're on that subject, I've seen *you* get your way as surely as Leah gets hers."

That was completely false, and irritating, too. "Well, if you think I'm just as nasty as Leah—"

"I didn't say that," said Jacob. "I said you're just as good at getting your way. Your method is completely different."

"I don't have a method," said Rachel. "I just ask if I want something, and sometimes Father says yes and sometimes he says no."

Jacob laughed. "Well, that explains why you keep doing it right in front of Leah! You have no idea, do you?"

"No idea of what?"

"Watch me," said Jacob.

He slid down from the rock he was sitting on, so that, seated on the ground, he was looking up into her eyes. But instead of raising his head to look at her forthrightly, he lowered his head, so he was looking up at her from under his eyebrows. Suddenly a man who had been manly was transformed into something . . . cute.

"Rachel," he said softly. "Do you know what would make me really happy?" His voice was small and sickeningly sweet.

"I don't do that!" she said.

He just grinned.

"Why do you want to marry me then, if I'm so *repulsive!*"

"It's not repulsive when you do it," said Jacob. "It's only repulsive when a grown man with a beard does it. When *you* do it it's absolutely charming. Well, a little childish, too, but as you said, you *are* still a child."

She leapt to her feet, embarrassed and angry. "I can see that you really hate me!"

His face at once grew solemn. "I only tell you the truth because I know you're the kind of person who hates flattery. Besides, it's not a flaw in you, and I'm not criticizing. If you think such a way of acting is wrong, then stop doing it—but don't blame me for seeing what you do."

"But I don't do that," said Rachel. "I hate girls who do that. I never treated you that way!"

"No, you never did," said Jacob. "And it's a good thing, too, because it wouldn't work on me. But you talk to your father that way all the time."

She sat back down. She thought about it. "Not as obviously as *you* made it look."

"No—but not as subtly as *you* seem to think."

"Father must think I'm horrible."

"Your father gives you every blessed thing you ever ask for, that he can possibly, decently give. You make him *glad* to give you your way. While Leah, who does the same thing with tears and petulance, makes him sad as he gives in to her. And it's not just his daughters. Laban thinks he's master of his house—and he *is* the master of his servants, all the men and women. But his children, he indulges them all shamelessly. I haven't met the youngest boy, Choraz, but from what I've seen, Laban has done a much better job with his daughters than with his sons."

Rachel dared not answer. She knew better than to criticize her brothers. If Father died before she was married to Jacob, she would be under their rule. She feared them in a way she had never feared her father.

"I don't mean to criticize them," said Jacob. "And that has

nothing to do with what's worrying me. Not that your brothers don't worry me."

"What's to worry about? Father likes you better than them." Which was the obvious truth. Jacob probably hadn't seen it, but Rachel knew quite well just how disgusted Father was with his two eldest boys. Choraz was the only son he was really proud of, which was why he sent him away, to get Choraz out from under the influence of Nahor and Terah. She could not remember Father ever looking at either of them with the same admiration and affection he showed when he looked at Jacob.

"What worries me about your brothers is how worried they are about *me*. They think I'm here to steal their inheritance by marrying their father's favorite daughter."

"I'm not his—that's just. . . ." But she couldn't finish the sentence, because it would not have been the truth.

"What worries me is Leah," said Jacob. "She's put herself in a box. She wants to learn the scriptures, but now she's rejected Bilhah as her maidservant—"

"That's just foolish! Bilhah is the only one of the girls who has the patience to . . . you know."

"Put up with her, I know. But Bilhah is not in bondage, and she has a right to study the scriptures on her own. This morning was the first time she ever did, because Leah was pouting about something and didn't come to my dooryard. So I set Bilhah to work copying. And I'm not going to stop letting her work at that, either. Because I know that's what Leah wants—to shut Bilhah out. And that's simply wrong."

"Well, now you get to find out just how stubborn Leah can be. Because she can keep a pout going forever."

"It won't make a difference to me."

"Just wait till she gets Father upset about how you and Bilhah are treating her."

"Just *you* wait till you see how little difference that makes," said Jacob. "Bilhah *will* keep up the copywork and the studying because she has a talent for it and because it's clear she loves the words of God and understands them. The way my mother always did."

"But that's no way to run a camp, letting servants pick and choose what jobs they'll do!"

"She isn't picking and choosing," said Jacob. "It's only an hour or two, and not every day. Besides, what other duties does she have, now that Leah refuses to have her?"

"No one else can put up with Leah."

"I think Zilpah will," said Jacob.

"Zilpah?" Rachel laughed. "She was assigned to *me*. Not that I want her, either!"

"Zilpah was assigned to you in order to spy on *me*," said Jacob.

Rachel looked at him narrowly. "Is that a guess, or did God tell you?"

"Zilpah told me."

"Well, she's a liar."

"Don't say that so easily, my sweet girl, when you didn't see her face as she told me about it."

"You always call me your 'sweet girl' when what you really mean is 'you stupid girl.'"

"But I never mean 'you stupid girl.' Not even when you're really, really stupid."

She looked at him sharply and saw that he was laughing silently.

"I don't know if I'm going to like being married to a man who ridicules me."

"What should I do, then, just gaze in perpetual rapture at your astonishing beauty?"

"Not all the time. Just whenever you think I'm stupid."

He laughed out loud this time. But then grew sober at once. "Leah is so unhappy. Our marriage weighs on her as a burden. The Lord showed her the way out of her misery by turning her heart toward the word of God. But now she's turned away from his word because it didn't give her the answers that she wanted. And out of envy of Bilhah—and of you."

That was a disquieting thought. Leah, envying Rachel. Oh, of course, she *always* did, but Jacob clearly meant something more. Did Leah envy her for having found a husband? Or did she envy Rachel for having found *this* husband?

"She has to live with her own choices," said Rachel, though her mind was on something else. "I wonder if Father realizes he *has* to find a husband for Leah before we marry."

"I'm sure the thought has occurred to him," said Jacob. "But marriage isn't what's going to make Leah happy."

"Nothing makes her happy because she doesn't want to be happy."

"Everyone wants to be happy, even if everything they choose to do keeps them from happiness," said Jacob firmly. "The trick is to get them to understand what will *make* them happy."

"And what will make Leah happy? I can't wait to hear, because believe me, this whole camp has been desperate to find out for as long as I can remember."

"The same thing that makes every other happy person

happy," said Jacob, as if the answer were obvious. "The love of God."

"Her love for God, or God's love for her?"

"They're the same," said Jacob. "We can't love God more than he loves us, and we can't love him in a different way from his love for us. That's just how things are."

"Well, then, anyway, that's between Leah and God."

"But the only time she's ever really reached out to God was through these books that have been entrusted to my care," said Jacob. "And because of how I bungled having Bilhah do copywork for me, I've made Leah feel angry and unwelcome. I've closed the books to her."

"She's closed the books to herself."

"Perhaps so, but she's too proud to back down."

"Then that's her problem, isn't it?" said Rachel. "I know that's heartless of me, but if I hadn't learned that years ago I'd be nothing but her personal slave by now. She can't apologize, not really, not and *mean* it. Once she's declared she won't do something, then she doesn't do it, until you give in to her."

"And giving in to her only makes her behave even worse the next time," said Jacob. "This is an interesting contradiction. If I don't give in to her, she'll be cut off from the word of God. But if I *do* give in to her, she'll be encouraged in her pride and selfishness, which will also cut her off from the word of God."

"Aren't lambs easy?" said Rachel.

"Yes," said Jacob emphatically. "But then, compared to women, *everything* is easy."

The discussion took a different turn, then—because Rachel made sure that it did. She was not interested in Jacob's view of how difficult women were. It seemed unfair to her that

Jacob would lump her and Leah together, along with every other female in the world, when the problem they were discussing was of Leah's making entirely.

How did *I* come into it?

But Rachel did not say this to Jacob. What would be the use? Whatever it was that men imagined about women, they did not change their minds just because a woman disagreed. Father was that way, and every other man Rachel had talked to in the camp. It's as if they thought that women were conducting a vast conspiracy to deceive men and make their lives difficult, so that anything a woman might say to simplify things had to be an attempt at deception.

If men would only listen to us, they'd find out that each one of us is different, and we're eager to teach you how to understand us. But I can't tell you how to understand Leah—I don't understand her either. And if you did understand her, poor foolish man, you would think you then understood all the rest of us, and you'd be hopelessly wrong. No wonder you despair of understanding women. The best you could ever hope for would be to understand *one* woman. And that's the goal none of you ever seems to try for.

CHAPTER 16

Leah could see that Father didn't want to talk to her, but she was too upset to wait.

"I'm busy," said Father.

"Yes, everything in the camp is more important than me." She walked away from him, and made it a point to stumble as she did.

"Why doesn't God send me a plague of locusts?" said Father to the servants he was supervising. "Then I'd have a chance of fighting them off."

When he talked like that, it meant that he was going to give in. And sure enough, in only a few moments he jogged up behind her and took her arm. "Come with me," he said. "Whatever it is, can it be so bad? You're healthy, aren't you?"

"It's Bilhah," said Leah. "And Jacob."

Father stopped walking. "What?"

There was such a tone of suspicion in his voice that she

was quite startled. It took a moment for her to realize what conclusion he had leapt to. But no, if she even hinted at such a thing, Father would be compelled by honor to do something dreadful and final. "No, no," said Leah. "I don't mean *that*."

"You don't mean what?" asked Father.

"Whatever you're thinking that made you sound like that. It's just . . . this morning I was sick, and I sent Bilhah to tell Jacob that I wouldn't be coming to read today."

"That was nice of you," said Father. "Not to keep him waiting."

"But then Bilhah didn't come back and she didn't come back and—so I went looking for her. I found her in Jacob's dooryard, reading and copying one of the holy books without me!"

By now they were at Father's tent. He ushered her inside.

"Well, that's good then," said Father. "She found a useful way to occupy her time."

"I see," said Leah, her heart sinking. Tears came unbidden to her eyes. "So you think it's all right that Bilhah's taken over something that was supposed to be for *me*."

"She's a servant," said Father. "She was serving."

"She was taking my place," said Leah, trying not to cry. She knew her words sounded selfish and foolish, but she also knew how much it had hurt her, to have Bilhah and Jacob treat her with such scorn. "She only learned in order to help me read, but now she's doing it on her own."

"I don't understand why that should bother you," said Father. "Truly, Leah, I'm sure no one meant any offense."

"No, no one ever means any offense," said Leah bitterly. "Why should it bother Leah? Why should Leah ever expect anything of her own? The great man comes to our camp, and of course he falls in love with beautiful Rachel and he's going to marry her, and the only thing Leah asked for was a chance to read the word of God in his books, only now even *that* is for Bilhah. What's left for me, Father? Isn't there anything I can call my own? Or am I to live as a spinster, on the charity of my brothers? You know how well they'll care for me after you're gone. Or do you expect me to go live with Jacob and Rachel when they both despise me, especially Jacob, who treats me like I don't even matter, who acts as if a servant girl is my equal? But then, he's right, isn't he. No, he's wrong, because I can't even make myself as useful as the servant girl. *She* can copy the holy books, and all I can do is hold it close to my face and squint until I have such a headache I feel like throwing up, and even then none of the words are meant for *me,* because even God sends Rachel dreams and a husband but he sends me *nothing.*" And with that, it was all too much to bear. Leah burst into sobs and sank down onto the carpets that covered the floor of Father's tent.

She felt Father's hand on her shoulder, but she shrugged him off. "I know you don't love me," she said. "I understand. How could you? How could anyone? It's Rachel that everyone loves. Don't deny it! Everybody else hates me, hates everything about me, looking at me, hearing me, serving me, having to help me, they all hate it and hate me and I don't even disagree with them, I hate me too, why shouldn't I?"

"Nobody hates you," said Father.

"It's a sin to lie," whispered Leah.

"I'll talk to Jacob."

"About what?" said Leah. "I already told Bilhah she wasn't my servant any more, but he just let her keep on copying as if it made no difference."

"Whom will I get to serve you now?" said Father.

"Sorry to *annoy* you, Father! After all, why should *any* servant be loyal to me! I should just get used to being betrayed, because I'm *nothing*."

"I don't think she—"

"No, *you* don't think she betrayed me because you weren't *there*, it didn't happen to *you*, it only happened to me, so it doesn't matter at all, does it!"

She knew she was being unfair, but she was so angry, and the words just came to her mind and she couldn't stop them. Well, maybe she could, but she didn't even want to try. He should *know* how much it hurt, he should *feel* it, and since nobody had any real understanding of her, she had to tell him, she had to make him *feel* what she felt.

"I'll talk to Jacob," said Father again.

"Oh, I can just hear you," said Leah. "Oh, Jacob, you have to understand, my poor blind daughter—"

"I never call you blind."

"My poor *tender-eyed* daughter Leah, she's such a big baby, she was crying today, we all have to be *so* careful with her, maybe it'll be better if you don't let Bilhah copy for a little while, till she feels better."

"Leah, that's not what—"

"That's exactly what you'd say! And I don't want it. I don't want him to do something because I *cried*. I can't help it that I cry. People cry when they're unhappy. Well, I'm unhappy *all the time*, and how often do you see me crying? Most of the time I pretend, just so nobody has to be bothered with me."

"Leah, I—"

"So you'll tell him not to get me upset and then he'll think of me the way everybody else in camp does, as a problem, poor Leah, not as a *person*. Not as somebody who has feelings like anybody else, somebody that should be treated with respect, because I don't deserve any respect, if I did deserve respect then *God* wouldn't have made me this way, would he? Or at least he'd give me some gift to make up for it. Like Rachel's dreams. *She* gets the dreams, when she already has the beauty and the good eyes, and I get *nothing*, not even my reading."

Father said nothing.

"I want Zilpah," said Leah.

"Zilpah is not appropriate to be the handmaiden of my daughter," said Father.

"Oh really? Then why was she assigned to Rachel?"

"She was? I didn't give my consent to that."

"Let Rachel have Bilhah. Let Bilhah go take care of sheep with her."

"Bilhah doesn't know anything about sheep."

"She didn't know anything about reading, either," said Leah. "So you just give her a few weeks, and pretty soon all the lambs will come when Bilhah calls, and they won't even know Rachel exists."

"I assign the servants in my house."

"I want Zilpah. Zilpah doesn't talk to me *patiently*, like being tender-eyed also made me stupid. She talks to me like a regular person."

"I don't think she's a good person, Leah," said Father.

"Then why do you keep her here?"

"Are you suggesting I should turn her away, with nothing?"

"I'm suggesting you should make her my handmaiden.

Because she's the only person in camp who is *almost* as much of a nothing as I am. So maybe she'll actually be loyal to me because she can't possibly aim for anything higher."

"Leah, please," said Father.

"Please what? What can I do for you, Father? What service do you want, except for me to go away and not cause you any trouble?" She burst into tears again. "I wish I had died the day I was born. Then you'd have only the one daughter, the one you love, the one everybody loves. You wouldn't have all these *problems,* you wouldn't have to try to find some man you could bribe into taking me off your hands—I'm not stupid, Father! I know that's how you plan to get me married. Only you've never found a man that needy!"

"I'll talk to Jacob," said Father. "That's all I can do."

"You can give me Zilpah, and make Rachel take that disloyal Bilhah!"

"Please go back to your tent," said Father. "Let me lead you back."

"Everyone will see I've been crying."

"Not if you cover your face."

"Oh, right, none of them will guess that I'm hiding something, if I cover my face!"

"Then wait here," said Father. "I'll send for Jacob. I'll talk to him."

"Please don't," said Leah. "I shouldn't have said anything." And she meant it. She thought of what Jacob would think of her, and it made her ashamed. "Just leave me alone, Father. Everybody leave me alone."

But she knew that was impossible. She couldn't even get from one end of the camp to the other without help. How could people possibly leave her alone?

Father left the tent. Leah cried in earnest then, but more quietly.

And in the midst of her crying, she found herself lamenting to God. "Why did you let me be born? I'm not good for anything at all, I make everybody unhappy, they all think I cry just to get my way but you know why I'm crying, I'm crying because I can't just die and have all of this *end*."

As usual, God said nothing.

"You don't hear me. You're just like everybody else, you don't even want to know I'm here. You speak to your prophets, you send dreams to my sister, but me, I'm nothing at all."

Then she remembered that for a moment she *had* felt the Wisdom of God come upon her. When the Lord told Enoch, "You will dwell in me, and I in you. So walk with me." The words had been spoken directly into her heart. God *had* given her a gift.

She simply had no idea what it meant.

Yet thinking about it ended her crying. She no longer felt sad and alone. She just felt . . . tired. Her eyes were weary with weeping. The inner room of Father's tent was dark. The air, though, was stiflingly hot. She felt as though she would never move again. Never *wanted* to move.

She awoke with someone jostling her shoulder. She did not remember where she was, but when she opened her eyes it was dark. No matter. She knew where she was from the smell—Father's tent, not her own. And from the smell, too, she recognized Zilpah. Also the strength of her hand, her roughness—not the namby-pamby way Bilhah always touched her, as if she were afraid Leah would break.

"Zilpah," murmured Leah.

"And they say you can't see," said Zilpah.

"I'm in my father's tent."

"Yes."

"Which means *you're* in my father's tent."

"I looked for you everywhere."

"But you're not allowed to come in here."

"This is where everyone said you went, the last time they saw you," said Zilpah.

"It doesn't matter. Is it dark out?" She opened her eyes and could see that the tent wall glowed with the red light of sunset. "You can't go out of here until it's dark."

"Of course I can. I'm your handmaiden now. I had to find you."

"It would be a scandal," said Leah. "And you know it." It occurred to Leah to wonder if that wasn't exactly what Zilpah wanted. Did she have some idea that if she was seen emerging from Father's tent, it would lead people to think she had the rights of a concubine? Did she imagine that would raise her status in the camp? Of course it wouldn't. It would only lower Father's.

"Well, what are we supposed to do? Just sit here?"

"Yes," said Leah. "*I* could go out. But then if you were found in here without me, that would be even worse. So we stay."

"Well then I wish I *hadn't* found you and *hadn't* wakened you."

"Next time you'll know."

"I've never been the handmaiden of the daughter of the prince."

"Father doesn't let people call him that."

"He's lord of this camp," said Zilpah. "Thank you for asking for me as your servant. Reuel said you did."

"Yes," said Leah.

"You saved me from something . . . something that I didn't want."

Why wouldn't she want to serve with Rachel? "Whoever is Rachel's handmaiden will go with her when she marries Jacob."

Zilpah gave a short, sharp, whispered laugh. "Oh, I don't think that was what anyone had in mind for me."

"So now you're with me, you'll never go off into another household because I'll never get married."

That sharp little laugh again. "Oh, mistress, that's just not true."

"No man wants to marry a blind wife."

"You're not blind," said Zilpah.

The ritual of reassurance. Not blind, tender-eyed, not blind, tender-eyed.

"And you're the daughter of a desert lord," said Zilpah. "And you're beautiful. What does it matter if you can't do needlework? The wife of a rich man doesn't *have* to do needlework. She just has to adorn her husband's life and produce babies for him while servants like me wait on her."

"No man will want me."

"Every woman has some man who wants her," said Zilpah, chuckling. "That's the one sure thing in this world. The only reason you don't know it is because you can't see the way they look at you. At me, at every woman."

"Not the really *old* women," said Leah.

"You think there aren't plenty of really old men panting after them?" said Zilpah. "Oh, when the time comes, there'll be no lack of men who want you. And that's without any kind of dowry. The only reason you don't already have a lot of suitors is you're so young. And also you look glum all the time. I never look glum, and so men look at *me* and want me, but I'm not half as beautiful as you."

Leah had heard all about what it was men looked at when they looked at Zilpah. But she liked hearing this, all the same. Because there was no hint of impatience in Zilpah's voice, the way there always was with Bilhah. Bilhah always thought Leah's fears and feelings were silly, a waste of time. But Zilpah seemed really to admire her, which was something Leah had never had before.

"I can't see myself. Or Rachel either. Or you. I don't really know what beauty is."

"For a young man, beauty is having a bosom and a willing smile. For a mature man, beauty is strength and cheerfulness and nice regular features, so you'll have healthy babies who won't be ugly."

Leah heard the part about a willing smile and cheerfulness. She knew what Zilpah was getting at.

"I've got nothing to be cheerful about."

"Of course not," said Zilpah. "Who does? Certainly not *me*. My mother went whoring around and I'm a fatherless girl with no money, born into bondage. What have I got to smile about? Except that my smile *is* my dowry. My smile makes men want me."

"I heard it was other features of yours."

"My 'other features' catch their eye, but if I look at them with an ugly face they go away. Mostly. But when I smile, they think I want *them*, and men love any woman who gives them a smile that says she likes them."

"Is that what Rachel did with Jacob?"

Zilpah laughed. "She *kissed* him. That's a lot better than a smile. But yes, she smiles all the time. She's a cheerful little girl."

Leah doubted greatly that if she smiled a lot she'd get anything like Rachel's results. After all, she *used* to be happy, back when she and Rachel were little and liked each other. She smiled a lot, but nobody but Father ever called her pretty. Still, it was nice to hear what Zilpah was saying. And maybe it was true. A little.

The tent walls weren't glowing anymore, and the night insects and birds were making their noise outside.

"I think we can go now," said Leah.

But when they stood up, Zilpah stumbled. "I left the lamp in your tent," she said. "It wasn't dark then."

It was Leah's turn to chuckle. "My turn to lead, then, I guess." She took Zilpah by the hand, and, feeling ahead of her with her other hand and with her toes, Leah quickly found the curtain separating the inner room from the outer one.

Just at that moment, though, a light appeared in the outer room, and there were voices. Father and Jacob.

Zilpah seemed perfectly ready to go ahead, but Leah pushed her quietly back into the farthest corner of the inner room. When Zilpah started to whisper something, Leah covered her mouth. Nothing could be said. Zilpah should not be found here.

And besides. Leah wanted to hear what was said in the other room.

If Father later found them here, Leah could simply say that she hadn't wanted to get Zilpah in trouble. That was true enough, wasn't it?

She felt Zilpah's breath in her ear. "This is not a good idea," said Zilpah in the softest possible whisper.

Leah knew Zilpah was right. She knew she might not like what Father had to say. But she also knew that this might be her only chance to find out how Father talked about her behind her back. If he, too, betrayed her, then . . . then she would know. And knowledge was good. Even bad knowledge. Even knowledge that broke your heart. Better to know than to be a fool, believing someone loved you when he didn't.

The conversation was boring enough at first—Jacob was full of reports about the sheep, about various shepherds. Leah barely knew them—they weren't often in the camp and had little enough to do with her even when they were.

Finally, though, the businesslike chat ended.

"I need to talk to you about Leah," said Father.

"I know," said Jacob. "I'm worried about her."

"So am I," said Father.

"She makes herself so unhappy, being jealous all the time."

"She was once the cheerfulest child," said Father. "I wish you could have seen her when she was little. The light of my life. And so good to her little sister. Like Rachel's own tiny mother." Father laughed. But Leah could tell that he was also emotional. There was a catch in his voice. There was a pause, too, as if he were wiping away a tear.

He *did* love her. Or at least, he loved her when she was little.

"The rivalry between the sisters makes them both unhappy," said Jacob. "I wish there were some way to put an end to it."

"Well, it's not really *between* the sisters," said Father. "I don't think Rachel even knows there's a rivalry."

Leah seethed for a moment, but Jacob's answer cheered her. "The only reason Rachel thinks there isn't a rivalry is because she always wins."

Father laughed. "Is that how it looks to you? Believe me, it's Leah who gets her way. She cries, it breaks my heart. I spoil her."

"Rachel gets her way every bit as much as Leah does," said Jacob. "How else to explain the way you let her do things no other desert lord would ever let a daughter do?"

"If I didn't let her go out with the shepherds, you wouldn't have met her at that well," said Father dryly.

"The difference between Rachel and Leah is that when Rachel gets her way, she makes you like her for it, while Leah makes you pity her. That's why Rachel wins every time, between the sisters. Getting their way doesn't make either of them particularly happy. But even when she gets her way, Leah can see that everyone likes Rachel more than they like her, and so she feels like she loses every time."

"I see you've solved all our problems," said Father, getting downright testy.

"I wish I could!" said Jacob. "Because it's going to be my problem, too."

"Oh, really?"

"Yes," said Jacob. "I'm going to marry a little girl who thinks that all she has to do to get her way is smile."

Leah nodded. Yes. Jacob saw *right through* Rachel! He was the only one who ever had.

"Leah was unhappy today," said Father. "When you had Bilhah copying for you."

"I could tell," said Jacob.

"I've assigned Bilhah to serve Rachel now. To be her hand-maid."

"Good," said Jacob. "Because Rachel doesn't want her. So I can still have her to do copy work for several hours a day."

Leah felt Zilpah jab her slightly with her elbow. "Copy work I bet," Zilpah whispered in her ear.

Leah jabbed her back, and harder. She might detest Bilhah, but the girl was *not* like Zilpah, always thinking about what men wanted. If Bilhah was asked by Jacob to do copy work, then copying is what she'd do.

"It makes Leah unhappy," said Father. "So I ask you not to have Bilhah do this work. I'll have Reuel teach someone else to read, if you need help that way."

"Bilhah is already trained, and she's good at it."

"It makes Leah unhappy."

"Only because Leah is selfish," said Jacob.

It stung. She felt her face flush.

"When it comes to the holy books," said Jacob, "those are my birthright. No other man but me can say who copies them and who does not, or who can even lay eyes on them."

There was a sharpness in Jacob's tone, along with the hard edge of his words. Leah knew that Father would not like either.

"You're my guest. I can determine how my servants work, and where, and with whom."

"Indeed you can," said Jacob. "But there is nothing more important to me than the word of God. I have put myself into your service in order to earn the right to marry your daughter. That means that my time does not belong to me. For seven years I won't be able to copy these books. That's a perilously long time. They fade. The papyrus cracks."

"Papyrus," snorted Father. "Clay is better! In a fire, clay only gets harder! The impressions of the stylus never fade!"

"But to carry all the books I have, if they were written on clay," said Jacob, "it would take two carts."

"What are two carts?" said Father expansively.

"Two more than I have," said Jacob. "So I need to keep the copy work going. Bilhah is already trained."

"But as I said, Leah doesn't want her doing it, so . . ."

"So you'll put the selfish whim of an angry girl before keeping the word of God alive for another generation?"

There it was. Proof that Jacob hated her. Leah's eyes stung.

"I'll put the peace and good order of my house ahead of anything else," said Father.

"Very well," said Jacob. "Then I'll have to ask Bilhah what she wants."

"What?" said Father angrily.

"She's a free girl," said Jacob. "It's one of the reasons I love and admire you so much, Father Laban. The orphaned relative of a low servant of yours, and when the servant runs away, you keep the orphan. Your generosity is legendary. But she already tried to leave your service once. I brought her back, but not to be treated as a bondservant. If you won't allow her to help with the copying while she's in your care, then I will offer her my protection, in order to let her keep on with this work."

"You'd take away the handmaiden I intended to give my daughter to follow her into marriage?"

"Bilhah is not yours to give," said Jacob. "She's free to choose. But I'd rather she stayed in your protection. If she's in mine, where would I have for her to sleep, except the outer chamber of my tent?"

Leah understood Jacob's game now. And he criticized her and Rachel for always getting their way.

"I see that you mean to force this issue," said Father coldly.

"I mean to protect the words of God by copying them," said Jacob. "I would not be worthy of my birthright if I made any other choice."

"What about Leah, then?"

"I hope she'll keep coming to me to learn from the holy books," said Jacob. "She's already learned much from them."

"She won't come back, if Bilhah's there."

"Yes she will," said Jacob.

"No I won't," whispered Leah softly.

It was Zilpah's turn to elbow her for making noise. This would not have been a good moment for them to be discovered.

"You don't know Leah."

"I know the Spirit of God," said Jacob. "She has tasted from the cup of Wisdom. She'll be back for another sip, and then another."

"You don't know how proud and stubborn she is."

"I know exactly how proud and stubborn she is," said Jacob. "It's her only sin. But the Wisdom of the Lord has already spoken to her and invited her to walk with God. She is good at heart. She'll repent of her stubbornness and her pride, and with a broken heart she will come back to the word of the Lord."

Father said nothing for a moment. Then: "Is this a prophecy?"

"If you mean, did God tell me this, then no. But I saw how

her face lit up with joy when she felt the Wisdom of the Lord in her heart. Of course the Enemy at once tried to twist the experience and make it mean something else, tried to distract her with anger and confusion. But she knows. She has *tasted* it. She's a good girl, Laban. Her heart is pure and she seeks to serve God. She'll master her anger and she'll forget her jealousy and she'll come to me again for another taste."

"And you think she'll sit down beside Bilhah, when she knows you deliberately let Bilhah continue copying and reading against my will?"

"Against Leah's will, you mean," said Jacob.

"My request then, for Leah's sake."

"She will sit down next to Bilhah and speak kindly to her, because she knows that Bilhah did her no wrong, and you can't hear the word of God if there's injustice in your heart."

"Then God must have few indeed to hear him these days," said Laban.

"That is the truth," said Jacob.

"You seem to have made a particular study of Leah," said Laban.

"She seeks the word of the Lord," said Jacob. "It makes us kin to each other. It makes us friends."

"Could it make you more than that?" asked Laban.

"What do you mean?" asked Jacob.

"You don't already know? I thought you knew everything." But Laban laughed when he said it.

"Are you suggesting that I . . ."

"Rachel has no interest in the holy books. Has she?"

"Not yet," said Jacob.

"The words of our covenant were that you would work for me seven years to marry my daughter."

"Rachel," said Jacob.

"But the *word* was 'daughter.'"

Zilpah's elbow again. But Leah didn't need prodding to realize what Father was offering. It was humiliating, that he should try to pressure Jacob into marrying her when he obviously didn't love her. And yet even as she knew that Jacob would refuse, and that Father was wrong to do it, she felt a momentary thrill as she imagined what her life might be like if Jacob were to say, Yes, I never thought of it, but yes, Leah is the one who loves the holy books, *she* is the one I should love and marry at the end of my seven years.

Jacob made no answer.

"I just thought," said Father, "not *instead* of Rachel, but . . . a man can have two wives."

"No," said Jacob. "Not me. My father had only one wife— Rebekah was enough for him. I want a marriage like that. A love like that. Even when my father was blind in his old age, he looked at her with such love—and Mother, the way she felt about him."

"Your grandfather had three wives," said Father. "It did him no harm."

"No harm?" Jacob laughed. "Hagar and her boy Ishmael were the most dangerous thing that ever happened in my father's life. Jealousy between women—your daughters already have a rivalry every bit as sharp as my father's with Ishmael."

"Or yours with Esau."

"So far neither of your daughters has threatened to kill the other, thank the Lord," said Jacob.

"Never mind then," said Father. "I just thought—you

seemed to care about Leah, that's all. A father wants his daughter to marry a man who cares about her."

"I do care about her," said Jacob.

"As the sister of your wife-to-be," said Father.

"As a daughter of God," said Jacob. "God loves her and longs for her to turn her heart to him and serve him. She longs to serve God, if once she can get control of herself and change her jealous heart. I'm the keeper of the holy books. I love her for loving the word of God."

"Jacob, my brother, my son-to-be," said Father, "that is a great gift in my beloved daughter's life. You will yet be a blessing to both my girls. You have my blessing when it comes to Bilhah copying. Her mornings are yours, and you needn't take her into your protection, she has mine. As for Leah, well, she'll be angry and heartbroken, but since you have so much confidence that she'll overcome these things, I will trust in your judgment on this."

"I could not ask any more of my beloved brother and father," said Jacob.

"I place both my daughters' happiness in your hands."

And with that, both men and the lamp left the outer room.

Leah and Zilpah waited only a few moments before they made their way through the dark tent to the front entrance. Father might come back quickly, and they had to be gone before he came into his inner chamber to sleep.

Leah could hear Father and Jacob still talking, and led Zilpah out into the darkness in another direction. But after only a few paces, Leah was lost in the dark—there were few sounds to guide her now. So Zilpah took over, picking her way by the light of a thin moon, until at last, still wordless, they entered Leah's tent.

A lamp already burned there. "I left it here for you," said Zilpah. "I don't want you to be sorry that I'm your hand-maiden now."

"Thank you," said Leah.

"I think Jacob was a fool to turn you down," said Zilpah.

"He's not a fool," said Leah, trying not to be sharp with the girl. After all, Zilpah was obviously trying to be loyal to her. "Every word he said was true."

Zilpah started to speak—or at least took in a breath as if she meant to speak. But instead she held her silence. Perhaps she saw something in Leah's face that stilled her.

"I need to be alone," said Leah.

"You haven't had supper," said Zilpah.

"Could you go and fetch it for me?" asked Leah. "Bring it to me in a bowl and leave it just outside my inner room. You can sleep in the outer room tonight. Please?"

"Of course, mistress," said Zilpah.

In a moment she was gone.

Leah walked quickly into her inner chamber and knelt on the carpets there. "O Lord," she said. "Let Jacob's words be true. Let me be the good girl he told my father I am. Help me not to be jealous. Help me to be worthy of the Wisdom you gave me."

She couldn't help herself. As she spoke the words softly, tears flowed down her cheeks. But they were not the hot tears of anger. They were tears of shame and sorrow. "I've been so selfish," she said. "But I'm angry. Help me not to be angry. I'm sad, and I don't want to be sad. I'm *lonely* and I don't want to be alone."

Then her grief at all she had realized tonight got the better of her, and she could not speak. Once again she wept, lying on carpet, alone in an inner chamber. But this time the tears were different. This time her tears were offered up to God. To God and to Jacob, who had asked for them, who had believed in her when nobody else did, not even herself.

"Father," she whispered. "Lord God my father. Help me know how to walk with you."

PART IX

SEVEN
YEARS

CHAPTER 17

Bilhah was beginning to produce the same kind of small, fine handwriting that she saw on the scrolls. Instead of laboriously drawing each character, the letters seemed to flow directly out of her hand.

Her back grew tired, though, so every little while when the brush ran out of ink, she dipped it into the water, set it aside, and then got up and stretched and walked around.

It was on one such morning, when Jacob was already gone to see Rachel—or, rather, to tend to the animals that Rachel merely happened to be watching over—that Leah and Zilpah came into the dooryard.

Immediately Bilhah was filled with dread. What sort of confrontation were they planning? There was the scroll she was copying—the sayings of Noah—on the low table. Though she could not imagine what they might do to it, the scroll was her responsibility. She strode swiftly toward it, meaning to get between Leah and Zilpah and the writing table, when to her surprise Leah sank to her knees.

"Is Jacob here?" asked Leah.

Bilhah glanced at Zilpah, who was neither smirking nor simpering. Zilpah's dress was not low-necked; or perhaps it was, but she wore another cloth around her neck that completely concealed her bosom. Leah might prefer Zilpah to Bilhah for a handmaiden, but she had never had to tell *Bilhah* to dress more modestly.

"He's not here," said Bilhah. "He left me to copy this scroll till noon."

Leah lowered her head. "Sister Bilhah," she said.

The familiar address was baffling. Was Leah mocking her?

"I've come to ask your forgiveness for my treatment of you."

Bilhah's heart sank. Was Leah now going to demand that Bilhah give up the copying and come back to be her handmaiden?

"There's nothing to forgive," said Bilhah.

"That's what I told her," said Zilpah quietly.

Leah stiffened, and Zilpah looked out over the dooryard fence, as if she had spotted some bird or lizard doing something endlessly fascinating.

Leah went on. "I accused you wrongly. And I tried to stop you from doing this work. I see now that the work you do for Jacob is the most important work in this camp, and for me to try to stop you is the same as if I tried to stop God."

Bilhah tried to see if Leah was being sarcastic, but with her head downturned there was no way to read her face.

"If my copying were that important," said Bilhah, "they would have someone important doing it."

Leah shook her head and lifted her face. "It's the work that makes the worker important, not the other way around."

What could Bilhah do, except respond as if Leah meant every word? "If forgiveness from me is needed, then I forgive you freely. I hope you will also forgive me for having . . ."

She was not altogether sure what Leah might expect her to apologize for, so she hesitated. She would have thought of something, but Leah removed the necessity.

"You have done no wrong, but thank you for trying to make a balance between us."

Leah rose gracefully to her feet. Now that they were on the same level again, Bilhah could see that there was something different about Leah's face. Had she been crying? No. Her eyes weren't puffy or reddened. Yet there was some kind of transformation.

"Come, Zilpah," said Leah. "Our business here is done until Jacob returns."

"You could stay and wait," said Bilhah impulsively. "He's bound to return before noon to put the book away."

"No, we have work to do," said Leah.

Zilpah, with an expressionless face, said, "She's teaching me to read."

"I'm also working on teaching stones to sing," said Leah.

For a moment Bilhah looked back and forth between the two girls, trying to understand whether they were quarreling or . . .

Joking. Leah and Zilpah both burst into laughter.

Bilhah smiled, but she didn't know what was funny.

"It's not going very well," said Zilpah.

"I need better eyes—I never draw the letters the same twice," said Leah.

"And I need a better head," said Zilpah.

"But we're getting there."

"Letter by letter," said Zilpah.

"Except the ones that I don't really remember."

"Those are my favorites," said Zilpah. "Because we get to make up new shapes every time, and then guess."

Bilhah was baffled. Leah didn't joke with anyone. Bilhah had tried now and then to introduce some kind of playfulness to their conversations, but Leah did not respond to wit, especially at her own expense. Now she was bantering with Zilpah, and it was partly about Leah's tender eyes, and there was no sign of anger. What, exactly, had happened? Had Zilpah done something to her? No, there was nothing a bondservant could do to compel her mistress.

If Leah had been like this with *me*, we might have become friends, and I would still be her handmaiden.

But the memory of Leah's tantrums and accusations was too fresh. Bilhah thought of her time with Leah as a failure, a defeat; to see Zilpah now succeeding didn't make her any happier. If I had been a better friend or servant, perhaps I might have deserved to be Leah's friend, as Zilpah now is.

"Can I help you with the teaching?" asked Bilhah. "I remember all the letters because I use them every day."

She inwardly winced at her own words. She had meant her mention of daily writing to explain—to excuse—why she remembered the more rarely-used letters that Leah apparently had forgotten. But her explanation was also a reminder of her work as Jacob's copyist, and though Leah had just apologized, Bilhah well knew how easily she could be set off on another round of resentment and, if it went deep enough, rage.

But when Leah shook her head, it was without a trace of

snappishness. "No, we're making slow progress, and in truth I think we've got all the letters right, now."

"Why not show me, and I can confirm it?" asked Bilhah.

"That's a good idea," said Leah. "Zilpah, can you write the letters on the ground for Bilhah to see?"

Now Zilpah looked at Bilhah with real anger.

Bilhah thought she knew why. "Everyone who reads and writes was once a beginner," she said.

Zilpah rolled her eyes. Bilhah noticed that she said nothing, gave no sign of her annoyance, not even with an irritable sigh.

Yet Leah, with her finely tuned senses, knew that something was amiss. Maybe it was just Zilpah's hesitation. "Come now, Zilpah, even your worst letters are better than the best of mine."

Zilpah dropped to her knees and arched her back to stretch out her hands. In the process, the cloth she had been wearing around her neck slipped off her shoulders and Bilhah could see that this was one of the least modest of her dresses that she wore. And when she bent over to write in the dirt, she kept her head back, so the view down her dress was as clear as possible. This made no sense at all to Bilhah—there were no men here. It could only be a gesture of defiance; but of what? To whom? Bilhah was the only one who could see.

But apparently that wasn't true. While Leah named the letters and Zilpah drew them—forming them well enough, for a beginner—Leah picked up the shawl and redraped it to cover Zilpah's breasts. "Zilpah doesn't like dressing modestly," said Leah. "She keeps testing me to see if I'll notice. She thinks I'm blind."

"I only have one beauty," said Zilpah softly.

"Yes," said Leah. "A good heart."

"All right, two beauties," said Zilpah.

And then the two of them laughed again.

And finally Bilhah realized—Zilpah wasn't showing contempt at all. She was helping Leah learn how to deal with her disobedience as friendly teasing instead of infuriating defiance. It was something that no one had ever dared with Leah, to tease her. Well, Bilhah *tried,* but Leah had quickly taught her that it wasn't worth the trouble. Now she was getting lessons in being a normal person. But how ironic, to be getting them from someone as strange as Zilpah.

"That one is backward," said Bilhah. "It faces the other way."

"I *knew* something was wrong with it," said Leah, shaking her head.

Zilpah rubbed it out and drew it again, facing the right way.

"You have them all," said Bilhah. "You're doing well."

"Thank you, mistress," said Zilpah.

Her tone was so offensively snide that Bilhah wanted to say something really vile in reply, but Leah had come to make peace and Bilhah refused to be the one to break it. "I didn't mean to be condescending," said Bilhah. "I'm sorry."

Leah laughed. "Someone else needs joking lessons!" she said. "Zilpah's helping me learn how to take things as a joke."

Zilpah also smiled—but there was a sauciness to the smile that made it clear to Bilhah that they were *not* friends.

"It's a good skill to have," said Bilhah. "When something is *meant* as a joke."

"I don't know," said Leah. "I'm pretty sure Zilpah usually means the things she says every bit as nastily as they sound.

But if I *take* them as friendly gibes, we don't have a quarrel, and Zilpah gets the satisfaction of thinking she got away with something."

Zilpah's face went stiff. "If my mistress is displeased . . ." she began.

Leah laughed. "You see? *Everybody* has times when they don't get the joke."

Bilhah laughed too, watching Zilpah force herself to pretend to be amused at having been caught at her game. "Humor is so hard sometimes," said Bilhah. "Nobody's ever sure whether it's funny or not."

"But that's when it's funniest," said Leah. "When the other person isn't absolutely sure, but still has to laugh so as not to seem spiteful and easily provoked. It lets you be mean *and* get a reputation for cleverness."

Zilpah put on a half-smile and raised her eyebrows at Bilhah, as if to say, See what I have to put up with?

But Bilhah had no sympathy. Leah had apparently made some kind of vow to avoid having tantrums—but that didn't mean she'd stopped noticing when someone was being offensive to her. For the first time in a long time, Bilhah rather liked Leah. So whatever she was doing, it worked.

"Well, since you've learned the letters," said Bilhah, "why don't you both sit with me, and as I copy, I'll read the book phrase by phrase. Then the two of you can watch me write it out or read it from the original and Zilpah will see how the letters go."

"Thank you," said Leah. "If you're sure Jacob won't mind."

"He said that it's good for people to hear the words of God, with open heart and mind."

"Maybe that's why Zilpah dresses as she does," said Leah, straightening the shawl once again. "To show how open her heart is."

"Very funny," said Zilpah. But she soon joined in with Leah's and Bilhah's laughter.

Bilhah read, then, phrase by phrase. Since it was a book of sayings, there was no story to explain. Leah began to ask questions, to which Bilhah had no answers; but within a very little while, they were discussing with some animation what Noah might have meant by this or that saying; and Zilpah, too, joined in, though as often as not it was to be skeptical about whether Noah knew what he was talking about. Still, she wasn't hostile—she seemed to be sincere enough in the things she said.

All in all, it was a good morning.

Then noon came, and with it, Jacob. He came up behind them while they were discussing whether Noah's condemnation of drunkards was so vehement because drinking wine to excess was really all that bad, or merely because he himself had drunk too much from time to time and saw it as his own vice, and his harsh words were really directed at himself.

"Can't both be true?" Jacob asked, and that's when Bilhah first realized he was there, standing just beyond the dooryard fence behind them.

Leah was the only one who seemed not to be startled or even surprised at Jacob's coming. "I hope it's all right that Bilhah is reading to us," said Leah.

"I'm delighted that she is," said Jacob, "and happy that you came." He walked to the opening and came into the dooryard. "And Zilpah, are those your letters drawn in the dirt?"

"No, Jacob," said Leah. "They're the same letters you and Bilhah use."

It took Jacob a long second before he realized that Leah was joking. But his laughter, when it came, was all the more generous for the delay. "Well, there wouldn't be much point in making up your own letters that no one else could read, I guess," he said.

"We're trying not to interfere with Bilhah's copying," said Leah. "And when we discuss the words of the prophet Noah, I'm afraid it's the blind leading the blind."

"No one is blind," said Jacob, "when the Wisdom leads the way."

"But this morning, Wisdom was apparently off doing her laundry," said Leah. "At least as far as *my* understanding was concerned."

"Even Wisdom needs clean laundry," said Jacob solemnly.

"That was so wise," said Leah, "that I hope you'll let Bilhah write it down."

"Not in the sayings of Noah," said Bilhah. "Jacob says it's absolutely wrong to add things just because we think our words will improve on what the prophet wrote."

"I think some scribes have done a bit of alteration in the past," said Jacob. "But we can only copy the words we have. If I started trying to guess which words were genuine, I'd end up guessing wrong often enough that I'd only make it worse."

"So," said Leah, "that must mean we need to start writing down a new book. The sayings of Jacob."

"That would be a book with many words and little wisdom," said Jacob.

"Good practice for writing, then," said Zilpah dryly. "We wouldn't get distracted by trying to understand it."

Jacob laughed, and so did Leah and Bilhah, and the smile that then crossed Zilpah's face seemed genuine.

CHAPTER 18

Zilpah succeeded in avoiding Reuel for more than a week. It was easy enough—all she had to do was be extraordinarily attentive to Leah. She knew that whatever Reuel had to say, he wouldn't say in front of Jacob's daughter.

But it was inevitable that he'd catch her alone. Zilpah expected him to intercept her when she was carrying water, but instead he fell in beside her in the earliest light of dawn, when Zilpah was coming back to the tent from her morning privacy. "You think you're clever," said Reuel.

"I think you weren't so smart," said Zilpah, "conspiring with Nahor and Terah against their father."

"Not against their father."

"Against the man their father trusts better than them," said Zilpah. "I think it's pretty nearly the same thing."

"I'm not a good enemy to have," said Reuel.

"Better to have you as an enemy," said Zilpah, "than to trust you as a friend."

He seized her arm and gripped tightly. Painfully.

"Laban won't live forever, and then you'll be in my hands again."

"Not if Laban sends me with Leah when she marries."

"Leah will never marry," said Reuel. "No man wants her."

"They will," said Zilpah. "I'll make sure of it. Especially now that I know you mean to punish me for refusing to betray Jacob by spying on him as Rachel's handmaid."

"You can spy on him as Leah's handmaiden now, if you know what's good for you."

"But all that Jacob and Leah ever discuss is the holy books," said Zilpah. "Find another traitor."

"I'm not a traitor," said Reuel. "I'm Laban's good servant. This camp prospers under my hand. But Laban is getting older, and one day there'll be a new master here. It's a foolish steward who doesn't befriend the heir."

"But when the heir is an adder, it's a disloyal steward who puts him near the master's bed."

"What a clever saying. Does it come from one of Jacob's books? Or are you so good at reading the words of God now that he whispers new proverbs to you privately?"

Zilpah tried to pull away. "Leah will be expecting me."

"Leah doesn't wake up until well after dawn," said Reuel.

"I do when I hear loud talking," said Leah.

She was standing in the door of her tent. It was probably the first time Zilpah had been grateful to see her mistress.

They had not been talking loudly. But even whispers carried in the still dawn air, and Leah heard better than most.

"Forgive us if we woke you with our conversation," said Reuel, suddenly careful. He also let go of Zilpah's arm.

Zilpah made a point of rubbing it. Leah couldn't see well, but she could see big movements.

"It's so kind of you," said Leah, "to help Zilpah find her way back in the darkness. Or did you also help her make water? I just wondered why you were so attentive to my handmaiden."

"I asked her how you were doing," said Reuel.

"So she's spying on me? Oh, Reuel, you're so wise to make sure you know *everything* that's going on in camp. For instance, Zilpah and I are going to my father's tent now, to suggest to him that it's time he found a new steward. One who actually serves Father, instead of my worthless elder brothers."

Reuel abruptly strode to Leah and took her by the arms— perhaps not as roughly as he had handled Zilpah, but then again, her words were a dire threat to the man, and Zilpah knew that men got stupider and more violent when they were afraid.

"If you were listening so carefully, Leah," said Reuel, whispering right into Leah's face, "then you must have heard me remind Zilpah that someday it will be Nahor who rules over you, not your father."

Leah looked upward into his face, and Zilpah rather admired the way her face showed no fear.

"Father will find me a husband," said Leah, "before Rachel is married. He would never shame me."

"Your father will send *me* to find you a husband," said Reuel.

"Not after he hears what Zilpah and I have to say," said Leah.

"He'll never hear it, because you'll never say it."

This had gone on long enough, Zilpah decided. Her mother had told her many times how to stop a man who was determined to get his own way by force. "When they're angry, they don't think with their heads," Mother said. "You have to hit them where they're thinking so their brain can take over."

By the time Zilpah got close to them, she was already holding a fist-sized stone. She also had the neckline of her gown as open as she could make it.

She leaned in close to Leah, knowing that at that angle, Reuel could see down her dress. With his attention there, he wouldn't notice much else. "Mistress," she said urgently, "you'd better believe Reuel. He's too clever and dangerous to let a couple of girls interfere with his plans. We need him as our friend."

Leah looked at her with a face that could start a fire. But Zilpah met her with her sauciest I'm-just-teasing grin, and Leah changed her reply before it came out of her mouth. "You're right," Leah said. "I don't know what I was thinking."

"Do you two think I'm so stupid that I'll believe this pretense?"

"We don't think you're stupid, Reuel," said Zilpah, sliding between him and Leah. Her breasts pressed against Reuel's belly. "But I hope there's more than one way to be your friend."

"If you think I'm going to fall for your false promises," Reuel began.

But at that moment Zilpah swung the stone with all her

strength, smashing it into Reuel's crotch. The man cried out in agony and collapsed.

Zilpah immediately grabbed Leah's hand and began to pull her.

"I can't go that fast!" said Leah.

"Yes you can," said Zilpah. "Even pain like that only stops a man for a few moments. We need to get to your father."

"What'll you do when I fall down, drag me the rest of the way?"

Zilpah slowed down a little. Leah wasn't running now. She could keep up without stumbling.

"I thought for a minute you really were going to seduce him," said Leah.

"That old toad? He doesn't even remember what women are for."

"Doesn't matter what he remembers," said Leah. "After what you just did, I'm afraid he's going to end up a eunuch."

"That would take more than a stone," said Zilpah.

"Father had better believe us," said Leah. "Because if he doesn't, Reuel's going to have his vengeance."

"That's when he'll become a eunuch," said Zilpah.

The two girls laughed.

In the end, though, it didn't matter whether Father believed them. He had his doubts, but when he sent a servant to fetch Reuel to hear his side of the story, Reuel was nowhere to be found. After a little searching, they learned that Reuel had left on horseback, with a few silver baubles and a bundle of fine clothing.

"I take that as a full confession on his part," said Laban. "What he stole is worthless to me. I wouldn't waste time trying to track him down to kill him. But the horse has value."

Soon he had a half dozen riders out searching for Reuel, with strict instructions on how to deal with him.

"I just wonder how he managed to get astride a horse," said Leah.

"I hope it trots all the way to wherever he's going," said Zilpah.

Within an hour, a couple of riders returned. They led the horse Reuel had taken. Most of the clothes and trinkets were with them also; they laid them out at Laban's feet.

"As you said, sir, we left him wearing the very richest clothing."

"Good," said Laban. "The robbers on the road will take care of him for us, when they demand his silver and he has none to give them."

Whether this was what happened or not, they never heard from Reuel again.

And a week later, Nahor and Terah had to sit in their father's tent and watch as Laban made Jacob the steward of his camp, master of all his flocks and herds. "If you two boys want anything," said Laban, "just ask Jacob. He'll give to you according to what we can afford, and based on what you have earned."

"Earned?" asked Terah feebly.

"Shut up, you fool," said Nahor.

"Listen to your brother," said Laban. "By 'earned,' I mean that the two of you are going to work as shepherds until you actually know something about the business of this camp. If you slack off, if you don't work and learn, I will cut you off without an inheritance."

So it was that Jacob became master in Laban's house,

second only to Laban himself, and Laban's two older sons began to learn the shepherds' craft from their cousin.

Jacob and Laban both knew who had been their benefactors in Reuel's attempt to betray them. Zilpah didn't know what this might mean for Leah, but for her it meant that both Jacob and Laban now treated her with more respect, greeting her by name and showing her other signs of favor. She had nicer clothing to wear—although the necklines were always to Leah's specifications. The other servants in the camp no longer treated her with contempt, and the rude names were no longer said openly in Zilpah's presence.

Zilpah's mother was moved to a tent of her own, and her duties were lighter and included no indignities. If Mother knew that it was Zilpah's courage and loyalty to Laban that had won her this new treatment, she never gave a sign of it. Instead, she acted as if these privileges were hers by right, and long overdue. "I always told you," she said to Zilpah, "that one day they'd realize my true worth in this camp."

Zilpah didn't bother insisting on whose value was being recognized. Her mother was happy, and so was she.

CHAPTER 19

At first Leah felt as though she was spending every day pretending to be someone else. She would catch herself becoming angry over some slight, and then stop herself, force herself to be silent. Often the best choice was simply to walk away, to go back and hide in her tent. There she would brood about the offense—someone assuming she was incapable of doing a task, or someone expecting her to know something that only people with good vision could possibly know.

Or someone praising Rachel's beauty and then falling silent when they realized Leah could hear—didn't they know that praise for Rachel was never an offense to Leah unless they showed so plainly that they thought Leah could not bear to hear it?

However it happened, whatever it was, Leah would hold her tongue and go back to her tent. There she would find that

Zilpah was little help. "You *should* be angry, mistress, they had no right!" Only Zilpah rarely understood what it was that had hurt her feelings, and often added her own inadvertent insults to the original hurt. But even at those times, Leah controlled herself, and instead of flying into a rage at Zilpah, she would ask her to run an errand, or tell her that she needed to sleep.

Zilpah wasn't stupid. She knew that Leah was getting rid of her because she had given offense. For a while she even asked, "What did I say? Tell me so I won't do it again!"

But Leah did not want to teach Zilpah how not to offend her. She wanted to teach herself how not to be offended.

She knew perfectly well what people were saying, because several women made it a point to be sure she overheard them: "There goes Leah, off to pout inside her tent again." "Well, at least that's better than her having a fit over nothing the way she usually does."

And it *was* better. The camp was more peaceful. Of course, this realization led Leah to have the obvious childish, spiteful thought: Things would be even better if I were thoughtful enough to get sick and die.

But that kind of thinking led nowhere, she knew that. It had nothing to do with walking with the Lord.

So in her brooding, instead of going over and over again how unkind people were, she would try to find excuses for them. Sometimes there was no excuse—they had clearly meant to hurt her, and it had worked. But most of the time there was no intent to offend.

When someone thought she knew something that only people with good vision could know—who it was who was visiting the camp, for instance, or how the first buds were coming out on the trees—then wasn't that a good thing?

Wasn't it proof that they had forgotten that her vision was bad?

And when they made allowances that she didn't need, and offered to help her to do things she was perfectly capable of doing, wasn't that good, too? They were just trying to help, to make her life easier.

As she trained herself to think this way, she stopped feeling hurt and angry so often. She began to be able to say, "Thank you for offering to help, but this is a job I like to do myself." Or she'd say, "It's so silly, because I know most people *can* see it, but I just can't make out things that far away." At first they almost cowered, expecting her correction to turn into a rage. But gradually they realized that she wasn't going to rage at them over such things, and then they responded more naturally, too.

It was with Zilpah that she practiced speaking kindly. It didn't come naturally to her—of that she was ashamed, now that she recognized it. And Zilpah's response was to ask her very specific questions about her malady. "Why can you see perfectly well what dress I'm carrying, but you can't see the bruise on my forehead from the stone that stupid boy threw?"

Then Leah would explain that the dress was brightly colored, and she recognized the bold striped pattern. But the bruise was not so very different in color, and the edges were gradual. "To my eyes, it's just a shadow, if I can see it at all."

"So you can see colors but only if they're really different?"

"If I get very, very close then I can see almost everything. But from farther away, everything is just different smears of color—in bright light, that is. When it's dark, then I'm almost completely blind."

Having somebody listen while she explained things was

nice—she remembered that she had had a few such conversations with Bilhah, too. And, like Bilhah, Zilpah took some care to remember what she had been told. She made fewer mistakes. She began to know when help was needed and when it wasn't. And, perhaps most important, she began explaining to other people what Leah's actual limitations were—and what they were not.

When Bilhah had tried to do this, Leah had furiously told her to stop. "I don't want you gossiping about me! Can't I have any privacy in this camp?" Now, though, Leah realized that the more people knew about her tenderness of sight, the better they'd understand her.

Of course, all this did not happen at once. There were still rages in the first few months, and now and then in the first few years. Times when someone's deliberate offense hurt her so badly that she lost control and her temper flared.

Then she would weep bitterly afterward, ashamed before the Lord and before the people of the camp. They all knew she was trying to be different now, so when she lost her temper she was sure they all said, She'll never change, she's always going to be that way. But at least the poor dear is trying! It's better than it was!

Her refuge was always the holy books. She came every morning, and even though it was hard to face Bilhah for the first few weeks, she would concentrate on the words themselves, playing them in her mind for as long as she could. The method was a good one: Bilhah reading a phrase, and then silently copying out the words on the new scroll. It gave Leah time to let the words sink in, to ponder them. She could think much faster than Bilhah could write, so it was as if each phrase held its own sermon or story as it worked out in Leah's mind.

Bilhah never became friendly or warm, and Zilpah commented on it afterward until Leah asked her to stop. "I hurt her," said Leah. "Why should she be warm?"

"Because she's nobody, for one thing," said Zilpah. "Not as big a nobody as *me* but still a nobody, and you're the lord's daughter, so she should consider herself lucky she gets to read to you!"

"She's copying the word of God. I consider myself lucky that I get to sit by her and hear the words as she reads."

"Honestly, mistress, sometimes you take this business about being kind all the time *way* too far."

"I don't think I *can* take it too far," said Leah.

Zilpah teased, of course. "Oh, yes, Robber Man, please take everything I own. And wouldn't you like to beat me with sticks for a while?"

"I mean with the people of the camp," said Leah. "I've been unkind for so long, I think it won't hurt me to try a little harder. And Bilhah isn't nobody. Neither are you. When we're there listening to the word of God, he's talking to us all the same."

"Gods don't pay attention to girls like me," said Zilpah.

"Not gods," said Leah. "How long have you been in this camp, and you still talk about gods?"

"All my life, and yes, gods. Doesn't your father have those two gods he brings out at festival time?"

"They aren't gods, they're just statues representing the Lord and his great Angel. So we remember who it is we're praying to."

"So what do the prophets do, hold those statues up to their ears to hear what the gods are saying?"

"God, not gods," said Leah. "It's the word of God, the Lord, and the prophets hear inside their hearts, weren't you listening when Jacob explained it?"

"I heard him talk about that dream he had of a ladder leading into heaven and all the angels praising the chief god and singing . . . whatever it was they sang."

"Not the chief god, the *only* God."

"Oh really? Then why call him 'the most high God' unless there are gods that aren't so high?"

"Zilpah, how can you listen to the words of the prophets and still know absolutely nothing about what they say?"

"I *try* to listen," Zilpah answered honestly. "But a girl can think her own thoughts, can't she?"

"Or fall asleep," said Leah.

"Only the once!"

"Only the once that you fell over," said Leah. "What about the dozen times that you snored a little sitting up?"

"I never."

"You often."

But it was all right that Zilpah didn't listen all that well. She was a different person, with her own desires and thoughts. The words would have their effect even if she didn't listen closely. The day would come when she would realize what she was hearing.

Just as the words came to mean more to Leah. The more she understood, the more she realized how *little* she had understood before. She wanted to go back and read everything again. But instead of demanding it, as she would have before—she could imagine herself going to her father and wailing about how unfair it was that *she* could never go back and reread things the way Bilhah could whenever she wanted—she told herself, it's good to know that even what I've already heard, I haven't truly heard because I didn't understand it. There are years ahead, till Jacob leaves and takes these books with him. Perhaps then I can think back and remember things that I didn't understand at the time, and the Wisdom of God will make them clear to me.

God could not have invited me to walk with him, if he didn't mean to show me the path. So even when the books are gone, I must believe that God will not forget me.

It was the confidence, that peace that came from the quiet hours of listening and thinking and even, occasionally, understanding with perfect clarity, that sustained her through her own failures and through the difficult times when she succeeded in curbing her temper.

And after a while, the miracle happened. She was no longer pretending. She really *didn't* get angry. She couldn't remember why she ever had. There was no reason for it. She was not ill-treated.

Finally it dawned on her: She had never really been angry at the people around her, the poor things. She had been angry at her own blindness. She had been angry at God for his unfairness. And now she wasn't angry because she no longer wished for things to be different. Her eyes were as they were. They kept her from doing certain things. But the things that mattered most to her, she could do just fine. Tender eyes would not keep her from walking in God's path.

She was no longer pretending to be someone else. Nor could she honestly say that she had become a new person—though she knew that some people spoke of her that way. She was still the same Leah she had always been. Only now she was not trying to make everyone pretend that she was the equal of Rachel. She was content to be herself. Most of the time, anyway.

If she still cried herself to sleep some nights, that was nobody's business but her own. It's not as if the pain of her limitations had gone away. She just didn't let it make her angry anymore. And she no longer used it to get her father to do her bidding.

The years went by and she got older. She developed a woman's body. And her father began allowing serious suitors to come and see her. She was pleased that the men he brought were not chosen because they were so desperate that any miserable blind girl would do. They were men of real stature in the Haran or, one of them at least, in Byblos. And some of them were still young, not older men looking for a replacement for a dead wife or, worse yet, a young second wife who would have to live under the domination of the living first wife. Father was showing her real respect.

And she strove to merit his respect, meeting the men gracefully, speaking candidly about the condition of her eyes and how it limited her—and how it didn't. She had told Father that she preferred to explain it herself, instead of having it talked about when she wasn't there. "Whatever you say, Father, they *will* assume that it's worse than you're admitting. But if I say it myself, explaining it simply, then they'll be able to see that I really *can* do the things I say I can do. And they'll also learn that I'm honest and that I'm not stupid, I can talk clearly to a man without false modesty or shame."

"Did it ever occur to you that decent girls don't talk to prospective suitors on their first visit?"

"Because they have nothing to say and for them to talk would only reveal their ignorance."

Father laughed at that, and let her speak.

But after each such meeting, it would come down to the same thing: "Father, I don't think he would be happy with a wife who worships the true and living God of Abraham and Isaac."

"Do you think I'd bring them here if they hadn't already promised that you could worship as you wish?"

"Father, they say it, and they may even think they mean it, but when they take part in the public rituals and their wife makes a point of not being there, how long before they start asking me and then begging me and then demanding that I not shame them?"

"What do you know about how men act?" Father retorted.

"Am I wrong?"

"Men are different from each other, not all the same."

"It doesn't matter. Because there's not one of these men that would let me raise my children to serve the God of Abraham and him only."

And to that, Father had no answer. Except the obvious one. "Leah, there's only one Jacob, and he's promised to your sister."

"I don't want my sister's husband. He's my teacher. He's a prophet of God. That's all he is to me, and that's enough. He can keep on being those things to me after he's married Rachel."

"He can if I'm able to talk him into staying here. I don't want him to go off and take Rachel away, but I think he's going to want to make his fortune and how can he do that as my steward?"

"Well that's easy," said Leah. "Change the terms of his bondage. Allow him to keep a certain portion of the increase of the flocks, and allow him to take men into his own service. Let him build up his household in the shadow of yours."

"But he's a proud man, and that would be a gift."

"He's been your steward for how many years now? And have you prospered? Have your flocks increased to such a degree that you now have men roaming far and wide through the grasslands?"

"A portion of the increase. Now that's a thought. To keep him here with Rachel. Not in bondage, then, and not even as a steward. More like a . . ."

"A son?"

"Partner," said Father. "I already have all the sons I need. Sometimes I think I have a few extras, though that's an evil thing for a father to say."

Leah didn't think it was evil, just accurate, but she kept that thought to herself.

"But we were talking about your husband. Leah, there aren't a lot of men who worship only the true God, and not the version of God called Ba'al."

"I know."

"If you're determined to marry only a man who will let you raise your children as you were raised . . ."

"I intend to do a much better job than *that*."

Father looked really hurt.

"Father," she said impatiently, "I intend to raise my children without their mother being dead."

"Well, that's what your mother intended, too," said Father.

"And wouldn't it have been better if she had lived?"

He nodded and looked off into space. It embarrassed

Leah, to realize that she had been so insensitive as to make a kind of joke about the death of her mother when she was too young really to remember her. Father still loved her and missed her, and her death was a hard thing for him to have to talk about, and Leah hadn't known that till now.

"Father," said Leah. "I want to be a wife and mother. But I know it may never happen. I've always known that. I thought it would be my tender eyes that caused it, but if the cause of my loneliness is that I couldn't find a husband who would serve God, then I can bear it without rancor."

Father hugged her then, and wept a little. "Oh, Leah, I want you to be happy, especially now that you—took control of your life and . . ."

"And stopped making everybody else miserable?"

"You have become again the child I adored so much when you were little. I always understood why you were so frustrated and angry, and so I bore it, but I always prayed to the Lord and his Angel that you would be happy, and I see now that my prayer has been answered."

They spoke of these same things from time to time, a bit of it here, a bit of it there. Leah knew that Father was more and more anxious for her to marry before Rachel did. "I don't want tongues to have your name in derision."

"If I don't marry, then Rachel shouldn't be held captive to my solitude. I'm happy she has a husband who adores her, and such a man! She'll marry, I won't."

"You *will* marry," said Father. "It's impossible that we won't find the right man for you."

"You're so sweet, Papa," she said. "But I can bear it, as long as you promise me that you'll never make me depend on my brothers."

"They're different men now," said Father. "Work has been good for them."

"They're not different men," said Leah. "The only difference is that they've learned to hide what they really are from you."

"I see. Leah can change, but Nahor and Terah can't."

"They hate Jacob," said Leah simply.

"They love him! They've learned everything they know from him! Well, except for what they learned from me, I'd like to think."

"They aren't the grateful kind," said Leah. "But they know *you* want them to feel that way, so they pretend in order to make you happy."

"And you know this because they've taken you into their confidence?"

"Because of how they still treat the servants when no one's looking."

"Except you."

"Remember my eyes, Father. They don't think I can see, either, and I can't—but I can hear much better than they think, so I overhear them talking."

"They're plotting again, and you didn't tell me?"

"Not plotting, Father. Just complaining. Jacob had better be long gone from here before you die, Father, or their first act will be to kill him."

"They get angry sometimes, that's all."

"I think that can be said of most murderers, don't you think?"

"What do you know about murderers?" Father laughed at the thought. "Leah, I'll find you a husband, and you won't have to worry about living in Nahor's house."

And so it went, month after month. Father always promising to find a husband, Leah patiently meeting each inappropriate man. Now and then one of them would profess to be worshippers of the true God, but Leah would quickly find out that they had no idea who the true God was. "I'd rather marry a man who is honest about not believing in the Lord than a man who pretends he believes solely in order to fool you into giving me to him."

"Oh, no," said Laban. "Now you add *honesty* to the list of requirements?"

"It wasn't already on your list?"

"I'm not sure I know any honest men, at least not in Haran or Byblos.

"Keep searching, Papa. Miracles sometimes happen."

Then she went back to her study and contemplation and prayer. Back to trying to learn how to walk with the Lord.

CHAPTER 20

To Rachel it didn't seem like seven years. It didn't feel like waiting. It was just . . . life. Each day had a morning, a sunrise, a sunset, meals and sleep, and in between, work, the smell and music of the sheep and goats and cattle, the breezes and winds, the hot sun and the cold rain, the laughter and anger of shepherds, and through it all, Jacob, like the tree in whose shade the animals gathered during the heat of day, or the water they thirstily drank. He was not at the center of Rachel's life, he was at the center of *everyone's* life.

Of course he paid more attention to Rachel than to anyone else—but so had Father, all her life. So had everyone. She barely noticed it; only when someone else muttered or laughed about it did she realize that a man too busy to talk to anyone else always had time to talk to her, and not "later," when he had more time, but now. Aware of it, she tried not to abuse it, and more than once felt a little guilty when she realized that her urgent business had not really been all that urgent, after all. Still, she kept it in balance. Jacob was important to her. She was proud of him. Proud to have everyone know she belonged to him, at least by promise.

But what did it mean to belong to him? For six of the seven years, nothing at all. Didn't her life go on as it always had? Except that Leah was not so prickly and hard to get along with, except that her brothers Nahor and Terah were always in the camp now, and actually working, how was life different? Even having Bilhah in attendance was not a burden. She was an independent girl, never slavish. Instead of fawning over her the way her sisters-in-law, Asta and Deloch, made their servants do, Bilhah had duties of her own that had nothing to do with Rachel, and when they were together, it was more like fellow workers on a shared project than like mistress and handmaiden. Rachel wasn't sure they were friends, but they got along well.

Everything went well. Everything.

So why did it all have to change?

It began when Jacob announced that it had been six years since the agreement between him and Father for Rachel's hand in marriage. For Jacob to announce the date was not unusual—he kept the calendar of the camp, for the obvious reason that he was better with reading the stars and keeping the count of days than the priests in the nearby towns. As Jacob said to her once, "They're so impressed with their own knowledge of numbers and of the portents of stars that they forget it's all supposed to mean something about how long and short the days are, and how high the sun is at zenith, and how far south of true west and east at setting and rising."

None of which mattered to Rachel in the least, so the other dates he announced only mattered when they changed the routine of the camp. It's as if Jacob controlled the flow of time. When he said it was time for lambing, the lambs began to drop. When he announced that it was planting time for beans, the beans went into the ground. Leaves sprouted on limbs when he told them to. Even the locusts came when he said they would, and Rachel did not understand how he could know when they would be bad and when their coming would do little harm.

"They have a cycle," said Jacob. "Everything has a cycle, if you know what it is. Why should a man have to tell a *woman* that?"

"They *say* we're tied to the moon," said Rachel, "but that's nonsense. The time never comes on a woman at the exact same phase of the moon."

"A cycle of your own, and not perfect, either," said Jacob. "Because the things of human beings are never as perfect as the exact cycles of heaven."

"Why not?" said Rachel. "Didn't God make us too?"

"He also made us free," said Jacob. "So we don't follow our cycles so faithfully."

"If it were up to me, I'd have no cycle at *all*."

She had meant it frivolously, as a joke, but it made Jacob's face turn grave. "The cycle of women is the power of life. Creation by men is always slight. We make things that break. But women have the gift of God to make babies. That is as great as any priesthood, and no one has to ordain you to it, God fills the wombs of the women he chooses as his co-creators, and they bring forth fruit in their season, and their children grow up to have voices that can praise God."

"I think men have something to do with it," said Rachel. "If I'm wrong, there are a lot of rams and bulls and cocks and stallions who strut about nothing."

"Yes, the man struts, but the woman is the earth in which the seed grows. So don't speak ill of that cycle, painful and unclean as it may be. It's the great cycle of life, and God put the calendar of that life in every woman's body, as surely as he put it in the heavens."

It made her feel dreamy and wonderful to have him speak that way of the discomforts of her withdrawing days, when she was trapped in her tent, irritable and uncomfortable and untouchable, while Bilhah tended to her, bringing her meals and carrying away her rags for washing.

She and Jacob could talk about *anything*, and he would find reasons why they should honor and praise and thank the Lord; and yet it was still about her, too, and whatever she said seemed to make him think *she* was more wonderful than before. It was exhilarating to have a man so gifted by God, so respected by all the people in the camp, look to her as if she were somehow even more worthy of honor than he was.

And then it was the end of the sixth year of her betrothal, and now everything was changed.

Because each thing that happened was now happening for the last time. Shearing, lambing, bringing the flocks in, taking the flocks out, she could not help but say to herself, I do this for the last time this year. Next spring, next summer, next autumn I will not be coming out with the sheep, because a good wife of a powerful man does not come out and work with her hands. Does not let herself be familiar with the servants, the shepherds; they see her face, they show respect, but she doesn't take the lambs out of the shepherds' arms and minister to them herself. Nor does she bend over to harvest the beans, or carry a jar of water up from the well because everyone else is busy.

It put a touch of sadness into everything she did. But more than that, she began to be filled with dread. For she did not know yet what she would be doing instead, or whether she'd be good at it, or enjoy it. Because she had never seen her mother doing the things that the mistress of the camp should do, the only married women she knew at all well were Deloch and Asta, Nahor's and Terah's wives. But they were the wives of *sons*, not of lords of a camp, and they were not particularly good men at that—she loved her brothers, but she knew they were lazy, among several unvirtues. So their wives could hardly show Rachel what she was going to be.

When she spoke of this to Bilhah, once, the answer was quick—and a bit impertinent, but that was Bilhah's way. "I don't think you have to worry right away about assuming the duties of the mistress of a great camp."

"What do you mean? Jacob is a prince, a priest, the keeper of the books."

"He also is your father's overseer, and not the lord of anything, or the prince of anything. Where are his men? Who is owed bread at his table?"

"Jacob won't continue as Father's overseer," said Rachel. "He's only serving Father for my sake."

"Fine," said Bilhah. "But please tell me where he'll go, once you're married?"

In all her daydreaming and contemplation up in the hills for more than six years of betrothal, Rachel had never thought of that problem. Jacob couldn't go home—the threats of Esau were well-known. He had no herds of his own. For all that

Rachel could see, Jacob owned nothing but his clothing and the holy books.

"He can't stay here," said Rachel. "And why would he? He serves Father to earn *me*, and once he . . ."

"Once he *has* you," said Bilhah helpfully.

Has me, thought Rachel. Once he possesses me . . ."Well, then, I suppose *I'm* his . . . flock."

Bilhah tried, but she couldn't help but laugh at that. An easy laugh. Rachel wanted to tell her to stop it, but then Bilhah wouldn't know if it was her mistress telling her not to laugh, or her friend.

"He can't shear you," said Bilhah. "Lovely as your hair might be—and it is very nice hair—it doesn't grow fast enough."

"It can't be woven into cloth," said Rachel, playing the game with her.

"Well, it *can*, but it unravels so fast."

"And I wouldn't want to trust my life to a rope twisted out of my own hair."

"But if you put it in the stew along with lentils and greens," suggested Bilhah.

"Stringy," said Rachel.

"But flavorful."

When the jesting was over, though, Rachel had to face the fact that she had no idea what Jacob was planning, once they were married. Where would they go? Into some other man's service? Who but Laban would treat Jacob as the prophet, as the keeper of the Holy Books? Or was Jacob planning to go back to Beersheba and confront Esau, demand his inheritance?

If he does, how long will Esau let him live? Am I marrying

this great and good man, letting him take me away from the world I've known, only to become a widow in another land?

And what if Esau claims brother-right? Suppose he has someone murder Jacob, and then claims me as *his* bride? Father can't even come reclaim me—the bride-price was paid, and I would belong to Jacob's family, then.

My life only makes sense as Jacob's wife, not as his widow. And even as his wife, what are we, who are we, *where* are we? In this camp, Jacob will be the husband of the daughter of the lord of the camp. Anywhere else, and he's a man with no property and a pretty wife.

There are men who would kill him for a wife like me, if he has no coterie of armed men at his command. She remembered the story of Abraham and Sarah in Egypt—though she had also heard the story as if it happened to Isaac and Rebekah. The Lord protected them, drying up the wombs of the women of Egypt—or Abimelech—she would have to ask Jacob which was true.

For the first time, she wondered what it was like for the women of Egypt. *They* had not taken another man's wife into their household. And suddenly the Lord dried them up like raisins, taking away their very reason for life. The Lord had protected Abraham and Sarah, yes, but who was protecting these women? Who would replace the children they hadn't borne?

Perhaps the Lord, in his mercy, gave each of these women another year before they passed the age of bearing, so they lost no child by their temporary barrenness.

And it would have been a blessing, for the women who would die in their next childbirth. Being barren gave them extra months, or an extra year, of life. So for some it was merciful, and for others tragic.

Is there anything God can do in this world that is truly a blessing for everyone? A blessing for one man can be a cursing for another.

She thought of Nahor and Terah. What was Jacob to *them?* To Father, Jacob's coming was a blessing—his flocks and herds, now under Jacob's wise and energetic management, had expanded greatly, and his well-trained fighting men were able to protect them in farflung meadows and camps. For Father, a blessing. But for Nahor and Terah, Jacob's coming pointed up to Father just how wasteful and meaningless their lives were, how faithless they were to their wives. Everyone in camp knew of the time when Father railed at Nahor, "Jacob isn't even married, and yet he is perfectly faithful to Rachel, while you, who have a woman you can cover whenever you want, you can't keep yourself from sneaking off to the whores of Haran!"

Naturally, Nahor had denied everything, but Deloch was sullen for days, because Father's accusation was true. The worst thing, though, was that Father had no idea how such a comparison made Nahor and Terah hate Jacob. Why can't you be like my future son-in-law! Father said to them, and so Nahor and Terah grew angrier and angrier at Jacob.

So Jacob's coming was a blessing to Father, but a curse to Nahor and Terah.

Or was it?

Fearful of losing their inheritance, hadn't they come home? Hadn't they abandoned their friends in the city? Weren't they present in the lives of their children now? It was so funny and so sad when Terah didn't know which babies were his and which were Nahor's.

They were angry at Father and they hated Jacob for forcing them to do the work of their father's camp—but it made them into true shepherds, so that when Father died, they would know enough about the work of the camp to govern it, instead of turning everything over to a steward.

So Jacob's coming had made Nahor and Terah into better men. A blessing—though they hadn't wanted it.

What about me? thought Rachel. A blessing, to have this good man in my life. Surely God loves me to send me this husband.

And yet . . . everything I love about my life is going to be taken from me when this year ends. All my certainties will be replaced by uncertainty. If Jacob died today, it would break my heart—but it would not change my life for long. After we're married, though, if he dies, then as the widow of a poor man am I not also destroyed?

What a selfish thought. She was disgusted with herself for thinking it.

Why not think of Jacob? When he marries me, what dowry does he get? He might hope Father will give him herds and flocks of his own—and Father might, he's not an ungenerous man. But no dowry is owed. Jacob is entitled to nothing, he can count on nothing. For all these years, this man of such proud heritage has served as a bondsman in Father's household. A prince, bowed down . . . for my sake!

Am I a blessing in his life? He thinks I am. But in truth we're a mixed blessing to each other, bad along with good, sacrifices along with benefits.

So why do we do it?

She asked this aloud one time, when she and Leah were sitting together shelling beans into their aprons. "Why do we do it?"

"Do what?" asked Leah. "Or am I supposed to guess?"

In the old days, those words would have been nasty and Rachel would have fallen silent. But now Leah spoke them with a laugh, as if she enjoyed Rachel's habit of speaking as if everyone already knew what she had been thinking before she spoke.

"Marry," said Rachel. "It's so awful, how marriage changes things."

"It's about babies," said Leah. "Or didn't you hear of that?"

"It isn't *marriage* that makes the babies," said Rachel. "Or do the beasts have weddings we don't see?"

"Beasts rut in the fields," said Leah. "Humans marry."

"But why?" said Rachel. "Why can't we just . . . make the babies but stay at home with our parents? Why do I have to go off with Jacob and live as a stranger somewhere? It must have been awful for Rebekah."

"Not awful," said Leah. "Just hard."

"Oh, yes, as if you know." Rachel knew that in years past, her scornful tone would have caused a fight. Leah was so much better a sister and friend since she had taken to reading the holy books. So Rachel was able to speak more freely— almost like when they were little.

"You don't know either," said Leah—keeping her temper.

"I just thought—I just don't want to leave home."

"Well, first, what makes you think you're leaving? Where's Jacob going to go, anyway?"

"How can he stay? Is Father going to let me be married to the *steward?*"

Leah laughed. "He won't be steward, silly girl. He'll be Father's *son*. Sons inherit. Sons rule in their father's name."

"Nahor and Terah will hate that."

"Yes," said Leah. "It's a good thing neither one of them is a man of action, don't you think?"

"Jacob won't want to make enemies of them. He'll leave."

"As soon as he *can*, he'll leave," Leah said. "But he can't leave when he has *nothing*. How would you live?"

"It's frightening," said Rachel.

"But forget this idea about doing without marriage," said Leah. "It would never work."

"Why not?" said Rachel.

"Well, for one thing, if Father and Mother hadn't married, and we were just living with Mother, then when she died, where would we have gone?"

"With *her* father," said Rachel.

"But you've eliminated *all* fathers, haven't you?" said Leah. "And Mother's mother died in bearing Aunt Mirya. So our mother would have been an orphan."

"I know we need to marry," said Rachel. "I know it. I just wish . . ."

"You don't have to marry if you don't want to," said Leah. "Father's promise doesn't truly bind *you*. You're still young."

"Most girls my age are already married."

"My age, too," said Leah. "Does that make it the right time?"

"Maybe I'm just the wrong girl."

"Jacob thinks you're the only one."

"All he knows about me is my stupid pretty face."

"You've had plenty of chances to show him what else you are."

"It's the only thing he loves about me."

"If you think that, then you don't know Jacob."

"I *don't* know him." Only when she said it did she realize it was true.

"He knows *you* and he loves you," said Leah. "He marries the whole woman, not just the face."

"Why doesn't he marry *you?*" said Rachel. *"You're* the one filled with thoughts of God. You're the one who can read and write."

Leah said nothing.

Rachel realized what she had just said. "Oh, Leah, I never thought—do you love him? Do you wish you were marrying him?"

Leah laughed. "He knows you and loves you. He knows *me* and thinks very little of me, dear sister. When I marry, I want to marry a man who doesn't think I'm weak and foolish and vain and malicious."

"He doesn't think those things of you!"

"Jacob's not a man to lie, and those were his words."

"When did you have such a quarrel?"

"He didn't spout them all in a single list," said Leah. "But over the years, he's used those words, not to refer to *me*, of course, but the lesson was clear enough: You're like *this*, Leah, you're like *that*, now stop it."

"So he cares about you."

"The Lord knows how weak and unworthy I am. He brought Jacob here to love you, but to correct me. I only hope I've learned all that I *can* learn, before Jacob takes away not only you, but the Holy books as well."

"So you do think he'll leave."

"Someday, yes. Not the day after the wedding!"

"I'm not a *wife*," said Rachel. She meant that she was not a wifely kind of woman, but of course Leah had to tease her by pretending not to understand.

"No one is, until they are," said Leah.

"If you think that made sense . . ."

"I know who I'm talking to, Rachel," said Leah with a laugh. "I didn't expect it to make sense to *you*."

"I'll tell on you for being mean to me." That was part of the game these days, to make fun of how they used to be with each other, during the bad times.

"Father won't care," said Leah, "and God already knows. And they both forgive me."

"Whoever told you *that* doesn't know God!" said Rachel.

"Hush," said Leah, for the first time letting her voice show genuine warning.

"Leah," said Rachel softly. "Why do things have to change?"

"They always will."

"The sheep never change."

"Oh really? Then why do you watch them so closely?"

"They *do* things, stupid things, but no matter what they do, they're still sheep."

"Maybe that's how God looks at us," said Leah. "We do things, but we're still his children."

"Why did God make me such a happy child, if he only meant to change me into something else?"

"He sends us into the world as babies so we can *learn* to be people," said Leah.

"Well, I don't want to be people," said Rachel.

"You want to stay a baby forever?"

"I'm happy *now*."

"Why do you sound miserable?"

"Because God sent Jacob here to change *everything*."

"Because Jacob was willing to wait for you, you've had seven years without change. Thank God for those years, Rachel. And thank God for a good husband, when there are so many bad ones."

Rachel knew good advice when she heard it. "Why can't you snap at me and tell me I'm stupid?" she said. "Then I could get angry at you instead of having to pay attention to the wise things you say."

"Am I wise today?" said Leah. "Well, how nice. I can't wait for you to get smart enough to say wise things to *me*."

"The beans are done."

"That's why my fingers feel so empty as I shell them," said Leah.

"*My* beans are done."

"And mine are nearly done," said Leah. "But you can run off, little sister, and play with the other babies if you want."

Rachel stuck out her tongue.

"I'm not blind," said Leah. "I know a tongue-poke when I almost see it."

"Give me some of your beans," said Rachel. "I'll help you finish."

"Just remember," said Leah. "When you're married, you won't have *me* to remind you of how good your life is compared to mine."

"And you won't have *me* to accuse of being an ungrateful brat."

"I'll miss you so much," said Leah dryly.

"You *will*, you know," said Rachel.

"And you'll miss me," said Leah.

"Yes, but I *know* it."

"If you throw that bean at me, I'll take it all back."

"You see everything."

"I don't have to *see* when I know you so well."

Rachel wondered if anyone really knew anyone all that well.

I don't even know myself as well as Leah does, Rachel realized. I don't know anything or anybody. How am I supposed to be someone's wife and mother, when I'm such a hopelessly ignorant child?

Another year, Lord! Give me just another year!

Or two.

PART X

WARNINGS

CHAPTER 21

I t was a shearing day, when the normal duties of the camp were all set aside, except for a few who still prepared food and hauled water. Everyone else was bringing sheep in and out of the makeshift pens that covered all the land round about Padan-aram, except for those strong enough to hold the terrified sheep absolutely still, while those with dexterity and experience sliced away great fleeces of wool. Whether it was human blood or the blood of sheep, it was a mark of pride and cause for celebration when a whole shearing could be accomplished without any slicing of flesh. "Shearers, not butchers!" cried Laban. "That's what we are today!"

It was Laban who made the great show of leadership, thought Bilhah, but she knew from the comments of others that before Jacob came, there was blood in the wool most years, and usually roast mutton as their consolation for a fatal mistake in the shearing. There had never been a man lost, thank the Lord, but they heard of such things happening in other camps, a knife going awry and slicing someone's thigh. From such a wound the blood would flow so copiously that the victim would be dead in moments, and all the wool on the floor ruined. Who would wear a garment or even tread on a rug that was brown from the blood of a dead shepherd?

Under Jacob's leadership, though, they had practiced before the shearing began. Instead of plunging right in, the experienced ones talking the newer men and women through their work, Jacob had them act it out first, with no sheep at all, and then with a sheep but with sticks instead of knives.

That was how he was able to tell which men were too old now, their eyes too weak to go on shearing. It was hard on them to be turned out of the shearing shed and forced to go back to guiding the sheep in and out of the pens, but as Laban explained to the men who complained bitterly that first year, "I'd rather have you grumbling out here in the pens than dead with your blood all over the fleece. Or worse, with *my* blood all over, because you missed and slashed my belly open!"

By the third year, the complaints were over. Two clean years in a row were persuasion enough, and now, in Jacob's seventh spring shearing, the shearers were proud of being part of what they now called "the dance," when they went through the motions to make sure everyone was up to snuff, and give the newer ones a sense of what it felt like to do the job.

The "dance" had been yesterday. Today, the fleece was piling up, more than ever before, and cleaner and whiter, too. It was wealth they were carrying away to stack for carding, and under Jacob's leadership, everyone could see that his methods had led to prosperity beyond anyone's experience.

Bilhah's job, since she had never really become good with

the animals, was to haul water for the shearers to wash their hands, and for the whetstones they used to keep their blades sharp. She knew enough to stay back out of the way, pouring the water into the basins only when the shearers were between sheep.

She happened to be in the tent where Jacob was, oversee-ing the work of Terah, who had been commanded by his father to take a hand at shearing this year or see it cut off. Jacob had worked with him especially during the weeks before the shearing, to make sure he was ready, and Bilhah could see that Terah had, despite his complaints, learned well.

It was while she was watching Terah shear a sheep that Zilpah approached her, tapping her on the arm. "Talk to me when you come out," she whispered into Bilhah's ear.

Bilhah nodded, and dreaded keeping the appointment. Zilpah always acted as if she had all the important secrets of the universe to tell, when usually it was something quite ordi-nary or even unnecessary.

But Bilhah knew her judgment was unfair, even as she thought of it. Zilpah had changed in her years of service with Leah. She dressed more modestly, and without any particular flair. At first Bilhah had assumed it was because Zilpah was trying not to overshadow her mistress Leah—but in truth, under Zilpah's care Leah became more lovely, her hair always nicely arranged, her clothing always clean and well-chosen. There was little chance of Zilpah taking attention away from Leah now.

So Zilpah's modesty must arise from some other motive, and Bilhah had just about decided that it was actually Zilpah's nature to be modest, and her immodesty had been the result of her own fears and uncertainty. Whatever the reason for it, though, in the years since Zilpah became Leah's handmaid, she had turned into a woman of some grace and modesty.

I only think ill of her, thought Bilhah, because I resent the fact that she has prospered where I failed. Together, she and Leah have turned into good women, the one ready to take her place as a great lady, the other her honorable handmaiden. And I am . . . what? My lady is still a rough boyish girl who dislikes dressing as a grown woman, even though her wedding is not many months away. And when she does dress up to show her beauty—at feasts, or when her father asks it of her—it's someone else who tends to her, not her ostensible handmaiden, because I scarcely know how to do up my own hair, let alone a lady's.

Zilpah has shown me up.

And even though it annoys me, I can't bring myself to care enough to do anything about it. I could learn how to do hair, if I wanted to. But my real work is in Jacob's dooryard. I have copied so many books in these seven years—faithfully, and in a good hand—that surely I've exhausted his supply. How large a sack had he carried on his back when he came here all those years ago?

I have put the words down on scrolls, I have read them aloud to Leah and Zilpah and even, on rare occasions, to Rachel; and I have also written them in my heart. But no one can see such adornment. As I walk about the camp, the words of God don't draw anyone's eye to me, and no one sighs at my beauty when I pass them by. It's foolish of me to be envious of Zilpah and Leah, but I am. For are they not also as beautifully adorned in their hearts as I am? Are the scriptures not as much a part of their memory as they are of mine?

I should have learned from them, as Zilpah learned reading

from me. How will I ever marry, when there's nothing about me to recommend me to a man?

The sheep was finished, and Bilhah quickly filled the basins. She had learned what order to fill them in, so she wouldn't be in the way, and by the time she was done, the shearing of the next sheep had already begun.

Outside the tent, Zilpah was waiting, and fell into step beside her, reaching for the water jar.

"I can carry it," said Bilhah.

"Let it be that I'm helping you," said Zilpah.

"What's the great secret, Zilpah?"

"Leah is very worried and doesn't know what to do, and she needs your advice."

"She has only to ask. I see her nearly every day."

"It's a strange kind of question, and I think she's afraid to ask you, because it's about your mistress."

"About Rachel? They're sisters. They talk. They like each other. Why do they need us as go-betweens?"

"Leah's worried. Rachel seems not to realize that her wedding is coming nearer, only a few months away."

"You can be sure she hasn't forgotten."

"No, no," said Zilpah. "That's not the question. It's . . . Leah worries that . . . does Rachel know the ways of men and women?"

It took a moment for Bilhah to realize what the question meant. "She knows the way of rams and ewes," she said.

"Well, yes, of course, but . . . my mother explained things to me long ago," said Zilpah, "and there came a day when it was clear to me that Leah did *not* know anything, and so I offered to explain it to her. It came as quite a shock, and so now she's worried that Rachel seems so blithe about her wedding because she doesn't know what's expected of her."

"Rachel knows. She and Jacob even talk about it."

"What?"

"Not about themselves, but about . . . no, don't look so horrified, Zilpah! Jacob thought of this very problem, and made sure his own wife would not be taken by surprise. That's the kind of careful man he is."

"Well," said Zilpah. "But I wonder if he knows that much himself. Seven years here, and I've never heard anything about him lying with a woman. Have you?"

"Not a word," said Bilhah. "And he doesn't visit harlots in Haran or Byblos, either, or we'd hear tales from the men who travel with him."

"So how much does he even know?"

"It's none of our business, Zilpah," said Bilhah.

"My mistress is making it her business," said Zilpah.

"Then let her talk to Rachel and keep us out of it!"

Zilpah rolled her eyes.

Bilhah thought she understood. "Leah's too shy and modest to discuss it herself, but she can send you to me, and then expect me to—"

"She's *tried* to discuss it with Rachel, don't you see? And *I've* tried, and Rachel just walks away. She refuses to talk about it."

"What makes you think I'd do any better? If she doesn't want to talk about it, then—"

"Leah says it means that Rachel's frightened."

"Rachel isn't afraid of anything," said Bilhah. "Least of all Jacob. Her whole life revolves around him. She adores him. How can she possibly be afraid of him?"

"He's like a brother to her," said Zilpah. "That's what Leah's afraid of. They're so close that Leah thinks Rachel is afraid that marriage is going to ruin everything, and so she refuses to think about it or talk about how their love for each other has to change into something it hasn't been before."

"What makes you think she'll listen to *me* when she won't listen to her own sister? It's not as if I have any knowledge of it. You're the only one of the four of us who even knew her own mother, at least long enough to learn about marriage."

"I don't want you—I mean, Leah doesn't want you to talk to *Rachel*. She wants you to warn *Jacob*."

"Me? Jacob? I can't talk to Jacob about—"

"You're the only one who can."

"Then *no* one can."

"It would be extremely improper for the unmarried older sister of the bride to talk to Jacob about how unready Rachel is for their coming marriage. And as for me, I behaved in ways, when Jacob first came here, that make it very inappropriate for me to bring up such a topic, because he'll think I haven't changed since then. And don't ask."

"I wasn't going to," said Bilhah. Though of course she was.

"You work with him every day. With the holy books. You have no history of . . . provocation."

I'm plain and men don't think of love when they look at me, that's what you mean, thought Bilhah. Again she kept the words to herself.

"And you're Rachel's handmaiden. You have the right to speak plainly to her husband about private matters."

They reached the well and Zilpah lowered the bag to draw out water.

"Whoever her handmaiden is when she gets married, *she'll* have that right," said Bilhah, "but not me."

Zilpah laughed. "What do you mean? Do you think you *won't* be her handmaiden?"

"I'm free," said Bilhah. "I'm not Laban's, to be given away as a wedding present. I've *acted* as her handmaiden, that's all—and not very well, I might remind you, in case you're the only one who hasn't noticed."

"You could learn to do better if you cared."

"But I don't care," said Bilhah, "because I will *not* be her handmaiden after she's married, so there's no reason to learn it any better than she wants me to, and she's never wanted me to do more than I do."

"So what will you do when she marries Jacob?"

"I'll go to Byblos," said Bilhah, "and become a scribe."

The look of shock on Zilpah's face reminded Bilhah of why she had never spoken of this plan to anyone. "Women can't be scribes," said Zilpah.

"Obviously they can, since that's what I've been doing every morning for seven years."

"They can't get *paid* for it."

"Well I'm not going to do it for *free*," retorted Bilhah.

Zilpah shook her head. "What a pair you and Rachel are. Rachel refuses to admit she's about to get married, and you refuse to admit that you're stuck as somebody's servant as surely as I am."

"I'm free," said Bilhah fiercely.

"You're only free if you have choices," said Zilpah.

"I have choices."

"You have delusions," said Zilpah.

"Maybe I'll *marry* a scribe."

Zilpah sighed. "*Please* talk to Jacob and warn him about his bride."

"Warn him that she's beautiful and loves him devotedly?"

Zilpah flicked a drop of water in Bilhah's face. "Warn him that he's going to have a terrified, unready woman in his bed. Warn him that if he thinks she's ready, he might give her such a horrifying wedding night as will stand between them all the days of their lives."

"And this is the wisdom that has been stewed up in the pot of Leah's tent?"

"When a woman is terrified," said Zilpah, "her body isn't ready, and her husband can *hurt* her without meaning to. And then she'll be terrified forever after."

"Where did you hear that!" said Bilhah scornfully.

"From my mother. It happened to her, and she says it's happened to others. A woman who isn't filled with desire can't be *loved* that way, she can only be forced."

"And I'm supposed to talk like this with *Jacob?*"

"You will if you love Rachel."

"You and Leah can love Rachel and talk to Jacob. I won't do it."

"You are a selfish girl and a faithless friend." Zilpah turned to walk away.

Bilhah's face turned red in shame. "How could I explain anything to him when I don't have any idea what you're talking about!"

Zilpah turned around and looked at her witheringly. "Say what I said, and Jacob will understand."

"Have your mother talk to him!" Bilhah said. She hoisted the water jug onto her shoulder and walked back to the shearing shed.

Somehow she was letting Rachel down, she understood that, but she could not discuss this with Jacob. She could hardly bear to think of it herself. Until now, she had thought she knew everything about the ways of men and women. But now it seemed that there were things about women's bodies—about her own body—that Zilpah and Leah both knew, and Bilhah herself had no idea of.

Jacob couldn't hurt Rachel, ever. A good man like him, he'd *know*. Leah and Zilpah were worried about nothing. Or else they were trying to trick Bilhah into doing something outrageous. Was it a joke they were playing on her? Or was the joke on Rachel? Or on Jacob himself?

Whatever game they were playing, Bilhah wasn't going to play. There were things that even a slave handmaiden shouldn't be asked to do, and a free girl certainly didn't have to do them.

CHAPTER 22

The shearing was nearly done when Choraz came home, the little brother who had gone into the service of Prince Kedar. He came covered in glory, leading three armed men on horseback and five camels, four of them loaded with riches, and one of them bearing his wife, an Elamite woman who, he assured them all, was not captured in a raid but married him willingly, "from her father's house."

The woman's name was Hassaweh, or that's what Choraz called her, when he was speaking to them in Hebrew; talking between themselves, they spoke her language, which sounded strange, jabbery and whispery, both at once.

"Hassaweh is the glory of my tent!" cried Choraz for all to hear.

And so it was that after Choraz had hugged Father, and then helped his lady from her camel, it was Rachel's duty—because she was there, and Mother was dead, and Leah couldn't see well

315

enough—to embrace the haughty and beautiful woman and welcome her to the camp of Laban at Padan-aram.

Without a smile, Hassaweh looked around her and said to Rachel, in heavily accented Hebrew, "I see many tents, but not a hundred, and many animals, but not ten thousand."

Rachel was surprised at the woman's ignorance; if Choraz had told her the size of his father's camp and herds, then what kind of wife would speak in a way that suggested she doubted his honesty?

"Perhaps you're not used to shepherds' ways," said Rachel, speaking quietly.

"Perhaps not," said Hassaweh, "if one sheep counts as ten, and a single tent as five."

This was too much to bear. Rachel didn't even try to keep the scorn out of her voice. "If the herds and flocks were all here at once, they'd starve in two days. Father keeps them widely scattered through the hills and plains of Syria, and each flock is watched over by men enough to dwell in the tents that you don't see here."

Hassaweh held very still. "This is something that a shepherd's wife would know without asking," she said.

Rachel realized it was a question. "Yes," she said. "But not a warrior's wife."

For the first time, Hassaweh looked at her, face to face. "You have saved me from embarrassing myself in front of this company."

Privately, Rachel thought that a good wife would not have said anything to disparage her husband's father even if her calculation of their poverty had been correct. But she kept this view to herself. If Hassaweh was humble enough to admit she'd been wrong, and to be grateful that Rachel had corrected her before she blundered in front of the whole company, that spoke well enough of her manners.

This raised her higher in Rachel's esteem than Deloch and Asta, the wives of Choraz's older brothers Nahor and Terah. Rachel could not remember them ever thanking anyone for anything—least of all for sparing them from embarrassment. Of course, that was partly because they seemed to have no concept of what embarrassment *was*.

"Welcome to the camp of my father Laban," said Rachel. "As wife of my brother Choraz, you are my sister." And then, very softly, leaning in so only Hassaweh could hear, she added, "And I assure you that you have married the best of my brothers."

Hassaweh greeted that with a low chuckle. "I have no doubt that I have married the best of men," she said.

"There are so many ways to judge a man," said Rachel. "Perhaps God has blessed both you and me with the man who is best in the ways that matter most to us."

"You're married?" said Hassaweh. "Choraz said that neither of his sisters had a husband."

"Soon to be married," said Rachel.

"Ah, yes. You're the daughter who is going to marry the bondservant."

Without waiting for a response, Hassaweh walked over to her husband and was presented to her new father-in-law.

Rachel was annoyed, but also amused. No one could say that Choraz had married a shy woman. Rachel rather envied her boldness, even as she resented her slighting reference to Jacob. But what could she expect? Rachel had no illusions about how her brothers must have depicted Jacob in their messages to Choraz.

A few moments later, Zilpah led Leah out to greet Choraz and meet his wife. Rachel hung back, to give Leah a chance to form her own impression of Hassaweh. But she was close enough to overhear Hassaweh's greeting: "Ah, Leah. You're the beautiful one, I see."

That one really stung, despite Rachel's lifelong confidence that she didn't care about beauty. It had been easy to believe this, because she was always recognized as the most beautiful of women.

So . . . what did Hassaweh mean by this? Did beauty mean something different in her country? Or was Hassaweh trying to be malicious toward Rachel? Did she mean to be over-heard? Or was she merely flattering Leah?

Rachel looked carefully at her older sister and realized that over the years, Leah had grown into a beauty, of a different sort than Rachel, but a beauty all the same. There was a glow to her face—a smile in her eyes even when there was none on her lips.

Why shouldn't a stranger come here and see Leah as being more beautiful than me? She's truly a woman, her mind full of wisdom and her heart full of faith in God. And what am I? A shepherd girl. Mine could easily seem a simple, homespun sort of beauty. In the eyes of a woman like Hassaweh, who has seen so much more of the world, perhaps what I have is a common kind of prettiness, while Leah's radiant grace is rarer and more highly valued.

And if that's so, isn't it what I've wished for so many times? That Leah be the beautiful one so Rachel could be left in peace?

Then a dark thought: Is this what Jacob sees, too? Over these years, has he come to see Leah as the more beautiful one? Does he regret having bargained for me? He is too honorable ever to say such a thing, not to me, not to anyone—after all, who is his confidante in camp, if not me?

She instantly answered her own question: Bilhah is with him almost every day, copying the holy books. Leah listens and learns, and Zilpah too is with them much of the time. While I alone remain ignorant of Jacob's birthright.

What was I thinking? For nearly seven years I've indulged myself, tending the sheep because it pleased me to wander through the hills and take care of these patient animals. Because Jacob spent so much of his time with me there, and talked to me with such respect, it never crossed my mind that I don't even know what he says to my sister and these two handmaidens, mine and hers. They share something that I'm left out of, and how can I possibly know that what I share with Jacob is more important to him than what he shares with them?

How beautiful is Leah in *his* eyes?

Rachel felt her eyes stinging with tears. How absurd! I don't know what Hassaweh meant by what she said, and I certainly don't know that Jacob or anyone else would agree with her even if she meant it. And now I'm on the verge of weeping because someone said my sister was more beautiful than me.

If I feel this, now, at my age, how did Leah feel when she heard such things over and over again?

If I can't stop myself from feeling this way, at my age, how was it for Leah, when we were both little girls?

That was the thought that made the tears spill out onto her cheeks. Rachel quickly caught them with her sleeve, but when she looked up from wiping her face, she saw Hassaweh looking at her. No expression on her face, but looking quite steadily.

She meant me to hear, Rachel thought. She meant me to cry.

I don't like my brother's new wife very much.

And yet . . . hadn't Rachel learned something from Hassaweh's bit of praise for Leah? What was Hassaweh's intention—to make me cry, or to teach me something about myself and about my sister?

Or did she intend nothing at all?

Rachel couldn't take her eyes off Hassaweh. She stood so straight; she moved so gracefully. This is a great lady, thought Rachel. Everyone can see now that neither Leah nor I is graceful or even womanly. But how could we be? We had no lady mother to imitate and learn from. The only women in our lives were servants, until Terah and Nahor made their choices among the daughters of greedy or ambitious friends of Father's, and what would we possibly learn from *them?* Instead we learned to walk like shepherds.

Or rather, I did. Leah learned to walk . . . carefully. Perhaps that was all that Hassaweh meant by what she said. Leah moves like a lady, yes, her feet carefully and lightly stepping along the ground, while I run like a boy as often as not, and when I walk, I shamble and slouch . . . and now that I think about it, haven't several of the servants told me to stand up tall, and I just ignored them because . . . because I was already beautiful, so why did I need to change anything about myself?

Whether Hassaweh is malicious or merely foreign, I can still learn from her. Try to become more of the sort of wife that a great prince like Jacob can be proud of.

He *is* a great prince, even if he has no flocks of his own, or men to serve him.

He's a great prince because he has the birthright of Abraham, the holy books, which I have treated as if they were nothing. While I have shown that I value the very sheep that Jacob knows so much about, but owns none of. Is it possible . . . have I hurt Jacob with my lack of interest in his books? Was that why he never pressed me to come and study with my sister and our handmaidens? Because he thought I despised the treasure he had, and treasured that which he lacked?

What does he think of me? What does he think I think of *him?*

Why do I have to get married when I don't know anything about my husband and he knows nothing about me?

Her mind kept spinning the same questions, doubts, worries, and self-condemnations throughout the evening's feasting. It didn't help that Hassaweh was openly scornful of the way men and women ate separately. "Ever since I married him, Choraz and I have shared everything," she said. "Now, because we're here, he and I have to eat separately?"

The servants all busied themselves at serving the meal to the men in Father's dining tent, so they didn't have to show how shocked they were by Hassaweh's words. Rachel herself couldn't think of anything to say. She had thought of herself as a rebellious girl, shepherding with the men and caring little for dressing and acting like a lady. But in all her rebelliousness, it had never occurred to her to sit down and *dine* with Jacob.

"It's our way," said Leah. "Perhaps we prefer not to let our men see us dribbling muttonfat down our chins."

Hassaweh looked at her in momentary shock; then she laughed. "You're a sharp one, Leah," she said.

Leah smiled back at her, but Rachel knew that there was no amusement or friendship in the smile. Good. Leah doesn't like her.

Why is that good? Because I don't like her?

Don't I like her?

When Rachel got a chance, she took Leah aside and tried to find out what she thought of Hassaweh, but it was as if Leah didn't know the woman existed.

"I never thought it would be like this," said Leah, sounding a bit like her old petulant self. "All these years Choraz has been gone, but now that he's home, we don't even get to see him. Well, we *see* him, but that's all."

"I know," said Rachel. "I missed him so much when he left."

"He was so good to us before. And now he doesn't have time for us."

"Because he got married," said Rachel, trying to get the conversation back to Hassaweh.

"Well, I suppose we should have known he'd find a wife, though he should have asked Father."

"A younger son?" said Rachel. "He was lucky to find a wife who'd take him. He earned the right to have her by . . ."

"By what?" asked Leah. "I want to hear stories of his adventures! Is he truly a warrior? Was he in battles? Did he fight off brigands? Was his wealth captured from his enemies? Or a reward from someone he rescued? Or gifts from the man he served?"

"I imagine he's telling Father and Jacob and Nahor and Terah right now," said Rachel.

"And then we'll have to listen to the stories the servants tell."

"Jacob will tell us, and without exaggerating," said Rachel.

Leah chuckled dryly. "He'll tell *you*, you mean."

"He talks to you every day!"

"He listens to the reading of scripture," said Leah. "He talks about the scripture. He would never spend that sacred time talking about the adventures of a desert warrior."

Rachel could not figure out how to feel about that. Clearly Leah was saying that Rachel would have the advantage of hearing about Choraz's stories and Leah wouldn't; but that was only because what Leah shared with Jacob was so sacred and holy that it couldn't be profaned with the tales of a mere man of war. *That* was for the ears of children.

No, no, don't be so resentful, don't . . . *brood* about this, Rachel told herself.

And then realized that this was precisely the way Leah used to work herself into such rages, noticing everything that might possibly put her at a disadvantage and assuming that everybody *meant* to make her feel bad.

"What do you think of Hassaweh?" asked Rachel.

"If she makes Choraz happy, then I'm glad she married him," said Leah. "Come on, let's go back inside and find out what the servants are overhearing." Leah immediately headed back inside the kitchen tent.

That was the end of Rachel's chance to gossip about Hassaweh.

She went to bed that night brooding about all her mistakes, worrying that she had become the kind of woman that Jacob would only marry as a duty, because he had promised to take her before he knew what a miserable, empty-headed, unladylike woman she would grow up to be.

CHAPTER 23

In the morning, Rachel's fears seemed childish to her. Choraz was home and she was glad of it. He had married, and the lady was exotic and beautiful and fascinating—of course Choraz loved her, and of course Rachel would come to love her too. All the rest was the nonsense in the mind of a little girl who was nervous about getting married. She was sure of it.

Then, as she combed some of the sleep-tousles out of her hair, the flap of her inner chamber opened and Hassaweh stepped in, blinking her eyes in the darkness.

"Good morning," said Rachel. If her voice sounded a little cold it was only because . . . well, because she was put out that someone would come in without being announced or at least coughing.

"I'm sorry if this isn't how one enters a tent," said Hassaweh. "In my father's house there were doors."

"That's a door you just came through," said Rachel.

"But . . . how do you lock it?"

"In camp, a closed door is a locked door."

"Ah," said Hassaweh. "Then I have achieved the miraculous power to unlock a door with a touch of my hand." She smiled, then sat down on the thickest pile of rugs—again, without invitation.

"Did you sleep well?" asked Rachel, determined, now that the surprise of being barged in on was over, to become friends with her favorite brother's wife.

"I slept *alone*," said Hassaweh.

"So did I," said Rachel.

Hassaweh squinted at her. "Are you mocking me?"

"I don't think so," said Rachel. "I doubt I'm clever enough to mock a lady like you."

Hassaweh laughed. "And thus you prove yourself wrong with such clever mockery."

Rachel was genuinely flustered. "I didn't mean to . . . I don't know why I said that . . ."

Hassaweh shook her head. "No, no, now I see it's true. As I was told, you really are a little girl still."

Rachel didn't know how to take this. Absolved of mocking her, but now dismissed as a child?

"Who told you that? When Choraz was last here, I *was* a little girl."

"And he was a little boy." Hassaweh laughed. "I wish I could have known him then. Before he had blooded his blade."

The words sent a chill down Rachel's spine. She wasn't sure if it was thrilling or appalling, how casually Hassaweh spoke of it. "Is Choraz such a killer, then?"

"A mighty warrior," said Hassaweh. "But also a little boy. Who's the strongest? Who can run fastest? Who can cut deepest? So much competition. But his men love him. The ones he brought with him, they came even though he forbade them."

"So they love him but don't obey him."

"'If you need me and I'm far away, how will I be able to serve you?'" Hassaweh quoted. "These are free men that Choraz could have killed or sold into slavery when he captured them. Instead they serve him, because they know quality when they see it."

Rachel thought of the first time she saw Jacob. How different he was from all other men. Like a lion among dogs. Did Choraz look that way to Hassaweh?

There was no way to ask *that* question, so instead Rachel asked the obvious one. "Why did you visit me so early in the morning?"

"Because your sister and her handmaiden and *your* handmaiden are gathered in the dooryard of your husband, reciting from arcane scrolls and scratching papyrus till it bleeds black."

Rachel laughed. It was the first time she'd heard anyone be really clever, and it was funny, to think of Bilhah's writing as if it were an injury to the scroll.

"And I had no intention of breaking fast with my husband's brother's wives. I'm sure they serve the purpose for which they were obtained—your brothers have anthills of children, apparently, swarming madly about the camp."

"Most of the children belong to the servants."

"Out and about, underfoot?" Hassaweh seemed genuinely surprised. Which made Rachel wonder where servants kept their children in whatever city she came from.

"What city are you from?" asked Rachel.

"One you've never heard of," said Hassaweh.

"Try me. I don't live in a cave."

"Axeptemantex," said Hassaweh. Or at least that was what Rachel thought she heard.

Rachel smiled and shook her head. "Back to the cave with me."

"No one speaks the language of the Medes," Hassaweh said. "My ancestors conquered on horseback, but soon enough they lived like the people they conquered. Only their language did they keep. So when I saw your brother, I thought: This is the kind of warrior that once my own forefathers were. It made me curious, as if by knowing him I'd come to know myself as I might have been."

"And who did you find yourself to be?"

"I found myself to be a woman, like any other woman, because he was a man, like any other man."

The words had such bitterness in them that Rachel wasn't sure she had understood. "Then why did you marry him?"

"Oh, you never find this out until you're married," said Hassaweh. "You'll see."

"What will I see?"

"Before they marry you, they're so kind, so attentive. So . . ." She said a word in her own language. "Like a loving servant. Though I admit that your husband is the first I heard of who actually *became* a servant to win the woman he loved."

"Jacob might enter into service for a time," said Rachel softly, "but he is always a prince, the keeper of the birthright of Abraham."

Hassaweh waved her hand airily. "I'm sure you're right." Then she chuckled dryly.

"But you think that even Jacob will be like all other men?"

"It's all a show," said Hassaweh. "I will love you forever. I will be so tender with you."

"Choraz *is* careful of you," said Rachel.

"For show. Outdoors, where others can see."

"Does he . . . hit you?"

Hassaweh laughed. "No, he's not such a fool as *that*. He's a man, but he also knows who and what *I* am."

"What are you?" asked Rachel. As long as she brought it up.

"I'm a woman that you only hit once," said Hassaweh.

Rachel decided to be a bit perverse. "Are you that easily broken?"

Hassaweh hooted with laughter. It surprised Rachel that this aloof lady could laugh so loudly. "You're a sharp one. Maybe you'll be able to tame yours as well as I tamed mine."

"But I don't intend to tame him," said Rachel. "He isn't wild."

"You'll see," said Hassaweh. "Tell me about rams and ewes, shepherd girl. Tell me about bulls and cows."

Rachel turned away her face. "You don't need me to explain such things."

"I didn't grow up among animals!" said Hassaweh. "But all I meant was this: Tell me what the ewe does, when the ram comes at her?"

"She . . . stands there . . . and then she . . . runs away."

"Men are rams, only they think that every woman is always in heat."

Rachel tried again to understand what she was saying. "Has Choraz been unfaithful to you?"

"Do you think I want him to father some other woman's

brats? That's the bitter choice: A man will love the woman who bears him sons. So you have to keep him coming to *you* when the desire comes on him. Or when his friends goad him to show how manly he is. That's the best time, I can assure you," she said, and from her tone of voice Rachel knew she meant it was the worst. "Always in their cups at such times," said Hassaweh. "Stinking and fumbling until they either fall asleep or throw up. But *you* don't want to shame him in front of his friends, so you cry out in *ecstasy* as if he had just transported you to heaven."

Rachel blushed. She had heard servant women cry out sometimes in their tents and once, when she was young, she had told her Father, "We must go help," and Father laughed and said, "Nine months later is when we go to help a woman in such distress." At the time, Rachel had thought that Father's laughter meant that the woman was not really in pain. Was it possible that she *was* in pain, but Father didn't care?

"Why are you telling me this?" asked Rachel.

"Because, shepherd girl, I saw your holy man. How softly he speaks. Yet I also see he has the body of a mighty man of war. Otherwise, your brothers would have killed him long ago, don't you see?"

"No," said Rachel. "My brothers aren't murderers."

"Not yet," said Hassaweh. "Your husband, your shepherd, your *ram*, he talks to you so gently, doesn't he? Listens to you attentively. Are you warm enough? Cool enough? Hungry? Thirsty? Tired?"

Rachel shook her head. "Jacob knows that I know how to fetch water when I'm thirsty."

Hassaweh rolled her eyes and lolled back on the rugs.

"Worse yet. He's not even *trying*. Who can doubt how he'll be after you're married."

"How will he be?" asked Rachel, defiantly.

"He'll take what he wants. Whether you want it or not. Whether you like it or not. And when he's finished with his own pleasure he'll toss you aside. If you're pregnant, he'll leave you alone for a while. If you're not, he'll come at you till you are. You're not a person to him, Rachel, little sister. You're a lovely garden he's been given in order to plant his seed. You're dirt under his feet, until his garden starts to grow."

"Do you have any children?" asked Rachel.

Hassaweh smiled broadly. "Not yet," she said. "But Choraz says he's glad of it, because he loves me *so much* that he doesn't want to have to leave me alone at night." Hassaweh's smile turned nasty. "You can guess how long *that* attitude will last. I think maybe a year, and then if I'm not carrying his child, he'll start to look for someone else."

"He wouldn't divorce you!"

"He wouldn't have to," said Hassaweh. "He just takes another wife. I'm the senior wife, yes . . . until the second one bears him a son. Then she becomes the mother of his heir, and what am I? No, you can be sure that I'll bear him a son or die trying. It's the only way a woman can keep her place in her husband's house."

Rachel knew this was true, but no one had ever said it in quite those words. It made it seem ugly and unfair.

"But a shepherd girl like you," said Hassaweh, "you won't have any trouble bearing children. I'd worry about your sister. She seems so . . . frail. While you're . . . well, robust. Your arms are so strong. Your face is so *brown*. They tell me you're out of doors all the time. Like a servant."

"Jacob and I know every lamb in the flock," said Rachel icily.

"Yes, well, the only flock *he'll* care about is the one that comes out of your body. And the only herding he'll care about is herding *you*."

"Why do you hate Jacob? What has he ever done to you?"

Hassaweh looked genuinely surprised. "I don't hate him. I don't even know him." She smiled. "I know *you*, though. Well enough to like you. I don't want you to be surprised. I don't want you to spend your wedding night weeping because now you know what your husband really is, and it's too late to put a stop to it."

"Put a stop to what?"

"To submitting to the bondage of your husband. You have a good and generous father. So did I. So you think your husband will treat you as your father did. But he won't."

"He'll treat me better."

Hassaweh got to her feet. "Come here, into the outer chamber. There's more light."

She led the way into the front room and pulled back the flap on the door to let in more light.

Then, to Rachel's surprise, Hassaweh pulled her dress up to her shoulders, baring her torso.

"See the bruises?" asked Hassaweh. "Here. Here. But don't touch them. They hurt me, being so fresh."

Now Rachel could see that what looked like birthmarks in the slanting light of early morning were angry bruises. "I thought you said he never hit you."

"No," said Hassaweh. "He never has. He never will. Don't you understand? These are the bruises he gave me during *love*."

Rachel turned away, appalled. She had never heard any of the other women complain of such things. Perhaps it was something they all knew, but preferred not to speak of. "Why haven't I heard of such things before?"

"Perhaps because no one loves you enough to tell you," said Hassaweh. "Or maybe they just suppose that it's the fate of all women, and it will happen to you whether they warn you or not. Better to be married and suffer. Besides, with any luck you'll get pregnant right away, and then you'll have some peace."

"Please put down your dress."

"Don't like looking at the marks of your brother's tender affection, eh? Women are so foolish, when they admire a man because he's so *strong*. The stronger he is, the worse he can hurt you."

Not Jacob, thought Rachel. He would never do anything that he thought would hurt me.

"I heard there was a little bit of pain, the first time."

"I heard that, too," said Hassaweh. She laughed bitterly. "You should have looked for a weak man. A grateful man. A man who wouldn't dare to offend your father. You could tame him then. Rule in your own house. I had men like that after me, and I scorned them all. I set my heart on Choraz, the mighty warrior from the desert. What a fool I was. And you, desert girl. You think I haven't heard the story of this man coming to you when you were—what, eleven years old? Twelve? A child—and he kissed you. Don't you see? A strong man from the desert, and he looks for a *child*, someone he can overpower easily. Someone he can pick up and toss about however and whenever he wants. A plaything. Your Jacob

332

wasn't looking for a woman to be his *wife*. He was looking for a girl to be his . . . ewe."

Hassaweh might mean what she said, but she was wrong. Jacob was not like that. "I think," said Rachel, "that it is disloyal of me to listen to someone speak that way of the man I'm going to marry."

"Oh, of course. Be loyal!" Hassaweh winked. "Think of me however you like. We'll talk again *after* your wedding. Then you'll know who your true friend is." Hassaweh laughed. "Your lucky sister Leah! So beautiful, so frail—just the sort of woman that brutish men find irresistible. Yet because she's nearly blind, she gets to keep her freedom. She won't die in childbirth."

"She'll get married," said Rachel loyally.

"Not very likely," said Hassaweh. "Or she'd be married already, wouldn't she?"

"Leah *will* have children," said Rachel. "She'll be a wonderful mother."

"It all comes back to that problem with men, doesn't it?" said Hassaweh. "We need what they have. But to get it, we have to subject ourselves to them. That's how the gods have arranged things, so we must endure it."

Hassaweh slipped out of the tent so quickly that it was almost as if she were fleeing. And perhaps she was, because only a few moments later, Bilhah came in.

"What was Hassaweh doing in your tent, Lady Rachel?" she asked. And then, "Why are you crying?"

But Rachel had no answer. Was she crying because she had never had anyone be so wantonly cruel to her as Hassaweh had been, shaming her with nakedness and slandering her husband and her brother? Or because she feared that

Hassaweh was right about everything, and she was about to lose her happiness.

I already feared it, thought Rachel. I didn't know why, but I feared it. I knew that I didn't want to get married.

"What is it?" said Bilhah. "You never cry."

"Why do I have to get married right now?" said Rachel.

"Not for weeks yet," said Bilhah.

"Why can't I wait?"

"But you're nearly nineteen years old."

"I'm not ready," whispered Rachel. "I don't know if I'll ever be ready."

"What did Hassaweh say to you?" asked Bilhah.

"Nothing."

"You weren't crying before, and then she visited your tent and I come in and you're weeping like . . . like . . ."

"Like a baby."

"Like a widow," said Bilhah.

"She told me about marriage," said Rachel.

"The most she could have told you about is *her* marriage," said Bilhah. "She doesn't know anything about how *yours* will be. Nobody does. Except why shouldn't it be wonderful? Is there a better man in the world than Jacob?"

Rachel couldn't explain, because she'd have to repeat the awful things that Hassaweh had said, and it would shame her even to say the words.

"I'll tell you then, in case you haven't noticed," said Bilhah. "Jacob is wise and noble, faithful and holy. And he's also a master of men—they're eager to follow him, they *love* him. And strong enough that even the bulls don't argue with him."

Yes, even the bulls and stallions fear him, obey him. What

chance have I, then, if a man like that decides he wants to make use of me harshly, the way Choraz uses Hassaweh?

But she said nothing. Instead she fled into her inner chamber and sent Bilhah for water, so she could wash her face before she left her tent this morning.

"I came because Choraz is looking for you," said Bilhah. "He wants to see you."

"I don't want to see him," said Rachel. "Not right now, I mean. Not till I've washed."

"All right," said Bilhah.

But Rachel didn't hear her going away.

"Are you still here, Bilhah?"

"Lady Rachel," said Bilhah. "Please don't believe everything that woman says. She doesn't know you or any of us. She's a stranger, and she's made you cry."

"Thank you for your counsel," said Rachel. "Now please fetch me water."

Now she could hear Bilhah leave.

She's right. It's all lies. For some reason, Hassaweh wants me to fear the whole idea of marriage.

Or she wants to warn me.

Or make me fear Jacob.

I don't fear him. But marriage, I fear that. What if I . . . become like Hassaweh? Like Asta or Deloch?

Or what if I simply die, as Mother did? As Bilhah's mother did?

What if Mother died because she wanted to? Because married life, even with a good man like Father, was so awful?

Why can't things stay as they are?

CHAPTER 24

Bilhah knew she had to do something. Talk to someone. She had never seen Rachel so upset. If only she could talk to Jacob about it. But what could she tell *him* about Rachel? Didn't Jacob see her every day? Wasn't he blessed with the spirit of Wisdom? He must already know what was wrong. Or else it was the will of God that he *not* know. Either way, what could Bilhah say to him?

Oh, Jacob, in case you haven't noticed, Rachel is working herself into some kind of frenzy over the idea of marrying you. Zilpah noticed it first, and I certainly noticed it today. Yes, she weeps at the thought of marrying you. You didn't detect this in your conversations with her for hours every day? Well, aren't you the unobservant one.

Of course he knew.

So it would be all right. Bilhah didn't have to do anything about Rachel, except encourage her.

Even as she reached this conclusion, she knew it was false. She could feel it—an emptiness inside her that told her that she *knew* she had to do something.

Was this how the spirit of Wisdom whispered to a woman like Bilhah? Would the voice of God seem like hunger? Indigestion? Not likely.

And yet here she was in front of Laban's tent.

"He's busy," said the woman who was waiting at the door.

Bilhah almost walked away. "He's always busy."

"He's talking to Choraz."

"How much could they have to say to each other after being apart for nine years?" said Bilhah. "I'll wait."

"I'm ahead of you in line," said the woman.

"I can see that."

"Tell me what you want to see him for."

"I have to confess something to him."

The woman leaned in, pretending not to be eager. "What?"

"I've been minding my own business so much, it's starting to cause trouble in the camp."

It took the woman a moment to realize that it was a rebuke. "Aren't you the clever one," she said dryly.

They waited in silence for a long time. Now and then, there was a burst of laughter from inside the tent. But Bilhah couldn't make out any words.

Finally the woman stood up. "Some of us have too much work to do to spend the whole morning waiting outside Lord Laban's tent."

"I'm doing my work right here," said Bilhah.

"What work are *you* doing?"

Bilhah grinned at her.

The woman smiled sourly. "Oh. Yes. Minding your own

business. And to think I've missed so many chances to be amused by your wit."

Bilhah waited alone for a little while longer, when she was wakened by someone's foot prodding her.

"Oh," she said, sitting up. "I fell asleep."

"So that's it," said Nahor. "And here we thought you were dead."

Terah grinned at her. "Unless you spent the night here."

"She must have stayed up all night doing her work," said Nahor. "How else would she have time to take a nap in front of Father's tent?"

Bilhah said nothing, but looked right into their eyes, looking first at Nahor, then at Terah, then back to Nahor. Apparently they found either her silence or her gaze disconcerting, because they gave up and went inside.

Bilhah meant to stay awake, but either Nahor and Terah spent only a few moments inside the tent or she dozed again, because they seemed to emerge right away, Choraz with them.

"Look, Choraz," said Terah. "We're so prosperous here that Father can afford to feed girls who just lie about in the shade of his tent."

Bilhah looked up into Choraz's eyes. He studied her for a moment, then stepped back inside the tent.

When he came back out, Laban was with him.

"Choraz says you're worried about something, Bilhah," said Laban.

Bilhah looked again at Choraz and gave him a wan smile. "Thank you," she said.

Choraz nodded and led his older brothers away from the tent.

"Come inside, Bilhah," said Laban.

Sitting just inside the tent, it took Bilhah only a few moments to tell her concern. What Zilpah had said about Rachel not knowing what she needed to know, and then Rachel crying after talking to Hassaweh.

"She's afraid of the marriage, sir," said Bilhah. "And when I encourage her, it does no good."

"Because you're not married," said Laban.

"Hassaweh's married, and she made it worse."

"An interesting woman, this wife of my son Choraz," said Laban.

"Sir, you must talk to her. What if she doesn't want to marry Jacob?"

Laban looked at her as if she were insane. "My promise is given."

"I know," said Bilhah. "But if she's terrified, would you force her to go ahead?"

"What's to be terrified about? People get married all the time."

"She never saw her own mother and father as husband and wife," said Bilhah. "So what marriages has she seen? The marriages of servants, of course. Do you think that will reassure her?"

"Her brothers are married," said Laban dismissively.

Bilhah said nothing, while she let Laban realize what he had just said.

"Well, I suppose that isn't very reassuring either, is it," said Laban. "Nothing wrong with the girls, though—they have lots of babies."

"And they and their husbands are constantly quarreling. And it's well known that your sons used to go to Byblos and—"

"In Byblos they conducted business," said Laban coldly. "Or do you listen to idle gossip?"

"Does Rachel?"

Laban sighed. "She knows that Jacob is a better man than Nahor and Terah."

"But is he a better husband? She's afraid, sir. Talk to her. Or would you have her weeping all the way through her wedding?"

"And talking to Hassaweh didn't help?" said Laban hopefully.

"Made it worse, sir."

He touched his forehead and sighed. "What can a man do, when women decide to have a fit about something? She's always been a sensible girl till now." His voice suddenly got louder. "For seven years, she couldn't figure things out? Now suddenly it's time to panic?"

"I don't know if I'd be any different, sir," said Bilhah. "It's one thing to know it's coming far in the future. Something else when it's coming in a few weeks."

"I'll talk to her."

"Thank you, sir."

"Unless you can get her calmed down first," said Laban.

"If I thought I could, I wouldn't have bothered you, sir."

"Leah was always the problem child," said Laban. "Not Rachel."

"Maybe now it's Rachel's turn," said Bilhah.

"Why did God make her so beautiful, and not make her desire marriage?"

But Laban seemed to be asking God, or maybe just himself. Bilhah didn't attempt to answer.

PART XI

WEDDINGS

CHAPTER 25

Leah knew that something was wrong, but she couldn't figure out what it was. Everything seemed normal. Choraz was home, of course, which made some difference, but it wasn't as though he was actually around. During the weeks before Rachel's wedding he was out with his men—and Nahor and Terah—visiting all the outlying herds and flocks.

Likewise, Hassaweh made sure she was the center of attention whenever she felt like it, but that didn't interfere with Leah's life in any noticeable way. And Hassaweh seemed to have provided Asta and Deloch with someone new to resent, which meant that they left Leah and Rachel alone.

Mornings, Leah and Zilpah and Bilhah spent together in Jacob's dooryard, copying and reading. That was still a peaceful time, as it had been almost from the start. In the seven years that Jacob had been here, Leah had heard every word of every book, and now they were well through the second pass, with Bilhah making yet another copy.

As for Leah herself, during those hours she lived in the world of Adam and Eve and Seth, Enoch and Zion, Noah and his family, Shem and Melchizedek, Abraham and Sarah, Isaac and Rebekah. She no longer listened to the words of the Lord in a desperate search for some message to herself. Now she understood that the Lord said to his children in every age whatever they needed to know, whatever they could bear to hear.

What I need, he will tell me. Meanwhile, I'm still learning how to follow his path. Still trying to get control of myself so I can be his true daughter and servant.

She knew she was coming closer than ever before.

So . . . why was she so ill at ease? What was it that worried her and woke her in the morning, to lie there brooding in the darkness?

When the Lord didn't answer her questions, she decided he meant her to figure things out herself. So she began paying more attention to what went on around her. There was, of course, the normal amount of tension between Bilhah and Zilpah—the two of them never really understood each other, and why should they? Leah had long since figured out that neither one of them was a servant by nature, and both of them seethed sometimes at the course of their lives. But she could do nothing to solve that, except to treat them both fairly, and study the scriptures with them in hopes that God would bring peace to their souls.

Jacob also seemed to be preoccupied, but from what Leah could sense—the times he stiffened or grew more alert, the way he turned away when something disgusted him—she knew exactly what was bothering *him*. Choraz's homecoming worried him. Well, that wasn't hard to figure out. Jacob knew that Terah and Nahor resented him, and Choraz's arrival shortly before Rachel's wedding couldn't be mere coincidence. Choraz had been sent for, and it had something to do with Jacob.

But Leah knew that Jacob had nothing to fear from Choraz. He might have become a man of warfare, but he was still Choraz, and he would do nothing to harm the man that Rachel loved. Besides, if Choraz did take it into his head to try to do battle with Jacob, he would soon find out how the Lord strengthens the arm of his servant. Wasn't Jacob the man that the Lord had shown a vision of heaven? A man who had seen the angels going to and fro between heaven and earth had nothing to fear from a mere soldier, however bloody his sword. The only way Choraz could kill Jacob or drive him away would be if God wanted it to happen.

The flocks and herds were prospering. The servants were eager for the festivities surrounding the wedding, even though the preparations caused more work for everyone.

Leah wondered for a while if her unease was caused by the tender way everyone was treating her—the older sister who would stand there unmarried at her younger sister's wedding. Leah didn't even bother to reassure them—her heart was at peace when it came to marriage. Leah was in the hands of the Lord—if he wanted her to marry, there would be a husband. Meanwhile, she would rejoice at her sister's wedding, and be happy to have Jacob for a brother.

Perhaps I'm so restless and fretful because I'm going to die. Couldn't that be the message the Lord has for me? Now that Rachel is getting married, and I'm not, perhaps God will bring me home and relieve me of this blurred and shadowed life. To see God with clear eyes! But that would be perfect happiness—why would a premonition of my death wake me in the night, full of anxiety? No, that wasn't what was bothering her.

It could only be Rachel.

As far as Leah could see, Rachel was behaving as she normally did—all the same routines, in and out of camp, tending to the flocks. It was as if the wedding weren't even happening. That, of course, was unusual—most girls, even servant girls, became excited in the days before they married, chatted constantly, gave away their childish toys, put on womanly airs, walked about as if in a dream.

There was none of that with Rachel. If anything she grew quieter and kept to herself even more than usual.

But when Leah thought about it, when she paid special attention to Rachel, she realized that what she was feeling was not her own fear, it was her sister's. Rachel was full of dread and yet dared not show it.

Leah could hear it in the trembling of Rachel's breath from time to time. In the fidgeting of her fingers. In the slump of her shoulders. The silent sigh that had just the slightest catch in it. The way Rachel hung back when Jacob was near. The slowness of her steps, where once she would have run.

Rachel is unhappy, so I'm unhappy. That's what's been waking me up in the darkness.

Once she realized what the problem was, Leah wasted no time. She rose at once from where she sat in Jacob's dooryard.

Bilhah and Zilpah both stopped what they were doing and looked up at her expectantly.

"Go ahead without me," Leah said to Bilhah. "Zilpah, will you help me find Rachel?"

In a few moments they were walking along the path that wound through the hills to the nearby flock that Rachel would be tending. "Stay close, mistress," said Zilpah. "The path drops away steeply here on the right."

"If I hold tightly enough to you, then at least if I fall and die, I won't die alone."

"Very funny," said Zilpah. "The question is whether you can hold on as strongly as I can shove away."

"Let's see!" said Leah. She feinted toward the edge of the path.

Zilpah's effort to break free was half-hearted at best—she didn't dare use her full strength, Leah knew, for fear that in their horseplay she'd accidently push Leah off the edge.

"All right," said Leah. "I'll be good."

"Oh, *that* will be a nice change."

They walked in silence for a while.

"Lady Leah," said Zilpah. "Why are we looking for Rachel?"

"Because I have to talk with her."

"What about?"

"I'm worried about her."

"Well, aren't we all!"

"Are we? All of us? I've heard no talk about it."

"People don't talk about the wedding near you, Mistress," said Zilpah.

"I know," said Leah. "Isn't that silly?"

"In the old days, they would have avoided the topic for fear of launching you on a tantrum," said Zilpah. "But now, it's because they don't want to hurt your feelings."

"Well, what is everyone worried about?"

"Not *everyone*," said Zilpah. "I meant—all of us who actually know how frightened Rachel is."

"And who is that?"

"Me," said Zilpah. "Bilhah, not that *she* ever talks about Lady Rachel behind her back. Hassaweh and Choraz. And your father. Not that he confides in me, either. But you can see how he watches her and gets thoughtful."

No, I *can't* see that, thought Leah. But that was nothing new.

"So with all of you concerned about Rachel, I have nothing to worry about?"

"Hardly," said Zilpah. "Rachel's not talking to anybody. Your father has tried several times to get her to come to his tent and talk to him about the wedding, but she just blushes and refuses. Or when he presses her and she promises to come, then she just . . . doesn't do it."

"And she doesn't say why?"

"I think she's terrified. From what Hassaweh said. From what I saw myself. I think she's afraid of . . . but what does it matter what I think? She won't talk to me about it, so I don't know any more than you. You'll see."

And, for once, Leah *did* see. Rachel greeted them cheerfully enough, but after Zilpah withdrew, when Leah tried to make cheerful conversation with Rachel, she turned back to the sheep she was examining.

"Rachel," said Leah.

"What?" asked Rachel, a little impatiently. "Can't you see I'm working?"

"I can see you're working at a task that could be done tomorrow as easily as today. Or next week. Or next month."

"Well, next month I won't be *doing* this, will I?"

"I don't know," said Leah. "What are you and Jacob planning?"

"*We're* not planning anything," said Rachel.

"Have you asked him what he's planning?"

"No."

"Let me guess. When he tries to talk about it, you do to him what you're doing to me."

"I'm not doing anything to you."

"You're making it very clear you want me to go away and leave you alone."

"And yet you don't go."

"That's because I love you so much, my darling sister."

"Oh, I see," said Rachel. "They've all gotten together and chosen *you* to come talk to me about how happy I should be before my wedding."

"Nobody got together with anybody."

"Why don't I believe you?"

"Because you're as dumb as two rocks in the road. Nobody's talking to me about you or the wedding because they're afraid they'll hurt my feelings."

Rachel said nothing.

"You didn't think of that, did you?" said Leah.

Rachel sighed. "No. Sorry if my wedding is making things hard for you."

"Ah, there's the snotty-voiced sister that I was looking for."

"I didn't ask for this conversation, Leah."

"Look, Rachel," said Leah. "I don't know what's going on, but it's plain that you're suffering and Zilpah tells me you won't talk to anybody about it."

"There's no 'it' to talk about."

"Good. Then you can go right to Father and tell him that."

"I already have."

"But you haven't *explained* it to him," said Leah. "You haven't told him in detail exactly what it is you aren't feeling, which is keeping you from being excited about your wedding like a normal bride."

"I'm not normal," said Rachel. "You go tell him that."

"Father loves you," said Leah. "He won't make you marry Jacob if you don't want to."

Rachel sighed.

"What do you *want*, Rachel?"

"I want you to leave me alone. Father will be furious when he finds out you came all the way out here. You could have fallen. The path isn't safe for somebody who can't see the ground clearly."

"Lead me back," said Leah.

"Zilpah can lead you."

"You take me or I'll throw a tantrum."

"Don't be stupid. You don't do that anymore."

"You think I've forgotten how?"

"I don't care whether you have or not."

"Rachel, come back with me and talk to Father."

"You plan to drag me?"

"Who's throwing a tantrum, anyway?" said Leah.

"Not me."

"Yes you. What do you think this act of yours is? 'Leave me alone. Let me suffer in silence. I won't talk to anybody. Nothing's wrong.'"

"I'm saying good-bye to my life, is that all right with you?"

"What was that? An answer?" Leah laughed. "Well, that was a nice try, but I don't believe it. Saying good-bye to your life? You're getting married, you're not dying."

"I *am* dying," said Rachel. "The girl I've always been, she's going to be dead and gone. She's never coming back. So leave me alone to say good-bye to that life."

"Fine, that's worth an hour of quiet reflection, not this pout that's been going on for weeks."

"I'm not pouting."

"Not *visibly*," said Leah. "But you must remember that I'm the one who can sense things that the eye can't see."

"Even things that don't exist."

"For instance, do you think Jacob isn't worried about you?"

"If he were, he would have said something."

"What, for instance? Don't you understand that he can't? You're making such a show of being miserable before the wedding, what is he supposed to think? He's with you every day, for hours at a time—"

"Speaking of which, he should be here any time. So I can't go with you."

"And you don't talk to him about what's bothering you. No doubt he thinks that you've decided you'd rather marry a rich warrior, some man like Choraz."

"That's just stupid."

"Talk to Jacob, if you won't talk to Father."

"I don't even want to talk to you."

"Then let me put it another way," said Leah. "I'm doing a good job of being happy for you. But it's all completely wasted if you aren't even happy for yourself."

"Please, please, Leah, leave me alone."

"I won't leave you alone."

Rachel turned back to the sheep.

"How many days till the wedding, Rachel?"

"I don't know."

"Everyone else does. What will you wear?"

"Some dress. They're making it for me."

"Everyone else has seen it. Not you, though, right?"

"I'll see it when they fit it on me."

In despair, Leah closed her eyes and prayed silently. Help me, Lord God, to say what Rachel needs to hear.

"What are you doing?" said Rachel.

"Praying for you," said Leah.

Rachel said nothing.

"I love you, Rachel," said Leah. "I want you to be happy."

Silence from Rachel.

"God sent his prophet to be your husband. You were chosen."

Rachel actually shuddered.

"What's *wrong?*" demanded Leah.

"Was I chosen?" said Rachel. "By God?"

"You know you were."

"Or did I just dream it up, because I wanted to be like Rebekah?"

"Jacob's real. I know, I've seen him."

"No you haven't," said Rachel. "All you've seen is a blur." And then she giggled at her own joke.

Giggled, but it was as if she had opened a dam. Suddenly she began to cry. And not just quiet tears. She cried as if someone she loved had just died.

Leah sat down in the grass beside her and put her arms around her. Rachel let her do it and cried into her shoulder.

Until she slid down and cried in Leah's lap. All the while, Leah stroked her, patted her, but said nothing.

It went on for a long time. Leah hadn't known Rachel was capable of so much emotion.

But no one can cry forever, and after a while Rachel was still.

"Please, Rachel, tell me why you're grieving."

Rachel shook her head.

"Then talk to Father. Whatever it is you want, you know he'll do it for you."

She shook her head again.

Then, suddenly, words came into Leah's mind and she said them without thinking. "If you talk to Father, everything will work out exactly as the Lord desires."

Rachel did not shake her head.

Instead she sat up and looked at Leah. "What happened?" she said.

"What do you mean?"

"You said that like . . . like a man. Like Father. As if you had *authority*."

Leah didn't want to claim any authority. "They weren't my words," she said.

Rachel was silent a long time. Finally: "I don't know anything about God."

"That's silly, of course you do."

"I know about God the way a child does. Not like you and the other girls."

"We've read books," said Leah. "But the spirit of Wisdom can touch every heart."

"Not mine," said Rachel. "My heart repels wisdom, like rain off a tent roof."

"But if you reach out and touch it, Wisdom will come in."

"I'm so frightened, Leah," said Rachel.

"Talk to Father."

"What can he do? He's given his word. I gave *my* word."

"I just know . . . I know what I said. I know it's from God. If you talk to Father, it will work out the way God wants it to."

Rachel laughed miserably. "But I want it to work out the way *I* want it to."

"Give the Lord a chance. Maybe you both want the same thing."

"I don't think so. Because I want to be fourteen again. I want to be fourteen forever."

"Why fourteen?"

"Because it was after Jacob got here. After we became friends again. Before Choraz married . . . whoever. It was a good time."

"There'll be other good times, Rachel."

"Did God tell you that?"

"No."

"Then shut up, please," said Rachel. But she hugged Leah as she said it, so Leah knew that she meant it in the nicest possible way.

"Please lead me back to camp, Rachel," said Leah.

"I will."

"And you'll talk to Father?"

"I will."

CHAPTER 26

Father was more understanding than Rachel could ever have hoped. Perhaps because she had never faced his anger, she dreaded it more than anyone else in camp. Yet to her surprise, he wasn't angry at all, or if he was he didn't show it.

"Of course you're afraid," said Father. "Do you think I haven't seen how your attitude has turned so glum these past weeks? It's as if my happy little girl had been replaced by a leftover mourner from someone's funeral."

"But I love Jacob, Father. Except for you and Leah, I love him more than anyone else in the world!"

"Well, there's the problem," said Laban. "Your father and your sister shouldn't come before your husband."

"He's not my husband yet."

"No, he's not."

"He's served the seven years," said Rachel. "You should

355

let him stay, but not as a bondsman. I'll still be promised to him. And in a few months or a year or . . ."

"Rachel, you know how quickly the days pass. How do you know you won't feel the same in a year? Or in two years?"

"I won't. I'll be older and . . ."

"If you don't keep your promise to him now, Rachel, how do you know he'll keep his promise to you?"

"So you're saying I have to marry him now or never?"

"Not at all," said Father. "I'm saying that I'll do my best to get you what you want—a postponement of your wedding, and yet Jacob would stay here, waiting for you, contented. But it might not be possible. Jacob may decide to reject what I offer him."

"Do you think he will?"

"I offer him the best that God has given me. Only the schedule of delivery would be changed. If he rejects it, then he's unworthy of you."

"The Lord brought him here," said Rachel. "And Leah promised me . . ."

"Promised you what?"

"The spirit of Wisdom whispered to her," said Rachel. "That if I talked to you, everything would work out as the Lord desires."

Father put his arm around her. "That's a solemn promise. But beware—a promise like that says nothing about what *you* want, only what the Lord wants you to have."

"But if the Lord didn't want me to have Jacob as my husband, why would he have brought him here? Why would I have had my dream of him?"

"You have to decide for yourself, Rachel. Perhaps if you

refuse to keep the promise to marry him day after tomorrow, the Lord will take back the gift he offered you."

"But doesn't everything come from the Lord?" asked Rachel. "My dreams, Jacob—but my fear also. A warning—doesn't that come from the Lord too, just like a promise?"

"I'm not a prophet," said Laban. "I'm not even a scholar. You should speak to Jacob if you want answers to questions like that."

"How can I tell him . . . myself? You have to tell me what God wants me to do."

"God wants you to be happy. He wants you to make choices, and then live with the results of the choices you made. And if they were wrong choices, then you make the best of them."

"So you're saying I should keep the promise I made to Jacob," said Rachel.

"No, I didn't say—"

"But I was a child then, Father! What did I know about marriage? Nobody told me anything. Now I know . . . more than I wanted to ever know."

"Marriage isn't so awful," said Father. "Your mother and I loved each other very much. It was marriage that gave us our wonderful children."

"We're not so wonderful, Papa. Choraz kills men in battle. Leah is half blind. Terah and Nahor—well, you know. And me—"

"Yes, what is your fatal flaw?"

"I'm a coward. And an oathbreaker."

"Not a breaker of oaths. A delayer of weddings."

Rachel laughed in spite of herself. "You make me sound not quite so awful as I deserve."

"Why don't we do this?" said Laban. "Let's leave the preparations for the wedding in place. Say nothing to anyone. But you and Leah will sleep in this outer room of my tent on the eve of the wedding. If you decide on the very day that you want to go ahead, then you can do it, and no one needs to know that you ever thought of delaying the wedding."

"But what if I can't? Then it will come as a shock to Jacob and he'll think I betrayed him."

"What difference does it make *when* he finds out? I'll propose a change in our agreement that lets you delay the wedding. He's a poor man. What if I ask him to continue as steward of all my flocks and herds, in exchange for a portion of the increase? Half of the new lambs and calves and kids and foals, for each year until you marry him?"

"Half?" In the short run, that wouldn't be a crippling cost, but if it went on for too many years, Jacob would end up with half of her brothers' inheritance.

"If you keep delaying the wedding, then you'll end up costing me a great deal," said Father with a smile.

"I won't delay so very long, Father. The Lord will help me get ready."

"Well, wouldn't it have been nice if he'd helped you get ready for *this* day."

"What if Jacob won't wait? He's already spent seven years. I know from things he's said to me that he doesn't want to be like Abraham was, an old, old man before his sons were born."

"There's always that possibility," said Laban. "What would you do then? If Jacob married someone else first, but then returned to marry you as his second wife?"

"That would be terrible! What if it was someone like . . .

Asta? Or even Hassaweh? As the first wife! She'd think she had a right to rule over me."

"Where do you get these ideas?" said Father. "The husband rules both wives equally. What matters is which wife the husband loves best. And how could that be anyone but you?"

"No," said Rachel. "No other wife. I'd rather never marry him than have to share him with another."

"Sarah shared Abraham with her handmaiden, Hagar."

"Oh, don't remind me of *that* story. Hagar ended up being thrown out of the camp and set to wander and die in the wilderness! If the angel hadn't saved her—"

"My example was badly chosen," said Father. "Never mind. I'll make my offer to him. If he refuses and says he'll go off and marry someone else, what should I tell him?"

"Tell him that he has the right to do that. But I'll never marry anyone else. I'll stay here forever in your camp, with Leah. She and I will be old spinsters together, and we'll tell our brothers' grandchildren about the prophet from the desert who was *almost* our husband. I mean *my* husband."

"That might be the exact choice you're making, Rachel, my dear. Between Jacob and never marrying at all."

"You think he'll be that angry?"

"Rachel, please, think about it. The story of Jacob's service to win the hand of Laban's beautiful daughter is already a legend. How quickly will the story spread that Laban doesn't keep his word? What man will come to bargain with me for either of my daughters then?"

"You don't mean that this will hurt *Leah!*"

Father shook his head. "Rachel, your sister is very beautiful, but her eyes are no good. And even though you know and I know how sweet-tempered she's become, the stories of her shrewishness are still out there. If no one came to ask for her hand after you fail to marry Jacob, it will be the same number as came to court her for the past three years."

Rachel was already emotional, so tears came easily to her eyes. "Poor Leah! She'd be such a wonderful wife!"

"If the Lord wants her to be married, she will be," said Father. "But I'm not a prophet. I have no miracles in me. I'm not going to go out and bribe some miserable greedy fellow to marry her for pride's sake. She wouldn't have such a man anyway, and then I'd be famous as the man who had *two* daughters who refused to marry according to their father's bargain."

"You're angry with me."

"I'm just being honest. But I wouldn't have you marry against your will, just to keep me from being embarrassed in the neighborhood. My embarrassment will last a little while, but an unhappy marriage is the rest of your life."

Father stood up and headed for the door. "Stay here until your eyes don't look so weepy. And be content. Until the very last moment, you don't have to go ahead with the wedding if you don't want to."

"I think you're counting on my changing my mind and marrying him after all," said Rachel. "Will you be very angry if I don't?"

"I'm not counting on anything, my little gazelle. I'm opening every wall of the tent and seeing which way the wind blows."

As soon as he left the tent, Rachel wanted to run after him. I've made a terrible mistake! I'll go through with the wedding!

Because the worst thing she could think of would be the look of stricken disappointment on Jacob's face. Other men might be angry, but he would only be hurt. He would turn away from her. It *wouldn't* go on as it had before.

Well, I have that choice. I'll go through with it. As Father said, no one will ever know that I even thought of delaying the wedding.

CHAPTER 27

Leah sat in her tent and listened to her father carefully.
When he was through telling her, she could only shake
her head.

"Father, that's not even a plan. It's a desperate excuse for
Rachel's fearfulness."

"If you had seen how unhappy she was—"

"Father, I *did* see. That's why I tried so hard to get her to
talk to you."

"Well, she did, and this is where things stand."

"Do you think that Jacob is the kind of man you can put
off the bargain by paying him in cattle and sheep? I'll tell you
what Jacob will think: If I do what Laban suggests, then in half
the stories I'll be the fool who got tricked out of his wedding
day, and in the other half, I'll be a man who married Laban's
daughter in order to get half his flocks and herds."

"I knew your hearing was unusually acute, Leah, but I

never knew you could hear a man's thoughts before he even thought them."

"Father, Jacob will come forward tomorrow expecting to marry your daughter. Instead you're going to come out and renegotiate the bargain. At what point in the ceremony do you intend to do that? And how will he spend the rest of his day? His wedding *night?* Are you *trying* to turn the house of Abraham into our enemies?"

"Well what would you have me do?"

"Go to him now. Talk to him. Tell him about Rachel's fears. Tell him what you told her. Tell him everything."

"How will that help our problem, Leah? It won't make Rachel any happier about getting married, *and* she'll be angry with me for breaking my promise *not* to speak to Jacob in advance. And Jacob will *still* be a man who has no one in his bed on his wedding night. Finding out you're being treated like a fool the day before your wedding isn't all that much better than finding out at the wedding. Especially since Rachel might change her mind and go ahead with it and leave Jacob none the wiser."

"That's your mistake, Father. You think you can fool a prophet of God."

Father buried his face in his hands. "I'm not going to force Rachel to marry against her will."

"Be honest with Jacob," said Leah. "He deserves nothing less."

"I wish I didn't see my miserable sons behind this whole problem," said Father.

That came as a complete surprise to Leah. "What do you mean?"

"Why did Choraz come home when he did? I think Nahor

or Terah or both of them sent him a message to get here and prevent the wedding."

"Why would they even care?"

"In case you haven't noticed, I set Jacob as overseer of all my household—above them. No doubt they remember the stories of how Jacob tricked Esau out of his birthright. So when he marries my daughter Rachel, and given that my sons are idiots, naturally they'll think Jacob is out to steal their inheritance."

"Then they don't know Jacob."

"They don't know *me*," said Father. "Because when they were still chasing after harlots in Byblos and gambling away as much of my wealth as I ever put in their hands, I came *this* close to disinheriting them and leaving everything to Choraz and Jacob and whoever you ended up marrying."

"Father! You couldn't do that to your own sons."

"But I could. Better that than to watch them try to rule a great household when they never bothered to learn anything about how it's done! It doesn't matter now, anyway. I managed to convince them that I meant what I said, and so they've stayed close to home, raised their children, and learned from Jacob how to be good husbandmen. Now they're almost worth leaving my inheritance to."

"Obviously they hate and fear Jacob—they wouldn't be Nahor and Terah if they didn't," said Leah. "But what does that have to do with Choraz?"

"Think about it," said Father. "What can Choraz do that Nahor and Terah have never been able to do?"

"Hold two thoughts in his head at the same time?"

"Very funny," said Father. "He's a man of war. He kills people."

Leah felt the blood pound in her ears. "What are you accusing your sons of?"

"You know them, Leah! Just because that was Nahor's and Terah's plan doesn't mean Choraz ever had any intention of doing such a thing. But you yourself said that Rachel's worries didn't become really awful until Choraz's wife regaled her with stories of just how awful husbands are."

"You mean Choraz *wanted* her to tell Rachel that he was a brutal husband?"

"It crossed my mind. We all knew Choraz as a sweet and gentle boy, clever and strong, but kind. If *his* wife was brutalized by marriage, then how could Rachel expect Jacob to be any different?"

"Well, there's the part about Jacob being a prophet."

"And there's the part about Rachel being a frightened girl, and Hassaweh being a glamorous woman of the city."

"So you think Choraz was trying his own method of preventing the wedding?" asked Leah.

"I suspect it. It's *possible.* And that really galls me. I don't want to force Rachel into an unhappy marriage. But I also don't want Choraz and Terah and Nahor to think they managed to manipulate their father into keeping Jacob out of the family."

"Well, they *have,* haven't they?" asked Leah. "Rachel's putting off the wedding, according to plan. I'm going to give them a piece of my mind!"

"For heaven's sake, Leah! Right now we're trying to keep open the possibility of the wedding going forward as planned. It won't help anything if you start railing on your brothers about their treacherous intentions."

"What if the wedding *does* go forward? Will Nahor and Terah decide to go ahead with their original plan?"

"Of course not," said Father. "They never had the stomach for murder. That's why they sent for Choraz. And Choraz isn't about to kill his sister's husband. He became a warrior, not a monster."

"I have a headache, Father," said Leah.

"So do I," said Father. "In fact, I have three or four of them, all at once, pounding around in my head, trying to get me to drown myself in a bucket of water for relief." He stood there for a moment longer, though. Leah thought it was just because he was in pain. "Choraz won't hurt the husband of his sister," he said thoughtfully. "I suppose that would apply to the husband of *any* sister."

"He only has two," said Leah.

Father chuckled and left the tent.

It was only later, as Leah was busy working with Zilpah on the winter blanket she was hemming to give Rachel as a wedding gift, that it occurred to her what Father might be planning.

But it was absurd. Father couldn't possibly think that Jacob would put up with a substitution of one sister for the other.

Nor would *I* allow it! Just because I've curbed my temper for the past few years doesn't mean I don't still have one.

It would solve half of Father's problems, though. Jacob would be married to Laban's daughter, right on schedule. Not the daughter he wanted, but a daughter's a daughter, yes? And from the moment Jacob accepted the substitution, he would be Laban's son-in-law, so Choraz wouldn't raise a hand against him. It would all be accomplished—*and* Rachel wouldn't have to marry right now, just as she wants.

At least that's how Father might see it. He might even imagine that, with Leah having spent most mornings in Jacob's dooryard for so many years, they might have fallen in love with each other.

Well, think again, Father. It's all study and teaching in that dooryard. Not like the tender little idylls of love that Jacob and Rachel enact most days out in the hills.

And Rachel would never sit still for it, either. It's one thing to delay the wedding and quite something else to have Jacob marry someone else. Just propose it, and Rachel will be out of her tent and drinking the wedding cup with Jacob as originally planned.

Then it dawned on her. No, no, Leah, you fool. *That* is Father's plan.

"What are you smiling about?" asked Zilpah. "How crooked your hemming stitch is?"

"It's not crooked, it's straighter than yours," said Leah.

"You're not smiling because your stitches are straight, either," said Zilpah.

"I was smiling because I think my father has figured out a way to make sure Rachel overcomes her fears and marries Jacob tomorrow."

"Is she still upset over whatever nonsense it was that Hassaweh told her?"

"You know she is, Zilpah," said Leah. "Since you're the champion collector of gossip in the camp."

"I'm glad my talents are appreciated," said Zilpah. "But at least I have the virtue of *telling* the gossip only to you."

"What do the people in the camp think is going to happen?"

"They think Laban is going to make sure his daughter keeps her promise to Jacob. Even though he spoils her terribly, they can't imagine that he'd shame himself in front of the whole world by backing out of a wedding promise."

"Father would never *make* Rachel do anything," said Leah. "Or me, either."

"Yes, well, remember that *they* all think of Laban as very strong and fierce when he's angry. They think this is the sort of thing that will earn Rachel her father's wrath for the first time in her life."

"They certainly guessed wrong about that."

"And yet you're smiling because your father has figured out a way to get Rachel married after all."

"That's right," said Leah. "The only question is whether I'm willing to play *my* part in the game."

"Are you?"

"No," said Leah.

"Then you're free to tell me what the game is," said Zilpah.

"There's no game. Just a little seed of an idea in Father's head. But I intend to pluck it out before it sprouts."

"Can I watch?"

"If you can see through tent walls."

"I'm left out of all the best gossip," said Zilpah.

"Sorry to inconvenience you."

Zilpah laughed. "You just hemmed the blanket to your apron."

In consternation, Leah picked up the blanket's edge. Her apron didn't come with it. "You're such a liar, Zilpah."

"Oh, weren't they sewn together? Foolish me."

"Just remember, in the dark I sew much better than you."

"Yes, but in the light you sew exactly the way you do in the dark."

"Everyone has their own special abilities," said Leah.

They went back to their work, content with their easy camaraderie.

As Leah worked, though, the thought kept preying on her. What if Father really does intend to try to get Jacob to marry me instead of Rachel? And what if Rachel really is so afraid of marriage that she goes along with it, for the sake of keeping the promise?

Would Jacob accept me?

Would I accept Jacob?

In all these years, she had never allowed herself to think of Jacob that way. If such thoughts arose, she stifled them as quickly as possible. He belonged to Rachel. God had brought him here for Rachel to marry, and for Leah to have the scriptures. There was a clear wall between the two roles of disciple and wife, and Leah was happy with the side of the wall she dwelt on.

But what if, what if, what if? What if Jacob said to Father, This must be the will of God? What if he said, in all these years I've come to see Leah as she really is. She's become a true disciple. She is the wife that the keeper of the birthright of Abraham needs as his companion. She'll help me to teach our children the law of God and all the stories of scripture. I welcome her as my wife. Rachel's fears were sent to her by God, for truly I came here to be Leah's husband. For Rachel can marry anyone, but only I have seen Leah's true worth and only I am her proper helpmeet.

The story she was spinning out in her mind was so sweet to her that it filled her eyes with tears.

And then she forced herself to remember that none of this was possible, that neither Jacob nor Rachel would ever go along with such a thing, and hopes like this were vain.

Even admitting that she hoped to marry her sister's husband filled her with shame, both for the disloyalty of it and how pathetic it was. Such a tragic figure I've already become. Yes, children, your great-aunt Leah was secretly in love with your grandfather Jacob, and she spent all her life wishing that he had loved her instead of Rachel. Could there be any more miserable life than that, to be pitied by every generation of her family, forever?

The thought made her angry, and so the tears stopped.

"Well, I'm glad that little summer shower is over," said Zilpah.

"What are you talking about?" said Leah.

"*I'm* not blind. I know tears falling on a blanket when I see them."

"I was thinking about how much I'll miss my sister after she's married."

"Oh, that's such a lie," said Zilpah.

"I really allow you far too much freedom in the way you talk to me."

"It's Jacob you'll miss."

That was so dead on the mark that Leah wondered for a moment if she had inadvertently spoken her thoughts out loud.

"For seven years you've listened to the scriptures in his dooryard every morning," said Zilpah. "When that stops, it's going to change your life a lot more than losing the sister who was always out in the hills somewhere petting the animals."

Ah. So Leah's heart had not been *so* transparent after all. "We've read all the books twice anyway," said Leah. "It's time to spend my mornings doing something else anyway."

"Like repeating them from memory?"

"What do you mean?"

"Haven't you been memorizing them?" asked Zilpah innocently.

"Not . . . *memorizing* them. But I think about them, yes."

"And say them over to yourself. Over and over. Your lips even move when you sew."

"I never really thought about it," said Leah. "Perhaps I *have* memorized some passages."

"I thought you were doing it on purpose," said Zilpah. "So you could always have your own copy of the holy books with you even after Jacob leaves with Rachel."

"I wish I *had* been doing that," said Leah. "Now all I'll have is a few passages, and those I probably remember all wrong."

"I'd wager you have the whole thing in your head, every word."

"No doubt. The problem is getting the words back out of my head in the right order."

"Now, really, tell me," said Zilpah. "What were you crying about?"

"I'm as bad as Rachel," said Leah. "I don't want things to change, and they're going to. Everything's going to be different, and I wish I had faith enough to trust what the Lord whispered to me—that everything was going to work out according to his plan."

"Oh, you can be sure of *that*," said Zilpah. "Since everything always works out according to the will of the . . . of the Lord."

Leah knew she had been about to say, by habit, "the will of the gods." Leah was never quite sure just how much of a believer Zilpah had become, even after years of studying the scripture alongside her and Bilhah. But she didn't make an issue of it.

"What worries you," Zilpah went on, "is whether you and the Lord will agree on what happens to be best for you."

"Oh, I'm much more pessimistic than that," said Leah. "I think the Lord is controlling what happens to Rachel and Jacob very, very carefully. But I don't think it makes a bit of difference in his plans what happens to me. I think he already changed my life in the only way that matters, and so he's done with me until it's time for me to die."

"Well, I'm glad you're so content with the knowledge that you're not the center of creation," said Zilpah. "It would be so crowded if *both* of us tried to occupy that spot."

"Oh, yes, God is building all his plans around you," said Leah.

"Making me a slave in Laban's house is all part of the plan," said Zilpah. "So when a great desert prince carries me off to bear him sons, it will seem all the more miraculous, and everyone will say, It could only have been God's will that Zilpah lived such a wonderful romantic love story."

Leah laughed. Too enthusiastically apparently, because now Zilpah was acting hurt.

"Oh, don't be offended," said Leah. "The only reason I laughed was because I thought I was the only one who thought that way."

"So we really *are* both in the center of creation," said Zilpah sourly.

"Don't worry. Since we're both making up stories no one else will see, there's plenty of room for both of us in the picture."

"Not a chance," said Zilpah. "I'm not sharing *my* imaginary desert prince with *anybody.*"

"Well, then, you're selfish and you don't deserve to have one."

Zilpah laughed. "Oh, I *hope* we don't get the life we *deserve,*" she said. "God wouldn't be that cruel."

CHAPTER 28

All morning, all afternoon of the wedding day, the air was filled with the smell of roasting meat for the feast and the sounds of frantic busyness and frolicking children. The boys and girls of the camp could sense the excitement of the adults, and with fewer duties to keep them busy, they acted out what everyone was feeling, going from games to japes to quarrels to tears in moments.

Only a few people realized that there was something seriously wrong with the wedding plans. And the three of them were sitting together in Laban's tent, arguing and, in Rachel's and Leah's case, taking turns crying.

"It isn't going to work," said Leah. "Jacob will know it's me the moment I walk out there."

"No he won't," said Laban.

"What's the point, anyway?" said Leah. "If Rachel wants

to marry him, then let her marry him. If she doesn't want to, then why go through a false ceremony?"

"It won't be a false ceremony," said Father. "Rachel will stand here in the tent and hear every word. She'll make the oaths and covenants as surely as if she were out there, and if she decides to go through with the wedding night, then she'll be truly married to Jacob."

"Then let her go out and stand there with Jacob herself!"

Rachel wept again. "I can't I can't I can't."

"Well, if you can't manage to stand there and say a few words," said Leah, "you don't deserve to marry him."

"It's not the words," said Rachel. "It's *lying* with him. And if I say the words, then I have to . . . lie with him."

"That's just the point," said Laban. "The ceremony is necessary, but it's not the actual wedding. You're not married until you lie together as husband and wife. And then you *are* married, whether you said the words or not."

"So every harlot in Byblos had a hundred husbands," said Leah.

"I won't hear indecency from my daughter," said Laban sternly. "And I said *as husband and wife,* if you'll recall."

"What's the point?" Leah asked again.

"You're *trying* not to understand. It's the *public* ceremony where a refusal to go ahead with the wedding would cause a scandal. So we'll have that ceremony—no scandal! What happens in Jacob's tent tonight—"

"What *won't* happen," said Rachel miserably.

"Is private. And quiet. No scandal. No public spectacle."

"Father, there's going to be a scandal, no matter what you do," said Leah.

Rachel cried again.

"It postpones the decision," said Laban.

"I'm not going to change my mind," said Rachel. "Especially if it was my *sister* who actually went through the ceremony."

"Oh," said Laban. "It bothers you that someone else would stand up with Jacob? Even though she's actually standing in for *you?*"

Leah shook her head. "Rachel, what is it, you don't want him, but you also don't want him ever to marry anyone else?"

"I *do* want to marry him. Someday."

Laban sighed noisily. "So now we begin the whole conversation again, for the third time."

"Oh, do it then!" cried Rachel. "I want to die."

"Why not just swallow hard," said Leah, "put on the dress, and go out there and marry the man?"

"I can't I can't I can't."

* * *

The piper changed from a jig to a more stately tune as the door to Laban's tent parted, and Laban came out.

But Laban was alone.

He walked to Jacob, who was already standing under the canopy that had been erected in Laban's dooryard. The jar of wine stood on a low table, with a rough clay cup for the bride and groom to share. Two small statues also stood on the table—one representing God and the other the great angel of his presence. Jacob looked askance at what some might take to be idols, though Laban had assured him many times over the years that they were nothing of the kind.

Laban had no intention of discussing the statues again now. "A moment's word with you, Jacob," said Laban.

Jacob stepped with him toward the door of the tent. "Is she afraid?" Jacob asked. "Let me talk to her."

"She *is* afraid, but your talking to her would only make her more nervous. You know how it is—the most important day in her life, and she absolutely knows she's going to do it all wrong and embarrass her. She's really very shy. It's part of the reason she's more at home with the flocks than in the camp."

"I know," said Jacob.

"If she's going to get through this, she has to feel that no one's staring at her."

"Everybody stares at the bride," said Jacob.

"That's why she begged me to let her use a thick, heavy veil. Like the one your mother used to wear."

Jacob smiled and shook his head. "If it makes her feel better to pretend that she's Rebekah in the old story, I don't mind."

"She's been crying all morning," said Laban. "She's hoarse. Can't be helped."

"Would you please assure her that if she doesn't want to, she doesn't have to lie with me tonight? As long as she comes to my tent, the marriage will be complete in everyone's eyes, and we can take as long as she needs to overcome her fear."

"That's very gracious of you," said Laban. "I'll tell her you said that."

Laban returned to the tent.

A few minutes later, he emerged again, this time with the bride on his arm. A veil of white wool covered her head, but it must have been transparent from the inside, because she walked surefootedly until she stood beside her husband to be.

Laban himself performed the ceremony, since he was the

priest of his household, as well as its master. He poured the wine into the cup and then prayed over it, asking the blessing of God upon his daughter and this good man that the Lord had brought to her. He slipped the cup under the veil for the bride to drink, and then gave it to Jacob, who drained the rest of the wine.

Then she walked three times around him, not led by anyone, showing that she chose of her own free will to make this man the center of her life. If she trembled and stepped with exaggerated care, that was only to be expected—rumor had it that the poor girl had been crying all week in fear of this very ceremony. Or of *something,* if the cruder rumors were to be believed.

"The cup that seals our marriage," said Jacob, "will never serve wine to any lips but ours." He dashed the cup to the ground, and it broke into shards, which he then ground into the earth with his sandaled foot, until the pieces were too small, too mingled with the dirt, for anyone to attempt to reassemble them.

When all the words were said, all the rituals acted out, Jacob turned to her and softly said, "That wasn't so bad, was it, Rachel? Now can't you let us see your lovely face?"

"Please no," she whispered. "Please."

She stumbled. Laban at once sprang to her side. "I told you," he whispered to Jacob. "She's so frightened she can hardly stand up. Everyone looking at her—that's what frightens her *most.*"

"Then won't it be hard for her to be shown to the guests at the feast?" asked Jacob quietly.

"Maybe she'll work up the courage to come let you show

her off at the feast. But if not, then she'll come to your tent tonight."

Jacob chuckled. To his bride he said, "Whatever you want, my love." And to Laban, he added, "I hope your wine is good and strong, so the guests will *think* they saw both a bride and groom at the feast."

Laban laughed, too, then helped his trembling daughter back to the tent.

CHAPTER 29

Inside the tent, Rachel helped Leah pull off the veil and remove the dress. Both of them were weeping, as silently as possible, while they did it.

"So who is married to him," Rachel finally whispered, when the dress was off. "You or me?"

"You or no one," said Leah.

"It *should* be you," said Rachel. "I don't deserve him. I didn't even have the courage to . . . *You're* the one who's strong enough to . . . He's a prophet, you're the one who knows the scriptures."

"You're the one who saw him in a vision," said Leah.

"You're the one who was born to be a prophet's wife," said Rachel. Though her words could hardly be understood, her voice was so distorted by her weeping.

"I wasn't born to be anyone's wife."

"He's going to be so angry at me tonight," said Rachel.

"Not if you go to him as his true wife. You said the words here inside the tent, didn't you?"

"But I didn't walk around him or drink the wine," said Rachel.

"Go to him tonight and lie with him," said Leah. "Every married woman in the world has done it."

"I'd go to him as a coward and a deceiver," said Rachel.

"I think *I'm* the one who just deceived him."

"Only because I'm such a coward."

"Between the two of us," said Leah, "we make one completely wretched woman."

Rachel began to laugh in the midst of her crying. "We're not even good enough to be *bad* by ourselves."

"We probably didn't even fool anybody," said Leah. "How hard will it be for them to figure out that Leah wasn't there to watch her own sister's wedding?" Then she gave a short, bitter laugh. "Though come to think of it, it probably won't surprise anyone at all. Poor miserable older sister, shamed by having her beautiful younger sister married before her, can't even show her face at the wedding."

"Well, you *didn't* show your face," said Rachel. Which set off another bout of quiet but slightly hysterical laughing.

They huddled alone in the tent for a long time. Not until the feast was well under way did their father come to them.

"Well, that's done," said Laban.

"Done?" asked Leah. "You mean people actually believed it was Rachel?"

"Of course," said Laban. "You're the same height. Your voices sound alike."

"Not very much," said Leah.

"Nobody said a thing," said Laban. "Except to cluck their

tongues about how shy Rachel is. And you're just as happy to be missing the feast, since there have been more than a few jests from your brothers about a wedding night spent with a bride dressed in a thick woollen curtain."

"Thank you for telling us that, Father," said Leah. "But just between us, I think that having no bride at all will make his wedding night even more inconvenient."

Rachel's answer was to bury her face in the rugs.

"As for that," said Laban, "I have a plan."

"I hope it doesn't involve me any further," said Leah.

"It involves you completely," said Laban. He glanced at Rachel and then smiled thinly at Leah. "We've had a wedding. The question of exactly who got married is still up in the air. So here's my thought. Rachel isn't ready to get married. But her older sister is."

"Am I?" said Leah.

"So tonight, I'll take my veiled daughter to Jacob's tent," said Laban. "If Rachel wants to be the daughter under the veil, so be it. But if she doesn't, then Leah will go in and offer herself. If Jacob accepts her, then we've followed proper custom and the older daughter is married first. How can anyone make a scandal out of that?"

"Jacob won't accept me," said Leah. "I'm sure he'll be very kind about it, but he'll send me away."

"Ah, but that's why my plan is so brilliant. He'll see that *I* did everything I could to keep my promise, including sending him my older daughter, whose value he and I both know better than any other men alive."

Leah held her tongue.

"So he can't be angry with me," Laban went on. "He can't be angry at Leah for offering herself in her sister's place. As a sort of sacrifice. How can the son of Isaac complain about *that*? And he can't be angry at Rachel, because *she* can't help being so afraid. No shame, no scandal."

"No shame for *you*, you mean," said Leah. "Plenty of shame for Rachel and me."

"No! None at all," said Laban. "What shame?"

"Well, Rachel will be ashamed that she was afraid to marry a prophet of God," said Leah. "Right, Rachel?"

Still face down in the rugs, Rachel nodded.

"And I'll be ashamed because I offered myself to this man without any invitation from him, and of course he rejected me."

"He hasn't rejected you yet," said Laban.

"But he will."

"It won't be a *rejection*," said Laban. "It will be an opportunity that he chose not to accept."

Leah laughed nastily at her father's imaginary distinction between two versions of the same thing.

Laban leaned close to his older daughter and whispered in her ear, "If sending you to Jacob doesn't get Rachel out of this tent, nothing will."

Rachel rolled over and sat up. For a moment, they thought she had heard them. Then they thought the stratagem had already worked.

"Yes," said Rachel. "Send her. She's the one that Jacob should marry. He'll see that and accept her."

"No he won't," said Leah. "He's been crazy with love for you for seven years. Do you think that will just go away because another woman shows up in his tent?"

"But the spirit of Wisdom will guide him," said Rachel.

"He'll choose you. But if he doesn't, then I'll know that it's truly the will of God that I marry him."

"So," said Laban, "if he sends Leah back, you'll go to him? Tonight?"

"Yes," said Rachel. "Because then I'll know it's the will of God."

CHAPTER 30

Leah knew that for the servants' weddings, there were often loud revelries outside the wedding tent, with plenty of lewd jests. But for his daughter's wedding, Father had forbidden any such vulgar activity. He had specifically forbidden his sons to leave their tents, and had posted men to watch from a distance to make sure no one disturbed Jacob's nuptial tent.

So there was no one to look closely at her as her father led her from his own tent to Jacob's.

"I'll be waiting outside," said Laban. "If he sends you back out."

"*When* he sends me," said Leah.

"God will guide him," said Laban.

"If the Lord of heaven is running this wedding, wouldn't he have arranged for somebody to tell somebody else the truth?"

"That's your job right now," said Laban.

Inside the tent, to Leah's surprise, there was no lamp burning.

"It's dark," she said.

"I didn't want you to feel shy with me," said Jacob. "Did your father tell you what I said? There's no need for us to do anything but sleep tonight, if you prefer."

No, Father hadn't mentioned it. "Jacob, don't you know who I am?" asked Leah.

"I think you're the same woman who stood with me under the canopy today," said Jacob.

So he *had* noticed that it wasn't Rachel inside the veil. "I am, if you'll have me. Father brought me here tonight to fulfil the bargain, even though I'm a poor substitute."

There was a long pause. In the darkness, Leah listened for Jacob's breathing, his movement, to tell her what he was feeling. Wrath? Pity?

He took a couple of quick steps, his bare feet making little noise on the rugs. Surely he wasn't going to strike her for daring to come to his tent in Rachel's place—not that she wouldn't deserve it.

But instead, his hands took her by the shoulders and gently removed the veil from her. Then he pulled her to him, his hands strong but kind.

She heard his breath change, felt the slight wind of his movement as he bowed over her. His cheek brushed hers. His lips moved along her cheek until they found her own lips. He kissed her.

"Then you accept me?" she whispered. "After seven years of service, you'll be content with *me*?"

"What God has given me, I would be ungrateful to refuse," he whispered. "Will you accept *me* tonight? I'm content to wait, if you prefer."

Leah's head spun with giddiness. He had accepted her!

Something she had never allowed herself even to dream of. Despite Rachel's dream, Jacob had been brought here for her.

"No," said Leah.

Jacob relaxed his grip and started to pull away.

"I mean, no, there's no need to wait," said Leah. "As you said, what God has given me, I would be ungrateful to refuse."

"You'll have to help me," said Jacob. "I've never done this before."

"Neither have I," said Leah.

"No," said Jacob. "I mean, I've never undressed a woman."

Leah laughed lightly. "I can take care of that part."

"Then . . . please do it . . . now. If you don't mind my making you do all the hard work on the first night of our marriage."

"May all your commands bring me so much joy, Husband," she said.

"May God help me learn how to bring you joy every day, Wife," he answered.

After that, few words were said. For Leah, though, the silence was full of music. The sound of his breath and her own breath, mingling. The feeling of his rough hands on her smooth skin, and his own smooth skin under her hands. The smells of their bodies and the woollen rugs and the desert air on this beautiful, musical, magical night.

* * *

And then it was morning.

She woke before him and lay there in the darkness of the tent and whispered a soft prayer of thanks for this great blessing God had given her. She prayed also that Rachel would be given happiness to equal her own.

Sometime during her prayer Jacob woke up—she could tell, from the difference in his breathing, though he didn't move.

When her prayer ended with a soft "amen," Jacob reached out and touched her. "What's this about, child? I thought I heard you praying for yourself by name."

"Not for myself," said Leah, wondering what he had thought he heard, amid her whispering.

And then, with a wave of sickness passing through her body, she realized what he had heard.

"O Lord God," she whispered, "let it not be true."

"Let what not be true?" asked Jacob. He got up and walked to the flap that separated his inner chamber from the outer one.

"Jacob, you know who I am, don't you? You told me you did last night. You told me that you know who I am."

"What are you talking about?" he said. "What are you upset about?"

Then the curtain parted and light came into the chamber, and even though he was too far away for Leah to see anything more of him than a blur in the shape of a man, she knew that he could see her clearly.

"I thought you accepted me," she said. "You said you accepted me."

"What have you done?" said Jacob softly. No, coldly.

"Rachel was frightened," said Leah. "Father brought me to offer myself as a substitute. I said so. I—how could you not know it was me?"

"It was dark," said Jacob. His voice was soft, but sharp as

a blade. "Dark, because your father said Rachel was so shy, afraid to be looked at. But I see now that it was for another purpose. To make a fool of me."

"How could you mistake me for her?" said Leah. "Even in the dark, our voices aren't so alike. We don't move alike, we don't use the same words, you've heard our voices a thousand times and you couldn't tell it was me?"

"I couldn't *see*," said Jacob.

"So what?" said Leah. "I can't ever see anybody, and I have no trouble telling them apart."

"Very clever," said Jacob. "I'm sure you'll have an answer for everything. But the truth is very plain. I served Laban seven years for the hand of Rachel, and on my wedding night, he brought you instead, in the darkness."

"He was waiting outside for you to send me away, if you didn't want me," said Leah. "And Rachel . . . she was waiting for you to decide. Which of us you wanted."

"I decided seven years ago. By what sign did I lead you or anyone else to think that I might have changed my mind?"

"No sign, nothing, you did nothing, you said nothing. But Rachel was so frightened, and Father was afraid that we'd be shamed in front of—"

"But tricking me into marrying the wrong daughter, *that* doesn't shame him?" Jacob laughed bitterly. "Get dressed. I need to go find my wife."

"*I'm* your wife," said Leah.

"A woman who sneaks into a man's tent and offers him her body might be many things, but she is *not* a wife."

"I stood beside you, I walked around you, I drank from the cup with you," said Leah. "And when I came here I told you I was a poor substitute, and you said you accepted me. I am no harlot, and if you treat me as one then let God choose between your injustice and mine."

Jacob seemed not to have heard her. "So Rachel was part of this deception, too? Whose idea was it? Did Laban compel you? Or was it your idea? Why did Rachel go along with it? She loves me—I know she does."

"Yes, she does," said Leah. "But she was terrified of marriage. Things that people told her. Hassaweh."

"Rachel's not a fool—why would she believe anything *that* woman said?"

"Why wouldn't she believe her dearest brother's wife?" said Leah. "But yes, go find her, Jacob, because when you accepted me last night, Rachel must have thought—her heart must be broken."

"If she has a heart," said Jacob. "If anyone in your family has a heart."

And then he was gone.

Leah got up and looked around for clothing, but then she realized that she had nothing but the wedding dress to wear. If Jacob had loved her, if he had known what she thought he knew, then she could have worn that dress proudly out of his tent. But he hated her, he believed she had tricked him, he as much as called her a harlot. She could never put on that dress again.

But she also couldn't put on a man's clothing, and she couldn't leave the tent naked as she now was.

So she waited, weeping and praying, for Jacob to return or for Zilpah to come for her. Or would it be Bilhah? Had Father told their handmaidens who it was who was going into Jacob's tent last night?

"O God in heaven," she prayed. "How could you let this

happen? You put the words into my mouth, that if Rachel went to Father, everything would happen according to your will. Was this what you wanted? For me to give myself to a husband who hates me? Who thinks I'm a harlot, a deceiver? Why couldn't you let me die as a baby instead of living this terrible life?"

Then she wept again. And prayed again, and wept again, until finally she heard someone come into the tent.

It was Bilhah.

"What happened here?" asked Bilhah. "What are you doing in Jacob's tent? And . . . naked?"

Leah could only weep more bitterly, as Bilhah reached her own conclusion and fled from her.

She was praying again when Zilpah came, carrying clothing for her.

"It's too late to pray for God to let you die as a baby," said Zilpah. "Why do you waste God's time with prayers that even he can't answer?"

"Leave me alone," said Leah.

"I brought you clothes."

"Leave them."

"And a pot, just in case you drank any liquid yesterday that you don't want to leave just anywhere this morning."

Leah resigned herself to her fate and got up from the rugs. Zilpah quickly slid a dress over her head and helped her pull it down all around.

"Is there anyone outside watching?"

"That's really two questions," said Zilpah. "In answer to the first question, yes, everybody knows what happened last night. In one version or another. But the answer to the second question is, no, there's nobody outside the tent to watch you leave. Your father banned everyone from the area."

"Which means they'll all be watching from a distance," said Leah. "Which version do people believe? That I'm a harlot? That I stole my sister's husband?"

"Nobody's putting out the harlot one," said Zilpah. "You're the first one to say anything of the kind."

"No I'm not," said Leah.

"The first one *I* heard," Zilpah corrected herself. "There are a few people saying that it's a shame you stole your sister's husband. Those are the ones who are sure Jacob will divorce you immediately. But most people are saying your father forced you both to go along with tricking Jacob. So they think you're nothing worse than an obedient daughter. Then again, there are those who remember how you used to get your father to give you your way, so they combine the stories into one where you threw tantrums until your father gave in and set up this elaborate trick. Of course, in *every* version Jacob comes out looking dumb as your thumb, not to be able to tell the difference between you and Rachel."

"It was dark," said Leah bitterly. "All girls are beautiful in the dark."

"Not all," said Zilpah cheerfully. "One thinks, for instance, of girls with goiters. And amputated limbs. Not to mention lepers. But I get your point."

"Thank you for telling me the truth about what people are saying," said Leah.

"Let them say whatever they want. You should hear what they say about *me*."

Leah pressed her lips together rather than say the hurtful truth that came immediately to her mind—that she must have sunk low indeed, to have someone with Zilpah's reputation think it would comfort her that her own was no worse.

Still, Leah's silence must have contained the message. "For what it's worth," said Zilpah, "I might have a reputation for being free with my body. But no man has ever had possession of me, and no man will, until and unless I have a husband."

"Then we truly are equal," said Leah. "Until my husband puts me aside. I pray that such shame will never come to you."

"I doubt it will ever come to you, either," said Zilpah.

"What else *can* he do? How can Jacob stay married to a woman he thinks tricked him into lying with her?"

Zilpah actually laughed out loud. "Are you serious? If men refused to stay married to women who tricked them, the human race would die out in a few generations."

Annoying as Zilpah's matter-of-fact attitude might be, it had a calming effect—as Zilpah no doubt intended. And since she had already named the worst, it dispelled Leah's dread of facing the world in her shame.

Or so she thought. She was calm enough walking to her own tent with Zilpah helping to guide her. But once inside, she was soon back to wishing she could die rather than go outside and face others again.

It was a long and terrible morning, but the worst moment was when Bilhah came in, looking for the wedding dress.

"I don't have it," said Leah. "I left it in Jacob's tent."

"You walked back here naked?" said Bilhah snidely.

"Zilpah brought me this," said Leah, too miserable even to protest Bilhah's impudent attitude. Besides, Bilhah was a free woman. She could say whatever she liked.

"I just want you to know," said Bilhah, "how bitterly Rachel wept all night last night, thinking she had lost Jacob."

What right did Bilhah have to try to make her feel worse than she already did? Leah couldn't stop herself from retorting, "How appropriate. She wept bitterly all day yesterday, thinking she might have to marry him."

"I hope you someday have a night like the one Rachel had last night," said Bilhah. "A night when you believe that the man you love has tossed you aside in favor of your own *sister*."

"What an excellent witch you are," said Leah. "Your curse will certainly be granted every night for the rest of my life."

Bilhah might have glared at her, for all Leah could see. All that mattered was that she left.

But soon Leah's anger at Bilhah faded and was replaced by compassion for Rachel—last night must have been terrible for her.

I didn't mean it, Rachel. Please, God, let her see that I didn't mean this to happen.

* * *

Zilpah brought her food and drink, twice. Otherwise, it was late afternoon before Leah talked with anyone else. Father came to the tent and sank wearily and sadly onto the rugs. Then he reached out his arms for Leah. She collapsed into his arms, weeping all over again, as if it had all just happened. She could bear Bilhah's hostility and Zilpah's matter-of-factness, but Father's compassion destroyed her composure completely.

When she was done, or at least quiet enough for him to talk, he began telling her what his day's work had been.

"First thing you have to know is, Jacob was fair to you. Oh, at first he doubted what you said, but the point is, he *told* me what you said. And I explained to him that because you could never count on your eyes to tell you who's who, it wouldn't have occurred to you that he couldn't tell one sister from the other just because it was dark. And when he repeated your conversation as best he could remember it, it became plain to all of us that you believed you had told him who you were."

"Who's 'all of us'?" asked Leah. "Please tell me Terah and Nahor weren't there."

"Of course they weren't," said Laban. "Am I insane? Jacob was there, and Rachel. And me. That's all."

"I wish you had included Bilhah," said Leah. "She thinks I'm evil. She even cursed me."

"Did she? Then I'll have her out of this camp in the morning."

"No, no, Father," said Leah. "Please don't. She's angry because she thinks I betrayed Rachel. She'd be a poor friend to Rachel if she didn't feel that way."

"You and Jacob, two of a kind. More worried that no harm comes to the person who injured you—though in his case, you're only the person he *thought* injured him. Till I explained."

"What did you explain?"

"That it was all my idea—which it was. But there was Rachel, and he obviously loves her, and the only way out of this mess was to have her marry him—which you can be sure she thinks is an *excellent* idea today, the silly selfish child. So I couldn't very well tell him that all of this was about trying to get his beloved Rachel to overcome her terror and marry him."

"What *did* you tell him?"

"That it's our custom to make sure the eldest daughter is married first. That I made you go to him so we wouldn't be shamed in front of all our neighbors. So Rachel doesn't have to explain to him why she couldn't bear the thought of sleeping with him, and you could."

"That version intersects with the truth here and there."

"It isn't truth I'm after, it's peace. So here's how it stands. Next week, he marries Rachel. And serves seven more years because, after all, that's the established bride-price around here."

"Seven years! He'll hate me."

"No he won't. How was he going to support even *one* wife, let alone two? This time, I'll give him a couple of servants of his own, to tend his own flocks. Which I'll give him. Nothing big, mind you. Nothing to inspire my ridiculous sons to any acts of violence against the Lord's anointed. But enough that if he tends his flocks as well as he tends my own, he'll leave here after seven years with enough to support a family."

"So you didn't offer him half the younglings?" asked Leah.

"That was while I was thinking it would be only a year before Rachel married him. Now he'll be with us seven more years—if I gave him half my younglings each year, and he didn't give me back half of *his*, within seven years he'd be the rich lord and I'd be the one with a small fraction of the great man's herd."

"That's why I don't like numbers," said Leah. "That doesn't even make sense. How could he ever have more than half?"

"Never mind," said Laban. "Just believe me, he would."

Something dawned on her. "If he's serving another seven years—two wives—"

"What are you asking?"

"He's not putting me away?"

"No! Never! What were you thinking? *He* may not have known what was going on, but *you* entered his tent as a married woman going to her husband, and if he tried to make a public claim that it was anything else, I couldn't stop Choraz from killing him. I wouldn't even try."

"Oh," said Leah. "So he's going to keep me as his wife because otherwise he'd be killed."

"He's going to keep you as his wife because he's a man of honor. And because you, too, were acting in good faith . . . which he now understands."

"Or agrees to pretend to believe."

"You weren't there, and I was, so my version is the true one."

"Or the kind one."

"Leah," said Laban. "You know I didn't set out to get you a husband by trickery, though that's the version everybody's going to hear. What do I care? In another few years I'll be dead—"

"What?"

"No, I'm perfectly healthy, but *everybody* dies, and I'm a lot closer to it than I used to be, that's all I meant. In a few years I'll be dead and then I'll be with God, who knows the truth of what happened, and what do I care what the world says about me then? My point was, I didn't set out to get you a husband by trickery. Neither did you. Things just happened, step by step. Very unreasonable, unlikely things happened, because they gradually came to seem perfectly logical at the time. Do you know why?"

"We're really stupid?"

"I see the hand of God in all of this."

Leah shook her head. "God can't be blamed for *this* mess."

"If it's a mess, then you're right, he can't be blamed. But what if it isn't a mess?"

"What do you mean?"

"What if God meant for both you and Rachel to be married to this man?"

"Then why didn't he give us *both* dreams of him? For that matter, when Jacob was having his vision of the ladder into heaven, why didn't God tell him right then, Go to Padan-aram and marry both daughters of Laban? Yes, the blind one too!"

"That's just the point," said Father. "God directs what happens, but he also lets us make our own choices. Jacob arrived here as the kind of man who would fall in love with the pretty shepherd girl, but pay little attention to the sister with tender eyes. But after seven years, he knows your true value."

"He hates me, Father."

"Well, yes, probably, at the moment. Not *hates*, probably, but he's certainly annoyed at the whole business. My point is that God gave us all choices—Rachel didn't *have* to work herself into such a lather over her fears, did she?—and we took them, but since he knew the choices we'd make, he was able to set things up exactly the way he wanted."

"Or else he doesn't care what we do, and we made this web ourselves and then got stuck on it like a bunch of flies."

"Usually that would be the likeliest answer. But you forget that Jacob is a prophet, and the keeper of the birthright, and part of the promise to Abraham was that his descendants would be as numerous as the sands of the sea, as the stars in the heavens. So far, how many descendants does he have? But with two wives going at it with Jacob, maybe some of that numerousness can finally get started."

"With Rachel's children lording it over mine, because she's the favorite wife."

"You have a head start," said Father. "So with any luck—or with the favor of the Lord—yours will be the firstborn son."

"And my lastborn, too."

"I doubt that."

"I'm not likely to get a second chance to conceive one."

"Leah, do you think I wasn't looking out for you? Rachel's wedding will be a week from now so that you can have your full week with him. And after that, he's promised me that he'll do his duty and give you every chance to have more children."

Leah began to cry again.

"What now?" said Father. "I thought you'd be happy to know he's promised to treat you as a real wife."

"I am happy, Father. Thank you."

"So why the tears?"

"Because last night he lay with me as if he loved me. From now on, he'll lie with me because it's his duty. I'll know the difference. And I'll know that whenever he's with Rachel, it will be the other way for her. Always with love."

"If he ever mistreats you, you just tell me and—"

"No, Father. You don't understand. He'll never *mistreat* me. He just won't *love* me."

Father looked at her in growing comprehension. "Leah. Oh, my poor darling. Oh, Leah." He held her tightly. "I never realized. Until now. Oh, dear Leah, you're in love with him, aren't you? You truly love him."

"I didn't deceive him, Papa," Leah said through her tears. "I loved him, yes, but I never would have tricked him. You know that, don't you?"

"Of course I know that," said Father. "Of course I know. And you know something else? He'll come to love you. He will."

"Why should he?" asked Leah. "The Lord may have maneuvered us all so that I'd be one of his wives and bear some of his sons and daughters. But why should God care whether I actually have a husband who loves me? After all, Father, I'm the one the Lord chose to be born half blind. Clearly my happiness isn't very high on his tally of things to care about."

"Leah, you poor thing, it hasn't been an easy life for you. But you *are* alive, and you have a husband that you love, even if he's angry at you right now. You'll have children—you'll see. The Lord will give you so many blessings . . . the thing is, right now, it just won't do you any good to be angry at the Lord. Even if it hurts his feelings, it's not going to stop him from doing whatever is best for you. So you might as well trust in him that even the things that seem bad are really for the best."

"I know," said Leah.

"Of course you know," said Laban. "You've been reading the holy books."

"He'll never let me near them again," said Leah.

"Yes he will."

"He only let me study them because he had Bilhah doing his copywork."

"Right," said Father. "And until you have sons old enough to read and write a good hand, she'll probably go right on doing it."

"Bilhah will?"

"Didn't I tell you? I'm giving you Zilpah to be your hand-maiden to take with you into your marriage. And I'm giving Bilhah to Rachel."

"You can't give Bilhah to anybody. She's a free woman."

"Right, yes, technically I *hired* her. But she didn't make a fuss about it. Where else would she go? Besides, she's so sure that Rachel has been badly treated—as if Rachel didn't *start* the whole mess—anyway, Bilhah is full of compassion for her poor, injured mistress. She would have insisted on staying with her even if I had forbidden it."

"I'm glad Rachel will have a friend."

"And so will you."

Leah laughed at that. "Zilpah? I suppose she's a friend. But you won't find her fighting for me the way Bilhah's standing up for poor Rachel."

"Won't I?" said Father. "You should have seen how she went straight to the worst gossips in camp—and you can be sure Zilpah knows who they *all* are—and laid down the law about what will and won't be said about you in this camp. I've never seen her so . . . fiery."

"Oh."

"Yes," said Father. "Whether you *feel* you do or not, you *have* a loyal friend."

"Well, that's something, I guess," said Leah.

"It's not everything, but yes, it's *something*. And a husband is something."

Leah hugged him tighter. "And a father who loves me, that's everything."

"No," said Father. "That's just 'something,' too. A whole bunch of somethings, that's what everything is."

His words were so absurd that Leah couldn't help laughing, and this time with real mirth.

"I never thought I'd hear that sound again," said Father. "Leah, laughing as if she were really enjoying herself."

PART XII

WIVES

CHAPTER 31

There was another wedding in the camp at Padan-aram, only a week after the first. This time the husband placed the veil over the bride's face himself. There was no doubt about whom he was marrying.

This time the bride did not tremble. She stood boldly to drink from the cup and to say the words she had to say, and when she walked around her husband, she did it, not three times, but seven.

At the feast, Jacob brought his new bride out for the company to cheer her, and they did it heartily. A few attempts at ribald humor were made, but her brother Choraz made it clear that there would be no more of that, and so there wasn't.

That night, Jacob fetched Rachel from her father's tent himself, and when they came inside his own tent, he kept a lamp burning. "I know you're shy," he said. "But I have to see you."

"I was afraid before," Rachel answered. "But then I learned that there was something I feared worse than marrying you."

"What was that?"

"Not marrying you," said Rachel.

By morning she had learned what a liar Hassaweh was.

* * *

That night her sister Leah slept very little. But it was not from jealousy. She would never begrudge Rachel the love of Jacob—it was Rachel's from the moment of that first kiss at the well, and Leah had never aspired to supplant her sister.

No, Leah was awake because she spent the night in prayer. For that morning she had awoken feeling nauseated, and hadn't been able to keep any food down until early afternoon.

She knew that it might be nothing more than the turbulence of her feelings about her husband's wedding that day—certainly the gossips of the camp would be speculating that Leah had induced the vomiting as an excuse to stay away from Rachel's wedding. Let them talk. Leah knew better.

She prayed for her nausea to mean what she wanted so desperately for it to mean. Let it be a boychild in her womb that made her feel like this—for she knew some women were sick right from the time when their husband's seed first took root inside the womb.

"O Lord," she prayed, "look upon my affliction. Let me bear him a son. Then my husband will love me."

AFTERWORD

I never intended the story of Rachel and Leah to be broken up among multiple volumes. It happened against my will.

I had no problem with keeping *Sarah* and *Rebekah* to one book each. But unlike either of those books, the story of Rachel and Leah has four very strong female characters who needed separate development. I had to create a network of attitudes and experiences for each of the six pairings. That takes time—measured both in book pages and writing time.

About halfway through writing this novel, I realized that there was no way to carry the story through to the logical ending place: Rachel's death after the birth of Benjamin. For a while I tried to bring it to an end at the point where Bilhah and Zilpah are given to Jacob as concubines, but that will now be one of the major events in the next book in the Women of Genesis series, *The Wives of Israel*. What finally worked for this book was to close the story when all the anticipation of the marriage is brought to its messy and painful fruition on Leah's wedding night.

Because this book ended up being one of the most difficult writing projects of my career, it didn't fit into my writing schedule as I had planned. Instead of writing it in the summer of 2003, the bulk of it became a project for the winter of 2004—precisely at the time when I began teaching two writing courses at Southern Virginia University. SVU is located three hours by car from my home in Greensboro. I had planned to commute with the company of books on tape, but I simply couldn't afford to take that much time away from writing.

Instead, our resident webwright, Scott Allen (you can see his work on my websites, *www.hatrack.com, www.nauvoo.com, www.ornery.org, www.strongverse.com,* and *www.taleswapper.com),* put his laptop in the trunk of my Crown Vic and drove me up highway 220 and I-81 twice a week. While I taught three hours of classes, he hooked into the SVU computer system in the office of my coteacher, Robert Stoddard, and worked on our websites.

For some inexplicable reason, it turned out that throughout the semester, I was only able to really concentrate and solve the writing problems of this novel while I was working on my laptop in the car during those drives. So about three-fourths of this novel was written within arm's reach of Scott Allen. I have *never* written a book with somebody else in the room until now. I'm just glad he's even more of an introvert than I am—he was perfectly content to drive in silence for hours on end.

Meanwhile, we got to know every McDonald's and Subway between Greensboro and Buena Vista. Thanks, Scott, for service above and beyond the call of your official job description—loose as that already was!

This book is dedicated to Robert and D'Ann Stoddard. It's a wonderful thing when a dear friend from bachelor days marries a woman that becomes as good a friend as he is. Over the past decades, Kristine and I have come to think of Robert and D'Ann as some of the dearest friends in our lives. But until the fall of 2003, we only got to see them when we went to Los Angeles—or, occasionally, when Robert's job at UCLA took him to Washington DC on a lobbying expedition. Now he teaches at the new LDS-oriented Southern Virginia University (which took over the name and campus of what used to be a women's college, which had long occupied a one-time resort in the Shenandoah Valley), so we get to see Robert and D'Ann far more often than before—to our delight.

For those who don't know, Robert was my collaborator on many theatrical projects when we were both in college. Steeped in musical comedy, Robert arrived at BYU in 1969 armed with extraordinary talent as a composer, writer, and performer—and almost as much ambition as I had. Once we started working together, we both produced some of the best work in our theatrical writing careers, though Robert never really needed *me*—he does brilliant work on his own.

Robert's ties with my career, as well as my life, are many. For instance, my book *Folk of the Fringe* began as a project to write a post-apocalyptic musical drama with Robert. We have some of the songs written, and all we're waiting for is my script for *Pageant Wagon*.

The very book you're holding is owed to a collaboration from our college days. I wrote the play *Stone Tables*, about Moses and Aaron, while I was a missionary in Brazil, and sent it off to Charles W. Whitman, my favorite professor and good friend in the BYU theatre department. Dr. Whitman (sorry, I can never call him by any other name; it would be like giving the Pope a nickname) immediately put it on the mainstage production schedule for the winter of 1973, and wrote back to tell me that Robert Stoddard—with whom I had already collaborated on several projects before my mission—was writing the music for the songs.

Songs? What songs?

I had written the play in verse—still my preferred form. (Yes, that's right. I also wrote a long set of poetic essays in heroic couplets. I may never recover from my one-sided love affairs with William Shakespeare and Alexander Pope. "One-sided" because, as far as I know, neither one of them has ever bothered to read anything of mine.) Seeing the words so nicely lined up in rows, Dr. Whitman made the connection I hadn't made. It was Robert's music—edgy, dramatic, powerful—that elevated the production to real event status at BYU that winter. It was so successful they held it over for a couple of weeks, and were still turning people away from packed houses at the end. I missed all of that, being a missionary in Brazil—they don't let you go home just because you have a big opening night. But I've heard recordings and I knew all of the actors anyway, either before or after my mission.

Years later, determined to get Robert's brilliant music before the public, I made a deal with Deseret Book (the parent company of Shadow Mountain, which published this volume in hardcover) to record and publish a CD of Robert's and my music from *Stone Tables*, to be marketed along with a novelization of the play, which I would write.

That book marked my return to writing adaptations of

scriptural stories. That's what half my playwriting in college consisted of, but in those days I knew I was writing for a Mormon audience. Now, with *Stone Tables*, I deliberately opened the book to any reader who cared about the story of Moses, Aaron, and Miriam, whether Christian, Muslim, Jewish, or unbeliever. I don't require the reader to believe—or disbelieve—that God is speaking to these characters. What matters is that *they* believe it, and act accordingly.

Stone Tables as a novel worked—to my satisfaction, anyway—and so it was only natural to look for a chance to do it again. That's when I contacted Deseret Book's then-competitor in the LDS publishing market, Bookcraft, where publisher Cory Maxwell made a deal with me over the phone for six books, the three "Women of Genesis" (*Sarah, Rebekah,* and *Rachel and Leah*) and three others about women in the Book of Mormon. Whereupon Bookcraft promptly sold itself to Deseret Book and these books became Shadow Mountain novels. (Later, TOR, my science fiction publisher, acquired the rights to at least the first two books in the series in mass market paperback.)

Fortunately, Cory Maxwell was acquired right along with Bookcraft, and he is still my publisher for this series of scripture-based novels. Kristine and I consider him, along with his boss, the inestimable and delightful Sheri Dew, to be friends as well as collaborators in the publishing biz.

In fact, just to take this full circle, Sheri Dew, the chief of the creative end of Deseret Book (i.e., she's in charge of everything that directly affects me except signing the checks), has theatrical roots—and back in college days, she was part of a USO tour of Alaskan military bases where the pianist was none other than . . . Robert Stoddard. There are twelve million Mormons, but apparently we all still know each other.

Anyway, this network of connections between Robert Stoddard and this book made it obvious to me that this book should be dedicated to him and D'Ann, who know more than a little bit about how two strangers can create a marriage that is more than the sum of its parts. In a book like this, which is about marriage, I couldn't think of anyone more appropriate to receive the dedication. However, I can assure you that Robert never married any of D'Ann's sisters.

There are several others who contributed to this novel, besides those already mentioned. My wife, Kristine, read every chapter as soon as I managed to squeeze it out of my head, and made many good suggestions and corrections. I also showed the chapters to Erin Absher and, between her cruises, Kathryn H. Kidd, who were both very helpful, even though they were reading chapters sometimes weeks apart. It's a good thing they both had Genesis chapter 29 to help them keep continuity.

Parts of the book were also written in the home of my cousin Mark and his wife Margaret, whose generosity seems to know no boundaries—and believe me, I've tested them strenuously.

Besides Sheri and Cory, we've had other good friends at Deseret Book who've been of great help in creating this series. Richard Peterson is the editor who makes sure that errors in this series are rare—though I remain responsible for any that survive. On previous books we've taken great pleasure in working with Emily Watts and Kathie Terry, who have both moved on to other work while this book was still aborning. We'll miss working with them.

And thanks to Tom Doherty, my publisher at TOR and still the best friend a writer's career could ever have, for picking up these out–of-genre books and keeping them alive in mass-market paperback editions.

It's probably absurd to thank Mel Gibson, who has no idea this book even exists, but if these books are ever adapted for film or television productions, it will be because he opened the door to serious, faithful film adaptations of scripture with his brilliant and courageous production of *The Passion of the Christ.* Even though at this writing, Hollywood seems determined to treat *The Passion* as a fluke and continue to ignore the huge audience for well-written, well-performed, well-filmed scriptural movies, that might change, and if it does, it will be because he opened the door.

In the end, though, this novel is owed to the people who have taught me what marriage is. My parents, Willard and Peggy Card, created the first of many marriages I've had a chance to observe and learn from, but observation is never enough. It wasn't until Kristine Allen agreed to form a new family with me that I began to really understand how this sort of thing is supposed to be done. Unfortunately, she didn't get a prophet as a husband—they're rather thin on the ground, I'm afraid—and nothing about our lives together has been anything like what she might have expected when we made that bargain twenty-seven years ago, but together we've faced enough challenges that I might actually know what I'm talking about when I try to write about what marriage means in the lives of women and men.

When it comes to the next book, though, our kids— Geoffrey, Emily, and Zina—won't have been any help at all. Where are the terrible sibling rivalries that might have prepared me to write about parents trying to raise Joseph and his brothers? Nor has any of them wiped out an entire middle-eastern village in order to avenge the rape of their sister. And as for Judah and his daughter-in-law . . . let's just leave that one alone. Mind you, I'm not complaining. The last thing a parent wants is to raise children with lives as interesting as Jacob's had.

READER'S GROUP

GUIDE

The stories of the women who went before us teach us something of our own lives, and never more so than in Orson Scott Card's novel *Rachel and Leah*. In this fascinating work of historical fiction, Card paints a vivid picture of the intertwined lives of four complicated women. Here we meet Leah, the oldest daughter of Laban, whose "tender eyes" prevent her from participating fully in the work and social structure of her father's camp; Rachel, the spoiled younger daughter, who is from Leah's perspective the petted and privileged beauty of the family; Bilhah, an orphan who is not quite a slave but not really a family member and searching to fit in; and Zilpah, who knows only how to use her beauty to manipulate men and who longs for something better than the life of drudgery and servitude into which she was born.

Into their lives comes Jacob, a handsome and charismatic kinsman who is clearly fated to be Rachel's husband. But that doesn't prevent the other three women from seeking for a way to be a part of his life.

Card captures vividly the anguish, the fear, and the techniques women probably had to employ to succeed in the Old Testament world. Beyond that, his portrayal of the power of religion—especially of the word of God—infuses the book with an epic feeling that transcends most fiction.

* * *

The questions that follow were created to stimulate thought and discussion about Rachel and Leah. *We hope this guide will enrich your experience and be a helpful starting point for meaningful discussion.*

1. It's interesting that the first chapter of a book titled *Rachel and Leah* would feature as its focus a different woman entirely. Why do you think Card began this story with Bilhah? What does this show us about how our lives in mortality are intertwined with the stories of others?

2. In chapter 3, Rachel describes to her father a vision she has had, and he dismisses it as too vague and unclear to be real. Later events prove the truth of the vision. Have you ever had spiritual experiences with meanings that were not fully clear until later on? Why does God teach us in this way at times?

3. What is your first impression of Jacob? Is he someone you would be interested in knowing better, after seeing his encounter with Rachel at the well?

4. With the introduction of Zilpah in chapter 5, we have now met all four of Jacob's future wives. Was it a surprise to you to see how young they all were when Jacob first joined Laban's household? What feelings from your own adolescent

years are you reminded of by their squabblings? What changes in their attitudes and behavior took place in each over the seven years leading to the first marriage? Which of the four women would you be likeliest to identify with?

5. In chapter 8, Leah summons the courage to ask Jacob to help her find in the holy books answers to her deepest questions. He tells her he knows "what it means to be alive when God seems to have no purpose for you." What experiences might he have had to make him feel this way? Have you ever experienced such feelings yourself? Have the scriptures had answers for you?

6. Leah's questions in chapter 11 about her handicap raise the issue of God's love for us and his willingness to intervene in our lives. What purpose might Leah's suffering serve for her? How does God's scriptural invitation to "walk with me" affect Leah? What difference would it make in our own questioning if we would accept that invitation?

7. Zilpah tells Leah, "I'm always happy," to which Leah retorts, "You can't just decide to be happy." Whom do you believe? Is happiness a choice? Is anger? What can we learn from Leah and Zilpah about how much control we have over our feelings and emotions? Jacob makes a statement that holds one key: "Everyone wants to be happy, even if everything they choose to do keeps them from happiness. The trick is to get them to understand what will *make* them happy." What is it in your experience that contributes to happiness?

8. In chapter 22 we meet Choraz, the third brother of Rachel and Leah, and his wife, Hasseweh. What do you make of Hasseweh? Have you ever met someone who resembles her? What might her motives be in trying to frighten Rachel

out of marrying Jacob? What does this show about how the adversary exploits our weaknesses?

9. What do you think of Laban's plan, in chapters 27 and 28, for sparing Rachel from the marriage that is frightening her so?

10. The book ends on a somewhat somber note. Card plans to write a sequel to be titled *The Wives of Israel*. If you were creating the sequel, what would you have happen with each of these characters and their relationships with each other?

11. What aspects of Card's writing do you most admire? Is there anything in his style or his portrayal of these people and the era in which they lived that makes you uneasy?